Books by Ernest Hemingway

THE COMPLETE SHORT STORIES

THE GARDEN OF EDEN

DATELINE: TORONTO

THE DANGEROUS SUMMER

SELECTED LETTERS

THE ENDURING HEMINGWAY

THE NICK ADAMS STORIES

ISLANDS IN THE STREAM

THE FIFTH COLUMN AND FOUR STORIES OF THE SPANISH CIVIL WAR

BY-LINE: ERNEST HEMINGWAY

A MOVEABLE FEAST

THREE NOVELS

THE SNOWS OF KILIMANJARO AND OTHER STORIES

THE HEMINGWAY READER

THE OLD MAN AND THE SEA

ACROSS THE RIVER AND INTO THE TREES

FOR WHOM THE BELL TOLLS

THE SHORT STORIES OF ERNEST HEMINGWAY

TO HAVE AND HAVE NOT

GREEN HILLS OF AFRICA

WINNER TAKE NOTHING

DEATH IN THE AFTERNOON

IN OUR TIME

A FAREWELL TO ARMS

MEN WITHOUT WOMEN

THE SUN ALSO RISES

THE TORRENTS OF SPRING

ERNEST HEMINGWAY

FOR WHOM THE BELL TOLLS

SCRIBNER PAPERBACK FICTION
PUBLISHED BY SIMON & SCHUSTER
NEW YORK LONDON TORONTO SYDNEY TOKYO SINGAPORE

SCRIBNER PAPERBACK FICTION
Simon & Schuster Inc.
Rockefeller Center
1230 Avenue of the Americas
New York, NY 10020

This book is a work of fiction. Names, characters, places, and
incidents either are products of the author's imagination or are used
fictitiously. Any resemblance to actual events or locales or persons,
living or dead, is entirely coincidental.

Copyright 1940 by Ernest Hemingway
Copyright renewed © 1968 by Mary Hemingway
All rights reserved, including the right of reproduction
in whole or in part in any form.

First Scribner Paperback Fiction Edition 1995

SCRIBNER PAPERBACK FICTION and design
are trademarks of Simon & Schuster Inc.
Manufactured in the United States of America

7   9   10   8   6

ISBN 0-684-80335-6

This book is for

MARTHA GELLHORN

No man is an *Iland,* intire of it selfe; every man
is a peece of the *Continent,* a part of the *maine;* if a
Clod bee washed away by the *Sea, Europe* is the lesse,
as well as if a *Promontorie* were, as well as if a *Mannor*
of thy *friends* or of *thine owne* were; any mans *death*
diminishes *me,* because I am involved in *Mankinde;* And
therefore never send to know for whom the *bell* tolls;
It tolls for *thee.*   JOHN DONNE

CHAPTER ONE

HE LAY flat on the brown, pine-needled floor of the forest, his chin on his folded arms, and high overhead the wind blew in the tops of the pine trees. The mountainside sloped gently where he lay; but below it was steep and he could see the dark of the oiled road winding through the pass. There was a stream alongside the road and far down the pass he saw a mill beside the stream and the falling water of the dam, white in the summer sunlight.

"Is that the mill?" he asked.

"Yes."

"I do not remember it."

"It was built since you were here. The old mill is farther down; much below the pass."

He spread the photostated military map out on the forest floor and looked at it carefully. The old man looked over his shoulder. He was a short and solid old man in a black peasant's smock and gray iron-stiff trousers and he wore rope-soled shoes. He was breathing heavily from the climb and his hand rested on one of the two heavy packs they had been carrying.

"Then you cannot see the bridge from here."

"No," the old man said. "This is the easy country of the pass where the stream flows gently. Below, where the road turns out of sight in the trees, it drops suddenly and there is a steep gorge—"

"I remember."

"Across this gorge is the bridge."

"And where are their posts?"

"There is a post at the mill that you see there."

The young man, who was studying the country, took his glasses from the pocket of his faded, khaki flannel shirt, wiped the lenses with a handkerchief, screwed the eyepieces around until the boards of the mill showed suddenly clearly and he saw the wooden bench beside the door; the huge pile of sawdust that rose behind the open shed where the circular saw was, and a stretch of the flume that brought the logs down from the mountainside on the other bank of the stream. The stream showed clear and smooth-looking in the glasses and, below the curl of the falling water, the spray from the dam was blowing in the wind.

"There is no sentry."

"There is smoke coming from the millhouse," the old man said. "There are also clothes hanging on a line."

"I see them but I do not see any sentry."

"Perhaps he is in the shade," the old man explained. "It is hot there now. He would be in the shadow at the end we do not see."

"Probably. Where is the next post?"

"Below the bridge. It is at the roadmender's hut at kilometer five from the top of the pass."

"How many men are here?" He pointed at the mill.

"Perhaps four and a corporal."

"And below?"

"More. I will find out."

"And at the bridge?"

"Always two. One at each end."

"We will need a certain number of men," he said. "How many men can you get?"

"I can bring as many men as you wish," the old man said. "There are many men now here in the hills."

"How many?"

"There are more than a hundred. But they are in small bands. How many men will you need?"

"I will let you know when we have studied the bridge."

"Do you wish to study it now?"

"No. Now I wish to go to where we will hide this explosive until it is time. I would like to have it hidden in utmost security at a distance no greater than half an hour from the bridge, if that is possible."

"That is simple," the old man said. "From where we are going, it will all be downhill to the bridge. But now we must climb a little in seriousness to get there. Are you hungry?"

"Yes," the young man said. "But we will eat later. How are you called? I have forgotten." It was a bad sign to him that he had forgotten.

"Anselmo," the old man said. "I am called Anselmo and I come from Barco de Avila. Let me help you with that pack."

The young man, who was tall and thin, with sun-streaked fair hair, and a wind- and sun-burned face, who wore the sun-faded flannel shirt, a pair of peasant's trousers and rope-soled shoes, leaned over, put his arm through one of the leather pack straps and swung the heavy pack up onto his shoulders. He worked his arm through the other strap and settled the weight of the pack against his back. His shirt was still wet from where the pack had rested.

"I have it up now," he said. "How do we go?"

"We climb," Anselmo said.

Bending under the weight of the packs, sweating, they climbed steadily in the pine forest that covered the mountainside. There was no trail that the young man could see, but they were working up and around the face of the mountain and now they crossed a small stream and the old man went steadily on ahead up the edge of the rocky stream bed. The climbing now was steeper and more difficult, until finally the stream seemed to drop down over the edge of a smooth granite ledge that rose above them and the old man waited at the foot of the ledge for the young man to come up to him.

"How are you making it?"

"All right," the young man said. He was sweating heavily and his thigh muscles were twitchy from the steepness of the climb.

"Wait here now for me. I go ahead to warn them. You do not want to be shot at carrying that stuff."

"Not even in a joke," the young man said. "Is it far?"

"It is very close. How do they call thee?"

"Roberto," the young man answered. He had slipped the pack off and lowered it gently down between two boulders by the stream bed.

"Wait here, then, Roberto, and I will return for you."

"Good," the young man said. "But do you plan to go down this way to the bridge?"

"No. When we go to the bridge it will be by another way. Shorter and easier."

"I do not want this material to be stored too far from the bridge."

"You will see. If you are not satisfied, we will take another place."

"We will see," the young man said.

He sat by the packs and watched the old man climb the ledge. It was not hard to climb and from the way he found hand-holds without searching for them the young man could see that he had climbed it many times before. Yet whoever was above had been very careful not to leave any trail.

The young man, whose name was Robert Jordan, was extremely hungry and he was worried. He was often hungry but he was not usually worried because he did not give any importance to what happened to himself and he knew from experience how simple it was to move behind the enemy lines in all this country. It was as simple to move behind them as it was to cross through them, if you had a good guide. It was only giving importance to what happened to you if you were caught that made it difficult; that and deciding whom to trust. You had to trust the people you worked with completely or not at all, and you had to make decisions about the trusting. He was not worried about any of that. But there were other things.

This Anselmo had been a good guide and he could travel wonderfully in the mountains. Robert Jordan could walk well enough himself and he knew from following him since before daylight that the old man could walk him to death. Robert Jordan trusted the man, Anselmo, so far, in everything except judgment. He had not yet had an opportunity to test his judgment, and, anyway, the judgment was his own responsibility. No, he did not worry about Anselmo and the problem of the bridge was no more difficult than many other problems. He knew how to blow any sort of bridge that you could name and he had blown them of all sizes and constructions. There was enough explosive and all equipment in the two packs to blow this bridge properly even if it were twice as big as Anselmo reported it, as he remembered it when he had walked over it on his way to La Granja on a walking trip in 1933, and as Golz had read him the description of it night before last in that upstairs room in the house outside of the Escorial.

"To blow the bridge is nothing," Golz had said, the lamplight on his scarred, shaved head, pointing with a pencil on the big map. "You understand?"

"Yes, I understand."

"Absolutely nothing. Merely to blow the bridge is a failure."

"Yes, Comrade General."

"To blow the bridge at a stated hour based on the time set for the attack is how it should be done. You see that naturally. That is your right and how it should be done."

Golz looked at the pencil, then tapped his teeth with it.

Robert Jordan had said nothing.

"You understand that is your right and how it should be done," Golz went on, looking at him and nodding his head. He tapped on the map now with the pencil. "That is how I should do it. That is what we cannot have."

"Why, Comrade General?"

"Why?" Golz said, angrily. "How many attacks have you seen and you ask me why? What is to guarantee that my orders are not changed? What is to guarantee that the attack is not annulled? What is to guarantee that the attack is not postponed? What is to guarantee that it starts within six hours of when it should start? Has *any* attack ever been as it should?"

"It will start on time if it is your attack," Robert Jordan said.

"They are never my attacks," Golz said. "I make them. But they are not mine. The artillery is not mine. I must put in for it. I have never been given what I ask for even when they have it to give. That is the least of it. There are other things. You know how those people are. It is not necessary to go into all of it. Always there is something. Always some one will interfere. So now be sure you understand."

"So when is the bridge to be blown?" Robert Jordan had asked.

"After the attack starts. As soon as the attack has started and not before. So that no reinforcements will come up over that road." He pointed with his pencil. "I must know that nothing will come up over that road."

"And when is the attack?"

"I will tell you. But you are to use the date and hour only as an indication of a probability. You must be ready for that time. You will blow the bridge after the attack has started. You see?" he indicated with the pencil. "That is the only road on which they can bring up reinforcements. That is the only road on which they can get up tanks, or artillery, or even move a truck toward the pass which I attack. I must know that bridge is gone. Not before, so it can be repaired if the attack is postponed. No. It must go when the attack starts and I must know it is gone. There are only two sentries. The man who will go with you has just come from there. He is a very reliable man, they say. You will see. He has people in the mountains. Get as many men as you need. Use as few as possible, but use enough. I do not have to tell you these things."

"And how do I determine that the attack has started?"

"It is to be made with a full division. There will be an aerial bombardment as preparation. You are not deaf, are you?"

"Then I may take it that when the planes unload, the attack has started?"

"You could not always take it like that," Golz said and shook his head. "But in this case, you may. It is my attack."

"I understand it," Robert Jordan had said. "I do not say I like it very much."

"Neither do I like it very much. If you do not want to undertake it, say so now. If you think you cannot do it, say so now."

"I will do it," Robert Jordan had said. "I will do it all right."

"That is all I have to know," Golz said. "That nothing comes up over that bridge. That is absolute."

"I understand."

"I do not like to ask people to do such things and in such a way," Golz went on. "I could not order you to do it. I understand what you may be forced to do through my putting such conditions. I explain very carefully so that you understand and that you understand all of the possible difficulties and the importance."

"And how will you advance on La Granja if that bridge is blown?"

"We go forward prepared to repair it after we have stormed the pass. It is a very complicated and beautiful operation. As complicated and as beautiful as always. The plan has been manufactured in Madrid. It is another of Vicente Rojo, the unsuccessful professor's, masterpieces. I make the attack and I make it, as always, not in sufficient force. It is a very possible operation, in spite of that. I am much happier about it than usual. It can be successful with that bridge eliminated. We can take Segovia. Look, I show you how it goes. You see? It is not the top of the pass where we attack. We hold that. It is much beyond. Look— Here— Like this——"

"I would rather not know," Robert Jordan said.

"Good," said Golz. "It is less of baggage to carry with you on the other side, yes?"

"I would always rather not know. Then, no matter what can happen, it was not me that talked."

"It is better not to know," Golz stroked his forehead with the pencil. "Many times I wish I did not know myself. But you do know the one thing you must know about the bridge?"

"Yes. I know that."

"I believe you do," Golz said. "I will not make you any little speech. Let us now have a drink. So much talking makes me very thirsty, Comrade Hordan. You have a funny name in Spanish, Comrade Hordown."

"How do you say Golz in Spanish, Comrade General?"

"Hotze," said Golz grinning, making the sound deep in his throat as though hawking with a bad cold. "Hotze," he croaked. "Comrade Heneral Khotze. If I had known how they pronounced Golz in Spanish I would pick me out a better name before I come to war here. When I think I come to command a division and I can pick out any name I want and I pick out Hotze. Heneral Hotze. Now it is too late to change. How do you like *partizan* work?" It was the Russian term for guerilla work behind the lines.

"Very much," Robert Jordan said. He grinned. "It is very healthy in the open air."

"I like it very much when I was your age, too," Golz said. "They tell me you blow bridges very well. Very scientific. It is only hearsay. I have never seen you do anything myself. Maybe nothing ever happens really. You really blow them?" he was teasing now. "Drink this," he handed the glass of Spanish brandy to Robert Jordan. "You *really* blow them?"

"Sometimes."

"You better not have any sometimes on this bridge. No, let us not talk any more about this bridge. You understand enough now about that bridge. We are very serious so we can make very strong jokes. Look, do you have many girls on the other side of the lines?"

"No, there is no time for girls."

"I do not agree. The more irregular the service, the more ir- regular the life. You have very irregular service. Also you need a haircut."

"I have my hair cut as it needs it," Robert Jordan said. He would be damned if he would have his head shaved like Golz. "I have enough to think about without girls," he said sullenly.

"What sort of uniform am I supposed to wear?" Robert Jordan asked.

"None," Golz said. "Your haircut is all right. I tease you. You are very different from me," Golz had said and filled up the glasses again.

"You never think about only girls. I never think at all. Why should I? I am *Général Sovietique*. I never think. Do not try to trap me into thinking."

Some one on his staff, sitting on a chair working over a map on a drawing board, growled at him in the language Robert Jordan did not understand.

"Shut up," Golz had said, in English. "I joke if I want. I am so se- rious is why I can joke. Now drink this and then go. You under- stand, huh?"

"Yes," Robert Jordan had said. "I understand."

They had shaken hands and he had saluted and gone out to the staff car where the old man was waiting asleep and in that car they had ridden over the road past Guadarrama, the old man still asleep, and up the Navacerrada road to the Alpine Club hut where he, Robert Jordan, slept for three hours before they started.

That was the last he had seen of Golz with his strange white face that never tanned, his hawk eyes, the big nose and thin lips and the shaven head crossed with wrinkles and with scars. Tomor- row night they would be outside the Escorial in the dark along the road; the long lines of trucks loading the infantry in the darkness; the men, heavy loaded, climbing up into the trucks; the machine- gun sections lifting their guns into the trucks; the tanks being run up on the skids onto the long-bodied tank trucks; pulling the Di- vision out to move them in the night for the attack on the pass. He would not think about that. That was not his business. That was Golz's business. He had only one thing to do and that was what he should think about and he must think it out clearly and take everything as it came along, and not worry. To worry was as bad as to be afraid. It simply made things more difficult.

He sat no by the stream watching the clear water flowing between the rocks and, across the stream, he noticed there was a thick bed of watercress. He crossed the stream, picked a double handful, washed the muddy roots clean in the current and then sat down again beside his pack and ate the clean, cool green leaves and the crisp, peppery-tasting stalks. He knelt by the stream and, pushing his automatic pistol around on his belt to the small of his back so that it would not be wet, he lowered himself with a hand on each of two boulders and drank from the stream. The water was achingly cold.

Pushing himself up on his hands he turned his head and saw the old man coming down the ledge. With him was another man, also in a black peasant's smock and the dark gray trousers that were almost a uniform in that province, wearing rope-soled shoes and with a carbine slung over his back. This man was bareheaded. The two of them came scrambling down the rock like goats.

They came up to him and Robert Jordan got to his feet.

"Salud, Camarada," he said to the man with the carbine and smiled.

"Salud," the other said, grudgingly. Robert Jordan looked at the man's heavy, beard-stubbled face. It was almost round and his head was round and set close on his shoulders. His eyes were small and set too wide apart and his ears were small and set close to his head. He was a heavy man about five feet ten inches tall and his hands and feet were large. His nose had been broken and his mouth was cut at one corner and the line of the scar across the upper lip and lower jaw showed through the growth of beard over his face.

The old man nodded his head at this man and smiled.

"He is the boss here," he grinned, then flexed his arms as though to make the muscles stand out and looked at the man with the carbine in a half-mocking admiration. "A very strong man."

"I can see it," Robert Jordan said and smiled again. He did not like the look of this man and inside himself he was not smiling at all.

"What have you to justify your identity?" asked the man with the carbine.

Robert Jordan unpinned a safety pin that ran through his pocket flap and took a folded paper out of the left breast pocket of his flannel shirt and handed it to the man, who opened it, looked at it doubtfully and turned it in his hands.

So he cannot read, Robert Jordan noted.

"Look at the seal," he said.

The old man pointed to the seal and the man with the carbine studied it, turning it in his fingers.

"What seal is that?"

"Have you never seen it?"

"No."

"There are two," said Robert Jordan. "One is S. I. M., the service of the military intelligence. The other is the General Staff."

"Yes, I have seen that seal before. But here no one commands but me," the other said sullenly. "What have you in the packs?"

"Dynamite," the old man said proudly. "Last night we crossed the lines in the dark and all day we have carried this dynamite over the mountain."

"I can use dynamite," said the man with the carbine. He handed back the paper to Robert Jordan and looked him over. "Yes. I have use for dynamite. How much have you brought me?"

"I have brought you no dynamite," Robert Jordan said to him evenly. "The dynamite is for another purpose. What is your name?"

"What is that to you?"

"He is Pablo," said the old man. The man with the carbine looked at them both sullenly.

"Good. I have heard much good of you," said Robert Jordan.

"What have you heard of me?" asked Pablo.

"I have heard that you are an excellent guerilla leader, that you are loyal to the republic and prove your loyalty through your acts, and that you are a man both serious and valiant. I bring you greetings from the General Staff."

"Where did you hear all this?" asked Pablo. Robert Jordan registered that he was not taking any of the flattery.

"I heard it from Buitrago to the Escorial," he said, naming all the stretch of country on the other side of the lines.

"I know no one in Buitrago nor in Escorial," Pablo told him.

"There are many people on the other side of the mountains who were not there before. Where are you from?"

"Avila. What are you going to do with the dynamite?"

"Blow up a bridge."

"What bridge?"

"That is my business."

"If it is in this territory, it is my business. You cannot blow bridges close to where you live. You must live in one place and operate in another. I know my business. One who is alive, now, after a year, knows his business."

"This is my business," Robert Jordan said. "We can discuss it together. Do you wish to help us with the sacks?"

"No," said Pablo and shook his head.

The old man turned toward him suddenly and spoke rapidly and furiously in a dialect that Robert Jordan could just follow. It was like reading Quevedo. Anselmo was speaking old Castilian and it went something like this, "Art thou a brute? Yes. Art thou a beast? Yes, many times. Hast thou a brain? Nay. None. Now we come for something of consummate importance and thee, with thy dwelling place to be undisturbed, puts thy fox-hole before the interests of humanity. Before the interests of thy people. I this and that in the this and that of thy father. I this and that and that in thy this. *Pick up that bag.*"

Pablo looked down.

"Every one has to do what he can do according to how it can be truly done," he said. "I live here and I operate beyond Segovia. If you make a disturbance here, we will be hunted out of these mountains. It is only by doing nothing here that we are able to live in these mountains. It is the principle of the fox."

"Yes," said Anselmo bitterly. "It is the principle of the fox when we need the wolf."

"I am more wolf than thee," Pablo said and Robert Jordan knew that he would pick up the sack.

"Hi. Ho . . . ," Anselmo looked at him. "Thou art more wolf than me and I am sixty-eight years old."

He spat on the ground and shook his head.

"You have that many years?" Robert Jordan asked, seeing that now, for the moment, it would be all right and trying to make it go easier.

"Sixty-eight in the month of July."

"If we should ever see that month," said Pablo. "Let me help you with the pack," he said to Robert Jordan. "Leave the other to the old man." He spoke, not sullenly, but almost sadly now. "He is an old man of great strength."

"I will carry the pack," Robert Jordan said.

"Nay," said the old man. "Leave it to this other strong man."

"I will take it," Pablo told him, and in his sullenness there was a sadness that was disturbing to Robert Jordan. He knew that sadness and to see it here worried him.

"Give me the carbine then," he said and when Pablo handed it to him, he slung it over his back and, with the two men climbing ahead of him, they went heavily, pulling and climbing up the granite shelf and over its upper edge to where there was a green clearing in the forest.

They skirted the edge of the little meadow and Robert Jordan, striding easily now without the pack, the carbine pleasantly rigid over his shoulder after the heavy, sweating pack weight, noticed that the grass was cropped down in several places and signs that picket pins had been driven into the earth. He could see a trail through the grass where horses had been led to the stream to drink and there was the fresh manure of several horses. They picket them here to feed at night and keep them out of sight in the timber in the daytime, he thought. I wonder how many horses this Pablo has?

He remembered now noticing, without realizing it, that Pablo's trousers were worn soapy shiny in the knees and thighs. I wonder if he has a pair of boots or if he rides in those *alpargatas,* he thought. He must have quite an outfit. But I don't like that sadness, he thought. That sadness is bad. That's the sadness they get before they quit or before they betray. That is the sadness that comes before the sell-out.

Ahead of them a horse whinnied in the timber and then, through the brown trunks of the pine trees, only a little sunlight coming down through their thick, almost-touching tops, he saw the corral made by roping around the tree trunks. The horses had their heads pointed toward the men as they approached, and at the foot of a tree, outside the corral, the saddles were piled together and covered with a tarpaulin.

As they came up, the two men with the packs stopped, and Robert Jordan knew it was for him to admire the horses.

"Yes," he said. "They are beautiful." He turned to Pablo. "You have your cavalry and all."

There were five horses in the rope corral, three bays, a sorrel, and a buckskin. Sorting them out carefully with his eyes after he had seen them first together, Robert Jordan looked them over individually. Pablo and Anselmo knew how good they were and while Pablo stood now proud and less sad-looking, watching them lovingly, the old man acted as though they were some great surprise that he had produced, suddenly, himself.

"How do they look to you?" he asked.

"All these I have taken," Pablo said and Robert Jordan was pleased to hear him speak proudly.

"That," said Robert Jordan, pointing to one of the bays, a big stallion with a white blaze on his forehead and a single white foot, the near front, "is much horse."

He was a beautiful horse that looked as though he had come out of a painting by Velásquez.

"They are all good," said Pablo. "You know horses?"

"Yes."

"Less bad," said Pablo. "Do you see a defect in one of these?"

Robert Jordan knew that now his papers were being examined by the man who could not read.

The horses all still had their heads up looking at the man. Robert Jordan slipped through between the double rope of the corral and slapped the buckskin on the haunch. He leaned back against the ropes of the enclosure and watched the horses circle the corral, stood watching them a minute more, as they stood still, then leaned down and came out through the ropes.

"The sorrel is lame in the off hind foot," he said to Pablo, not looking at him. "The hoof is split and although it might not get worse soon if shod properly, she could break down if she travels over much hard ground."

"The hoof was like that when we took her," Pablo said.

"The best horse that you have, the white-faced bay stallion, has a swelling on the upper part of the cannon bone that I do not like."

"It is nothing," said Pablo. "He knocked it three days ago. If it were to be anything it would have become so already."

He pulled back the tarpaulin and showed the saddles. There were two ordinary vaquero's or herdsman's saddles, like American stock saddles, one very ornate vaquero's saddle, with hand-tooled leather and heavy, hooded stirrups, and two military saddles in black leather.

"We killed a pair of *guardia civil,*" he said, explaining the military saddles.

"That is big game."

"They had dismounted on the road between Segovia and Santa Maria del Real. They had dismounted to ask papers of the driver of a cart. We were able to kill them without injuring the horses."

"Have you killed many civil guards?" Robert Jordan asked.

"Several," Pablo said. "But only these two without injury to the horses."

"It was Pablo who blew up the train at Arevalo," Anselmo said. "That was Pablo."

"There was a foreigner with us who made the explosion," Pablo said. "Do you know him?"

"What is he called?"

"I do not remember. It was a very rare name."

"What did he look like?"

"He was fair, as you are, but not as tall and with large hands and a broken nose."

"Kashkin," Robert Jordan said. "That would be Kashkin."

"Yes," said Pablo. "It was a very rare name. Something like that. What has become of him?"

"He is dead since April."

"That is what happens to everybody," Pablo said, gloomily. "That is the way we will all finish."

"That is the way all men end," Anselmo said. "That is the way men have always ended. What is the matter with you, man? What hast thou in the stomach?"

"*They* are very strong," Pablo said. It was as though he were talking to himself. He looked at the horses gloomily. "You do not realize how strong they are. I seem them always stronger, always better armed. Always with more material. Here am I with horses like these. And what can I look forward to? To be hunted and to die. Nothing more."

"You hunt as much as you are hunted," Anselmo said.

"No," said Pablo. "Not any more. And if we leave these mountains now, where can we go? Answer me that? Where now?"

"In Spain there are many mountains. There are the Sierra de Gredos if one leaves here."

"Not for me," Pablo said. "I am tired of being hunted. Here we are all right. Now if you blow a bridge here, we will be hunted. If they know we are here and hunt for us with planes, they will find us. If they send Moors to hunt us out, they will find us and we must go. I am tired of all this. You hear?" He turned to Robert Jordan. "What right have you, a foreigner, to come to me and tell me what I must do?"

"I have not told you anything you must do," Robert Jordan said to him.

"You will though," Pablo said. "There. There is the badness."

He pointed at the two heavy packs that they had lowered to the ground while they had watched the horses. Seeing the horses had seemed to bring this all to a head in him and seeing that Robert Jordan knew horses had seemed to loosen his tongue. The three of them stood now by the rope corral and the patchy sunlight shone on the coat of the bay stallion. Pablo looked at him and then pushed with his foot against the heavy pack. "There is the badness."

"I come only for my duty," Robert Jordan told him. "I come under orders from those who are conducting the war. If I ask you to help me, you can refuse and I will find others who will help me. I have not even asked you for help yet. I have to do what I am ordered to do and I can promise you of its importance. That I am a foreigner is not my fault. I would rather have been born here."

"To me, now, the most important is that we be not disturbed here," Pablo said. "To me, now, my duty is to those who are with me and to myself."

"Thyself. Yes," Anselmo said. "Thyself now since a long time. Thyself and thy horses. Until thou hadst horses thou wert with us. Now thou art another capitalist more."

"That is unjust," said Pablo. "I expose the horses all the time for the cause."

"Very little," said Anselmo scornfully. "Very little in my judgment. To steal, yes. To eat well, yes. To murder, yes. To fight, no."

"You are an old man who will make himself trouble with his mouth."

"I am an old man who is afraid of no one," Anselmo told him. "Also I am an old man without horses."

"You are an old man who may not live long."

"I am an old man who will live until I die," Anselmo said. "And I am not afraid of foxes."

Pablo said nothing but picked up the pack.

"Nor of wolves either," Anselmo said, picking up the other pack. "If thou art a wolf."

"Shut thy mouth," Pablo said to him. "Thou art an old man who always talks too much."

"And would do whatever he said he would do," Anselmo said, bent under the pack. "And who now is hungry. And thirsty. Go on, guerilla leader with the sad face. Lead us to something to eat."

It is starting badly enough, Robert Jordan thought. But Anselmo's a man. They are wonderful when they are good, he thought. There is no people like them when they are good and when they go bad there is no people that is worse. Anselmo must have known what he was doing when he brought us here. But I don't like it. I don't like any of it.

The only good sign was that Pablo was carrying the pack and that he had given him the carbine. Perhaps he is always like that, Robert Jordan thought. Maybe he is just one of the gloomy ones.

No, he said to himself, don't fool yourself. You do not know how he was before; but you do know that he is going bad fast and without hiding it. When he starts to hide it he will have made a decision. Remember that, he told himself. The first friendly thing he does, he will have made a decision. They are awfully good horses, though, he thought, beautiful horses. I wonder what could make me feel the way those horses make Pablo feel. The old man was right. The horses made him rich and as soon as he was rich he wanted to enjoy life. Pretty soon he'll feel bad because he can't join the Jockey Club, I guess, he thought. Pauvre Pablo. Il a manqué son Jockey.

That idea made him feel better. He grinned, looking at the two bent backs and the big packs ahead of him moving through the trees. He had not made any jokes with himself all day and now that he had made one he felt much better. You're getting to be as all the rest of them, he told himself. You're getting gloomy, too. He'd certainly been solemn and gloomy with Golz. The job had overwhelmed him a little. Slightly overwhelmed, he thought. Plenty overwhelmed. Golz was gay and he had wanted him to be gay too before he left, but he hadn't been.

All the best ones, when you thought it over, were gay. It was much better to be gay and it was a sign of something too. It was like having immortality while you were still alive. That was a complicated one. There were not many of them left though. No, there were not many of the gay ones left. There were very damned few of them left. And if you keep on thinking like that, my boy, you won't be left either. Turn off the thinking now, old timer, old comrade. You're a bridge-blower now. Not a thinker. Man, I'm hungry, he thought. I hope Pablo eats well.

CHAPTER TWO

THEY had come through the heavy timber to the cup-shaped upper end of the little valley and he saw where the camp must be under the rim-rock that rose ahead of them through the trees.

That was the camp all right and it was a good camp. You did not see it at all until you were up to it and Robert Jordan knew it could not be spotted from the air. Nothing would show from above. It was as well hidden as a bear's den. But it seemed to be little better guarded. He looked at it carefully as they came up.

There was a large cave in the rim-rock formation and beside the opening a man sat with his back against the rock, his legs stretched out on the ground and his carbine leaning against the rock. He was cutting away on a stick with a knife and he stared at them as they came up, then went on whittling.

"Hola," said the seated man. "What is this that comes?"

"The old man and a dynamiter," Pablo told him and lowered the pack inside the entrance to the cave. Anselmo lowered his pack, too, and Robert Jordan unslung the rifle and leaned it against the rock.

"Don't leave it so close to the cave," the whittling man, who had blue eyes in a dark, good-looking lazy gypsy face, the color of smoked leather, said. "There's a fire in there."

"Get up and put it away thyself," Pablo said. "Put it by that tree."

The gypsy did not move but said something unprintable, then, "Leave it there. Blow thyself up," he said lazily. "'Twill cure thy diseases."

"What do you make?" Robert Jordan sat down by the gypsy. The gypsy showed him. It was a figure four trap and he was whittling the crossbar for it.

"For foxes," he said. "With a log for a dead-fall. It breaks their backs." He grinned at Jordan. "Like this, see?" He made a motion of the framework of the trap collapsing, the log falling, then shook his head, drew in his hand, and spread his arms to show the fox with a broken back. "Very practical," he explained.

"He catches rabbits," Anselmo said. "He is a gypsy. So if he catches rabbits he says it is foxes. If he catches a fox he would say it was an elephant."

"And if I catch an elephant?" the gypsy asked and showed his white teeth again and winked at Robert Jordan.

"You'd say it was a tank," Anselmo told him.

"I'll get a tank," the gypsy told him. "I will get a tank. And you can say it is what you please."

"Gypsies talk much and kill little," Anselmo told him.

The gypsy winked at Robert Jordan and went on whittling.

Pablo had gone in out of sight in the cave. Robert Jordan hoped he had gone for food. He sat on the ground by the gypsy and the afternoon sunlight came down through the tree tops and was warm on his outstretched legs. He could smell food now in the cave, the smell of oil and of onions and of meat frying and his stomach moved with hunger inside of him.

"We can get a tank," he said to the gypsy. "It is not too difficult."

"With this?" the gypsy pointed toward the two sacks.

"Yes," Robert Jordan told him. "I will teach you. You make a trap. It is not too difficult."

"You and me?"

"Sure," said Robert Jordan. "Why not?"

"Hey," the gypsy said to Anselmo. "Move those two sacks to where they will be safe, will you? They're valuable."

Anselmo grunted. "I am going for wine," he told Robert Jordan. Robert Jordan got up and lifted the sacks away from the cave entrance and leaned them, one on each side of a tree trunk. He knew what was in them and he never liked to see them close together.

"Bring a cup for me," the gypsy told him.

"Is there wine?" Robert Jordan asked, sitting down again by the gypsy.

"Wine? Why not? A whole skinful. Half a skinful, anyway."

"And what to eat?"

"Everything, man," the gypsy said. "We eat like generals."

"And what do gypsies do in the war?" Robert Jordan asked him.

"They keep on being gypsies."

"That's a good job."

"The best," the gypsy said. "How do they call thee?"

"Roberto. And thee?"

"Rafael. And this of the tank is serious?"

"Surely. Why not?"

Anselmo came out of the mouth of the cave with a deep stone basin full of red wine and with his fingers through the handles of three cups. "Look," he said. "They have cups and all." Pablo came out behind them.

"There is food soon," he said. "Do you have tobacco?"

Robert Jordan went over to the packs and opening one, felt inside an inner pocket and brought out one of the flat boxes of Russian cigarettes he had gotten at Golz's headquarters. He ran his thumbnail around the edge of the box and, opening the lid, handed them to Pablo who took half a dozen. Pablo, holding them in one of his huge hands, picked one up and looked at it against the light. They were long narrow cigarettes with pasteboard cylinders for mouthpieces.

"Much air and little tobacco," he said. "I know these. The other with the rare name had them."

"Kashkin," Robert Jordan said and offered the cigarettes to the gypsy and Anselmo, who each took one.

"Take more," he said and they each took another. He gave them each four more, they making a double nod with the hand holding the cigarettes so that the cigarette dipped its end as a man salutes with a sword, to thank him.

"Yes," Pablo said. "It was a rare name."

"Here is the wine." Anselmo dipped a cup out of the bowl and handed it to Robert Jordan, then dipped for himself and the gypsy.

"Is there no wine for me?" Pablo asked. They were all sitting together by the cave entrance.

Anselmo handed him his cup and went into the cave for another. Coming out he leaned over the bowl and dipped the cup full and they all touched cup edges.

The wine was good, tasting faintly resinous from the wineskin, but excellent, light and clean on his tongue. Robert Jordan drank it slowly, feeling it spread warmly through his tiredness.

"The food comes shortly," Pablo said. "And this foreigner with the rare name, how did he die?"

"He was captured and he killed himself."

"How did that happen?"

"He was wounded and he did not wish to be a prisoner."

"What were the details?"

"I don't know," he lied. He knew the details very well and he knew they would not make good talking now.

"He made us promise to shoot him in case he were wounded at the business of the train and should be unable to get away," Pablo said. "He spoke in a very rare manner."

He must have been jumpy even then, Robert Jordan thought. Poor old Kashkin.

"He had a prejudice against killing himself," Pablo said. "He told me that. Also he had a great fear of being tortured."

"Did he tell you that, too?" Robert Jordan asked him.

"Yes," the gypsy said. "He spoke like that to all of us."

"Were you at the train, too?"

"Yes. All of us were at the train."

"He spoke in a very rare manner," Pablo said. "But he was very brave."

Poor old Kashkin, Robert Jordan thought. He must have been doing more harm than good around here. I wish I would have known he was that jumpy as far back as then. They should have pulled him out. You can't have people around doing this sort of work and talking like that. That is no way to talk. Even if they accomplish their mission they are doing more harm than good, talking that sort of stuff.

"He was a little strange," Robert Jordan said. "I think he was a little crazy."

"But very dexterous at producing explosions," the gypsy said. "And very brave."

"But crazy," Robert Jordan said. "In this you have to have very much head and be very cold in the head. That was no way to talk."

"And you," Pablo said. "If you are wounded in such a thing as this bridge, you would be willing to be left behind?"

"Listen," Robert Jordan said and, leaning forward, he dipped himself another cup of the wine. "Listen to me clearly. If ever I should have any little favors to ask of any man, I will ask him at the time."

"Good," said the gypsy approvingly. "In this way speak the good ones. Ah! Here it comes."

"You have eaten," said Pablo.

"And I can eat twice more," the gypsy told him. "Look now who brings it."

The girl stooped as she came out of the cave mouth carrying the big iron cooking platter and Robert Jordan saw her face turned at an angle and at the same time saw the strange thing about her. She smiled and said, *"Hola,* Comrade," and Robert Jordan said, *"Salud,"* and was careful not to stare and not to look away. She set down the flat iron platter in front of him and he noticed her handsome brown hands. Now she looked him full in the face and smiled. Her teeth were white in her brown face and her skin and her eyes were the same golden tawny brown. She had high cheekbones, merry eyes and a straight mouth with full lips. Her hair was the golden brown of a grain field that has been burned dark in the sun but it was cut short all over her head so that it was but little longer than the fur on a beaver pelt. She smiled in Robert Jordan's face and put her brown hand up and ran it over her head, flattening the hair which rose again as her hand passed. She has a beautiful face, Robert Jordan thought. She'd be beautiful if they hadn't cropped her hair.

"That is the way I comb it," she said to Robert Jordan and laughed. "Go ahead and eat. Don't stare at me. They gave me this haircut in Valladolid. It's almost grown out now."

She sat down opposite him and looked at him. He looked back at her and she smiled and folded her hands together over her knees. Her legs slanted long and clean from the open cuffs of the trousers as she sat with her hands across her knees and he could see the shape of her small up-tilted breasts under the gray shirt. Every time Robert Jordan looked at her he could feel a thickness in his throat.

"There are no plates," Anselmo said. "Use your own knife." The girl had leaned four forks, tines down, against the sides of the iron dish.

They were all eating out of the platter, not speaking, as is the Spanish custom. It was rabbit cooked with onions and green peppers and there were chick peas in the red wine sauce. It was well cooked, the rabbit meat flaked off the bones, and the sauce was delicious. Robert Jordan drank another cup of wine while he ate. The girl watched him all through the meal. Every one else was watching his food and eating. Robert Jordan wiped up the last of the sauce in front of him with a piece of bread, piled the rabbit bones to one side, wiped the spot where they had been for sauce, then wiped his fork clean with the bread, wiped his knife and put it away and ate the bread. He leaned over and dipped his cup full of wine and the girl still watched him.

Robert Jordan drank half the cup of wine but the thickness still came in his throat when he spoke to the girl.

"How art thou called?" he asked. Pablo looked at him quickly when he heard the tone of his voice. Then he got up and walked away.

"Maria. And thee?"

"Roberto. Have you been long in the mountains?"

"Three months."

"Three months?" He looked at her hair, that was as thick and short and rippling when she passed her hand over it, now in embarrassment, as a grain field in the wind on a hillside. "It was shaved," she said. "They shaved it regularly in the prison at Valladolid. It has taken three months to grow to this. I was on the train. They were taking me to the south. Many of the prisoners were caught after the train was blown up but I was not. I came with these."

"I found her hidden in the rocks," the gypsy said. "It was when we were leaving. Man, but this one was ugly. We took her along but many times I thought we would have to leave her."

"And the other one who was with them at the train?" asked Maria. "The other blond one. The foreigner. Where is he?"

"Dead," Robert Jordan said. "In April."

"In April? The train was in April."

"Yes," Robert Jordan said. "He died ten days after the train."

"Poor man," she said. "He was very brave. And you do that same business?"

"Yes."

"You have done trains, too?"

"Yes. Three trains."

"Here?"

"In Estremadura," he said. "I was in Estremadura before I came here. We do very much in Estremadura. There are many of us working in Estremadura."

"And why do you come to these mountains now?"

"I take the place of the other blond one. Also I know this country from before the movement."

"You know it well?"

"No, not really well. But I learn fast. I have a good map and I have a good guide."

"The old man," she nodded. "The old man is very good."

"Thank you," Anselmo said to her and Robert Jordan realized suddenly that he and the girl were not alone and he realized too that it was hard for him to look at her because it made his voice change so. He was violating the second rule of the two rules for getting on well with people that speak Spanish; give the men tobacco and leave the women alone; and he realized, very suddenly, that he did not care. There were so many things that he had not to care about, why should he care about that?

"You have a very beautiful face," he said to Maria. "I wish I would have had the luck to see you before your hair was cut."

"It will grow out," she said. "In six months it will be long enough."

"You should have seen her when we brought her from the train. She was so ugly it would make you sick."

"Whose woman are you?" Robert Jordan asked, trying not to pull out of it. "Are you Pablo's?"

She looked at him and laughed, then slapped him on the knee.

"Of Pablo? You have seen Pablo?"

"Well, then, of Rafael. I have seen Rafael."

"Of Rafael neither."

"Of no one," the gypsy said. "This is a very strange woman. Is of no one. But she cooks well."

"Really of no one?" Robert Jordan asked her.

"Of no one. No one. Neither in joke nor in seriousness. Nor of thee either."

"No?" Robert Jordan said and he could feel the thickness coming in his throat again. "Good. I have no time for any woman. That is true."

"Not fifteen minutes?" the gypsy asked teasingly. "Not a quarter of an hour?" Robert Jordan did not answer. He looked at the girl, Maria, and his throat felt too thick for him to trust himself to speak.

Maria looked at him and laughed, then blushed suddenly but kept on looking at him.

"You are blushing," Robert Jordan said to her. "Do you blush much?"

"Never."

"You are blushing now."

"Then I will go into the cave."

"Stay here, Maria."

"No," she said and did not smile at him. "I will go into the cave now." She picked up the iron plate they had eaten from and the four forks. She moved awkwardly as a colt moves, but with that same grace as of a young animal.

"Do you want the cups?" she asked.

Robert Jordan was still looking at her and she blushed again.

"Don't make me do that," she said. "I do not like to do that."

"Leave them," they gypsy said to her. "Here," he dipped into the stone bowl and handed the full cup to Robert Jordan who watched the girl duck her head and go into the cave carrying the heavy iron dish.

"Thank you," Robert Jordan said. His voice was all right again, now that she was gone. "This is the last one. We've had enough of this."

"We will finish the bowl," the gypsy said. "There is over half a skin. We packed it in on one of the horses."

"That was the last raid of Pablo," Anselmo said. "Since then he has done nothing."

"How many are you?" Robert Jordan asked.

"We are seven and there are two women."

"Two?"

"Yes. The *mujer* of Pablo."

"And she?"

"In the cave. The girl can cook a little. I said she cooks well to please her. But mostly she helps the *mujer* of Pablo."

"And how is she, the *mujer* of Pablo?"

"Something barbarous," the gypsy grinned. "Something *very* barbarous. If you think Pablo is ugly you should see his woman. But brave. A hundred times braver than Pablo. But something barbarous."

"Pablo was brave in the beginning," Anselmo said. "Pablo was something serious in the beginning."

"He killed more people than the cholera," the gypsy said. "At the start of the movement, Pablo killed more people than the typhoid fever."

"But since a long time he is *muy flojo,* Anselmo said. "He is very flaccid. He is very much afraid to die."

"It is possible that it is because he has killed so many at the beginning," the gypsy said philosophically. "Pablo killed more than the bubonic plague."

"That and the riches," Anselmo said. "Also he drinks very much. Now he would like to retire like a *matador de toros.* Like a bullfighter. But he cannot retire."

"If he crosses to the other side of the lines they will take his horses and make him go in the army," the gypsy said. "In me there is no love for being in the army either."

"Nor is there in any other gypsy," Anselmo said.

"Why should there be?" the gypsy asked. "Who wants to be in an army? Do we make the revolution to be in an army? I am willing to fight but not to be in an army."

"Where are the others?" asked Robert Jordan. He felt comfortable and sleepy now from the wine and lying back on the floor of the forest he saw through the tree tops the small afternoon clouds of the mountains moving slowly in the high Spanish sky.

"There are two asleep in the cave," the gypsy said. "Two are on guard above where we have the gun. One is on guard below. They are probably all asleep."

Robert Jordan rolled over on his side.

"What kind of a gun is it?"

"A very rare name," the gypsy said. "It has gone away from me for the moment. It is a machine gun."

It must be an automatic rifle, Robert Jordan thought.

"How much does it weigh?" he asked.

"One man can carry it but it is heavy. It has three legs that fold. We got it in the last serious raid. The one before the wine."

"How many rounds have you for it?"

"An infinity," the gypsy said. "One whole case of an unbelievable heaviness."

Sounds like about five hundred rounds, Robert Jordan thought.

"Does it feed from a pan or a belt?"

"From round iron cans on the top of the gun."

Hell, it's a Lewis gun, Robert Jordan thought.

"Do you know anything about a machine gun?" he asked the old man.

"*Nada,*" said Anselmo. "Nothing."

"And thou?" to the gypsy.

"That they fire with much rapidity and become so hot the barrel burns the hand that touches it," the gypsy said proudly.

"Every one knows that," Anselmo said with contempt.

"Perhaps," the gypsy said. "But he asked me to tell what I know about a *máquina* and I told him." Then he added, "Also, unlike an ordinary rifle, they continue to fire as long as you exert pressure on the trigger."

"Unless they jam, run out of ammunition or get so hot they melt," Robert Jordan said in English.

"What do you say?" Anselmo asked him.

"Nothing," Robert Jordan said. "I was only looking into the future in English."

"That is seomthing truly rare," the gypsy said. "Looking into the future in *Ingles.* Can you read in the palm of the hand?"

"No," Robert Jordan said and he dipped another cup of wine. "But if thou canst I wish thee would read in the palm of my hand and tell me what is going to pass in the next three days."

"The *mujer* of Pablo reads in the hands," the gypsy said. "But she is so irritable and of such a barbarousness that I do not know if she will do it."

Robert Jordan sat up now and took a swallow of the wine.

"Let us see the *mujer* of Pablo now," he said. "If it is that bad let us get it over with."

"I would not disturb her," Rafael said. "She has a strong hatred for me."

"Why?"

"She treats me as a time waster."

"What injustice," Anselmo taunted.

"She is against gypsies."

"What an error," Anselmo said.

"She has gypsy blood," Rafael said. "She knows of what she speaks." He grinned. "But she has a tongue that scalds and that bites like a bull whip. With this tongue she takes the hide from any one. In strips. She is of an unbelievable barbarousness."

"How does she get along with the girl, Maria?" Robert Jordan asked.

"Good. She likes the girl. But let any one come near her seriously—" He shook his head and clucked with his tongue.

"She is very good with the girl," Anselmo said. "She takes good care of her."

"When we picked the girl up at the time of the train she was very strange," Rafael said. "She would not speak and she cried all the time and if any one touched her she would shiver like a wet dog. Only lately has she been better. Lately she has been much better. Today she was fine. Just now, talking to you, she was very good. We would have left her after the train. Certainly it was not worth being delayed by something so sad and ugly and apparently worthless. But the old woman tied a rope to her and when the girl thought she could not go further, the old woman beat her with the end of the rope to make her go. Then when she could not really go further, the old woman carried her over her shoulder. When the old woman could not carry her, I carried her. We were going up that hill breast high in the gorse and heather. And when I could no longer carry her, Pablo carried her. But what the old woman had to say to us to make us do it!" He shook his head at the memory. "It is true that the girl is long in the legs but is not heavy. The bones are light and she weighs little. But she weighs enough when we had to carry her and stop to fire and then carry her again with the old woman lashing at Pablo with the rope and carrying his rifle, putting it in his hand when he would drop the girl, making him pick her up again and loading the gun for him while she cursed him; taking the shells from his pouches and shoving them down into the magazine and cursing him. The dusk was coming well on then and when the night came it was all right. But it was lucky that they had no cavalry."

"It must have been very hard at the train," Anselmo said. "I was not there," he explained to Robert Jordan. "There was the band of Pablo, of El Sordo, whom we will see tonight, and two other bands of these mountains. I had gone to the other side of the lines."

"In addition to the blond one with the rare name—" the gypsy said.

"Kashkin."

"Yes. It is a name I can never dominate. We had two with a machine gun. They were sent also by the army. They could not get the gun away and lost it. Certainly it weighed no more than that girl and if the old woman had been over them they would have gotten it away." He shook his head remembering, then went on. "Never in my life have I seen such a thing as when the explosion was produced. The train was coming steadily. We saw it far away. And I had an excitement so great that I cannot tell it. We saw steam from it and then later came the noise of the whistle. Then it came chu-chu-chu-chu-chu-chu steadily larger and larger and then, at the moment of the explosion, the front wheels of the engine rose up and all of the earth seemed to rise in a great cloud of blackness and a roar and the engine rose high in the cloud of dirt and of the wooden ties rising in the air as in a dream and then it fell onto its side like a great wounded animal and there was an explosion of white steam before the clods of the other explosion had ceased to fall on us and the *máquina* commenced to speak ta-tat-tat-ta!" went the gypsy shaking his two clenched fists up and down in front of him, thumbs up, on an imaginary machine gun. "Ta! Ta! Tat! Tat! Tat! Ta!" he exulted. "Never in my life have I seen such a thing, with the troops running from the train and the *máquina* speaking into them and the men falling. It was then that I put my hand on the *máquina* in my excitement and discovered that the barrel burned and at that moment the old woman slapped me on the side of the face and said, 'Shoot, you fool! Shoot or I will kick your brains in!' Then I commenced to shoot but it was very hard to hold my gun steady and the troops were running up the far hill. Later, after we had been down at the train to see what there was to take, an officer forced some troops back toward us at the point of a pistol. He kept waving the pistol and shouting at them and we were all shooting at him but no one hit him. Then some troops lay down and commenced firing and the officer walked up and down behind them with his pistol and still we could not hit him and the *máquina* could not fire on him because of the position of the train. This officer shot two men as they lay and still they would not get up and he was cursing them and finally they got up, one two and three at a time and came running toward us and the train. Then they lay flat again and fired. Then we left, with the *máquina* still speaking over us as we left. It was then I found the girl where she had run from the train to the rocks and she ran with us. It was those troops who hunted us until that night."

"It must have been something very hard," Anselmo said. "Of much emotion."

"It was the only good thing we have done," said a deep voice. "What are you doing now, you lazy drunken obscene unsayable son of an unnameable unmarried gypsy obscenity? What are you doing?"

Robert Jordan saw a woman of about fifty almost as big as Pablo, almost as wide as she was tall, in black peasant skirt and waist, with heavy wool socks on heavy legs, black rope-soled shoes and a brown face like a model for a granite monument. She had big but nice looking hands and her thick curly black hair was twisted into a knot on her neck.

"Answer me," she said to the gypsy, ignoring the others.

"I was talking to these comrades. This one comes as a dynamiter."

"I know all that," the *mujer* of Pablo said. "Get out of here now and relieve Andrés who is on guard at the top."

"*Me voy,*" the gypsy said. "I go." He turned to Robert Jordan. "I will see thee at the hour of eating."

"Not even in a joke," said the woman to him. "Three times you have eaten today according to my count. Go now and send me Andrés.

"*Hola,*" she said to Robert Jordan and put out her hand and smiled. "How are you and how is everything in the Republic?"

"Good," he said and returned her strong hand grip. "Both with me and with the Republic."

"I am happy," she told him. She was looking into his face and smiling and he noticed she had fine gray eyes. "Do you come for us to do another train?"

"No," said Robert Jordan, trusting her instantly. "For a bridge."

"No es nada," she said. "A bridge is nothing. When do we do another train now that we have horses?"

"Later. This bridge is of great importance."

"The girl told me your comrade who was with us at the train is dead."

"Yes."

"What a pity. Never have I seen such an explosion. He was a man of talent. He pleased me very much. It is not possible to do another train now? There are many men here now in the hills. Too many. It is already hard to get food. It would be better to get out. And we have horses."

"We have to do this bridge."

"Where is it?"

"Quite close."

"All the better," the *mujer* of Pablo said. "Let us blow all the bridges there are here and get out. I am sick of this place. Here is too much concentration of people. No good can come of it. Here is a stagnation that is repugnant."

She sighted Pablo through the trees.

"Borracho!" she called to him. "Drunkard. Rotten drunkard!" She turned back to Robert Jordan cheerfully. "He's taken a leather wine bottle to drink alone in the woods," she said. "He's drinking all the time. This life is ruining him. Young man, I am very content that you have come." She clapped him on the back. "Ah," she said. "You're bigger than you look," and ran her hand over his shoulder, feeling the muscle under the flannel shirt. "Good. I am very content that you have come."

"And I equally."

"We will understand each other," she said. "Have a cup of wine."

"We have already had some," Robert Jordan said. "But, will you?"

"Not until dinner," she said. "It gives me heartburn." Then she sighted Pablo again. *"Borracho!"* she shouted. "Drunkard!" She turned to Robert Jordan and shook her head. "He was a very good man," she told him. "But now he is terminated. And listen to me about another thing. Be very good and careful about the girl. The Maria. She has had a bad time. Understandest thou?"

"Yes. Why do you say this?"

"I saw how she was from seeing thee when she came into the cave. I saw her watching thee before she came out."

"I joked with her a little."

"She was in a very bad state," the woman of Pablo said. "Now she is better, she ought to get out of here."

"Clearly, she can be sent through the lines with Anselmo."

"You and the Anselmo can take her when this terminates."

Robert Jordan felt the ache in his throat and his voice thickening. "That might be done," he said.

The *mujer* of Pablo looked at him and shook her head. "Ayee. Ayee," she said. "Are all men like that?"

"I said nothing. She is beautiful, you know that."

"No she is not beautiful. But she begins to be beautiful, you mean," the woman of Pablo said. "Men. It is a shame to us women that we make them. No. In seriousness. Are there not homes to care for such as her under the Republic?"

"Yes," said Robert Jordan. "Good places. On the coast near Valencia. In other places too. There they will treat her well and she can work with children. There are the children from evacuated villages. They will teach her the work."

"That is what I want," the *mujer* of Pablo said. "Pablo has a sickness for her already. It is another thing which destroys him. It lies on him like a sickness when he sees her. It is best that she goes now."

"We can take her after this is over."

"And you will be careful of her now if I trust you? I speak to you as though I knew you for a long time."

"It is like that," Robert Jordan said, "when people understand one another."

"Sit down," the woman of Pablo said. "I do not ask any promise because what will happen, will happen. Only if you will *not* take her out, then I ask a promise."

"Why if I would not take her?"

"Because I do not want her crazy here after you will go. I have had her crazy before and I have enough without that."

"We will take her after the bridge," Robert Jordan said. "If we are alive after the bridge, we will take her."

"I do not like to hear you speak in that manner. That manner of speaking never brings luck."

"I spoke in that manner only to make a promise," Robert Jordan said. "I am not of those who speak gloomily."

"Let me see thy hand," the woman said. Robert Jordan put his hand out and the woman opened it, held it in her own big hand, rubbed her thumb over it and looked at it, carefully, then dropped it. She stood up. He got up too and she looked at him without smiling.

"What did you see in it?" Robert Jordan asked her. "I don't believe in it. You won't scare me."

"Nothing," she told him. "I saw nothing in it."

"Yes you did. I am only curious. I do not believe in such things."

"In what do you believe?"

"In many things but not in that."

"In what?"

"In my work."

"Yes, I saw that."

"Tell me what else you saw."

"I saw nothing else," she said bitterly. "The bridge is very difficult you said?"

"No. I said it is very important."

"But it can be difficult?"

"Yes. And now I go down to look at it. How many men have you here?"

"Five that are any good. The gypsy is worthless although his intentions are good. He has a good heart. Pablo I no longer trust."

"How many men has El Sordo that are good?"

"Perhaps eight. We will see tonight. He is coming here. He is a very practical man. He also has some dynamite. Not very much, though. You will speak with him."

"Have you sent for him?"

"He comes every night. He is a neighbor. Also a friend as well as a comrade."

"What do you think of him?"

"He is a very good man. Also very practical. In the business of the train he was enormous."

"And in the other bands?"

"Advising them in time, it should be possible to unite fifty rifles of a certain dependability."

"How dependable?"

"Dependable within the gravity of the situation."

"And how many cartridges per rifle?"

"Perhaps twenty. Depending how many they would bring for this business. If they would come for this business. Remember thee that in this of a bridge there is no money and no loot and in thy reservations of talking, much danger, and that afterwards there must be a moving from these mountains. Many will oppose this of the bridge."

"Clearly."

"In this way it is better not to speak of it unnecessarily."

"I am in accord."

"Then after thou hast studied thy bridge we will talk tonight with El Sordo."

"I go down now with Anselmo."

"Wake him then," she said. "Do you want a carbine?"

"Thank you," he told her. "It is good to have but I will not use it. I go to look, not to make disturbances. Thank you for what you have told me. I like very much your way of speaking."

"I try to speak frankly."

"Then tell me what you saw in the hand."

"No," she said and shook her head. "I saw nothing. Go now to thy bridge. I will look after thy equipment."

"Cover it and that no one should touch it. It is better there than in the cave."

"It shall be covered and no one shall touch it," the woman of Pablo said. "Go now to thy bridge."

"Anselmo," Robert Jordan said, putting his hand on the shoulder of the old man who lay sleeping, his head on his arms.

The old man looked up. "Yes," he said. "Of course. Let us go."

CHAPTER THREE

THEY came down the last two hundred yards, moving carefully from tree to tree in the shadows and now, through the last pines of the steep hillside, the bridge was only fifty yards away. The late afternoon sun that still came over the brown shoulder of the mountain showed the bridge dark against the steep emptiness of the gorge. It was a steel bridge of a single span and there was a sentry box at each end. It was wide enough for two motor cars to pass and it spanned, in solid-flung metal grace, a deep gorge at the bottom of which, far below, a brook leaped in white water through rocks and boulders down to the main stream of the pass.

The sun was in Robert Jordan's eyes and the bridge showed only in outline. Then the sun lessened and was gone and looking up through the trees at the brown, rounded height that it had gone behind, he saw, now, that he no longer looked into the glare, that the mountain slope was a delicate new green and that there were patches of old snow under the crest.

Then he was watching the bridge again in the sudden short trueness of the little light that would be left, and studying its construction. The problem of its demolition was not difficult. As he watched he took out a notebook from his breast pocket and made several quick line sketches. As he made the drawings he did not figure the charges. He would do that later. Now he was noting the points where the explosive should be placed in order to cut the support of the span and drop a section of it into the gorge. It could be done unhurriedly, scientifically and correctly with a half dozen charges laid and braced to explode simultaneously; or it could be done roughly with two big ones. They would need to be very big ones, on opposite sides and should go at the same time. He sketched quickly and happily; glad at last to have the problem under his hand; glad at last actually to be engaged upon it. Then he shut his notebook, pushed the pencil into its leather holder in the edge of the flap, put the notebook in his pocket and buttoned the pocket.

While he had sketched, Anselmo had been watching the road, the bridge and the sentry boxes. He thought they had come too close to the bridge for safety and when the sketching was finished, he was relieved.

As Robert Jordan buttoned the flap of his pocket and then lay flat behind the pine trunk, looking out from behind it, Anselmo put his hand on his elbow and pointed with one finger.

In the sentry box that faced toward them up the road, the sentry was sitting holding his rifle, the bayonet fixed, between his knees. He was smoking a cigarette and he wore a knitted cap and blanket style cape. At fifty yards, you could not see anything about his face. Robert Jordan put up his field glasses, shading the lenses carefully with his cupped hands even though there was now no sun to make a glint, and there was the rail of the bridge as clear as though you could reach out and touch it and there was the face of the senty so clear he could see the sunken cheeks, the ash on the cigarette and the greasy shine of the bayonet. It was a peasant's face, the cheeks hollow under the high cheekbones, the beard stubbled, the eyes shaded by the heavy brows, big hands holding the rifle, heavy boots showing beneath the folds of the blanket cape. There was a worn, blackened leather wine bottle on the wall of the sentry box, there were some newspapers and there was no telephone. There could, of course, be a telephone on the side he could not see; but there were no wires running from the box that were visible. A telephone line ran along the road and its wires were carried over the bridge. There was a charcoal brazier outside the sentry box, made from an old petrol tin with the top cut off and holes punched in it, which rested on two stones; but he held no fire. There were some fire-blackened empty tins in the ashes under it.

Robert Jordan handed the glasses to Anselmo who lay flat beside him. The old man grinned and shook his head. He tapped his skull beside his eye with one finger.

"*Ya lo veo,*" he said in Spanish. "I have seen him," speaking from the front of his mouth with almost no movement of his lips in the way that is quieter than any whisper. He looked at the sentry as Robert Jordan smiled at him and, pointing with one finger, drew the other across his throat. Robert Jordan nodded but he did not smile.

The sentry box at the far end of the bridge faced away from them and down the road and they could not see into it. The road, which was broad and oiled and well constructed, made a turn to the left at the far end of the bridge and then swung out of sight around a curve to the right. At this point it was enlarged from the old road to its present width by cutting into the solid bastion of the rock on the far side of the gorge; and its left or western edge, looking down from the pass and the bridge, was marked and protected by a line of upright cut blocks of stone where its edge fell sheer away to the gorge. The gorge was almost a canyon here, where the brook, that the bridge was flung over, merged with the main stream of the pass.

"And the other post?" Robert Jordan asked Anselmo.

"Five hundred meters below that turn. In the roadmender's hut that is built into the side of the rock."

"How many men?" Robert Jordan asked.

He was watching the sentry again with his glasses. The sentry rubbed his cigarette out on the plank wall of the box, then took a leather tobacco pouch from his pocket, opened the paper of the dead cigarette and emptied the remnant of used tobacco into the pouch. The sentry stood up, leaned his rifle against the wall of the box and stretched, then picked up his rifle, slung it over his shoulder and walked out onto the bridge. Anselmo flattened on the ground and Robert Jordan slipped his glasses into his shirt pocket and put his head well behind the pine tree.

"There are seven men and a corporal," Anselmo said close to his ear. "I informed myself from the gypsy."

"We will go now as soon as he is quiet," Robert Jordan said. "We are too close."

"Hast thou seen what thou needest?"

"Yes. All that I need."

It was getting cold quickly now with the sun down and the light was failing as the afterglow from the last sunlight on the mountains behind them faded.

"How does it look to thee?" Anselmo said softly as they watched the sentry walk across the bridge toward the other box, his bayonet bright in the last of the afterglow, his figure unshapely in the blanket coat.

"Very good," Robert Jordan said. "Very, very good."

"I am glad," Anselmo said. "Should we go? Now there is no chance that he sees us."

The sentry was standing, his back toward them, at the far end of the bridge. From the gorge came the noise of the stream in the boulders. Then through this noise came another noise, a steady, racketing drone and they saw the sentry looking up, his knitted cap slanted back, and turning their heads and looking up they saw, high in the evening sky, three monoplanes in V formation, showing minute and silvery at that height where there still was sun, passing unbelievably quickly across the sky, their motors now throbbing steadily.

"Ours?" Anselmo asked.

"They seem so," Robert Jordan said but knew that at that height you never could be sure. They could be an evening patrol of either side. But you always said pursuit planes were ours because it made people feel better. Bombers were another matter.

Anselmo evidently felt the same. "They are ours," he said. "I recognize them. They are *Moscas.*"

"Good," said Robert Jordan. "They seem to me to be *Moscas,* too."

"They are *Moscas,*" Anselmo said.

Robert Jordan could have put the glasses on them and been sure instantly but he preferred not to. It made no difference to him who they were tonight and if it pleased the old man to have them be ours, he did not want to take them away. Now, as they moved out of sight toward Segovia, they did not look to be the green, red wing-tipped, low wing Russian conversion of the Boeing P32 that the Spaniards called *Moscas.* You could not see the colors but the cut was wrong. No. It was a Fascist Patrol coming home.

The sentry was still standing at the far box with his back turned.

"Let us go," Robert Jordan said. He started up the hill, moving carefully and taking advantage of the cover until they were out of sight. Anselmo followed him at a hundred yards distance. When they were well out of sight of the bridge, he stopped and the old man came up and went into the lead and climbed steadily through the pass, up the steep slope in the dark.

"We have a formidable aviation," the old man said happily.

"Yes."

"And we will win."

"We have to win."

"Yes. And after we have won you must come to hunt."

"To hunt what?"

"The boar, the bear, the wolf, the ibex——"

"You like to hunt?"

"Yes, man. More than anything. We all hunt in my village. You do not like to hunt?"

"No," said Robert Jordan. "I do not like to kill animals."

"With me it is the opposite," the old man said. "I do not like to kill men."

"Nobody does except those who are disturbed in the head," Robert Jordan said. "But I feel nothing against it when it is necessary. When it is for the cause."

"It is a different thing, though," Anselmo said. "In my house, when I had a house, and now I have no house, there were the tusks of boar I had shot in the lower forest. There were the hides of wolves I had shot. In the winter, hunting them in the snow. One very big one, I killed at dusk in the outskirts of the village on my way home one night in November. There were four wolf hides on the floor of my house. They were worn by stepping on them but they were wolf hides. There were the horns of ibex that I had killed in the high Sierra, and there was an eagle stuffed by an embalmer of birds of Avila, with his wings spread, and eyes as yellow and real as the eyes of an eagle alive. It was a very beautiful thing and all of those things gave me great pleasure to contemplate."

"Yes," said Robert Jordan.

"On the door of the church of my village was nailed the paw of a bear that I killed in the spring, finding him on a hillside in the snow, overturning a log with this same paw."

"When was this?"

"Six years ago. And every time I saw that paw, like the hand of a man, but with those long claws, dried and nailed through the palm to the door of the church, I received a pleasure."

"Of pride?"

"Of pride of remembrance of the encounter with the bear on that hillside in the early spring. But of the killing of a man, who is a man as we are, there is nothing good that remains."

"You can't nail his paw to the church," Robert Jordan said.

"No. Such a barbarity is unthinkable. Yet the hand of a man is like the paw of a bear."

"So is the chest of a man like the chest of a bear," Robert Jordan said. "With the hide removed from the bear, there are many similarities in the muscles."

"Yes," Anselmo said. "The gypsies believe the bear to be a brother of man."

"So do the Indians in America," Robert Jordan said. "And when they kill a bear they apologize to him and ask his pardon. They put his skull in a tree and they ask him to forgive them before they leave it."

"The gypsies believe the bear to be a brother to man because he has the same body beneath his hide, because he drinks beer, because he enjoys music and because he likes to dance."

"So also believe the Indians."

"Are the Indians then gypsies?"

"No. But they believe alike about the bear."

"Clearly. The gypsies also believe he is a brother because he steals for pleasure."

"Have you gypsy blood?"

"No. But I have seen much of them and clearly, since the movement, more. There are many in the hills. To them it is not a sin to kill outside the tribe. They deny this but it is true."

"Like the Moors."

"Yes. But the gypsies have many laws they do not admit to having. In the war many gypsies have become bad again as they were in olden times."

"They do not understand why the war is made. They do not know for what we fight."

"No," Anselmo said. "They only know now there is a war and people may kill again as in the olden times without a surety of punishment."

"You have killed?" Robert Jordan asked in the intimacy of the dark and of their day together.

"Yes. Several times. But not with pleasure. To me it is a sin to kill a man. Even Fascists whom we must kill. To me there is a great difference between the bear and the man and I do not believe the wizardry of the gypsies about the brotherhood with animals. No. I am against all killing of men."

"Yet you have killed."

"Yes. And will again. But if I live later, I will try to live in such a way, doing no harm to any one, that it will be forgiven."

"By whom?"

"Who knows? Since we do not have God here any more, neither His Son nor the Holy Ghost, who forgives? I do not know."

"You have not God any more?"

"No. Man. Certainly not. If there were God, never would He have permitted what I have seen with my eyes. Let *them* have God."

"They claim Him."

"Clearly I miss Him, having been brought up in religion. But now a man must be responsible to himself."

"Then it is thyself who will forgive thee for killing."

"I believe so," Anselmo said. "Since you put it clearly in that way I believe that must be it. But with or without God, I think it is a sin to kill. To take the life of another is to me very grave. I will do it whenever necessary but I am not of the race of Pablo."

"To win a war we must kill our enemies. That has always been true."

"Clearly. In war we must kill. But I have very rare ideas," Anselmo said.

They were walking now close together in the dark and he spoke softly, sometimes turning his head as he climbed. "I would not kill even a Bishop. I would not kill a proprietor of any kind. I would make them work each day as we have worked in the fields and as we work in the mountains with the timber, all of the rest of their lives. So they would see what man is born to. That they should sleep where we sleep. That they should eat as we eat. But above all that they should work. Thus they would learn."

"And they would survive to enslave thee again."

"To kill them teaches nothing," Anselmo said. "You cannot exterminate them because from their seed comes more with greater hatred. Prison is nothing. Prison only makes hatred. That all our enemies should learn."

"But still thou hast killed."

"Yes," Anselmo said. "Many times and will again. But not with pleasure and regarding it as a sin."

"And the sentry. You joked of killing the sentry."

"That was in joke. I would kill the sentry. Yes. Certainly and with a clear heart considering our task. But not with pleasure."

"We will leave them to those who enjoy it," Robert Jordan said. "There are eight and five. That is thirteen for those who enjoy it."

"There are many of those who enjoy it," Anselmo said in the dark. "We have many of those. More of those than of men who would serve for a battle."

"Hast thou ever been in a battle?"

"Nay," the old man said. "We fought in Segovia at the start of the movement but we were beaten and we ran. I ran with the others. We did not truly understand what we were doing, nor how it should be done. Also I had only a shotgun with cartridges of large buckshot and the *guardia civil* had Mausers. I could not hit them with buckshot at a hundred yards, and at three hundred yards they shot us as they wished as though we were rabbits. They shot much and well and we were like sheep before them." He was silent. Then asked, "Thinkest thou there will be a battle at the bridge?"

"There is a chance."

"I have never seen a battle without running," Anselmo said. "I do not know how I would comport myself. I am an old man and I have wondered."

"I will respond for thee," Robert Jordan told him.

"And hast thou been in many battles?"

"Several."

"And what thinkest thou of this of the bridge?"

"First I think of the bridge. That is my business. It is not difficult to destroy the bridge. Then we will make the dispositions for the rest. For the preliminaries. It will all be written."

"Very few of these people read," Anselmo said.

"It will be written for every one's knowledge so that all know, but also it will be clearly explained."

"I will do that to which I am assigned," Anselmo said. "But remembering the shooting in Segovia, if there is to be a battle or even much exchanging of shots, I would wish to have it very clear what I must do under all circumstances to avoid running. I remember that I had a great tendency to run at Segovia."

"We will be together," Robert Jordan told him. "I will tell you what there is to do at all times."

"Then there is no problem," Anselmo said. "I can do anything that I am ordered."

"For us will be the bridge and the battle, should there be one," Robert Jordan said and saying it in the dark, he felt a little theatrical but it sounded well in Spanish.

"It should be of the highest interest," Anselmo said and hearing him say it honestly and clearly and with no pose, neither the English pose of understatement nor any Latin bravado, Robert Jordan thought he was very lucky to have this old man and having seen the bridge and worked out and simplified the problem it would have been to surprise the posts and blow it in a normal way, he resented Golz's orders, and the necessity for them. He resented them for what they could do to him and for what they could do to this old man. They were bad orders all right for those who would have to carry them out.

And that is not the way to think, he told himself, and there is not you, and there are no people that things must not happen to. Neither you nor this old man is anything. You are instruments to do your duty. There are necessary orders that are no fault of yours and there is a bridge and that bridge can be the point on which the future of the human race can turn. As it can turn on everything that happens in this war. You have only one thing to do and you must do it. Only one thing, hell, he thought. If it were one thing it was easy. Stop worrying, you windy bastard, he said to himself. Think about something else.

So he thought about the girl Maria, with her skin, the hair and the eyes all the same golden tawny brown, the hair a little darker than the rest but it would be lighter as her skin tanned deeper, the smooth skin, pale gold on the surface with a darkness underneath.

Smooth it would be, all of her body smooth, and she moved awk-wardly as though there were something of her and about her that embarrassed her as though it were visible, though it was not, but only in her mind. And she blushed with he looked at her, and she sitting, her hands clasped around her knees and the shirt open at the throat, the cup of her breasts uptilted against the shirt, and as he thought of her, his throat was choky and there was a difficulty in walking and he and Anselmo spoke no more until the old man said, "Now we go down through these rocks and to the camp."

As they came through the rocks in the dark, a man spoke to them, "Halt. Who goes?" They heard a rifle bolt snick as it was drawn back and then the knock against the wood as it was pushed forward and down on the stock.

"Comrades," Anselmo said.

"What comrades?"

"Comrades of Pablo," the old man told him. "Dost thou not know us?"

"Yes," the voice said. "But it is an order. Have you the pass-word?"

"No. We come from below."

"I know," the man said in the dark. "You come from the bridge. I know all of that. The order is not mine. You must know the sec-ond half of a password."

"What is the first half then?" Robert Jordan said.

"I have forgotten it," the man said in the dark and laughed. "Go then unprintably to the campfire with thy obscene dy-namite."

"That is called guerilla discipline," Anselmo said. "Uncock thy piece."

"It is uncocked," the man said in the dark. "I let it down with my thumb and forefinger."

"Thou wilt do that with a Mauser sometime which has no knurl on the bolt and it will fire."

"This is a Mauser," the man said. "But I have a grip of thumb and forefinger beyond description. Always I let it down that way."

"Where is the rifle pointed?" asked Anselmo into the dark.

"At thee," the man said, "all the time that I descended the bolt. And when thou comest to the camp, order that some one should relieve me because I have indescribable and unprintable hunger and I have forgotten the password."

"How art thou called?" Robert Jordan asked.

"Agustín," the man said. "I am called Agustín and I am dying with boredom in this spot."

"We will take the message," Robert Jordan said and he thought how the word *aburmiento* which means boredom in Spanish was a word no peasant would use in any other language. Yet it is one of the most common words in the mouth of a Spaniard of any class.

"Listen to me," Agustín said, and coming close he put his hand on Robert Jordan's shoulder. Then striking a flint and steel together he held it up and blowing on the end of the cork, looked at the young man's face in its glow.

"You look like the other one," he said. "But something different. Listen," he put the lighter down and stood holding his rifle. "Tell me this. Is it true about the bridge?"

"What about the bridge?"

"That we blow up an obscene bridge and then have to obscenely well obscenity ourselves off out of these mountains?"

"I know not."

"*You* know not," Agustín said. "What a barbarity! Whose then is the dynamite?"

"Mine."

"And knowest thou not what it is for? Don't tell me tales."

"I know what it is for and so will you in time," Robert Jordan said. "But now we go to the camp."

"Go to the unprintable," Agustín said. "And unprint thyself. But do you want me to tell you something of service to you?"

"Yes," said Robert Jordan. "If it is not unprintable," naming the principal obscenity that had larded the conversation. The man, Agustín, spoke so obscenely, coupling an obscenity to every noun as an adjective, using the same obscenity as a verb, that Robert Jordan wondered if he could speak a straight sentence. Agustín laughed in the dark when he heard the word. "It is a way of speaking I have. Maybe it is ugly. Who knows? Each one speaks according to his manner. Listen to me. The bridge is nothing to me. As well the bridge as another thing. Also I have a boredom in these mountains. That we should go if it is needed. These mountains say nothing to me. That we should leave them. But I would say one thing. Guard well thy explosive."

"Thank you," Robert Jordan said. "From thee?"

"No," Agustín said. "From people less unprintably equipped than I."

"So?" asked Robert Jordan.

"You understand Spanish," Agustín said seriously now. "Care well for thy unprintable explosive."

"Thank you."

"No. Don't thank me. Look after thy stuff."

"Has anything happened to it?"

"No, or I would not waste thy time talking in this fashion."

"Thank you all the same. We go now to camp."

"Good," said Agustín, "and that they send some one here who knows the password."

"Will we see you at the camp?"

"Yes, man. And shortly."

"Come on," Robert Jordan said to Anselmo.

They were walking down the edge of the meadow now and there was a gray mist. The grass was lush underfoot after the pine-needle floor of the forest and the dew on the grass wet through their canvas rope-soled shoes. Ahead, through the trees, Robert Jordan could see a light where he knew the mouth of the cave must be.

"Agustín is a very good man," Anselmo said. "He speaks very filthily and always in jokes but he is a very serious man."

"You know him well?"

"Yes. For a long time. I have much confidence in him."

"And what he says?"

"Yes, man. This Pablo is bad now, as you could see."

"And the best thing to do?"

"One shall guard it at all times."

"Who?"

"You. Me. The woman and Agustín. Since he sees the danger."

"Did you think things were as bad as they are here?"

"No," Anselmo said. "They have gone bad very fast. But it was necessary to come here. This is the country of Pablo and of El

Sordo. In their country we must deal with them unless it is something that can be done alone."

"And El Sordo?"

"Good," Anselmo said. "As good as the other is bad."

"You believe now that he is truly bad?"

"All afternoon I have thought of it and since we have heard what we have heard, I think now, yes. Truly."

"It would not be better to leave, speaking of another bridge, and obtain men from other bands?"

"No," Anselmo said. "This is his country. You could not move that he would not know it. But one must move with much precautions."

CHAPTER FOUR

THEY came down to the mouth of the cave, where a light shone out from the edge of a blanket that hung over the opening. The two packs were at the foot of the tree covered with a canvas and Robert Jordan knelt down and felt the canvas wet and stiff over them. In the dark he felt under the canvas in the outside pocket of one of the packs and took out a leather-covered flask and slipped it in his pocket. Unlocking the long barred padlocks that passed through the grommet that closed the opening of the mouth of the packs, and untying the drawstring at the top of each pack, he felt inside them and verified their contents with his hands. Deep in one pack he felt the bundled blocks in the sacks, the sacks wrapped in the sleeping robe, and tying the strings of that and pushing the lock shut again, he put his hands into the other and felt the sharp wood outline of the box of the old exploder, the cigar box with the caps, each little cylinder wrapped round and round with its two wires (the lot of them packed as carefully as he had packed his collection of wild bird eggs when he was a boy), the stock of the submachine gun, disconnected from the barrel and wrapped in his leather jacket, the two pans and five clips in one of the inner pockets of the big pack-sack and the small coils of copper wire and the big coil of light insulated wire in the other. In the pocket with the wire he felt his pliers and the two wooden awls for making holes in the end of the blocks and then, from the last inside pocket, he took a big box of the Russian cigarettes of the lot he had from Golz's headquarters and tying the mouth of the pack shut, he pushed the lock in, buckled the flaps down and again covered both packs with the canvas. Anselmo had gone on into the cave.

Robert Jordan stood up to follow him, then reconsidered and, lifting the canvas off the two packs, picked them up, one in each hand, and started with them, just able to carry them, for the mouth of the cave. He laid one pack down and lifted the blanket aside, then with his head stooped and with a pack in each hand, carrying by the leather shoulder straps, he went into the cave.

It was warm and smoky in the cave. There was a table along one wall with a tallow candle stuck in a bottle on it and at the table were seated Pablo, three men he did not know, and the gypsy, Rafael. The candle made shadows on the wall behind the men and Anselmo stood where he had come in to the right of the table. The wife of Pablo was standing over the charcoal fire on the open fire hearth in the corner of the cave. The girl knelt by her stirring in an iron pot. She lifted the wooden spoon out and looked at Robert Jordan as he stood there in the doorway and he saw, in the glow from the fire the woman was blowing with a bellows, the girl's face, her arm and the drops running down from the spoon and dropping into the iron pot.

"What do you carry?" Pablo said.

"My things," Robert Jordan said and set the two packs down a little way apart where the cave opened out on the side away from the table.

"Are they not well outside?" Pablo asked.

"Some one might trip over them in the dark," Robert Jordan said and walked over to the table and laid the box of cigarettes on it.

"I do not like to have dynamite here in the cave," Pablo said.

"It is far from the fire," Robert Jordan said. "Take some cigarettes." He ran his thumbnail along the side of the paper box with the big colored figure of a warship on the cover and pushed the box toward Pablo.

Anselmo brought him a rawhide-covered stool and he sat down at the table. Pablo looked at him as though he were going to speak again, then reached for the cigarettes.

Robert Jordan pushed them toward the others. He was not looking at them yet. But he noted one man took cigarettes and two did not. All of his concentration was on Pablo.

"How goes it, gypsy?" he said to Rafael.

"Good," the gypsy said. Robert Jordan could tell they had been talking about him when he came in. Even the gypsy was not at ease.

"She is going to let you eat again?" Robert Jordan asked the gypsy.

"Yes. Why not?" the gypsy said. It was a long way from the friendly joking they had together in the afternoon.

The woman of Pablo said nothing and went on blowing up the coals of the fire.

"One called Agustín says he dies of boredom above," Robert Jordan said.

"That doesn't kill," Pablo said. "Let him die a little."

"Is there wine?" Robert Jordan asked the table at large, leaning forward, his hands on the table.

"There is little left," Pablo said sullenly. Robert Jordan decided he had better look at the other three and try to see where he stood.

"In that case, let me have a cup of water. Thou," he called to the girl. "Bring me a cup of water."

The girl looked at the woman, who said nothing, and gave no sign of having heard, then she went to a kettle containing water and dipped a cup full. She brought it to the table and put it down before him. Robert Jordan smiled at her. At the same time he sucked in on his stomach muscles and swung a little to the left on his stool so that his pistol slipped around on his belt closer to where he wanted it. He reached his hand down toward his hip pocket and Pablo watched him. He knew they all were watching him, too, but he watched only Pablo. His hand came up from the hip pocket with the leather-covered flask and he unscrewed the top and then, lifting the cup, drank half the water and poured very slowly from the flask into the cup.

"It is too strong for thee or I would give thee some," he said to the girl and smiled at her again. "There is little left or I would offer some to thee," he said to Pablo.

"I do not like anis," Pablo said.

The acrid smell had carried across the table and he had picked out the one familiar component.

"Good," said Robert Jordan. "Because there is very little left."

"What drink is that?" the gypsy asked.

"A medicine," Robert Jordan said. "Do you want to taste it?"

"What is it for?"

"For everything," Robert Jordan said. "It cures everything. If you have anything wrong this will cure it."

"Let me taste it," the gypsy said.

Robert Jordan pushed the cup toward him. It was a milky yellow now with the water and he hoped the gypsy would not take more than a swallow. There was very little of it left and one cup of it took the place of the evening papers, of all the old evenings in cafés, of all chestnut trees that would be in bloom now in this month, of the great slow horses of the outer boulevards, of book shops, of kiosques, and of galleries, of the Parc Montsouris, of the Stade Buffalo, and of the Butte Chaumont, of the Guaranty Trust Company and the Ile de la Cité, of Foyot's old hotel, and of being able to read and relax in the evening; of all the things he had enjoyed and forgotten and that came back to him when he tasted that opaque, bitter, tongue-numbing, brain-warming, stomach-warming, idea-changing liquid alchemy.

The gypsy made a face and handed the cup back. "It smells of anis but it is bitter as gall," he said. "It is better to be sick than have that medicine."

"That's the wormwood," Robert Jordan told him. "In this, the real absinthe, there is wormwood. It's supposed to rot your brain out but I don't believe it. It only changes the ideas. You should pour water into it very slowly, a few drops at a time. But I poured it into the water."

"What are you saying?" Pablo said angrily, feeling the mockery.

"Explaining the medicine," Robert Jordan told him and grinned. "I bought it in Madrid. It was the last bottle and it's lasted me three weeks." He took a big swallow of it and felt it coasting over his tongue in delicate anæsthesia. He looked at Pablo and grinned again.

"How's business?" he asked.

Pablo did not answer and Robert Jordan looked carefully at the other three men at the table. One had a large flat face, flat and brown as a Serrano ham with a nose flattened and broken, and the long thin Russian cigarette, projecting at an angle, made the face look even flatter. This man had short gray hair and a gray stubble of beard and wore the usual black smock buttoned at the neck. He looked down at the table when Robert Jordan looked at him but his eyes were steady and they did not blink. The other two were evidently brothers. They looked much alike and were both short, heavily built, dark haired, their hair growing low on their foreheads, dark-eyed and brown. One had a scar across his forehead above his left eye and as he looked at them, they looked back at him steadily. One looked to be about twenty-six or -eight, the other perhaps two years older.

"What are you looking at?" one brother, the one with the scar, asked.

"Thee," Robert Jordan said.

"Do you see anything rare?"

"No," said Robert Jordan. "Have a cigarette?"

"Why not?" the brother said. He had not taken any before. "These are like the other had. He of the train."

"Were you at the train?"

"We were all at the train," the brother said quietly. "All except the old man."

"That is what we should do now," Pablo said. "Another train."

"We can do that," Robert Jordan said. "After the bridge."

He could see that the wife of Pablo had turned now from the fire and was listening. When he said the word bridge every one was quiet.

"After the bridge," he said again deliberately and took a sip of the absinthe. I might as well bring it on, he thought. It's coming anyway.

"I do not go for the bridge," Pablo said, looking down at the table. "Neither me nor my people."

Robert Jordan said nothing. He looked at Anselmo and raised the cup. "Then we shall do it alone, old one," he said and smiled.

"Without this coward," Anselmo said.

"What did you say?" Pablo spoke to the old man.

"Nothing for thee. I did not speak to thee," Anselmo told him.

Robert Jordan now looked past the table to where the wife of Pablo was standing by the fire. She had said nothing yet, nor given any sign. But now she said something he could not hear to the girl and the girl rose from the cooking fire, slipped along the wall, opened the blanket that hung over the mouth of the cave and went out. I think it is going to come now, Robert Jordan thought. I believe this is it. I did not want it to be this way but this seems to be the way it is.

"Then we will do the bridge without thy aid," Robert Jordan said to Pablo.

"No," Pablo said, and Robert Jordan watched his face sweat. "Thou wilt blow no bridge here."

"No?"

"Thou wilt blow no bridge," Pablo said heavily.

"And thou?" Robert Jordan spoke to the wife of Pablo who was standing, still and huge, by the fire. She turned toward them and said, "I am for the bridge." Her face was lit by the fire and it was flushed and it shone warm and dark and handsome now in the firelight as it was meant to be.

"What do you say?" Pablo said to her and Robert Jordan saw the betrayed look on his face and the sweat on his forehead as he turned his head.

"I am for the bridge and against thee," the wife of Pablo said. "Nothing more."

"I am also for the bridge," the man with the flat face and the broken nose said, crushing the end of the cigarette on the table.

"To me the bridge means nothing," one of the brothers said. "I am for the *mujer* of Pablo."

"Equally," said the other brother.

"Equally," the gypsy said.

Robert Jordan watched Pablo and as he watched, letting his right hand hang lower and lower, ready if it should be necessary, half hoping it would be (feeling perhaps that were the simplest and easiest yet not wishing to spoil what had gone so well, knowing how quickly all of a family, all of a clan, all of a band, can turn against a stranger in a quarrel, yet thinking what could be done with the hand were the simplest and best and surgically the most sound now that this had happened), saw also the wife of Pablo standing there and watched her blush proudly and soundly and healthily as the allegiances were given.

"I am for the Republic," the woman of Pablo said happily. "And the Republic is the bridge. Afterwards we will have time for other projects."

"And thou," Pablo said bitterly. "With your head of a seed bull and your heart of a whore. Thou thinkest there will be an afterwards from this bridge? Thou hast an idea of that which will pass?"

"That which must pass," the woman of Pablo said. "That which must pass, will pass."

"And it means nothing to thee to be hunted then like a beast after this thing from which we derive no profit? Nor to die in it?"

"Nothing," the woman of Pablo said. "And do not try to frighten me, coward."

"Coward," Pablo said bitterly. "You treat a man as coward because he has a tactical sense. Because he can see the results of an idiocy in advance. It is not cowardly to know what is foolish."

"Neither is it foolish to know what is cowardly," said Anselmo, unable to resist making the phrase.

"Do you want to die?" Pablo said to him seriously and Robert Jordan saw how unrhetorical was the question.

"No."

"Then watch thy mouth. You talk too much about things you do not understand. Don't you see that this is serious?" he said almost pitifully. "Am I the only one who sees the seriousness of this?"

I believe so, Robert Jordan thought. Old Pablo, old boy, I believe so. Except me. You can see it and I see it and the woman read it in my hand but she doesn't see it, yet. Not yet she doesn't see it.

"Am I a leader for nothing?" Pablo asked. "I know what I speak of. You others do not know. This old man talks nonsense. He is an old man who is nothing but a messenger and a guide for foreigners. This foreigner comes here to do a thing for the good of the foreigners. For his good we must be sacrificed. I am for the good and the safety of all."

"Safety," the wife of Pablo said. "There is no such thing as safety. There are so many seeking safety here now that they make a great danger. In seeking safety now you lose all."

She stood now by the table with the big spoon in her hand.

"There is safety," Pablo said. "Within the danger there is the safety of knowing what chances to take. It is like the bullfighter who knowing what he is doing, takes no chances and is safe."

"Until he is gored," the woman said bitterly. "How many times have I heard matadors talk like that before they took a goring. How often have I heard Finito say that it is all knowledge and that the bull never gored the man; rather the man gored himself on the horn of the bull. Always do they talk that way in their arrogance before a goring. Afterwards we visit them in the clinic." Now she was mimicking a visit to a bedside, "'Hello, old timer. Hello,'" she boomed. Then, "'*Buenas, Compadre.* How goes it, Pilar?'" imitating the weak voice of the wounded bullfighter. "'How did this happen, Finito, *Chico,* how did this dirty accident occur to thee?'" booming it out in her own voice. Then talking weak and small, "'It is nothing, woman. Pilar, it is nothing. It shouldn't have happened. I killed him very well, you understand. Nobody could have killed him better. Then having killed him exactly as I should and him absolutely dead, swaying on his legs, and ready to fall of his own weight, I walked away from him with a certain amount of arrogance and much style and from the back he throws me this horn between the cheeks of my buttocks and it comes out of my liver.'" She commenced to laugh, dropping the imitation of the almost effeminate bullfighter's voice and booming again now. "You and your safety! Did I live nine years with three of the worst paid matadors in the world not to learn about fear and about safety? Speak to me of anything but safety. And thee. What illusions I put in thee and how they have turned out! From one year of war thou has become lazy, a drunkard and a coward."

"In that way thou hast no right to speak," Pablo said. "And less even before the people and a stranger."

"In that way will I speak," the wife of Pablo went on. "Have you not heard? Do you still believe that you command here?"

"Yes," Pablo said. "Here I command."

"Not in joke," the woman said. "Here I command! Haven't you heard *la gente?* Here no one commands but me. You can stay if you wish and eat of the food and drink of the wine, but not too bloody much, and share in the work if thee wishes. But here I command."

"I should shoot thee and the foreigner both," Pablo said sullenly.

"Try it," the woman said. "And see what happens."

"A cup of water for me," Robert Jordan said, not taking his eyes from the man with his sullen heavy head and the woman standing proudly and confidently holding the big spoon as authoritatively as though it were a baton.

"Maria," called the woman of Pablo and when the girl came in the door she said, "Water for this comrade."

Robert Jordan reached for his flask and, bringing the flask out, as he brought it he loosened the pistol in the holster and swung it on top of his thigh. He poured a second absinthe into his cup and took the cup of water the girl brought him and commenced to drip it into the cup, a little at a time. The girl stood at his elbow, watching him.

"Outside," the woman of Pablo said to her, gesturing with the spoon.

"It is cold outside," the girl said, her cheek close to Robert Jordan's, watching what was happening in the cup where the liquor was clouding.

"Maybe," the woman of Pablo said. "But in here it is too hot." Then she said, kindly, "It is not for long."

The girl shook her head and went out.

I don't think he is going to take this much more, Robert Jordan thought to himself. He held the cup in one hand and his other hand rested, frankly now, on the pistol. He had slipped the safety catch and he felt the worn comfort of the checked grip chafed almost smooth and touched the round, cool companionship of the trigger guard. Pablo no longer looked at him but only at the woman. She went on, "Listen to me, drunkard. You understand who commands here?"

"I command."

"No. Listen. Take the wax from thy hairy ears. Listen well. I command."

Pablo looked at her and you could tell nothing of what he was thinking by his face. He looked at her quite deliberately and then he looked across the table at Robert Jordan. He looked at him a long time contemplatively and then he looked back at the woman, again.

"All right. You command," he said. "And if you want he can command too. And the two of you can go to hell." He was looking the woman straight in the face and he was neither dominated by her nor seemed to be much affected by her. "It is possible that I am lazy and that I drink too much. You may consider me a coward but there you are mistaken. But I am not stupid." He paused. "That you should command and that you should like it. Now if you are a woman as well as a commander, that we should have something to eat."

"Maria," the woman of Pablo called.

The girl put her head inside the blanket across the cave mouth. "Enter now and serve the supper."

The girl came in and walked across to the low table by the hearth and picked up the enameled-ware bowls and brought them to the table.

"There is wine enough for all," the woman of Pablo said to Robert Jordan. "Pay no attention to what that drunkard says. When this is finished we will get more. Finish that rare thing thou art drinking and take a cup of wine."

Robert Jordan swallowed down the last of the absinthe, feeling it, gulped that way, making a warm, small, fume-rising, wet, chemical-change-producing heat in him and passed the cup for wine. The girl dipped it full for him and smiled.

"Well, did you see the bridge?" the gypsy asked. The others, who had not opened their mouths after the change of allegiance, were all leaning forward to listen now.

"Yes," Robert Jordan said. "It is something easy to do. Would you like me to show you?"

"Yes, man. With much interest."

Robert Jordan took out the notebook from his shirt pocket and showed them the sketches.

"Look how it seems," the flat-faced man, who was named Primitivo, said. "It is the bridge itself."

Robert Jordan with the point of the pencil explained how the bridge should be blown and the reason for the placing of the charges.

"What simplicity," the scarred-faced brother, who was called Andrés, said. "And how do you explode them?"

Robert Jordan explained that too and, as he showed them, he felt the girl's arm resting on his shoulder as she looked. The woman of Pablo was watching too. Only Pablo took no interest, sitting by himself with a cup of wine that he replenished by dipping into the big bowl Maria had filled from the wineskin that hung to the left of the entrance to the cave.

"Hast thou done much of this?" the girl asked Robert Jordan softly.

"Yes."

"And can we see the doing of it?"

"Yes. Why not?"

"You will see it," Pablo said from his end of the table. "I believe that you will see it."

"Shut up," the woman of Pablo said to him and suddenly remembering what she had seen in the hand in the afternoon she was wildly, unreasonably angry. "Shut up, coward. Shut up, bad luck bird. Shut up, murderer."

"Good," Pablo said. "I shut up. It is thou who commands now and you should continue to look at the pretty pictures. But remember that I am not stupid."

The woman of Pablo could feel her rage changing to sorrow and to a feeling of the thwarting of all hope and promise. She knew this feeling from when she was a girl and she knew the things that caused it all through her life. It came now suddenly and she put it away from her and would not let it touch her, neither her nor the Republic, and she said, "Now we will eat. Serve the bowls from the pot, Maria."

CHAPTER FIVE

ROBERT JORDAN pushed aside the saddle blanket that hung over the mouth of the cave and, stepping out, took a deep breath of the cold night air. The mist had cleared away and the stars were out. There was no wind, and, outside now of the warm air of the cave, heavy with smoke of both tobacco and charcoal, with the odor of cooked rice and meat, saffron, pimentos, and oil, the tarry, wine-spilled smell of the big skin hung beside the door, hung by the neck and the four legs extended, wine drawn from a plug fitted in one leg, wine that spilled a little onto the earth of the floor, settling the dust smell; out now from the odors of different herbs whose names he did not know that hung in bunches from the ceiling, with long ropes of garlic, away now from the copper-penny, red wine and garlic, horse sweat and man sweat dried in the clothing (acrid and gray the man sweat, sweet and sickly the dried brushed-off lather of horse sweat), of the men at the table, Robert Jordan breathed deeply of the clear night air of the mountains that smelled of the pines and of the dew on the grass in the meadow by the stream. Dew had fallen heavily since the wind had dropped, but, as he stood there, he thought there would be frost by morning.

As he stood breathing deep and then listening to the night, he heard first, firing far away, and then he heard an owl cry in the timber below, where the horse corral was slung. Then inside the cave he could hear the gypsy starting to sing and the soft chording of a guitar.

"I had an inheritance from my father," the artificially hardened voice rose harshly and hung there. Then went on:

> *"It was the moon and the sun*
> *"And though I roam all over the world*
> *"The spending of it's never done."*

The guitar thudded with chorded applause for the singer. "Good," Robert Jordan heard some one say. "Give us the Catalan, gypsy."

"No."

"Yes. Yes. The Catalan."

"All right," the gypsy said and sang mournfully,

> *"My nose is flat.*
> *"My face is black.*
> *"But still I am a man."*

"Olé!" some one said. "Go on, gypsy!"

The gypsy's voice rose tragically and mockingly.

> *"Thank God I am a Negro.*
> *"And not a Catalan!"*

"There is much noise," Pablo's voice said. "Shut up, gypsy."

"Yes," he heard the woman's voice. "There is too much noise. You could call the *guardia civil* with that voice and still it has no quality."

"I know another verse," the gypsy said and the guitar commenced.

"Save it," the woman told him.

The guitar stopped.

"I am not good in voice tonight. So there is no loss," the gypsy said and pushing the blanket aside he came out into the dark.

Robert Jordan watched him walk over to a tree and then come toward him.

"Roberto," the gypsy said softly.

"Yes, Rafael," he said. He knew the gypsy had been affected by the wine from his voice. He himself had drunk the two absinthes and some wine but his head was clear and cold from the strain of the difficulty with Pablo.

"Why didst thou not kill Pablo?" the gypsy said very softly.

"Why kill him?"

"You have to kill him sooner or later. Why did you not approve of the moment?"

"Do you speak seriously?"

"What do you think they all waited for? What do you think the woman sent the girl away for? Do you believe that it is possible to continue after what has been said?"

"That you all should kill him."

"*Qué va,*" the gypsy said quietly. "That is your business. Three or four times we waited for you to kill him. Pablo has no friends."

"I had the idea," Robert Jordan said. "But I left it."

"Surely all could see that. Every one noted your preparations. Why didn't you do it?"

"I thought it might molest you others or the woman."

"*Qué va.* And the woman waiting as a whore waits for the flight of the big bird. Thou art younger than thou appearest."

"It is possible."

"Kill him now," the gypsy urged.

"That is to assassinate."

"Even better," the gypsy said very softly. "Less danger. Go on. Kill him now."

"I cannot in that way. It is repugnant to me and it is not how one should act for the cause."

"Provoke him then," the gypsy said. "But you have to kill him. There is no remedy."

As they spoke, the owl flew between the trees with the softness of all silence, dropping past them, then rising, the wings beating quickly, but with no noise of feathers moving as the bird hunted.

"Look at him," the gypsy said in the dark. "Thus should men move."

"And in the day, blind in a tree with crows around him," Robert Jordan said.

"Rarely," said the gypsy. "And then by hazard. Kill him," he went on. "Do not let it become difficult."

"Now the moment is passed."

"Provoke it," the gypsy said. "Or take advantage of the quiet."

The blanket that closed the cave door opened and light came out. Some one came toward where they stood.

"It is a beautiful night," the man said in a heavy, dull voice. "We will have good weather."

It was Pablo.

He was smoking one of the Russian cigarettes and in the glow, as he drew on the cigarette, his round face showed. They could see his heavy, long-armed body in the starlight.

"Do not pay any attention to the woman," he said to Robert Jordan. In the dark the cigarette glowed bright, then showed in his hand as he lowered it. "She is difficult sometimes. She is a good woman. Very loyal to the Republic." The light of the cigarette jerked slightly now as he spoke. He must be talking with it in the corner of his mouth, Robert Jordan thought. "We should have no difficulties. We are of accord. I am glad you have come." The cigarette glowed brightly. "Pay no attention to arguments," he said. "You are very welcome here.

"Excuse me now," he said. "I go to see how they have picketed the horses."

He went off through the trees to the edge of the meadow and they heard a horse nicker from below.

"You see?" the gypsy said. "Now you see? In this way has the moment escaped."

Robert Jordan said nothing.

"I go down there," the gypsy said angrily.

"To do what?"

"*Qué va*, to do what. At least to prevent him leaving."

"Can he leave with a horse from below?"

"No."

"Then go to the spot where you can prevent him."

"Agustín is there."

"Go then and speak with Agustín. Tell him that which has happened."

"Agustín will kill him with pleasure."

"Less bad," Robert Jordan said. "Go then above and tell him all as it happened."

"And then?"

"I go to look below in the meadow."

"Good. Man. Good," he could not see Rafael's face in the dark but he could feel him smiling. "Now you have tightened your garters," the gypsy said approvingly.

"Go to Agustín," Robert Jordan said to him.

"Yes, Roberto, yes," said the gypsy.

Robert Jordan walked through the pines, feeling his way from tree to tree to the edge of the meadow. Looking across it in the darkness, lighter here in the open from the starlight, he saw the dark bulks of the picketed horses. He counted them where they were scattered between him and the stream. There were five. Robert Jordan sat down at the foot of a pine tree and looked out across the meadow.

I am tired, he thought, and perhaps my judgment is not good. But my obligation is the bridge and to fulfill that, I must take no useless risk of myself until I complete that duty. Of course it is sometimes more of a risk not to accept chances which are necessary to take but I have done this so far, trying to let the situation take its own course. If it is true, as the gypsy says, that they expected me to kill Pablo then I should have done that. But it was never clear to me that they did expect that. For a stranger to kill where he must work with the people afterwards is very bad. It may be done in action, and it may be done if backed by sufficient discipline, but in this case I think it would be very bad, although it was a temptation and seemed a short and simple way. But I do not believe anything is that short nor that simple in this country and, while I trust the woman absolutely, I could not tell how she would react to such a drastic thing. One dying in such a place can be very ugly, dirty and repugnant. You could not tell how she would react. Without the woman there is no organization nor any discipline here and with the woman it can be very good. It would be ideal if she would kill him, or if the gypsy would (but he will not) or if the sentry, Agustín, would. Anselmo will if I ask it, though he says he is against all killing. He hates him, I believe, and he already trusts me and believes in me as a representative of what he believes in. Only he and the woman really believe in the Republic as far as I can see; but it is too early to know that yet.

As his eyes became used to the starlight he could see that Pablo was standing by one of the horses. The horse lifted his head from grazing; then dropped it impatiently. Pablo was standing by the horse, leaning against him, moving with him as he swung with the length of the picket rope and patting him on the neck. The horse was impatient at the tenderness while he was feeding. Robert Jordan could not see what Pablo was doing, nor hear what he was saying to the horse, but he could see that he was neither unpicketing nor saddling. He sat watching him, trying to think his problem out clearly.

"Thou my big good little pony," Pablo was saying to the horse in the dark; it was the big bay stallion he was speaking to. "Thou lovely white-faced big beauty. Thou with the big neck arching like the viaduct of my pueblo," he stopped. "But arching more and much finer." The horse was snatching grass, swinging his head sideways as he pulled, annoyed by the man and his talking. "Thou art no woman nor a fool," Pablo told the bay horse. "Thou, oh, thou, thee, thee, my big little pony. Thou art no woman like a rock that is burning. Thou art no colt of a girl with cropped head and the movement of a foal still wet from its mother. Thou dost not insult nor lie nor not understand. Thou, oh, thee, oh my good big little pony."

It would have been very interesting for Robert Jordan to have heard Pablo speaking to the bay horse but he did not hear him because now, convinced that Pablo was only down checking on his horses, and having decided that it was not a practical move to kill him at this time, he stood up and walked back to the cave. Pablo stayed in the meadow talking to the horse for a long time. The horse understood nothing that he said; only, from the tone of the voice, that they were endearments and he had been in the corral all day and was hungry now, grazing impatiently at the limits of his picket rope, and the man annoyed him. Pablo shifted the picket pin finally and stood by the horse, not talking now. The horse went on grazing and was relieved now that the man did not bother him.

CHAPTER SIX

INSIDE the cave, Robert Jordan sat on one of the rawhide stools in a corner by the fire listening to the woman. She was washing the dishes and the girl, Maria, was drying them and putting them away, kneeling to place them in the hollow dug in the wall that was used as a shelf.

"It is strange," she said. "That El Sordo has not come. He should have been here an hour ago."

"Did you advise him to come?"

"No. He comes each night."

"Perhaps he is doing something. Some work."

"It is possible," she said. "If he does not come we must go to see him tomorrow."

"Yes. Is it far from here?"

"No. It will be a good trip. I lack exercise."

"Can I go?" Maria asked. "May I go too, Pilar?"

"Yes, beautiful," the woman said, then turning her big face, "Isn't she pretty?" she asked Robert Jordan. "How does she seem to thee? A little thin?"

"To me she seems very well," Robert Jordan said. Maria filled his cup with wine. "Drink that," she said. "It will make me seem even better. It is necessary to drink much of that for me to seem beautiful."

"Then I had better stop," Robert Jordan said. "Already thou seemest beautiful and more."

"That's the way to talk," the woman said. "You talk like the good ones. What more does she seem?"

"Intelligent," Robert Jordan said lamely. Maria giggled and the woman shook her head sadly. "How well you begin and how it ends, Don Roberto."

"Don't call me Don Roberto."

"It is a joke. Here we say Don Pablo for a joke. As we say the Señorita Maria for a joke."

"I don't joke that way," Robert Jordan said. "Camarada to me is what all should be called with seriousness in this war. In the joking commences a rottenness."

"Thou art very religious about thy politics," the woman teased him. "Thou makest no jokes?"

"Yes. I care much for jokes but not in the form of address. It is like a flag."

"I could make jokes about a flag. Any flag," the woman laughed. "To me no one can joke of anything. The old flag of yellow and gold we called pus and blood. The flag of the Republic with the purple added we call blood, pus and permanganate. It is a joke."

"He is a Communist," Maria said. "They are very serious *gente*."

"Are you a Communist?"

"No I am an anti-fascist."

"For a long time?"

"Since I have understood fascism."

"How long is that?"

"For nearly ten years."

"That is not much time," the woman said. "I have been a Republican for twenty years."

"My father was a Republican all his life," Maria said. "It was for that they shot him."

"My father was also a Republican all his life. Also my grandfather," Robert Jordan said.

"In what country?"

"The United States."

"Did they shoot them?" the woman asked.

"*Qué va*," Maria said. "The United States is a country of Republicans. They don't shoot you for being a Republican there."

"All the same it is a good thing to have a grandfather who was a Republican," the woman said. "It shows a good blood."

"My grandfather was on the Republican national committee," Robert Jordan said. That impressed even Maria.

"And is thy father still active in the Republic?" Pilar asked.

"No. He is dead."

"Can one ask how he died?"

"He shot himself."

"To avoid being tortured?" the woman asked.

"Yes," Robert Jordan said. "To avoid being tortured."

Maria looked at him with tears in her eyes. "My father," she said, "could not obtain a weapon. Oh, I am very glad that your father had the good fortune to obtain a weapon."

"Yes. It was pretty lucky," Robert Jordan said. "Should we talk about something else?"

"Then you and me we are the same," Maria said. She put her hand on his arm and looked in his face. He looked at her brown face and at the eyes that, since he had seen them, had never been as young as the rest of her face but that now were suddenly hungry and young and wanting.

"You could be brother and sister by the look," the woman said. "But I believe it is fortunate that you are not."

"Now I know why I have felt as I have," Maria said. "Now it is clear."

"*Qué va,*" Robert Jordan said and reaching over, he ran his hand over the top of her head. He had been wanting to do that all day and now he did it, he could feel his throat swelling. She moved her head under his hand and smiled up at him and he felt the thick but silky roughness of the cropped head rippling between his fingers. Then his hand was on her neck and then he dropped it.

"Do it again," she said. "I wanted you to do that all day."

"Later," Robert Jordan said and his voice was thick.

"And me," the woman of Pablo said in her booming voice. "I am expected to watch all this? I am expected not to be moved? One cannot. For fault of anything better; that Pablo should come back."

Maria took no notice of her now, nor of the others playing cards at the table by the candlelight.

"Do you want another cup of wine, Roberto?" she asked.

"Yes," he said. "Why not?"

"You're going to have a drunkard like I have," the woman of Pablo said. "With that rare thing he drank in the cup and all. Listen to me, *Inglés.*"

"Not *Inglés.* American."

"Listen, then, American. Where do you plan to sleep?"

"Outside. I have a sleeping robe."

"Good," she said. "The night is clear?"

"And will be cold."

"Outside then," she said. "Sleep thee outside. And thy materials can sleep with me."

"Good," said Robert Jordan.

"Leave us for a moment," Robert Jordan said to the girl and put his hand on her shoulder.

"Why?"

"I wish to speak to Pilar."

"Must I go?"

"Yes."

"What is it?" the woman of Pablo said when the girl had gone over to the mouth of the cave where she stood by the big wineskin, watching the card players.

"The gypsy said I should have——" he began.

"No," the woman interrupted. "He is mistaken."

"If it is necessary that I——" Robert Jordan said quietly but with difficulty.

"Thee would have done it, I believe," the woman said. "Nay, it is not necessary. I was watching thee. But thy judgment was good."

"But if it is needful——"

"No," the woman said. "I tell you it is not needful. The mind of the gypsy is corrupt."

"But in weakness a man can be a great danger."

"No. Thou dost not understand. Out of this one has passed all capacity for danger."

"I do not understand."

"Thou art very young still," she said. "You will understand." Then, to the girl, "Come, Maria. We are not talking more."

The girl came over and Robert Jordan reached his hand out and patted her head. She stroked under his hand like a kitten. Then he thought that she was going to cry. But her lips drew up again and she looked at him and smiled.

"Thee would do well to go to bed now," the woman said to Robert Jordan. "Thou hast had a long journey."

"Good," said Robert Jordan. "I will get my things."

CHAPTER SEVEN

HE WAS asleep in the robe and he had been asleep, he thought, for a long time. The robe was spread on the forest floor in the lee of the rocks beyond the cave mouth and as he slept, he turned, and turning rolled on his pistol which was fastened by a lanyard to one wrist and had been by his side under the cover when he went to sleep, shoulder and back weary, leg-tired, his muscles pulled with tiredness so that the ground was soft, and simply stretching in the robe against the flannel lining was voluptuous with fatigue. Waking, he wondered where he was, knew, and then shifted the pistol from under his side and settled happily to stretch back into sleep, his hand on the pillow of his clothing that was bundled neatly around his rope-soled shoes. He had one arm around the pillow.

Then he felt her hand on his shoulder and turned quickly, his right hand holding the pistol under the robe.

"Oh, it is thee," he said and dropping the pistol he reached both arms up and pulled her down. With his arms around her he could feel her shivering.

"Get in," he said softly. "It is cold out there."

"No. I must not."

"Get in," he said. "And we can talk about it later."

She was trembling and he held her wrist now with one hand and held her lightly with the other arm. She had turned her head away.

"Get in, little rabbit," he said and kissed her on the back of the neck.

"I am afraid."

"No. Do not be afraid. Get in."

"How?"

"Just slip in. There is much room. Do you want me to help you?"

"No," she said and then she was in the robe and he was holding her tight to him and trying to kiss her lips and she was pressing her face against the pillow of clothing but holding her arms close around his neck. Then he felt her arms relax and she was shivering again as he held her.

"No," he said and laughed. "Do not be afraid. That is the pistol."
He lifted it and slipped it behind him.

"I am ashamed," she said, her face away from him.

"No. You must not be. Here. Now."

"No, I must not. I am ashamed and frightened."

"No. My rabbit. Please."

"I must not. If thou dost not love me."

"I love thee."

"I love thee. Oh, I love thee. Put thy hand on my head," she said away from him, her face still in the pillow. He put his hand on her head and stroked it and then suddenly her face was away from the pillow and she was in his arms, pressed close against him, and her face was against his and she was crying.

He held her still and close, feeling the long length of the young body, and he stroked her head and kissed the wet saltiness of her eyes, and as she cried he could feel the rounded, firm-pointed breasts touching through the shirt she wore.

"I cannot kiss," she said. "I do not know how."

"There is no need to kiss."

"Yes. I must kiss. I must do everything."

"There is no need to do anything. We are all right. But thou hast many clothes."

"What should I do?"

"I will help you."

"Is that better?"

"Yes. Much. It is not better to thee?"

"Yes. Much better. And I can go with thee as Pilar said?"

"Yes."

"But not to a home. With thee."

"No, to a home."

"No. No. No. With thee and I will be thy woman."

Now as they lay all that before had been shielded was unshielded. Where there had been roughness of fabric all was smooth with a smoothness and firm rounded pressing and a long warm coolness, cool outside and warm within, long and light and closely holding, closely held, lonely, hollow-making with contours, happy-making, young and loving and now all warmly smooth with a hollowing, chest-aching, tight-held loneliness that was such that Robert Jordan felt he could not stand it and he said, "Hast thou loved others?"

"Never."

Then suddenly, going dead in his arms, "But things were done to me."

"By whom?"

"By various."

Now she lay perfectly quietly and as though her body were dead and turned her head away from him.

"Now you will not love me."

"I love you," he said.

But something had happened to him and she knew it.

"No," she said and her voice had gone dead and flat. "Thou wilt not love me. But perhaps thou wilt take me to the home. And I will go to the home and I will never be thy woman nor anything."

"I love thee, Maria."

"No. It is not true," she said. Then as a last thing pitifully and hopefully.

"But I have never kissed any man."

"Then kiss me now."

"I wanted to," she said. "But I know not how. Where things were done to me I fought until I could not see. I fought until—until—until one sat upon my head—and I bit him—and then they tied my mouth and held my arms behind my head—and others did things to me."

"I love thee, Maria," he said. "And no one has done anything to thee. Thee, they cannot touch. No one has touched thee, little rabbit."

"You believe that?"

"I know it."

"And you can love me?" warm again against him now.

"I can love thee more."

"I will try to kiss thee very well."

"Kiss me a little."

"I do not know how."

"Just kiss me."

She kissed him on the cheek.

"No."

"Where do the noses go? I always wondered where the noses would go."

"Look, turn thy head," and then their mouths were tight together and she lay close pressed against him and her mouth opened a little gradually and then, suddenly, holding her against him, he was happier than he had ever been, lightly, lovingly, exultingly, innerly happy and unthinking and untired and unworried and only feeling a great delight and he said, "My little rabbit. My darling. My sweet. My long lovely."

"What do you say?" she said as though from a great distance away.

"My lovely one," he said.

They lay there and he felt her heart beating against his and with the side of his foot he stroked very lightly against the side of hers.

"Thee came barefooted," he said.

"Yes."

"Then thee knew thou wert coming to the bed."

"Yes."

"And you had no fear."

"Yes. Much. But more fear of how it would be to take my shoes off."

"And what time is it now? *lo sabes?*"

"No. Thou hast no watch?"

"Yes. But it is behind thy back."

"Take it from there."

"No."

"Then look over my shoulder."

It was one o'clock. The dial showed bright in the darkness that the robe made.

"Thy chin scratches my shoulder."

"Pardon it. I have no tools to shave."

"I like it. Is thy beard blond?"

"Yes."

"And will it be long?"

"Not before the bridge. Maria, listen. Dost thou—?"

"Do I what?"

"Dost thou wish?"

"Yes. Everything. Please. And if we do everything together, the other maybe never will have been."

"Did you think of that?"

"No. I think it in myself but Pilar told me."

"She is very wise."

"And another thing," Maria said softly. "She said for me to tell you that I am not sick. She knows about such things and she said to tell you that."

"She told you to tell me?"

"Yes. I spoke to her and told her that I love you. I loved you when I saw you today and I loved you always but I never saw you before and I told Pilar and she said if I ever told you anything about anything, to tell you that I was not sick. The other thing she told me long ago. Soon after the train."

"What did she say?"

"She said that nothing is done to oneself that one does not accept and that if I loved some one it would take it all away. I wished to die, you see."

"What she said is true."

"And now I am happy that I did not die. I am so happy that I did not die. And you can love me?"

"Yes. I love you now."

"And I can be thy woman?"

"I cannot have a woman doing what I do. But thou art my woman now."

"If once I am, then I will keep on. Am I thy woman now?"

"Yes, Maria. Yes, my little rabbit."

She held herself tight to him and her lips looked for his and then found them and were against them and he felt her, fresh, new and smooth and young and lovely with the warm, scalding coolness and unbelievable to be there in the robe that was as familiar as his clothes, or his shoes, or his duty and then she said, frightenedly, "And now let us do quickly what it is we do so that the other is all gone."

"You want?"

"Yes," she said almost fiercely. "Yes. Yes. Yes."

CHAPTER EIGHT

IT WAS cold in the night and Robert Jordan slept heavily. Once he woke and, stretching, realized that the girl was there, curled far down in the robe, breathing lightly and regularly, and in the dark, bringing his head in from the cold, the sky hard and sharp with stars, the air cold in his nostrils, he put his head under the warmth of the robe and kissed her smooth shoulder. She did not wake and he rolled onto his side away from her and with his head out of the robe in the cold again, lay awake a moment feeling the long, seeping luxury of his fatigue and then the smooth tactile happiness of their two bodies touching and then, as he pushed his legs out deep as they would go in the robe, he slipped down steeply into sleep.

He woke at first daylight and the girl was gone. He knew it as he woke and, putting out his arm, he felt the robe warm where she had been. He looked at the mouth of the cave where the blanket showed frost-rimmed and saw the thin gray smoke from the crack in the rocks that meant the kitchen fire was lighted.

A man came out of the timber, a blanket worn over his head like a poncho. Robert Jordan saw it was Pablo and that he was smoking a cigarette. He's been down corralling the horses, he thought.

Pablo pulled open the blanket and went into the cave without looking toward Robert Jordan.

Robert Jordan felt with his hand the light frost that lay on the worn, spotted green balloon silk outer covering of the five-year-old down robe, then settled into it again. *Bueno,* he said to himself, feeling the familiar caress of the flannel lining as he spread his legs wide, then drew them together and then turned on his side so that his head would be away from the direction where he knew the sun would come. *Qué más da,* I might as well sleep some more.

He slept until the sound of airplane motors woke him.

Lying on his back, he saw them, a fascist patrol of three Fiats, tiny, bright, fast-moving across the mountain sky, headed in the direction from which Anselmo and he had come yesterday. The three passed and then came nine more, flying much higher in the minute, pointed formations of threes, threes and threes.

Pablo and the gypsy were standing at the cave mouth, in the shadow, watching the sky and as Robert Jordan lay still, the sky now full of the high hammering roar of motors, there was a new droning roar and three more planes came over at less than a thousand feet above the clearing. These three were Heinkel one-elevens, twin-motor bombers.

Robert Jordan, his head in the shadow of the rocks, knew they would not see him, and that it did not matter if they did. He knew they could possibly see the horses in the corral if they were looking for anything in these mountains. If they were not looking for anything they might still see them but would naturally take them for some of their own cavalry mounts. Then came a new and louder droning roar and three more Heinkel one-elevens showed coming steeply, stiffly, lower yet, crossing in rigid formation, their pounding roar approaching in crescendo to an absolute of noise and then receding as they passed the clearing.

Robert Jordan unrolled the bundle of clothing that made his pillow and pulled on his shirt. It was over his head and he was pulling it down when he heard the next planes coming and he pulled his trousers on under the robe and lay still as three more of the Heinkel bimotor bombers came over. Before they were gone over the shoulder of the mountain, he had buckled on his pistol, rolled the robe and placed it against the rocks and sat now, close against the rocks, tying his rope-soled shoes when the approaching droning turned to a greater clattering roar than ever before and nine more Heinkel light bombers came in echelons; hammering the sky apart as they went over.

Robert Jordan slipped along the rocks to the mouth of the cave where one of the brothers, Pablo, the gypsy, Anselmo, Agustín and the woman stood in the mouth looking out.

"Have there been planes like this before?" he asked.

"Never," said Pablo. "Get in. They will see thee."

The sun had not yet hit the mouth of the cave. It was just now shining on the meadow by the stream and Robert Jordan knew they could not be seen in the dark, early morning shadow of the trees and the solid shade the rocks made, but he went in the cave in order not to make them nervous.

"They are many," the woman said.

"And there will be more," Robert Jordan said.

"How do you know?" Pablo asked suspiciously.

"Those, just now, will have pursuit planes with them."

Just then they heard them, the higher, whining drone, and as they passed at about five thousand feet, Robert Jordan counted fifteen Fiats in echelon of echelons like a wild-goose flight of the V-shaped threes.

In the cave entrance their faces all looked very sober and Robert Jordan said, "You have not seen this many planes?"

"Never," said Pablo.

"There are not many at Segovia?"

"Never has there been, we have seen three usually. Sometimes six of the chasers. Perhaps three Junkers, the big ones with the three motors, with the chasers with them. Never have we seen planes like this."

It is bad, Robert Jordan thought. This is really bad. Here is a concentration of planes which means something very bad. I must listen for them to unload. But no, they cannot have brought up the troops yet for the attack. Certainly not before tonight or tomorrow night, certainly not yet. Certainly they will not be moving anything at this hour.

He could still hear the receding drone. He looked at his watch. By now they should be over the lines, the first ones anyway. He pushed the knob that set the second hand to clicking and watched it move around. No, perhaps not yet. By now. Yes. Well over by now. Two hundred and fifty miles an hour for those one-elevens anyway. Five minutes would carry them there. By now they're well beyond the pass with Castile all yellow and tawny beneath them now in the morning, the yellow crossed by white roads and spotted with the small villages and the shadows of the Heinkels moving over the land as the shadows of sharks pass over a sandy floor of the ocean.

There was no bump, bump, bumping thud of bombs. His watch ticked on.

They're going on to Colmenar, to Escorial, or to the flying field at Manzanares el Real, he thought, with the old castle above the lake with the ducks in the reeds and the fake airfield just behind the real field with the dummy planes, not quite hidden, their props turning in the wind. That's where they must be headed. They can't know about the attack, he told himself and something in him said, why can't they? They've known about all the others.

"Do you think they saw the horses?" Pablo asked.

"Those weren't looking for horses," Robert Jordan said.

"But did they see them?"

"Not unless they were asked to look for them."

"Could they see them?"

"Probably not," Robert Jordan said. "Unless the sun were on the trees."

"It is on them very early," Pablo said miserably.

"I think they have other things to think of besides thy horses," Robert Jordan said.

It was eight minutes since he had pushed the lever on the stop watch and there was still no sound of bombing.

"What do you do with the watch?" the woman asked.

"I listen where they have gone."

"Oh," she said. At ten minutes he stopped looking at the watch knowing it would be too far away to hear, now, even allowing a minute for the sound to travel, and said to Anselmo, "I would speak to thee."

Anselmo came out of the cave mouth and they walked a little way from the entrance and stood beside a pine tree.

"*Qué tal?*" Robert Jordan asked him. "How goes it?"

"All right."

"Hast thou eaten?"

"No. No one has eaten."

"Eat then and take something to eat at mid-day. I want you to go to watch the road. Make a note of everything that passes both up and down the road.

"I do not write."

"There is no need to," Robert Jordan took out two leaves from his notebook and with his knife cut an inch from the end of his pencil. "Take this and make a mark for tanks thus," he drew a slanted tank, "and then a mark for each one and when there are four, cross the four strokes for the fifth."

"In this way we count also."

"Good. Make another mark, two wheels and a box, for trucks. If they are empty make a circle. If they are full of troops make a straight mark. Mark for guns. Big ones, thus. Small ones, thus. Mark for cars. Mark for ambulances. Thus, two wheels and a box with a cross on it. Mark for troops on foot by companies, like this, see? A little square and then mark beside it. Mark for cavalry, like this, you see? Like a horse. A box with four legs. That is a troop of twenty horse. You understand? Each troop a mark."

"Yes. It is ingenious."

"Now," he drew two large wheels with circles around them and a short line for a gun barrel. "These are anti-tanks. They have rubber tires. Mark for them. These are anti-aircraft," two wheels with the gun barrel slanted up. "Mark for them also. Do you understand? Have you seen such guns?"

"Yes," Anselmo said. "Of course. It is clear."

"Take the gypsy with you that he will know from what point you will be watching so you may be relieved. Pick a place that is safe, not too close and from where you can see well and comfortably. Stay until you are relieved."

"I understand."

"Good. And that when you come back, I should know everything that moved upon the road. One paper is for movement up. One is for movement down the road."

They walked over toward the cave.

"Send Rafael to me," Robert Jordan said and waited by the tree. He watched Anselmo go into the cave, the blanket falling behind him. The gypsy sauntered out, wiping his mouth with his hand.

"*Qué tal?*" the gypsy said. "Did you divert yourself last night?"

"I slept."

"Less bad," the gypsy said and grinned. "Have you a cigarette?"

"Listen," Robert Jordan said and felt in his pocket for the cigarettes. "I wish you to go with Anselmo to a place from which he will observe the road. There you will leave him, noting the place in order that you may guide me to it or guide whoever will relieve him later. You will then go to where you can observe the saw mill and note if there are any changes in the post there."

"What changes?"

"How many men are there now?"

"Eight. The last I knew."

"See how many are there now. See at what intervals the guard is relieved at that bridge."

"Intervals?"

"How many hours the guard stays on and at what time a change is made."

"I have no watch."

"Take mine." He unstrapped it.

"What a watch," Rafael said admiringly. "Look at what complications. Such a watch should be able to read and write. Look at what complications of numbers. It's a watch to end watches."

"Don't fool with it," Robert Jordan said. "Can you tell time?"

"Why not? Twelve o'clock mid-day. Hunger. Twelve o'clock midnight. Sleep. Six o'clock in the morning, hunger. Six o'clock at night, drunk. With luck. Ten o'clock at night——"

"Shut up," Robert Jordan said. "You don't need to be a clown. I want you to check on the guard at the big bridge and the post on the road below in the same manner as the post and the guard at the saw mill and the small bridge."

"It is much work," the gypsy smiled. "You are sure there is no one you would rather send than me?"

"No, Rafael. It is very important. That you should do it very carefully and keeping out of sight with care."

"I believe I will keep out of sight," the gypsy said. "Why do you tell me to keep out of sight? You think I want to be shot?"

"Take things a little seriously," Robert Jordan said. "This is serious."

"Thou askest me to take things seriously? After what thou didst last night? When thou needest to kill a man and instead did what you did? You were supposed to kill one, not make one! When we have just seen the sky full of airplanes of a quantity to kill us back to our grandfathers and forward to all unborn grandsons including all cats, goats and bedbugs. Airplanes making a noise to curdle the milk in your mother's breasts as they pass over darkening the sky and roaring like lions and you ask me to take things seriously. I take them too seriously already."

"All right," said Robert Jordan and laughed and put his hand on the gypsy's shoulder. "*Don't* take them too seriously then. Now finish your breakfast and go."

"And thou?" the gypsy asked. "What do you do?"

"I go to see El Sordo."

"After those airplanes it is very possible that thou wilt find no-body in the whole mountains," the gypsy said. "There must have been many people sweating the big drop this morning when those passed."

"Those have other work than hunting guerillas."

"Yes," the gypsy said. Then shook his head. "But when they care to undertake that work."

"*Qué va,*" Robert Jordan said. "Those are the best of the German light bombers. They do not send those after gypsies."

"They give me a horror," Rafael said. "Of such things, yes, I am frightened."

"They go to bomb an airfield," Robert Jordan told him as they went into the cave. "I am almost sure they go for that."

"What do you say?" the woman of Pablo asked. She poured him a bowl of coffee and handed him a can of condensed milk.

"There is milk? What luxury!"

"There is everything," she said. "And since the planes there is much fear. Where did you say they went?"

Robert Jordan dripped some of the thick milk into his coffee from the slit cut in the can, wiped the can on the rim of the cup, and stirred the coffee until it was light brown.

"They go to bomb an airfield I believe. They might go to Escorial and Colmenar. Perhaps all three."

"That they should go a long way and keep away from here," Pablo said.

"And why are they here now?" the woman asked. "What brings them now? Never have we seen such planes. Nor in such quantity. Do they prepare an attack?"

"What movement was there on the road last night?" Robert Jordan asked. The girl Maria was close to him but he did not look at her.

"You," the woman said. "Fernando. You were in La Granja last night. What movement was there?"

"Nothing," a short, open-faced man of about thirty-five with a cast in one eye, whom Robert Jordan had not seen before, answered. "A few camions as usual. Some cars. No movement of troops while I was there."

"You go into La Granja every night?" Robert Jordan asked him.

"I or another," Fernando said. "Some one goes."

"They go for the news. For tobacco. For small things," the woman said.

"We have people there?"

"Yes. Why not? Those who work the power plant. Some others."

"What was the news?"

"*Pues nada*. There was nothing. It still goes badly in the north. That is not news. In the north it has gone badly now since the beginning."

"Did you hear anything from Segovia?"

"No, *hombre*. I did not ask."

"Do you go into Segovia?"

"Sometimes," Fernando said. "But there is danger. There are controls where they ask for your papers."

"Do you know the airfield?"

"No, *hombre*. I know where it is but I was never close to it. There, there is much asking for papers."

"No one spoke about these planes last night?"

"In La Granja? Nobody. But they will talk about them tonight certainly. They talked about the broadcast of Quiepo de Llano. Nothing more. Oh, yes. It seems that the Republic is preparing an offensive."

"That what?"

"That the Republic is preparing an offensive."

"Where?"

"It is not certain. Perhaps here. Perhaps for another part of the Sierra. Hast thou heard of it?"

"They say this in La Granja?"

"Yes, *hombre*. I had forgotten it. But there is always much talk of offensives."

"Where does this talk come from?"

"Where? Why from different people. The officers speak in the cafés in Segovia and Avila and the waiters note it. The rumors come running. Since some time they speak of an offensive by the Republic in these parts."

"By the Republic or by the Fascists?"

"By the Republic. If it were by the Fascists all would know of it. No, this is an offensive of quite some size. Some say there are two.

One here and the other over the Alto del León near the Escorial. Have you heard aught of this?"

"What else did you hear?"

"*Nada, hombre.* Nothing. Oh, yes. There was some talk that the Republicans would try to blow up the bridges, if there was to be an offensive. But the bridges are guarded."

"Art thou joking?" Robert Jordan said, sipping his coffee.

"No, *hombre,*" said Fernando.

"This one doesn't joke," the woman said. "Bad luck that he doesn't."

"Then," said Robert Jordan. "Thank you for all the news. Did you hear nothing more?"

"No. They talk, as always, of troops to be sent to clear out these mountains. There is some talk that they are on the way. That they have been sent already from Valladolid. But they always talk in that way. It is not to give any importance to."

"And thou," the woman of Pablo said to Pablo almost viciously. "With thy talk of safety."

Pablo looked at her reflectively and scratched his chin. "Thou," he said. "And thy bridges."

"What bridges?" asked Fernando cheerfully.

"Stupid," the woman said to him. "Thick head. *Tonto.* Take another cup of coffee and try to remember more news."

"Don't be angry, Pilar," Fernando said calmly and cheerfully. "Neither should one become alarmed at rumors. I have told thee and this comrade all that I remember."

"You don't remember anything more?" Robert Jordan asked.

"No," Fernando said with dignity. "And I am fortunate to remember this because, since it was but rumors, I paid no attention to any of it."

"Then there may have been more?"

"Yes. It is possible. But I paid no attention. For a year I have heard nothing but rumors."

Robert Jordan heard a quick, control-breaking sniff of laughter from the girl, Maria, who was standing behind him.

"Tell us one more rumor, Fernandito," she said and then her shoulders shook again.

"If I could remember, I would not," Fernando said. "It is beneath a man's dignity to listen and give importance to rumors."

"And with this we will save the Republic," the woman said.

"No. *You* will save it by blowing bridges," Pablo told her.

"Go," said Robert Jordan to Anselmo and Rafael. "If you have eaten."

"We go now," the old man said and the two of them stood up. Robert Jordan felt a hand on his shoulder. It was Maria. "Thou shouldst eat," she said and let her hand rest there. "Eat well so that thy stomach can support more rumors."

"The rumors have taken the place of the appetite."

"No. It should not be so. Eat this now before more rumors come." She put the bowl before him.

"Do not make a joke of me," Fernando said to her. "I am thy good friend, Maria."

"I do not joke at thee, Fernando. I only joke with him and he should eat or he will be hungry."

"We should all eat," Fernando said. "Pilar, what passes that we are not served?"

"Nothing, man," the woman of Pablo said and filled his bowl with the meat stew. "Eat. Yes, that's what you *can* do. Eat now."

"It is very good, Pilar," Fernando said, all dignity intact.

"Thank you," said the woman. "Thank you and thank you again."

"Are you angry at me?" Fernando asked.

"No. Eat. Go ahead and eat."

"I will," said Fernando. "Thank you."

Robert Jordan looked at Maria and her shoulders started shaking again and she looked away. Fernando ate steadily, a proud and dignified expression on his face, the dignity of which could not be affected even by the huge spoon that he was using or the slight dripping of juice from the stew which ran from the corners of his mouth.

"Do you like the food?" the woman of Pablo asked him.

"Yes, Pilar," he said with his mouth full. "It is the same as usual."

Robert Jordan felt Maria's hand on his arm and felt her fingers tighten with delight.

"It is for *that* that you like it?" the woman asked Fernando.

"Yes," she said. "I see. The stew; as usual. *Como siempre.* Things are bad in the north; as usual. An offensive here; as usual. That troops come to hunt us out; as usual. You could serve as a monument to as usual."

"But the last two are only rumors, Pilar."

"Spain," the woman of Pablo said bitterly. Then turned to Robert Jordan. "Do they have people such as this in other countries?"

"There are no other countries like Spain," Robert Jordan said politely.

"You are right," Fernando said. "There is no other country in the world like Spain."

"Hast thou ever seen any other country?" the woman asked him.

"Nay," said Fernando. "Nor do I wish to."

"You see?" the woman of Pablo said to Robert Jordan.

"Fernandito," Maria said to him. "Tell us of the time thee went to Valencia."

"I did not like Valencia."

"Why?" Maria asked and pressed Robert Jordan's arm again. "Why did thee not like it?"

"The people had no manners and I could not understand them. All they did was shout *ché* at one another."

"Could they understand thee?" Maria asked.

"They pretended not to," Fernando said.

"And what did thee there?"

"I left without even seeing the sea," Fernando said. "I did not like the people."

"Oh, get out of here, you old maid," the woman of Pablo said. "Get out of here before you make me sick. In Valencia I had the best time of my life. *Vamos!* Valencia. Don't talk to me of Valencia."

"What did thee there?" Maria asked. The woman of Pablo sat down at the table with a bowl of coffee, a piece of bread and a bowl of the stew.

"*Qué?* what did we there. I was there when Finito had a contract for three fights at the Feria. Never have I seen so many people. Never have I seen cafés so crowded. For hours it would be impossible to get a seat and it was impossible to board the tram cars. In Valencia there was movement all day and all night."

"But what did you do?" Maria asked.

"All things," the woman said. "We went to the beach and lay in the water and boats with sails were hauled up out of the sea by oxen.

The oxen driven to the water until they must swim; then harnessed to the boats, and, when they found their feet, staggering up the sand. Ten yokes of oxen dragging a boat with sails out of the sea in the morning with the line of the small waves breaking on the beach. That is Valencia."

"But what did thee besides watch oxen?"

"We ate in pavilions on the sand. Pastries made of cooked and shredded fish and red and green peppers and small nuts like grains of rice. Pastries delicate and flaky and the fish of a richness that was incredible. Prawns fresh from the sea sprinkled with lime juice. They were pink and sweet and there were four bites to a prawn. Of those we ate many. Then we ate *paella* with fresh sea food, clams in their shells, mussels, crayfish, and small eels. Then we ate even smaller eels alone cooked in oil and as tiny as bean sprouts and curled in all directions and so tender they disappeared in the mouth without chewing. All the time drinking a white wine, cold, light and good at thirty centimos the bottle. And for an end, melon. That is the home of the melon."

"The melon of Castile is better," Fernando said.

"*Qué va,*" said the woman of Pablo. "The melon of Castile is for self abuse. The melon of Valencia for eating. When I think of those melons long as one's arm, green like the sea and crisp and juicy to cut and sweeter than the early morning in summer. Aye, when I think of those smallest eels, tiny, delicate and in mounds on the plate. Also the beer in pitchers all through the afternoon, the beer sweating in its coldness in pitchers the size of water jugs."

"And what did thee when not eating nor drinking?"

"We made love in the room with the strip wood blinds hanging over the balcony and a breeze through the opening of the top of the door which turned on hinges. We made love there, the room dark in the day time from the hanging blinds, and from the streets there was the scent of the flower market and the smell of burned powder from the firecrackers of the *traca* that ran though the streets exploding each noon during the Feria. It was a line of fireworks that ran through all the city, the firecrackers linked together and the explosions running along on poles and wires of the tramways, exploding with great noise and a jumping from pole to pole with a sharpness and a cracking of explosion you could not believe.

"We made love and then sent for another pitcher of beer with the drops of its coldness on the glass and when the girl brought it, I took it from the door and I placed the coldness of the pitcher against the back of Finito as he lay, now, asleep, not having wakened when the beer was brought, and he said, 'No, Pilar. No, woman, let me sleep.' And I said, 'No, wake up and drink this to see how cold,' and he drank without opening his eyes and went to sleep again and I lay with my back against a pillow at the foot of the bed and watched him sleep, brown and dark-haired and young and quiet in his sleep, and drank the whole pitcher, listening now to the music of a band that was passing. You," she said to Pablo. "Do you know aught of such things?"

"We have done things together," Pablo said.

"Yes," the woman said. "Why not? And thou wert more man than Finito in your time. But never did we go to Valencia. Never did we lie in bed together and hear a band pass in Valencia."

"It was impossible," Pablo told her. "We have had no opportunity to go to Valencia. Thou knowest that if thou wilt be reasonable. But, with Finito, neither did thee blow up any train."

"No," said the woman. "That is what is left to us. The train. Yes. Always the train. No one can speak against that. That remains of all the laziness, sloth and failure. That remains of the cowardice of this moment. There were many other things before too. I do not want to be unjust. But no one can speak against Valencia either. You hear me?"

"I did not like it," Fernando said quietly. "I did not like Valencia."

"Yet they speak of the mule as stubborn," the woman said. "Clean up, Maria, that we may go."

As she said this they heard the first sound of the planes returning.

CHAPTER NINE

THEY stood in the mouth of the cave and watched them. The bombers were high now in fast, ugly arrow-heads beating the sky apart with the noise of their motors. They *are* shaped like sharks, Robert Jordan thought, the wide-finned, sharp-nosed sharks of the Gulf Stream. But these, wide-finned in silver, roaring, the light mist of their propellers in the sun, these do not move like sharks. They move like no thing there has ever been. They move like mechanized doom.

You ought to write, he told himself. Maybe you will again some time. He felt Maria holding to his arm. She was looking up and he said to her, "What do they look like to you, *guapa?*"

"I don't know," she said. "Death, I think."

"They look like planes to me," the woman of Pablo said. "Where are the little ones?"

"They may be crossing at another part," Robert Jordan said. "Those bombers are too fast to have to wait for them and have come back alone. We never follow them across the lines to fight. There aren't enough planes to risk it."

Just then three Heinkel fighters in V formation came low over the clearing coming toward them, just over the tree tops, like clattering, wing-tilting, pinch-nosed ugly toys, to enlarge suddenly, fearfully to their actual size; pouring past in a whining roar. They were so low that from the cave mouth all of them could see the pilots, helmeted, goggled, a scarf blowing back from behind the patrol leader's head.

"*Those* can see the horses," Pablo said.

"Those can see thy cigarette butts," the woman said. "Let fall the blanket."

No more planes came over. The others must have crossed farther up the range and when the droning was gone they went out of the cave into the open.

The sky was empty now and high and blue and clear.

"It seems as though they were a dream that you wake from,"

Maria said to Robert Jordan. There was not even the last almost unheard hum that comes like a finger faintly touching and leaving and touching again after the sound is gone almost past hearing.

"They are no dream and you go in and clean up," Pilar said to her. "What about it?" she turned to Robert Jordan. "Should we ride or walk?"

Pablo looked at her and grunted.

"As you will," Robert Jordan said.

"Then let us walk," she said. "I would like it for the liver."

"Riding is good for the liver."

"Yes, but hard on the buttocks. We will walk and thou—" She turned to Pablo. "Go down and count thy beasts and see they have not flown away with any."

"Do you want a horse to ride?" Pablo asked Robert Jordan.

"No. Many thanks. What about the girl?"

"Better for her to walk," Pilar said. "She'll get stiff in too many places and serve for nothing."

Robert Jordan felt his face reddening.

"Did you sleep well?" Pilar asked. Then said, "It is true that there is no sickness. There could have been. I know not why there wasn't. There probably still is God after all, although we have abolished Him. Go on," she said to Pablo. "This does not concern thee. This is of people younger than thee. Made of other material. Get on." Then to Robert Jordan, "Agustín is looking after thy things. We go when he comes."

It was a clear, bright day and warm now in the sun. Robert Jordan looked at the big, brown-faced woman with her kind, widely set eyes and her square, heavy face, lined and pleasantly ugly, the eyes merry, but the face sad until the lips moved. He looked at her and then at the man, heavy and stolid, moving off through the trees toward the corral. The woman, too, was looking after him.

"Did you make love?" the woman said.

"What did she say?"

"She would not tell me."

"I neither."

"Then you made love," the woman said. "Be as careful with her as you can."

"What if she has a baby?"

"That will do no harm," the woman said. "That will do less harm."

"This is no place for that."

"She will not stay here. She will go with you."

"And where will I go? I can't take a woman where I go."

"Who knows? You may take two where you go."

"That is no way to talk."

"Listen," the woman said. "I am no coward, but I see things very clearly in the early morning and I think there are many that we know that are alive now who will never see another Sunday."

"In what day are we?"

"Sunday."

"*Qué va,*" said Robert Jordan. "Another Sunday is very far. If we see Wednesday we are all right. But I do not like to hear thee talk like this."

"Every one needs to talk to some one," the woman said. "Before we had religion and other nonsense. Now for every one there should be some one to whom one can speak frankly, for all the valor that one could have one becomes very alone."

"We are not alone. We are all together."

"The sight of those machines does things to one," the woman said. "We are nothing against such machines."

"Yet we can beat them."

"Look," the woman said. "I confess a sadness to you, but do not think I lack resolution. Nothing has happened to my resolution."

"The sadness will dissipate as the sun rises. It is like a mist."

"Clearly," the woman said. "If you want it that way. Perhaps it came from talking that foolishness about Valencia. And that failure of a man who has gone to look at his horses. I wounded him much with the story. Kill him, yes. Curse him, yes. But wound him, no."

"How came you to be with him?"

"How is one with any one? In the first days of the movement and before too, he was something. Something serious. But now he is finished. The plug has been drawn and the wine has all run out of the skin."

"I do not like him."

"Nor does he like you, and with reason. Last night I slept with him." She smiled now and shook her head. *"Vamos a ver,"* she said. "I said to him, 'Pablo, why did you not kill the foreigner?'

"'He's a good boy, Pilar,' he said. 'He's a good boy.'

"So I said, 'You understand now that I command?'

"'Yes, Pilar. Yes,' he said. Later in the night I hear him awake and he is crying. He is crying in a short and ugly manner as a man cries when it is as though there is an animal inside that is shaking him.

"'What passes with thee, Pablo?' I said to him and I took hold of him and held him.

"'Nothing, Pilar. Nothing.'

"'Yes. Something passes with thee.'

"'The people,' he said. 'The way they left me. The *gente.*'

"'Yes, but they are with me,' I said, 'and I am thy woman.'

"'Pilar,' he said, 'remember the train.' Then he said, 'May God aid thee, Pilar.'

"'What are you talking of God for?' I said to him. 'What way is that to speak?'

"'Yes,' he said. 'God and the *Virgen.*'

"*'Qué va,* God and the *Virgen,'* I said to him. 'Is that any way to talk?'

"'I am afraid to die, Pilar,' he said. *'Tengo miedo de morir.* Dost thou understand?'

"'Then get out of bed,' I said to him. 'There is not room in one bed for me and thee and thy fear all together.'

"Then he was ashamed and was quiet and I went to sleep but, man, he's a ruin."

Robert Jordan said nothing.

"All my life I have had this sadness at intervals," the woman said. "But it is not like the sadness of Pablo. It does not affect my resolution."

"I believe that."

"It may be it is like the times of a woman," she said. "It may be it is nothing," she paused, then went on. "I put great illusion in the Republic. I believe firmly in the Republic and I have faith. I believe in it with fervor as those who have religious faith believe in the mysteries."

"I believe you."

"And you have this same faith?"

"In the Republic?"

"Yes."

"Yes," he said, hoping it was true.

"I am happy," the woman said. "And you have no fear?"

"Not to die," he said truly.

"But other fears?"

"Only of not doing my duty as I should."

"Not of capture, as the other had?"

"No," he said truly. "Fearing that, one would be so preoccupied as to be useless."

"You are a very cold boy."

"No," he said. "I do not think so."

"No. In the head you are very cold."

"It is that I am very preoccupied with my work."

"But you do not like the things of life?"

"Yes. Very much. But not to interfere with my work."

"You like to drink, I know. I have seen."

"Yes. Very much. But not to interfere with my work."

"And women?"

"I like them very much, but I have not given them much importance."

"You do not care for them?"

"Yes. But I have not found one that moved me as they say they should move you."

"I think you lie."

"Maybe a little."

"But you care for Maria."

"Yes. Suddenly and very much."

"I, too. I care for her very much. Yes. Much."

"I, too," said Robert Jordan, and could feel his voice thickening. "I, too. Yes." It gave him pleasure to say it and he said it quite formally in Spanish. "I care for her very much."

"I will leave you alone with her after we have seen El Sordo."

Robert Jordan said nothing. Then he said, "That is not necessary."

"Yes, man. It is necessary. There is not much time."

"Did you see that in the hand?" he asked.

"No. Do not remember that nonsense of the hand."

She had put that away with all the other things that might do ill to the Republic.

Robert Jordan said nothing. He was looking at Maria putting away the dishes inside the cave. She wiped her hands and turned and smiled at him. She could not hear what Pilar was saying, but as she smiled at Robert Jordan she blushed dark under the tawny skin and then smiled at him again.

"There is the day also," the woman said. "You have the night, but there is the day, too. Clearly, there is no such luxury as in Valencia in my time. But you could pick a few wild strawberries or something." She laughed.

Robert Jordan put his arm on her big shoulder. "I care for thee, too," he said. "I care for thee very much."

"Thou art a regular Don Juan Tenorio," the woman said, embarrassed now with affection. "There is a commencement of caring for every one. Here comes Agustín."

Robert Jordan went into the cave and up to where Maria was standing. She watched him come toward her, her eyes bright, the blush again on her cheeks and throat.

"Hello, little rabbit," he said and kissed her on the mouth. She held him tight to her and looked in his face and said, "Hello. Oh, hello. Hello."

Fernando, still sitting at the table smoking a cigarette, stood up, shook his head and walked out, picking up his carbine from where it leaned against the wall.

"It is very unformal," he said to Pilar. "And I do not like it. You should take care of the girl."

"I am," said Pilar. "That comrade is her *novio.*"

"Oh," said Fernando. "In that case, since they are engaged, I encounter it to be perfectly normal."

"I am pleased," the woman said.

"Equally," Fernando agreed gravely. *"Salud,* Pilar."

"Where are you going?"

"To the upper post to relieve Primitivo."

"Where the hell are you going?" Agustín asked the grave little man as he came up.

"To my duty," Fernando said with dignity.

"Thy duty," said Agustín mockingly. "I besmirch the milk of

thy duty." Then turning to the woman, "Where the un-nameable is this vileness that I am to guard?"

"In the cave," Pilar said. "In two sacks. And I am tired of thy obscenity."

"I obscenity in the milk of thy tiredness," Agustín said.

"Then go and befoul thyself," Pilar said to him without heat.

"Thy mother," Agustín replied.

"Thou never had one," Pilar told him, the insults having reached the ultimate formalism in Spanish in which the acts are never stated but only implied.

"What are they doing in there?" Agustín now asked confidentially.

"Nothing," Pilar told him. *"Nada.* We are, after all, in the spring, animal."

"Animal," said Agustín, relishing the word. "Animal. And thou. Daughter of the great whore of whores. I befoul myself in the milk of the springtime."

Pilar slapped him on the shoulder.

"You," she said, and laughed that booming laugh. "You lack variety in your cursing. But you have force. Did you see the planes?"

"I un-name in the milk of their motors," Agustín said, nodding his head and biting his lower lip.

"That's something," Pilar said. "That is really something. But really difficult of execution."

"At that altitude, yes," Agustín grinned. *"Desde luego.* But it is better to joke."

"Yes," the woman of Pablo said. "It is much better to joke, and you are a good man and you joke with force."

"Listen, Pilar," Agustín said seriously. "Something is preparing. It is not true?"

"How does it seem to you?"

"Of a foulness that cannot be worse. Those were many planes, woman. Many planes."

"And thou hast caught fear from them like all the others?"

"Qué va," said Agustín. "What do you think they are preparing?"

"Look," Pilar said. "From this boy coming for the bridges obviously the Republic is preparing an offensive. From these planes obviously the Fascists are preparing to meet it. But why show the planes?"

"In this war are many foolish things," Agustín said. "In this war there is an idiocy without bounds."

"Clearly," said Pilar. "Otherwise we could not be here."

"Yes," said Agustín. "We swim within the idiocy for a year now. But Pablo is a man of much understanding. Pablo is very wily."

"Why do you say this?"

"I say it."

"But you must understand," Pilar explained. "It is now too late to be saved by wiliness and he has lost the other."

"I understand," said Agustín. "I know we must go. And since we must win to survive ultimately, it is necessary that the bridges must be blown. But Pablo, for the coward that he now is, is very smart."

"I, too, am smart."

"No, Pilar," Agustín said. "You are not smart. You are brave. You are loyal. You have decision. You have intuition. Much decision and much heart. But you are not smart."

"You believe that?" the woman asked thoughtfully.

"Yes, Pilar."

"The boy is smart," the woman said. "Smart and cold. Very cold in the head."

"Yes," Agustín said. "He must know his business or they would not have him doing this. But I do not know that he is smart. Pablo I *know* is smart."

"But rendered useless by his fear and his disinclination to action."

"But still smart."

"And what do you say?"

"Nothing. I try to consider it intelligently. In this moment we need to act with intelligence. After the bridge we must leave at once. All must be prepared. We must know for where we are leaving and how."

"Naturally."

"For this—Pablo. It must be done smartly."

"I have no confidence in Pablo."

"In this, yes."

"No. You do not know how far he is ruined."

"*Pero es muy vivo.* He is very smart. And if we do not do this smartly we are obscenitied."

"I will think about it," Pilar said. "I have the day to think about it."

"For the bridges; the boy," Agustín said. "This he must know. Look at the fine manner in which the other organized the train."

"Yes," Pilar said. "It was really he who planned all."

"You for energy and resolution," Agustín said. "But Pablo for the moving. Pablo for the retreat. Force him now to study it."

"You are a man of intelligence."

"Intelligent, yes," Agustín said. "But *sin picardía.* Pablo for that."

"With his fear and all?"

"With his fear and all."

"And what do you think of the bridges?"

"It is necessary. That I know. Two things we must do. We must leave here and we must win. The bridges are necessary if we are to win."

"If Pablo is so smart, why does he not see that?"

"He wants things as they are for his own weakness. He wants to stay in the eddy of his own weakness. But the river is rising. Forced to a change, he will be smart in the change. *Es muy vivo.*"

"It is good that the boy did not kill him."

"*Qué va.* The gypsy wanted me to kill him last night. The gypsy is an animal."

"You're an animal, too," she said. "But intelligent."

"We are both intelligent," Agustín said. "But the talent is Pablo!"

"But difficult to put up with. You do not know how ruined."

"Yes. But a talent. Look, Pilar. To make war all you need is intelligence. But to win you need talent and material."

"I will think it over," she said. "We must start now. We are late." Then, raising her voice, "English!" she called. "*Inglés!* Come on! Let us go."

CHAPTER TEN

"LET US rest," Pilar said to Robert Jordan. "Sit down here, Maria, and let us rest."

"We should continue," Robert Jordan said. "Rest when we get there. I must see this man."

"You will see him," the woman told him. "There is no hurry. Sit down here, Maria."

"Come on," Robert Jordan said. "Rest at the top."

"I rest now," the woman said, and sat down by the stream. The girl sat by her in the heather, the sun shining on her hair. Only Robert Jordan stood looking across the high mountain meadow with the trout brook running through it. There was heather growing where he stood. There were gray boulders rising from the yellow bracken that replaced the heather in the lower part of the meadow and below was the dark line of the pines.

"How far is it to El Sordo's?" he asked.

"Not far," the woman said. "It is across this open country, down into the next valley and above the timber at the head of the stream. Sit thee down and forget thy seriousness."

"I want to see him and get it over with."

"I want to bathe my feet," the woman said and, taking off her rope-soled shoes and pulling off a heavy wool stocking, she put her right foot into the stream. "My God, it's cold."

"We should have taken horses," Robert Jordan told her.

"This is good for me," the woman said. "This is what I have been missing. What's the matter with you?"

"Nothing, except that I am in a hurry."

"Then calm yourself. There is much time. What a day it is and how I am contented not to be in pine trees. You cannot imagine how one can tire of pine trees. Aren't you tired of the pines, *guapa?*"

"I like them," the girl said.

"What can you like about them?"

"I like the odor and the feel of the needles under foot. I like the wind in the high trees and the creaking they make against each other."

"You like anything," Pilar said. "You are a gift to any man if you could cook a little better. But the pine tree makes a forest of boredom. Thou hast never known a forest of beech, nor of oak, nor of chestnut. Those are forests. In such forests each tree differs and there is character and beauty. A forest of pine trees is boredom. What do you say, *Inglés?*"

"I like the pines, too."

"*Pero, venga,*" Pilar said. "Two of you. So do I like the pines, but we have been too long in these pines. Also I am tired of the mountains. In mountains there are only two directions. Down and up and down leads only to the road and the towns of the Fascists."

"Do you ever go to Segovia?"

"*Qué va.* With this face? This is a face that is known. How would you like to be ugly, beautiful one?" she said to Maria.

"Thou art not ugly."

"*Vamos,* I'm not ugly. I was born ugly. All my life I have been ugly. You, *Inglés,* who know nothing about women. Do you know how an ugly woman feels? Do you know what it is to be ugly all your life and inside to feel that you are beautiful? It is very rare," she put the other foot in the stream, then removed it. "God, it's cold. Look at the water wagtail," she said and pointed to the gray ball of a bird that was bobbing up and down on a stone up the stream. "Those are no good for anything. Neither to sing nor to eat. Only to jerk their tails up and down. Give me a cigarette, *Inglés,*" she said and taking it, lit it from a flint and steel lighter in the pocket of her skirt. She puffed on the cigarette and looked at Maria and Robert Jordan.

"Life is very curious," she said, and blew smoke from her nostrils. "I would have made a good man, but I am all woman and all ugly. Yet many men have loved me and I have loved many men. It is curious. Listen, *Inglés,* this is interesting. Look at me, as ugly as I am. Look closely, *Inglés.*"

"Thou art not ugly."

"*Qué no?* Don't lie to me. Or," she laughed the deep laugh. "Has it begun to work with thee? No. That is a joke. No. Look at the ugliness. Yet one has a feeling within one that blinds a man while he loves you. You, with that feeling, blind him, and blind yourself. Then one day, for no reason, he sees you ugly as you really are and he is not blind any more and then you see yourself as ugly as he sees you and you lose your man and your feeling. Do you understand, *guapa?*" She patted the girl on the shoulder.

"No," said Maria. "Because thou art not ugly."

"Try to use thy head and not thy heart, and listen," Pilar said. "I am telling you things of much interest. Does it not interest you, *Inglés?*"

"Yes. But we should go."

"*Qué va,* go. I am very well here. Then," she went on, addressing herself to Robert Jordan now as though she were speaking to a classroom; almost as though she were lecturing. "After a while, when you are as ugly as I am, as ugly as women can be, then, as I say, after a while the feeling, the idiotic feeling that you are beautiful, grows slowly in one again. It grows like a cabbage. And then, when the feeling is grown, another man sees you and thinks you are beautiful and it is all to do over. Now I think I am past it, but it still might come. You are lucky, *guapa,* that you are not ugly."

"But I *am* ugly," Maria insisted.

"Ask *him,*" said Pilar. "And don't put thy feet in the stream because it will freeze them."

"If Roberto says we should go, I think we should go," Maria said.

"Listen to you," Pilar said. "I have as much at stake in this as thy Roberto and I say that we are well off resting here by the stream and that there is much time. Furthermore, I like to talk. It is the only civilized thing we have. How otherwise can we divert ourselves? Does what I say not hold interest for you, *Inglés?*"

"You speak very well. But there are other things that interest me more than talk of beauty or lack of beauty."

"Then let us talk of what interests thee."

"Where were you at the start of the movement?"

"In my town."

"Avila?"

"*Qué va,* Avila."

"Pablo said he was from Avila."

"He lies. He wanted to take a big city for his town. It was this town," and she named a town.

"And what happened?"

"Much," the woman said. "Much. And all of it ugly. Even that which was glorious."

"Tell me about it," Robert Jordan said.

"It is brutal," the woman said. "I do not like to tell it before the girl."

"Tell it," said Robert Jordan. "And if it is not for her, that she should not listen."

"I can hear it," Maria said. She put her hand on Robert Jordan's. "There is nothing that I cannot hear."

"It isn't whether you can hear it," Pilar said. "It is whether I should tell it to thee and make thee bad dreams."

"I will not get bad dreams from a story," Maria told her. "You think after all that has happened with us I should get bad dreams from a story?"

"Maybe it will give the *Inglés* bad dreams."

"Try it and see."

"No, *Inglés,* I am not joking. Didst thou see the start of the movement in any small town?"

"No," Robert Jordan said.

"Then thou hast seen nothing. Thou hast seen the ruin that now is Pablo, but you should have seen Pablo on that day."

"Tell it."

"Nay. I do not want to."

"Tell it."

"All right, then. I will tell it truly as it was. But thee, *guapa,* if it reaches a point that it molests thee, tell me."

"I will not listen to it if it molests me," Maria told her. "It cannot be worse than many things."

"I believe it can," the woman said. "Give me another cigarette, *Inglés,* and *vamonos.*"

The girl leaned back against the heather on the bank of the stream and Robert Jordan stretched himself out, his shoulders against the ground and his head against a clump of the heather. He reached out and found Maria's hand and held it in his, rubbing their two hands against the heather until she opened her hand and laid it flat on top of his as they listened.

"It was early in the morning when the *civiles* surrendered at the barracks," Pilar began.

"You had assaulted the barracks?" Robert Jordan asked.

"Pablo had surrounded it in the dark, cut the telephone wires, placed dynamite under one wall and called on the *guardia civil* to surrender. They would not. And at daylight he blew the wall open. There was fighting. Two *civiles* were killed. Four were wounded and four surrendered.

"We all lay on roofs and on the ground and at the edge of walls and of buildings in the early morning light and the dust cloud of the explosion had not yet settled, for it rose high in the air and there was no wind to carry it, and all of us were firing into the broken side of the building, loading and firing into the smoke, and from within there was still the flashing of rifles and then there was a shout from in the smoke not to fire more, and out came the four *civiles* with their hands up. A big part of the roof had fallen in and the wall was gone and they came out to surrender.

"'Are there more inside?' Pablo shouted.

"'There are wounded.'

"'Guard these,' Pablo said to four who had come up from where we were firing. 'Stand there. Against the wall,' he told the *civiles*. The four *civiles* stood against the wall, dirty, dusty, smoke-grimed, with the four who were guarding them pointing their guns at them and Pablo and the others went in to finish the wounded.

"After they had done this and there was no longer any noise of the wounded, neither groaning, nor crying out, nor the noise of shooting in the barracks, Pablo and the others came out and Pablo had his shotgun over his back and was carrying in his hand a Mauser pistol.

"'Look, Pilar,' he said. 'This was in the hand of the officer who killed himself. Never have I fired a pistol. You,' he said to one of the guards, 'show me how it works. No. Don't show me. Tell me.'

"The four *civiles* had stood against the wall, sweating and saying nothing while the shooting had gone on inside the barracks. They were all tall men with the faces of *guardias civiles,* which is the same model of face as mine is. Except that their faces were covered with the small stubble of this their last morning of not yet being shaved and they stood there against the wall and said nothing.

"'You,' said Pablo to the one who stood nearest him. 'Tell me how it works.'

"'Pull the small lever down,' the man said in a very dry voice. 'Pull the receiver back and let it snap forward.'

"'What is the receiver?' asked Pablo, and he looked at the four *civiles*. 'What is the receiver?'

"'The block on top of the action.'

"Pablo pulled it back, but it stuck. 'What now?' he said. 'It is jammed. You have lied to me.'

"'Pull it farther back and let it snap lightly forward,' the *civil* said, and I have never heard such a tone of voice. It was grayer than a morning without sunrise.

"Pablo pulled and let go as the man had told him and the block snapped forward into place and the pistol was cocked with the hammer back. It is an ugly pistol, small in the round handle, large and flat in the barrel, and unwieldy. All this time the *civiles* had been watching him and they had said nothing.

"'What are you going to do with us?' one asked him.

"'Shoot thee,' Pablo said.

"'When?' the man asked in the same gray voice.

"'Now,' said Pablo.

"'Where?' asked the man.

"'Here,' said Pablo. 'Here. Now. Here and now. Have you anything to say?'

"'*Nada,*' said the *civil*. 'Nothing. But it is an ugly thing.'

"'And you are an ugly thing,' Pablo said. 'You murderer of peasants. You who would shoot your own mother.'

"'I have never killed any one,' the *civil* said. 'And do not speak of my mother.'

"'Show us how to die. You, who have always done the killing.'

"'There is no necessity to insult us,' another *civil* said. 'And we know how to die.'

"'Kneel down against the wall with your heads against the wall,' Pablo told them. The *civiles* looked at one another.

"'Kneel, I say,' Pablo said. 'Get down and kneel.'

"'How does it seem to you, Paco?' one *civil* said to the tallest, who had spoken with Pablo about the pistol. He wore a corporal's stripes on his sleeves and was sweating very much although the early morning was still cool.

"'It is as well to kneel,' he answered. 'It is of no importance.'

"'It is closer to the earth,' the first one who had spoken said, trying to make a joke, but they were all too grave for a joke and no one smiled.

"'Then let us kneel,' the first *civil* said, and the four knelt, looking very awkward with their heads against the wall and their hands by their sides, and Pablo passed behind them and shot each in turn in the back of the head with the pistol, going from one to another and putting the barrel of the pistol against the back of their heads, each man slipping down as he fired. I can hear the pistol still, sharp and yet muffled, and see the barrel jerk and the head of the man drop forward. One held his head still when the pistol touched it. One pushed his head forward and pressed his forehead against the stone. One shivered in his whole body and his head was shaking. Only one put his hands in front of his eyes, and he was the last one, and the four bodies were slumped against the wall when Pablo turned away from them and came toward us with the pistol still in his hand.

"'Hold this for me, Pilar,' he said. 'I do not know how to put down the hammer,' and he handed me the pistol and stood there looking at the four guards as they lay against the wall of the barracks. All those who were with us stood there too, looking at them, and no one said anything.

"We had won the town and it was still early in the morning and no one had eaten nor had any one drunk coffee and we looked at each other and we were all powdered with dust from the blowing up of the barracks, as powdered as men are at a threshing, and I stood holding the pistol and it was heavy in my hand and I felt weak in the stomach when I looked at the guards dead there against the wall; they all as gray and as dusty as we were, but each one was now moistening with his blood the dry dirt by the wall where they lay. And as we stood there the sun rose over the far hills and shone now on the road where we stood and on the white wall of the barracks and the dust in the air was golden in that first sun and the peasant who was beside me looked at the wall of the barracks and what lay there and then looked at us and then at the sun and said, *'Vaya,* a day that commences.'

"'Now let us go and get coffee,' I said.

"'Good, Pilar, good,' he said. And we went up into the town to the Plaza, and those were the last people who were shot in the village."

"What happend to the others?" Robert Jordan asked. "Were there no other fascists in the village?"

"*Qué va,* were there no other fascists? There were more than twenty. But none was shot."

"What was done?"

"Pablo had them beaten to death with flails and thrown from the top of the cliff into the river."

"All twenty?"

"I will tell you. It is not so simple. And in my life never do I wish to see such a scene as the flailing to death in the plaza on the top of the cliff above the river.

"The town is built on the high bank above the river and there is a square there with a fountain and there are benches and there are big trees that give a shade for the benches. The balconies of the houses look out on the plaza. Six streets enter on the plaza and there is an arcade from the houses that goes around the plaza so that one can walk in the shade of the arcade when the sun is hot. On three sides of the plaza is the arcade and on the fourth side is the walk shaded by the trees beside the edge of the cliff with, far below, the river. It is three hundred feet down to the river.

"Pablo organized it all as he did the attack on the barracks. First he had the entrances to the streets blocked off with carts as though to organize the plaze for a *capea*. For an amateur bullfight. The fascists were all held in the *Ayuntamiento,* the city hall, which was the largest building on one side of the plaza. It was there the clock was set in the wall and it was in the buildings under the arcade that the club of the fascists was. And under the arcade on the sidewalk in front of their club was where they had their chairs and tables for their club. It was there, before the movement, that they were accustomed to take the apéritifs. The chairs and the tables were of wicker. It looked like a café but was more elegant."

"But was there no fighting to take them?"

"Pablo had them seized in the night before he assaulted the barracks. But he had already surrounded the barracks. They were all seized in their homes at the same hour the attack started. That was intelligent. Pablo is an organizer. Otherwise he would have had people attacking him at his flanks and at his rear while he was assaulting the barracks of the *guardia civil.*

"Pablo is very intelligent but very brutal. He had this of the village well planned and well ordered. Listen. After the assault was successful, and the last four guards had surrendered, and he had shot them against the wall, and we had drunk coffee at the café that always opened earliest in the morning by the corner from which the early bus left, he proceeded to the organization of the plaza. Carts were piled exactly as for a *capea* except that the side toward the river was not enclosed. That was left open. Then Pablo ordered the priest to confess the fascists and give them the necessary sacraments."

"Where was this done?"

"In the *Ayuntamiento,* as I said. There was a great crowd outside and while this was going on inside with the priest, there was some levity outside and shouting of obscenities, but most of the people were very serious and respectful. Those who made jokes were those who were already drunk from the celebration of the taking of the barracks and there were useless characters who would have been drunk at any time.

"While the priest was engaged in these duties, Pablo organized those in the plaza into two lines.

"He placed them in two lines as you would place men for a rope pulling contest, or as they stand in a city to watch the ending of a bicycle road race with just room for the cyclists to pass between, or as men stood to allow the passage of a holy image in a procession. Two meters was left between the lines and they extended from the door of the *Ayuntamiento* clear across the plaza to the edge of the cliff. So that, from the doorway of the *Ayuntamiento,* looking across the plaza, one coming out would see two solid lines of people waiting.

"They were armed with flails such as are used to beat out the grain and they were a good flail's length apart. All did not have flails, as enough flails could not be obtained. But most had flails obtained from the store of Don Guillermo Martín, who was a fascist and sold all sorts of agricultural implements. And those who did not have flails had heavy herdsman's clubs, or ox-goads, and some had wooden pitchforks; those with wooden tines that are used to fork the chaff and straw into the air after the flailing. Some had sickles and reaping hooks but these Pablo placed at the far end where the lines reached the edge of the cliff.

"These lines were quiet and it was a clear day, as today is clear, and there were clouds high in the sky, as there are now, and the plaza was not yet dusty for there had been a heavy dew in the night, and the trees cast a shade over the men in the lines and you could hear the water running from the brass pipe in the mouth of the lion and falling into the bowl of the fountain where the women bring the water jars to fill them.

"Only near the *Ayuntamiento,* where the priest was complying with his duties with the fascists, was there any ribaldry, and that came from those worthless ones who, as I said, were already drunk and were crowded around the windows shouting obscenities and jokes in bad taste in through the iron bars of the windows. Most of the men in the lines were waiting quietly and I heard one say to another, 'Will there be women?'

"And another said, 'I hope to Christ, no.'

"Then one said, 'Here is the woman of Pablo. Listen, Pilar. Will there be women?'

"I looked at him and he was a peasant dressed in his Sunday jacket and sweating heavily and I said, 'No, Joaquín. There are no women. We are not killing the women. Why should we kill their women?'

"And he said, 'Thanks be to Christ, there are no women and when does it start?'

"And I said, 'As soon as the priest finishes.'

"'And the priest?'

"'I don't know,' I told him and I saw his face working and the sweat coming down on his forehead. 'I have never killed a man,' he said.

"'Then you will learn,' the peasant next to him said. 'But I do not think one blow with this will kill a man,' and he held his flail in both hands and looked at it with doubt.

"'That is the beauty of it,' another peasant said. 'There must be many blows.'

"'*They* have taken Valladolid. *They* have Avila,' some one said. 'I heard that before we came into town.'

"'*They* will never take this town. *This* town is ours. We have struck ahead of them,' I said, 'Pablo is not one to wait for them to strike.'

"'Pablo is able,' another said. 'But in this finishing off of the *civiles* he was egoistic. Don't you think so, Pilar?'

"'Yes,' I said. 'But now all are participating in this.'

"'Yes,' he said. 'It is well organized. But why do we not hear more news of the movement?'

"'Pablo cut the telephone wires before the assault on the barracks. They are not yet repaired.'

"'Ah,' he said. 'It is for this we hear nothing. I had my news from the road mender's station early this morning.'

"'Why is this done thus, Pilar?' he said to me.

"'To save bullets,' I said. 'And that each man should have his share in the responsibility.'

"'That it should start then. That it should start.' And I looked at him and saw that he was crying.

"'Why are you crying, Joaquín?' I asked him. 'This is not to cry about.'

"'I cannot help it, Pilar,' he said. 'I have never killed any one.'

"If you have not seen the day of revolution in a small town where all know all in the town and always have known all, you have seen nothing. And on this day most of the men in the double line across the plaza wore the clothes in which they worked in the fields, having come into town hurriedly, but some, not knowing how one should dress for the first day of a movement, wore their clothes for Sundays or holidays, and these, seeing that the others, including those who had attacked the barracks, wore their oldest clothes, were ashamed of being wrongly dressed. But they did not like to take off their jackets for fear of losing them, or that they might be stolen by the worthless ones, and so they stood, sweating in the sun and waiting for it to commence.

"Then the wind rose and the dust was now dry in the plaza for the men walking and standing and shuffling had loosened it and it commenced to blow and a man in a dark blue Sunday jacket shouted 'Agua! Agua!' and the caretaker of the plaza, whose duty it was to sprinkle the plaza each morning with a hose, came and turned the hose on and commenced to lay the dust at the edge of the plaza, and then toward the center. Then the two lines fell back and let him lay the dust over the center of the plaza; the hose sweeping in wide arcs and the water glistening in the sun and the men leaning on their flails or the clubs or the white wood pitchforks and watching the sweep of the stream of water. And then, when the plaza was nicely moistened and the dust settled, the lines formed up again and a peasant shouted, 'When do we get the first fascist? When does the first one come out of the box?'

"'Soon,' Pablo shouted from the door of the *Ayuntamiento.* 'Soon the first one comes out.' His voice was hoarse from shouting in the assault and from the smoke of the barracks.

"'What's the delay?' some one asked.

"'They're still occupied with their sins,' Pablo shouted.

"'Clearly, there are twenty of them,' a man said.

"'More,' said another.

"'Among twenty there are many sins to recount.'

"'Yes, but I think it's a trick to gain time. Surely facing such an emergency one could not remember one's sins except for the biggest.'

"'Then have patience. For with more than twenty of them there are enough of the biggest sins to take some time.'

"'I have patience,' said the other. 'But it is better to get it over with. Both for them and for us. It is July and there is much work. We have harvested but we have not threshed. We are not yet in the time of fairs and festivals.'

"'But this will be a fair and festival today,' another said. 'The Fair of Liberty and from this day, when these are extinguished, the town and the land are ours.'

"'We thresh fascists today,' said one, 'and out of the chaff comes the freedom of this pueblo.'

"'We must administer it well to deserve it,' said another. 'Pilar,' he said to me, 'when do we have a meeting for organization?'

"'Immediately after this is completed,' I told him. 'In the same building of the *Ayuntamiento.*'

"I was wearing one of the three-cornered patent leather hats of the *guardia civil* as a joke and I had put the hammer down on the pistol, holding it with my thumb to lower it as I pulled on the trigger as seemed natural, and the pistol was held in a rope I had

around my waist, the long barrel stuck under the rope. And when
I put it on the joke seemed very good to me, although afterwards
I wished I had taken the holster of the pistol instead of the hat.
But one of the men in the line said to me, 'Pilar, daughter. It
seems to me bad taste for thee to wear that hat. Now we have fin-
ished with such things as the *guardia civil*.'

"'Then,' I said, 'I will take it off.' And I did.

"'Give it to me,' he said. 'It should be destroyed.'

"And as we were at the far end of the line where the walk runs
along the cliff by the river, he took the hat in his hand and sailed it off
over the cliff with the motion a herdsman makes throwing a stone underhand at the bulls to herd them. The hat sailed far out into space
and we could see it smaller and smaller, the patent leather shining in
the clear air, sailing down to the river. I looked back over the square
and at all the windows and all the balconies there were people
crowded and there was the double line of men across the square to the
doorway of the *Ayuntamiento* and the crowd swarmed outside against
the windows of that building and there was the noise of many people
talking, and then I heard a shout and some one said 'Here comes the
first one,' and it was Don Benito Garcia, the Mayor, and he came out
bareheaded walking slowly from the door and down the porch and
nothing happened; and he walked between the line of men with the
flails and nothing happened. He passed two men, four men, eight
men, ten men and nothing happened and he was walking between
that line of men, his head up, his fat face gray, his eyes looking
ahead and then flickering from side to side and walking steadily. And
nothing happened.

"From a balcony some one cried out, *'Qué pasa, cobardes?* What
is the matter, cowards?' and still Don Benito walked along between
the men and nothing happened. Then I saw a man three men down
from where I was standing and his face was working and he was
biting his lips and his hands were white on his flail. I saw him looking toward Don Benito, watching him come on. And still nothing
happened. Then, just before Don Benito came abreast of this man,
the man raised his flail high so that it struck the man beside him
and smashed a blow at Don Benito that hit him on the side of the
head and Don Benito looked at him and the man struck again
and shouted, 'That for you, *Cabron,'* and the blow hit Don Benito in

the face and he raised his hands to his face and they beat him until he fell and the man who had struck him first called to others to help him and he pulled on the collar of Don Benito's shirt and others took hold of his arms and with his face in the dust of the plaza, they dragged him over the walk to the edge of the cliff and threw him over and into the river. And the man who hit him first was kneeling by the edge of the cliff looking over after him and saying, 'The Cabron! The Cabron! Oh, the Cabron!' He was a tenant of Don Benito and they had never gotten along together. There had been a dispute about a piece of land by the river that Don Benito had taken from this man and let to another and this man had long hated him. This man did not join the line again but sat by the cliff looking down where Don Benito had fallen.

"After Don Benito no one would come out. There was no noise now in the plaza as all were waiting to see who it was that would come out. Then a drunkard shouted in a great voice, '*Qué salga el toro!* Let the bull out!'

"Then some one from by the windows of the *Ayuntamiento* yelled, 'They won't move! They are all praying!'

"Another drunkard shouted, 'Pull them out. Come on, pull them out. The time for praying is finished.'

"But none came out and then I saw a man coming out of the door.

"It was Don Federico González, who owned the mill and feed store and was a fascist of the first order. He was tall and thin and his hair was brushed over the top of his head from one side to the other to cover a baldness and he wore a nightshirt that was tucked into his trousers. He was barefooted as when he had been taken from his home and he walked ahead of Pablo holding his hands above his head, and Pablo walked behind him with the barrels of his shotgun pressing against the back of Don Federico González until Don Federico entered the double line. But when Pablo left him and returned to the door of the *Ayuntamiento,* Don Federico could not walk forward, and stood there, his eyes turned up to heaven and his hands reaching up as though they would grasp the sky.

"'He has no legs to walk,' some one said.

"'What's the matter, Don Federico? Can't you walk?' some one shouted to him. But Don Federico stood there with his hands up and only his lips were moving.

"'Get on,' Pablo shouted to him from the steps. 'Walk.'

"Don Federico stood there and could not move. One of the drunkards poked him in the backside with a flail handle and Don Federico gave a quick jump as a balky horse might, but still stood in the same place, his hands up, and his eyes up toward the sky.

"Then the peasant who stood beside me said, 'This is shameful. I have nothing against him but such a spectacle must terminate.' So he walked down the line and pushed through to where Don Federico was standing and said, 'With your permission,' and hit him a great blow alongside of the head with a club.

"Then Don Federico dropped his hands and put them over the top of his head where the bald place was and with his head bent and covered by his hands, the thin long hairs that covered the bald place escaping through his fingers, he ran fast through the double line with flails falling on his back and shoulders until he fell and those at the end of the line picked him up and swung him over the cliff. Never did he open his mouth from the moment he came out pushed by the shotgun of Pablo. His only difficulty was to move forward. It was as though he had no command of his legs.

"After Don Federico, I saw there was a concentration of the hardest men at the end of the lines by the edge of the cliff and I left there and I went to the Arcade of the *Ayuntamiento* and pushed aside two drunkards and looked in the window. In the big room of the *Ayuntamiento* they were all kneeling in a half circle praying and the priest was kneeling and praying with them. Pablo and one named *Cuatro Dedos,* Four Fingers, a cobbler, who was much with Pablo then, and two others were standing with shotguns and Pablo said to the priest, 'Who goes now?' and the priest went on praying and did not answer him.

"'Listen, you,' Pablo said to the priest in his hoarse voice, 'who goes now? Who is ready now?'

"The priest would not speak to Pablo and acted as though he were not there and I could see Pablo was becoming very angry.

"'Let us all go together,' Don Ricardo Montalvo, who was a land owner, said to Pablo, raising his head and stopping praying to speak.

"'*Qué va,*' said Pablo. 'One at a time as you are ready.'

"'Then I go now,' Don Ricardo said. 'I'll never be any more

ready.' The priest blessed him as he spoke and blessed him again as he stood up, without interrupting his praying, and held up a crucifix for Don Ricardo to kiss and Don Ricardo kissed it and then turned and said to Pablo, 'Nor ever again as ready. You *Cabron* of the bad milk. Let us go.'

"Don Ricardo was a short man with gray hair and a thick neck and he had a shirt on with no collar. He was bow-legged from much horseback riding. 'Good-by,' he said to all those who were kneeling. 'Don't be sad. To die is nothing. The only bad thing is to die at the hands of this *canalla.* Don't touch me,' he said to Pablo. 'Don't touch me with your shotgun.'

"He walked out of the front of the *Ayuntamiento* with his gray hair and his small gray eyes and his thick neck looking very short and angry. He looked at the double line of peasants and he spat on the ground. He could spit actual saliva which, in such a circumstance, as you should know, *Inglés,* is very rare and he said, *'Arriba España!* Down with the miscalled Republic and I obscenity in the milk of your fathers.'

"So they clubbed him to death very quickly because of the insult, beating him as soon as he reached the first of the men, beating him as he tried to walk with his head up, beating him until he fell and chopping at him with reaping hooks and the sickles, and many men bore him to the edge of the cliff to throw him over and there was blood now on their hands and on their clothing, and now began to be the feeling that these who came out were truly enemies and should be killed.

"Until Don Ricardo came out with that fierceness and calling those insults, many in the line would have given much, I am sure, never to have been in the line. And if any one had shouted from the line, 'Come, let us pardon the rest of them. Now they have had their lesson,' I am sure most would have agreed.

"But Don Ricardo with all his bravery did a great disservice to the others. For he aroused the men in the line and where, before, they were performing a duty and with no great taste for it, now they were angry, and the difference was apparent.

"'Let the priest out and the thing will go faster,' some one shouted.

"'Let out the priest.'

"'We've had three thieves, let us have the priest.'

"'Two thieves,' a short peasant said to the man who had shouted. 'It was two thieves with Our Lord.'

"'Whose Lord?' the man said, his face angry and red.

"'In the manner of speaking it is said Our Lord.'

"'He isn't my Lord; not in joke,' said the other. 'And thee hadst best watch thy mouth if thou dost not want to walk between the lines.'

"'I am as good a Libertarian Republican as thou,' the short peasant said. 'I struck Don Ricardo across the mouth. I struck Don Federico across the back. I missed Don Benito. But I say Our Lord is the formal way of speaking of the man in question and that it was two thieves.'

"'I obscenity in the milk of thy Republicanism. You speak of Don this and Don that.'

"'Here are they so called.'

"'Not by me, the *cabrones*. And thy Lord— Hi! Here comes a new one!'

"It was then that we saw a disgraceful sight, for the man who walked out of the doorway of the *Ayuntamiento* was Don Faustino Rivero, the oldest son of his father, Don Celestino Rivero, a land owner. He was tall and his hair was yellow and it was freshly combed back from his forehead for he always carried a comb in his pocket and he had combed his hair now before coming out. He was a great annoyer of girls, and he was a coward, and he had always wished to be an amateur bullfighter. He went much with gypsies and with bullfighters and with bull raisers and delighted to wear the Andalucian costume, but he had no courage and was considered a joke. One time he was announced to appear in an amateur benefit fight for the old people's home in Avila and to kill a bull from on horseback in the Andalucian style, which he had spent much time practising, and when he had seen the size of the bull that had been substituted for him in place of the little one, weak in the legs, he had picked out himself, he had said he was sick and, some said, put three fingers down his throat to make himself vomit.

"When the lines saw him, they commenced to shout, '*Hola,* Don Faustino. Take care not to vomit.'

"'Listen to me, Don Faustino. There are beautiful girls over the cliff.'

"'Don Faustino. Wait a minute and we will bring out a bull bigger than the other.'

"And another shouted, 'Listen to me, Don Faustino. Hast thou ever heard speak of death?'

"Don Faustino stood there, still acting brave. He was still under the impulse that had made him announce to the others that he was going out. It was the same impulse that had made him announce himself for the bullfight. That had made him believe and hope that he could be an amateur matador. Now he was inspired by the example of Don Ricardo and he stood there looking both handsome and brave and he made his face scornful. But he could not speak.

"'Come, Don Faustino,' some one called from the line. 'Come, Don Faustino. Here is the biggest bull of all.'

"Don Faustino stood looking out and I think as he looked, that there was no pity for him on either side of the line. Still he looked both handsome and superb; but time was shortening and there was only one direction to go.

"'Don Faustino,' some one called. 'What are you waiting for, Don Faustino?'

"'He is preparing to vomit,' some one said and the lines laughed.

"'Don Faustino,' a peasant called. 'Vomit if it will give thee pleasure. To me it is all the same.'

"Then, as we watched, Don Faustino looked along the lines and across the square to the cliff and then when he saw the cliff and the emptyness beyond, he turned quickly and ducked back toward the entrance of the *Ayuntamiento.*

"All the lines roared and some one shouted in a high voice, 'Where do you go, Don Faustino? Where do you go?'

"'He goes to throw up,' shouted another and they all laughed again.

"Then we saw Don Faustino coming out again with Pablo behind him with the shotgun. All of his style was gone now. The sight of the lines had taken away his type and his style and he came out now with Pablo behind him as though Pablo were cleaning a street and Don Faustino was what he was pushing ahead of him. Don Faustino came out now and he was crossing himself and praying and then he put his hands in front of his eyes and walked down the steps toward the lines.

"'Leave him alone,' some one shouted. 'Don't touch him.'

"The lines understood and no one made a move to touch Don Faustino and, with his hands shaking and held in front of his eyes, and with his mouth moving, he walked along between the lines.

"No one said anything and no one touched him and, when he was halfway through the lines, he could go no farther and fell to his knees.

"No one struck him. I was walking along parallel to the line to see what happened to him and a peasant leaned down and lifted him to his feet and said, 'Get up, Don Faustino, and keep walking. The bull has not yet come out.'

"Don Faustino could not walk alone and the peasant in a black smock helped him on one side and another peasant in a black smock and herdsman's boots helped him on the other, supporting him by the arms and Don Faustino walking along between the lines with his hands over his eyes, his lips never quiet, and his yellow hair slicked on his head and shining in the sun, and as he passed the peasants would say, 'Don Faustino, *buen provecho*. Don Faustino, that you should have a good appetite,' and others said, 'Don Faustino, *a sus ordenes*. Don Faustino at your orders,' and one, who had failed at bullfighting himself, said, 'Don Faustino. *Matador, a sus ordenes,*' and another said, 'Don Faustino, there are beautiful girls in heaven, Don Faustino.' And they walked Don Faustino through the lines, holding him close on either side, holding him up as he walked, with him with his hands over his eyes. But he must have looked through his fingers, because when they came to the edge of the cliff with him, he knelt again, throwing himself down and clutching the ground and holding to the grass, saying, 'No. No. No. Please. NO. Please. Please. No. No.'

"Then the peasants who were with him and the others, the hard ones of the end of the line, squatted quickly behind him as he knelt, and gave him a rushing push and he was over the edge without ever having been beaten and you heard him crying loud and high as he fell.

"It was then I knew that the lines had become cruel and it was first the insults of Don Ricardo and second the cowardice of Don Faustino that had made them so.

"'Let us have another,' a peasant called out and another peasant slapped him on the back and said, 'Don Faustino! What a thing! Don Faustino!'

"'He's seen the big bull now,' another said. 'Throwing up will never help him, now.'

"'In my life,' another peasant said, 'in my life I've never seen a thing like Don Faustino.'

"'There are others,' another peasant said. 'Have patience. Who knows what we may yet see?'

"'There may be giants and dwarfs,' the first peasant said. 'There may be Negroes and rare beasts from Africa. But for me never, never will there be anything like Don Faustino. But let's have another one! Come on. Let's have another one!'

"The drunkards were handing around bottles of anis and cognac that they had looted from the bar of the club of the fascists, drinking them down like wine, and many of the men in the lines were beginning to be a little drunk, too, from drinking after the strong emotion of Don Benito, Don Federico, Don Ricardo and especially Don Faustino. Those who did not drink from the bottles of liquor were drinking from leather wineskins that were passed about and one handed a wineskin to me and I took a long drink, letting the wine run cool down my throat from the leather *bota* for I was very thirsty, too.

"'To kill gives much thirst,' the man with the wineskin said to me.

"'*Qué va,*' I said. 'Hast thou killed?'

"'We have killed four,' he said, proudly. 'Not counting the *civiles*. Is it true that thee killed one of the *civiles*, Pilar?'

"'Not one,' I said. 'I shot into the smoke when the wall fell, as did the others. That is all.'

"'Where got thee the pistol, Pilar?'

"'From Pablo. Pablo gave it to me after he killed the *civiles.*'

"'Killed he them with this pistol?'

"'With no other,' I said. 'And then he armed me with it.'

"'Can I see it, Pilar? Can I hold it?'

"'Why not, man?' I said, and I took it out from under the rope and handed it to him. But I was wondering why no one else had come out and just then who should come out but Don Guillermo Martín from whose store the flails, the herdsman's clubs, and the wooden pitchforks had been taken. Don Guillermo was a fascist but otherwise there was nothing against him.

"It is true he paid little to those who made the flails but he charged little for them too and if one did not wish to buy flails from Don Guillermo, it was possible to make them for nothing more than the cost of the wood and the leather. He had a rude way of speaking and he was undoubtedly a fascist and a member of their club and he sat at noon and at evening in the cane chairs of their club to read *El Debate,* to have his shoes shined, and to drink vermouth and seltzer and eat roasted almonds, dried shrimps, and anchovies. But one does not kill for that, and I am sure if it had not been for the insults of Don Ricardo Montalvo and the lamentable spectacle of Don Faustino, and the drinking consequent on the emotion of them and the others, some one would have shouted, 'That Don Guillermo should go in peace. We have his flails. Let him go.'

"Because the people of this town are as kind as they can be cruel and they have a natural sense of justice and a desire to do that which is right. But cruelty had entered into the lines and also drunkenness or the beginning of drunkenness and the lines were not as they were when Don Benito had come out. I do not know how it is in other countries, and no one cares more for the pleasure of drinking than I do, but in Spain drunkenness, when produced by other elements than wine, is a thing of great ugliness and the people do things that they would not have done. Is it not so in your country, *Inglés?*"

"It is so," Robert Jordan said. "When I was seven years old and going with my mother to attend a wedding in the state of Ohio at which I was to be the boy of a pair of boy and girl who carried flowers——"

"Did you do that?" asked Maria. "How nice!"

"In this town a Negro was hanged to a lamp post and later burned. It was an arc light. A light which lowered from the post to the pavement. And he was hoisted, first by the mechanism which was used to hoist the arc light but this broke——"

"A Negro," Maria said. "How barbarous!"

"Were the people drunk?" asked Pilar. "Were they drunk thus to burn a Negro?"

"I do not know," Robert Jordan said. "Because I saw it only look-ing out from under the blinds of a window in the house which stood on the corner where the arc light was. The street was full of people and when they lifted the Negro up for the second time——"

"If you had only seven years and were in a house, you could not tell if they were drunk or not," Pilar said.

"As I said, when they lifted the Negro up for the second time, my mother pulled me away from the window, so I saw no more," Robert Jordan said. "But since I have had experiences which demonstrate that drunkenness is the same in my country. It is ugly and brutal."

"You were too young at seven," Maria said. "You were too young for such things. I have never seen a Negro except in a circus. Unless the Moors are Negroes."

"Some are Negroes and some are not," Pilar said. "I can talk to you of the Moors."

"Not as I can," Maria said. "Nay, not as I can."

"Don't speak of such things," Pilar said. "It is unhealthy. Where were we?"

"Speaking of the drunkenness of the lines," Robert Jordan said. "Go on."

"It is not fair to say drunkenness," Pilar said. "For, yet, they were a long way from drunkenness. But already there was a change in them, and when Don Guillermo came out, standing straight, near-sighted, gray-headed, of medium height, with a shirt with a collar button but no collar, standing there and crossing himself once and looking ahead, but seeing little without his glasses, but walking forward well and calmly, he was an appearance to excite pity. But some one shouted from the line, 'Here, Don Guillermo. Up here, Don Guillermo. In this direction. Here we all have your products.'

"They had had such success joking at Don Faustino that they could not see, now, that Don Guillermo was a different thing, and if Don Guillermo was to be killed, he should be killed quickly and with dignity.

"'Don Guillermo,' another shouted. 'Should we send to the house for thy spectacles?'

"Don Guillermo's house was no house, since he had not much money and was only a fascist to be a snob and to console himself that he must work for little, running a wooden-implement shop. He was a fascist, too, from the religiousness of his wife which he accepted as his own due to his love for her. He lived in an apartment in the building three houses down the square and when Don Guillermo stood there, looking near-sightedly at the lines, the double lines he knew he must enter, a woman started to scream from the balcony of the apartment where he lived. She could see him from the balcony and she was his wife.

"'Guillermo,' she cried. 'Guillermo. Wait and I will be with thee.'

"Don Guillermo turned his head toward where the shouting came from. He could not see her. He tried to say something but he could not. Then he waved his hand in the direction the woman had called from and started to walk between the lines.

"'Guillermo!' she cried. 'Guillermo! Oh, Guillermo!'" She was holding her hands on the rail of the balcony and shaking back and forth. 'Guillermo!'

"Don Guillermo waved his hand again toward the noise and walked into the lines with his head up and you would not have known what he was feeling except for the color of his face.

"Then some drunkard yelled, 'Guillermo!' from the lines, imitating the high cracked voice of his wife and Don Guillermo rushed toward the man, blindly, with tears now running down his cheeks and the man hit him hard across the face with his flail and Don Guillermo sat down from the force of the blow and sat there crying, but not from fear, while the drunkards beat him and one drunkard jumped on top of him, astride his shoulders, and beat him with a bottle. After this many of the men left the lines and their places were taken by the drunkards who had been jeering and saying things in bad taste through the windows of the *Ayuntamiento.*

"I myself had felt much emotion at the shooting of the *guardia civil* by Pablo," Pilar said. "It was a thing of great ugliness, but I had thought if this is how it must be, this is how it must be, and at least there was no cruelty, only the depriving of life which, as we all have learned in these years, is a thing of ugliness but also a necessity to do if we are to win, and to preserve the Republic.

"When the square had been closed off and the lines formed, I had admired and understood it as a conception of Pablo, although it seemed to me to be somewhat fantastic and that it would be necessary for all that was to be done to be done in good taste if it were not to be repugnant. Certainly if the fascists were to be executed by the people, it was better for all the people to have a part in it, and I wished to share the guilt as much as any, just as I hoped to share in the benefits when the town should be ours. But after Don Guillermo I felt a feeling of shame and distaste, and with the coming of the drunkards and the worthless ones into the lines, and the abstention of those who left the lines as a protest after Don Guillermo, I wished that I might disassociate myself altogether from the lines, and I walked away, across the square, and sat down on a bench under one of the big trees that gave shade there.

"Two peasants from the lines walked over, talking together, and one of them called to me, 'What passes with thee, Pilar?'

"'Nothing, man,' I told him.

"'Yes,' he said. 'Speak. What passes.'

"'I think that I have a belly-full,' I told him.

"'Us, too,' he said and they both sat down on the bench. One of them had a leather wineskin and he handed it to me.

"'Rinse out thy mouth,' he said and the other said, going on with the talking they had been engaged in, 'The worst is that it will bring bad luck. Nobody can tell me that such things as the killing of Don Guillermo in that fashion will not bring bad luck.'

"Then the other said, 'If it is necessary to kill them all, and I am not convinced of that necessity, let them be killed decently and without mockery.'

"'Mockery is justified in the case of Don Faustino,' the other said. 'Since he was always a farcer and was never a serious man. But to mock such a serious man as Don Guillermo is beyond all right.'

"'I have a belly-full,' I told him, and it was literally true because I felt an actual sickness in all of me inside and a sweating and a nausea as though I had swallowed bad sea food.

"'Then, nothing,' the one peasant said. 'We will take no further part in it. But I wonder what happens in the other towns.'

"'They have not repaired the telephone wires yet,' I said. 'It is a lack that should be remedied.'

"'Clearly,' he said. 'Who knows but what we might be better employed putting the town into a state of defense than massacring people with this slowness and brutality.'

"'I will go to speak with Pablo, I told them and I stood up from the bench and started toward the arcade that led to the door of the

Ayuntamiento from where the lines spread across the square. The lines now were neither straight nor orderly and there was much and very grave drunkenness. Two men had fallen down and lay on their backs in the middle of the square and were passing a bottle back and forth between them. One would take a drink and then shout, *'Viva la Anarquia!'* lying on his back and shouting as though he were a madman. He had a red-and-black handkerchief around his neck. The other shouted, *'Viva la Libertad!'* and kicked his feet in the air and then bellowed, *'Viva la Libertad!'* again. He had a red-and-black handkerchief too and he waved it in one hand and waved the bottle with the other.

"A peasant who had left the lines and now stood in the shade of the arcade looked at them in disgust and said, 'They should shout, "Long live drunkenness." That's all they believe in.'

"'They don't believe even in that,' another peasant said. 'Those neither understand nor believe in anything.'

"Just then, one of the drunkards got to his feet and raised both arms with his fists clenched over his head and shouted, 'Long live Anarchy and Liberty and I obscenity in the milk of the Republic!'

"The other drunkard who was still lying on his back, took hold of the ankle of the drunkard who was shouting and rolled over, so that the shouting drunkard fell with him, and they rolled over together and then sat up and the one who had pulled the other down put his arm around the shouter's neck and then handed the shouter a bottle and kissed the red-and-black handkerchief he wore and they both drank together.

"Just then, a yelling went up from the lines and, looking up the arcade, I could not see who it was that was coming out because the man's head did not show above the heads of those crowded about the door of the *Ayuntamiento.* All I could see was that some one was being pushed out by Pablo and Cuatro Dedos with their shotguns but I could not see who it was and I moved on close toward the lines where they were packed against the door to try to see.

"There was much pushing now and the chairs and the tables of the fascists' café had been overturned except for one table on which a drunkard was lying with his head hanging down and his mouth open and I picked up a chair and set it against one of the pillars and mounted on it so that I could see over the heads of the crowd.

"The man who was being pushed out by Pablo and Cuatro Dedos was Don Anastasio Rivas, who was an undoubted fascist and the fattest man in the town. He was a grain buyer and the agent for several insurance companies and he also loaned money at high rates of interest. Standing on the chair, I saw him walk down the steps and toward the lines, his fat neck bulging over the back of the collar band of his shirt, and his bald head shining in the sun, but he never entered them because there was a shout, not as of different men shouting, but of all of them. It was an ugly noise and was the cry of the drunken lines all yelling together and the lines broke with the rush of men toward him and I saw Don Anastasio throw himself down with his hands over his head and then you could not see him for the men piled on top of him. And when the men got up from him, Don Anastasio was dead from his head being beaten against the stone flags of the paving of the arcade and there were no more lines but only a mob.

"'We're going in,' they commenced to shout. 'We're going in after them.'

"'He's too heavy to carry,' a man kicked at the body of Don Anastasio, who was lying there on his face. 'Let him stay there.'

"'Why should we lug that tub of tripe to the cliff? Let him lie there.'

"'We are going to enter and finish with them inside,' a man shouted. 'We're going in.'

"'Why wait all day in the sun?' another yelled. 'Come on. Let us go.'

"The mob was now pressing into the arcade. They were shouting and pushing and they made a noise now like an animal and they were all shouting 'Open up! Open up!' for the guards had shut the doors of the *Ayuntamiento* when the lines broke.

"Standing on the chair, I could see in through the barred window into the hall of the *Ayuntamiento* and in there it was as it had been before. The priest was standing, and those who were left were kneeling in a half circle around him and they were all praying. Pablo was sitting on the big table in front of the Mayor's chair with his shotgun slung over his back. His legs were hanging down from the table and he was rolling a cigarette. Cuatro Dedos was sitting in the Mayor's chair with his feet on the table and he was smoking a cigarette. All the guards were sitting in different chairs of the administration, holding their guns. The key to the big door was on the table beside Pablo.

"The mob was shouting, 'Open up! Open up! Open up!' as though it were a chant and Pablo was sitting there as though he did not hear them. He said something to the priest but I could not hear what he said for the noise of the mob.

"The priest, as before, did not answer him but kept on praying. With many people pushing me, I moved the chair close against the wall, shoving it ahead of me as they shoved me from behind. I stood on the chair with my face close against the bars of the window and held on by the bars. A man climbed on the chair too and stood with his arms around mine, holding the wider bars.

"'The chair will break,' I said to him.

"'What does it matter?' he said. 'Look at them. Look at them pray.'

"His breath on my neck smelled like the smell of the mob, sour, like vomit on paving stones and the smell of drunkenness, and then he put his mouth against the opening in the bars with his head over my shoulder, and shouted, 'Open up! Open!' and it was as though the mob were on my back as a devil is on your back in a dream.

"Now the mob was pressed tight against the door so that those in front were being crushed by all the others who were pressing and from the square a big drunkard in a black smock with a red-and-black handkerchief around his neck, ran and threw himself against the press of the mob and fell forward onto the pressing men and then stood up and backed away and then ran forward again and threw himself against the backs of those men who were pushing, shouting, 'Long live me and long live Anarchy.'

"As I watched, this man turned away from the crowd and went and sat down and drank from a bottle and then, while he was sitting down, he saw Don Anastasio, who was still lying face down on the stones, but much trampled now, and the drunkard got up and went over to Don Anastasio and leaned over and poured out of the bottle onto the head of Don Anastasio and onto his clothes, and then he took a matchbox out of his pocket and lit several matches, trying to make a fire with Don Anastasio. But the wind was blowing hard now and it blew the matches out and after a little the big drunkard sat there by Don Anastasio, shaking his head and drinking out of the bottle and every once in a while, leaning over and patting Don Anastasio on the shoulders of his dead body.

"All this time the mob was shouting to open up and the man on the chair with me was holding tight to the bars of the window and shouting to open up until it deafened me with his voice roaring past my ear and his breath foul on me and I looked away from watching the drunkard who had been trying to set fire to Don Anastasio and into the hall of the *Ayuntamiento* again; and it was just as it had been. They were still praying as they had been, the men all kneeling, with their shirts open, some with their heads down, others with their heads up, looking toward the priest and toward the crucifix that he held, and the priest praying fast and hard and looking out over their heads, and in back of them Pablo, with his cigarette now lighted, was sitting there on the table swinging his legs, his shotgun slung over his back, and he was playing with the key.

"I saw Pablo speak to the priest again, leaning forward from the table and I could not hear what he said for the shouting. But the priest did not answer him but went on praying. Then a man stood up from among the half circle of those who were praying and I saw he wanted to go out. It was Don José Castro, whom every one called Don Pepe, a confirmed fascist, and a dealer in horses, and he stood up now small, neat-looking even unshaven and wearing a pajama top tucked into a pair of gray-striped trousers. He kissed the crucifix and the priest blessed him and he stood up and looked at Pablo and jerked his head toward the door.

"Pablo shook his head and went on smoking. I could see Don Pepe say something to Pablo but could not hear it. Pablo did not answer; he simply shook his head again and nodded toward the door.

"Then I saw Don Pepe look full at the door and realized that he had not known it was locked. Pablo showed him the key and he stood looking at it an instant and then he turned and went and knelt down again. I saw the priest look around at Pablo and Pablo grinned at him and showed him the key and the priest seemed to realize for the first time that the door was locked and he seemed as though he started to shake his head, but he only inclined it and went back to praying.

"I do not know how they could not have understood the door was locked unless it was that they were so concentrated on their praying and their own thoughts; but now they certainly understood and they understood the shouting and they must have known now that all was changed. But they remained the same as before.

"By now the shouting was so that you could hear nothing and the drunkard who stood on the chair with me shook with his hands at the bars and yelled, 'Open up! Open up!' until he was hoarse.

"I watched Pablo speak to the priest again and the priest did not answer. Then I saw Pablo unsling his shotgun and he reached over and tapped the priest on the shoulder with it. The priest paid no attention to him and I saw Pablo shake his head. Then he spoke over his shoulder to Cuatro Dedos and Cuatro Dedos spoke to the other guards and they all stood up and walked back to the far end of the room and stood there with their shotguns.

"I saw Pablo say something to Cuatro Dedos and he moved over two tables and some benches and the guards stood behind them with their shotguns. It made a barricade in that corner of the room. Pablo leaned over and tapped the priest on the shoulder again with the shotgun and the priest did not pay attention to him but I saw Don Pepe watching him while the others paid no attention but went on praying. Pablo shook his head and, seeing Don Pepe looking at him, he shook his head at Don Pepe and showed him the key, holding it up in his hand. Don Pepe understood and he dropped his head and commenced to pray very fast.

"Pablo swung his legs down from the table and walked around it to the big chair of the Mayor on the raised platform behind the long council table. He sat down in it and rolled himself a cigarette, all the time watching the fascists who were praying with the priest. You could not see any expression on his face at all. The key was on the table in front of him. It was a big key of iron, over a foot long. Then Pablo called to the guards something I could not hear and one guard went down to the door. I could see them all praying faster than ever and I knew that they all knew now.

"Pablo said something to the priest but the priest did not answer. Then Pablo leaned forward, picked up the key and tossed it underhand to the guard at the door. The guard caught it and Pablo smiled at him. Then the guard put the key in the door, turned it, and pulled the door toward him, ducking behind it as the mob rushed in.

"I saw them come in and just then the drunkard on the chair with me commenced to shout 'Ayee! Ayee! Ayee!' and pushed his head forward so I could not see and then he shouted 'Kill them! Kill them! Club them! Kill them!' and he pushed me aside with his two arms and I could see nothing.

"I hit my elbow into his belly and I said, 'Drunkard, whose chair is this? Let me see.'

"But he just kept shaking his hands and arms against the bars and shouting, 'Kill them! Club them! Club them! that's it. Club them! Kill them! *Cabrones! Cabrones! Cabrones!*'

"I hit him hard with my elbow and said, '*Cabron!* Drunkard! Let me see.'

"Then he put both his hands on my head to push me down and so he might see better and leaned all his weight on my head and went on shouting, 'Club them! that's it. Club them!'

"'Club yourself,' I said and I hit him hard where it would hurt him and it hurt him and he dropped his hands from my head and grabbed himself and said. '*No hay derecho, mujer.* This, woman, you have no right to do.' And in that moment, looking through the bars, I saw the hall full of men flailing away with clubs and striking with flails, and poking and striking and pushing and heaving against people with the white wooden pitchforks that now were red and with their tines broken, and this was going on all over the room while Pablo sat in the big chair with his shotgun on his knees, watching, and they were shouting and clubbing and stabbing and men were screaming as horses scream in a fire. And I saw the priest with his skirts tucked up scrambling over a bench and those after him were chopping at him with the sickles and the reaping hooks and then some one had hold of his robe and there was another scream and another scream and I saw two men chopping into his back with sickles while a third man held the skirt of his robe and the priest's arms were up and he was clinging to the back of a chair and then the chair I was standing on broke and the drunkard and I were on the pavement that smelled of spilled wine and vomit and the drunkard was shaking his finger at me and saying, '*No hay derecho, mujer, no hay derecho.* You could have done me an injury,' and the people were trampling over us to get into the hall of the *Ayuntamiento* and all I could see was legs of people going in the doorway and the drunkard sitting there facing me and holding himself where I had hit him.

"That was the end of the killing of the fascists in our town and I was glad I did not see more of it and, but for that drunkard, I would have seen it all. So he served some good because in the *Ayuntamiento* it was a thing one is sorry to have seen.

"But the other drunkard was something rarer still. As we got up after the breaking of the chair, and the people were still crowding into the *Ayuntamiento*, I saw this drunkard of the square with his red-and-black scarf, again pouring something over Don Anastasio. He was shaking his head from side to side and it was very hard for him to sit up, but he was pouring and lighting matches and then pouring and lighting matches and I walked over to him and said, 'What are you doing, shameless?'

" '*Nada, mujer, nada,*' he said. 'Let me alone.'

"And perhaps because I was standing there so that my legs made a shelter from the wind, the match caught and a blue flame began to run up the shoulder of the coat of Don Anastasio and onto the back of his neck and the drunkard put his head up and shouted in a huge voice, 'They're burning the dead! They're burning the dead'

" 'Who?' somebody said.

" 'Where?' shouted some one else.

" 'Here,' bellowed the drunkard. 'Exactly here!'

"Then some one hit the drunkard a great blow alongside the head with a flail and he fell back, and lying on the ground, he looked up at the man who had hit him and then shut his eyes and crossed his hands on his chest, and lay there beside Don Anastasio as though he were asleep. The man did not hit him again and he lay there and he was still there when they picked up Don Anastasio and put him with the others in the cart that hauled them all over to the cliff where they were thrown over that evening with the others after there had been a cleaning up in the *Ayuntamiento*. It would have been better for the town if they had thrown over twenty or thirty of the drunkards, especially those of the red-and-black scarves, and if we ever have another revolution I believe they should be destroyed at the start. But then we did not know this. But in the next days we were to learn.

"But that night we did not know what was to come. After the

slaying in the *Ayuntamiento* there was no more killing but we could not have a meeting that night because there were too many drunkards. It was impossible to obtain order and so the meeting was postponed until the next day.

"That night I slept with Pablo. I should not say this to you, *guapa,* but on the other hand, it is good for you to know everything and at least what I tell you is true. Listen to this, *Inglés.* It is very curious.

"As I say, that night we ate and it was very curious. It was as after a storm or a flood or a battle and every one was tired and no one spoke much. I, myself, felt hollow and not well and I was full of shame and a sense of wrongdoing and I had a great feeling of oppression and of bad to come, as this morning after the planes. And certainly, bad came within three days.

"Pablo, when we ate, spoke little.

"'Did you like it, Pilar?' he asked finally with his mouth full of roast young goat. We were eating at the inn from where the busses leave and the room was crowded and people were singing and there was difficulty serving.

"'No,' I said. 'Except for Don Faustino, I did not like it.'

"'I liked it,' he said.

"'All of it?' I asked him.

"'All of it,' he said and cut himself a big piece of bread with his knife and commenced to mop up gravy with it. 'All of it, except the priest.'

"'You didn't like it about the priest?' because I knew he hated priests even worse than he hated fascists.

"'He was a disillusionment to me,' Pablo said sadly.

"So many people were singing that we had to almost shout to hear one another.

"'Why?'

"'He died very badly,' Pablo said. 'He had very little dignity.'

"'How did you want him to have dignity when he was being chased by the mob?' I said. 'I thought he had much dignity all the time before. All the dignity that one could have.'

"'Yes,' Pablo said. 'But in the last minute he was frightened.'

"'Who wouldn't be?' I said. 'Did you see what they were chasing him with?'

"'Why would I not see?' Pablo said. 'But I find he died badly.'

"'In such circumstances any one dies badly,' I told him. 'What do you want for your money? Everything that happened in the *Ayuntamiento* was scabrous.'

"'Yes,' said Pablo. 'There was little organization. But a priest. He has an example to set.'

"'I thought you hated priests.'

"'Yes,' said Pablo and cut some more bread. 'But a *Spanish* priest. A *Spanish* priest should die very well.'

"'I think he died well enough,' I said. 'Being deprived of all formality.'

"'No,' Pablo said. 'To me he was a great disillusionment. All day I had waited for the death of the priest. I had thought he would be the last to enter the lines. I awaited it with great anticipation. I expected something of a culmination. I had never seen a priest die.'

"'There is time,' I said to him sarcastically. 'Only today did the movement start.'

"'No,' he said. 'I am disillusioned.'

"'Now,' I said. 'I suppose you will lose your faith.'

"'You do not understand, Pilar,' he said. 'He was a *Spanish* priest.'

"'What people the Spaniards are,' I said to him. And what a people they are for pride, eh, *Inglés?* What a people."

"We must get on," Robert Jordan said. He looked at the sun. "It's nearly noon."

"Yes," Pilar said. "We will go now. But let me tell you about Pablo. That night he said to me, 'Pilar, tonight we will do nothing.'

"'Good,' I told him. 'That pleases me.'

"'I think it would be bad taste after the killing of so many people.'

"'*Qué va*', I told him. 'What a saint you are. You think I lived years with bullfighters not to know how they are after the Corrida?'

"'Is it true, Pilar?' he asked me.

"'When did I lie to you?' I told him.

"'It is true, Pilar, I am a finished man this night. You do not reproach me?'

"'No, *hombre,*' I said to him. 'But don't kill people every day, Pablo.'

"And he slept that night like a baby and I woke him in the morning at daylight but I could not sleep that night and I got up and sat in a chair and looked out of the window and I could see the square in the moonlight where the lines had been and across the square the trees shining in the moonlight, and the darkness of their shadows, and the benches bright too in the moonlight, and the scattered bottles shining, and beyond the edge of the cliff where they had all been thrown. And there was no sound but the splashing of the water in the fountain and I sat there and I thought we have begun badly.

"The window was open and up the square from the Fonda I could hear a woman crying. I went out on the balcony standing there in my bare feet on the iron and the moon shone on the faces of all the buildings of the square and the crying was coming from the balcony of the house of Don Guillermo. It was his wife and she was on the balcony kneeling and crying.

"Then I went back inside the room and I sat there and I did not wish to think for that was the worst day of my life until one other day."

"What was the other?" Maria asked.

"Three days later when the fascists took the town."

"Do not tell me about it," said Maria. "I do not want to hear it. This is enough. This was too much."

"I told you that you should not have listened," Pilar said. "See. I did not want you to hear it. Now you will have bad dreams."

"No," said Maria. "But I do not want to hear more."

"I wish you would tell me of it sometime," Robert Jordan said.

"I will," Pilar said. "But it is bad for Maria."

"I don't want to hear it," Maria said pitifully. "Please, Pilar. And do not tell it if I am there, for I might listen in spite of myself."

Her lips were working and Robert Jordan thought she would cry.

"Please, Pilar, do not tell it."

"Do not worry, little cropped head," Pilar said. "Do not worry. But I will tell the *Inglés* sometime."

"But I want to be there when he is there," Maria said. "Oh, Pilar, do not tell it at all."

"I will tell it when thou art working."

"No. No. Please. Let us not tell it at all," Maria said.

"It is only fair to tell it since I have told what we did," Pilar said. "But you shall never hear it."

"Are there no pleasant things to speak of?" Maria said. "Do we have to talk always of horrors?"

"This afternoon," Pilar said, "thou and *Inglés*. The two of you can speak of what you wish."

"Then that the afternoon should come," Maria said. "That it should come flying."

"It will come," Pilar told her. "It will come flying and go the same way and tomorrow will fly, too."

"This afternoon," Maria said. "This afternoon. That this afternoon should come."

CHAPTER ELEVEN

As THEY came up, still deep in the shadow of the pines, after dropping down from the high meadow into the wooden valley and climbing up it on a trail that paralleled the stream and then left it to gain, steeply, the top of a rim-rock formation, a man with a carbine stepped out from behind a tree.

"Halt," he said. Then, *"Hola,* Pilar. Who is this with thee?"

"An *Inglés,"* Pilar said. "But with a Christian name—Roberto. And what an obscenity of steepness it is to arrive here."

"Salud, Camarada," the guard said to Robert Jordan and put out his hand. "Are you well?"

"Yes," said Robert Jordan. "And thee?"

"Equally," the guard said. He was very young, with a light build, thin, rather hawk-nosed face, high cheekbones and gray eyes. He wore no hat, his hair was black and shaggy and his handclasp was strong and friendly. His eyes were friendly too.

"Hello, Maria," he said to the girl. "You did not tire yourself?"

"Qué va, Joaquín," the girl said. "We have sat and talked more than we have walked."

"Are you the dynamiter?" Joaquín asked. "We have heard you were here."

"We passed the night at Pablo's," Robert Jordan said. "Yes, I am the dynamiter."

"We are glad to see you," Joaquín said. "Is it for a train?"

"Were you at the last train?" Robert Jordan asked and smiled.

"Was I not," Joaquín said. "That's where we got this," he grinned at Maria. "You are pretty now," he said to Maria. "Have they told thee how pretty?"

"Shut up, Joaquín, and thank you very much," Maria said. "You'd be pretty with a haircut."

"I carried thee," Joaquín told the girl. "I carried thee over my shoulder."

"As did many others," Pilar said in the deep voice. "Who didn't carry her? Where is the old man?"

"At the camp."

"Where was he last night?"

"In Segovia."

"Did he bring news?"

"Yes," Joaquín said, "there is news."

"Good or bad?"

"I believe bad."

"Did you see the planes?"

"Ay," said Joaquín and shook his head. "Don't talk to me of that. Comrade Dynamiter, what planes were those?"

"Heinkel one eleven bombers. Heinkel and Fiat pursuit," Robert Jordan told him.

"What were the big ones with the low wings?"

"Heinkel one elevens."

"By any names they are as bad," Joaquín said. "But I am delaying you. I will take you to the commander."

"The commander?" Pilar asked.

Joaquín nodded seriously. "I like it better than 'chief'," he said. "It is more military."

"You are militarizing heavily," Pilar said and laughed at him.

"No," Joaquín said. "But I like military terms because it makes orders clearer and for better discipline."

"Here is one according to thy taste, *Inglés,*" Pilar said. "A very serious boy."

"Should I carry thee?" Joaquín asked the girl and put his arm on her shoulder and smiled in her face.

"Once was enough," Maria told him. "Thank you just the same."

"Can you remember it?" Joaquín asked her.

"I can remember being carried," Maria said. "By you, no. I remember the gypsy because he dropped me so many times. But I thank thee, Joaquín, and I'll carry thee sometime."

"I can remember it well enough," Joaquín said. "I can remember holding thy two legs and thy belly was on my shoulder and thy head over my back and thy arms hanging down against my back."

"Thou hast much memory," Maria said and smiled at him. "I remember nothing of that. Neither thy arms nor thy shoulders nor thy back."

"Do you want to know something?" Joaquín asked her.

"What is it?"

"I was glad thou wert hanging over my back when the shots were coming from behind us."

"What a swine," Maria said. "And was it for this the gypsy too carried me so much?"

"For that and to hold onto thy legs."

"My heroes," Maria said. "My saviors."

"Listen, *guapa,*" Pilar told her. "This boy carried thee much, and in that moment thy legs said nothing to any one. In that moment only the bullets talked clearly. And if he would have dropped thee he could soon have been out of range of the bullets."

"I have thanked him," Maria said. "And I will carry him sometime. Allow us to joke. I do not have to cry, do I, because he carried me?"

"I'd have dropped thee," Joaquín went on teasing her. "But I was afraid Pilar would shoot me."

"I shoot no one," Pilar said.

"*No hace falta,*" Joaquín told her. "You don't need to. You scare them to death with your mouth."

"What a way to speak," Pilar told him. "And you used to be such a polite little boy. What did you do before the movement, little boy?"

"Very little," Joaquín said. "I was sixteen."

"But what, exactly?"

"A few pairs of shoes from time to time."

"Make them?"

"No. Shine them."

"*Qué va,*" said Pilar. "There is more to it than that." She looked at his brown face, his lithe build, his shock of hair, and the quick heel-and-toe way that he walked. "Why did you fail at it?"

"Fail at what?"

"What? You know what. You're growing the pigtail now."

"I guess it was fear," the boy said.

"You've a nice figure," Pilar told him. "But the face isn't much. So it was fear, was it? You were all right at the train."

"I have no fear of them now," the boy said. "None. And we have seen much worse things and more dangerous than the bulls. It is clear no bull is as dangerous as a machine gun. But if I were in the ring with one now I do not know if I could dominate my legs."

"He wanted to be a bullfighter," Pilar explained to Robert Jordan. "But he was afraid."

"Do you like the bulls, Comrade Dynamiter?" Joaquín grinned, showing white teeth.

"Very much," Robert Jordan said. "Very, very much."

"Have you seen them in Valladolid?" asked Joaquín.

"Yes. In September at the feria."

"That's my town," Joaquín said. "What a fine town but how the *buena gente,* the good people of that town, have suffered in this war." Then, his face grave, "There they shot my father. My mother. My brother-in-law and now my sister."

"What barbarians," Robert Jordan said.

How many times had he heard this? How many times had he watched people say it with difficulty? How many times had he seen their eyes fill and their throats harden with the difficulty of saying my father, or my brother, or my mother, or my sister? He could not remember how many times he had heard them mention their dead in this way. Nearly always they spoke as this boy did now; suddenly and apropos of the mention of the town and always you said, "What barbarians."

You only heard the statement of the loss. You did not see the father fall as Pilar made him see the fascists die in that story she had told by the stream. You knew the father died in some courtyard, or against some wall, or in some field or orchard, or at night, in the lights of a truck, beside some road. You had seen the lights of the car from the hills and heard the shooting and afterwards you had come down to the road and found the bodies. You did not see the mother shot, nor the sister, nor the brother. You heard about it; you heard the shots; and you saw the bodies.

Pilar had made him see it in that town.

If that woman could only write. He would try to write it and if he had luck and could remember it perhaps he could get it down as she told it. God, how she could tell a story. She's better than Quevedo, he thought. He never wrote the death of any Don Faustino as well as she told it. I wish I could write well enough to write that story, he thought. What we did. Not what the others did to us. He knew enough about that. He knew plenty about that behind the lines. But you had to have known the people before. You had to know what they had been in the village.

Because of our mobility and because we did not have to stay afterwards to take the punishment we never knew how anything really ended, he thought. You stayed with a peasant and his family. You came at night and ate with them. In the day you were hidden and the next night you were gone. You did your job and cleared out. The next time you came that way you heard that they had been shot. It was as simple as that.

But you were always gone when it happened. The *partizans* did their damage and pulled out. The peasants stayed and took the punishment. I've always known about the other, he thought. What we did to them at the start. I've always known it and hated it and I have heard it mentioned shamelessly and shamefully, bragged of, boasted of, defended, explained and denied. But that damned woman made me see it as though I had been there.

Well, he thought, it is part of one's education. It will be quite an education when it's finished. You learn in this war if you listen. You most certainly did. He was lucky that he had lived parts of ten years in Spain before the war. They trusted you on the language, principally. They trusted you on understanding the language completely and speaking it idiomatically and having a knowledge of the different places. A Spaniard was only really loyal to his village in the end. First Spain of course, then his own tribe, then his province, then his village, his family and finally his trade. If you knew Spanish he was prejudiced in your favor, if you knew his province it was that much better, but if you knew his village and his trade you were in as far as any foreigner ever could be. He never felt like a foreigner in Spanish and they did not really treat him like a foreigner most of the time; only when they turned on you.

Of course they turned on you. They turned on you often but they always turned on every one. They turned on themselves, too. If you had three together, two would unite against one, and then the two would start to betray each other. Not always, but often enough for you to take enough cases and start to draw it as a conclusion.

This was no way to think; but who censored his thinking? Nobody but himself. He would not think himself into any defeatism. The first thing was to win the war. If we did not win the war everything was lost. But he noticed, and listened to, and remembered everything. He was serving in a war and he gave absolute loyalty and as complete a performance as he could give while he was serving. But nobody owned his mind, nor his faculties for seeing and hearing, and if he were going to form judgments he would form them afterwards. And there would be plenty of material to draw them from. There was plenty already. There was a little too much sometimes.

Look at the Pilar woman, he thought. No matter what comes, if there is time, I must make her tell me the rest of that story. Look at her walking along with those two kids. You could not get three better-looking products of Spain than those. She is like a mountain and the boy and the girl are like young trees. The old trees are all cut down and the young trees are growing clean like that. In spite of what has happened to the two of them they look as fresh and clean and new and untouched as though they had never heard of misfortune. But according to Pilar, Maria has just gotten sound again. She must have been in an awful shape.

He remembered a Belgian boy in the Eleventh Brigade who had enlisted with five other boys from his village. It was a village of about two hundred people and the boy had never been away from the village before. When he first saw the boy, out at Hans' Brigade Staff, the other five from the village had all been killed and the boy was in very bad shape and they were using him as an orderly to wait on table at the staff. He had a big, blond, ruddy Flemish face and huge awkward peasant hands and he moved, with the dishes, as powerfully and awkwardly as a draft horse. But he cried all the time. All during the meal he cried with no noise at all.

You looked up and there he was, crying. If you asked for the wine, he cried and if you passed your plate for stew, he cried; turning away his head. Then he would stop; but if you looked up at him, tears would start coming again. Between courses he cried in the kitchen. Every one was very gentle with him. But it did no good. He would have to find out what became of him and whether he ever cleared up and was fit for soldiering again.

Maria was sound enough now. She seemed so anyway. But

he was no psychiatrist. Pilar was the psychiatrist. It probably had been good for them to have been together last night. Yes, unless it stopped. It certainly had been good for him. He felt fine today; sound and good and unworried and happy. The show looked bad enough but he was awfully lucky, too. He had been in others that announced themselves badly. Announced themselves; that was thinking in Spanish. Maria was lovely.

Look at her, he said to himself. Look at her.

He looked at her striding happily in the sun; her khaki shirt open at the neck. She walks like a colt moves, he thought. You do not run onto something like that. Such things don't happen. Maybe it never did happen, he thought. Maybe you dreamed it or made it up and it never did happen. Maybe it is like the dreams you have when some one you have seen in the cinema comes to your bed at night and is so kind and lovely. He'd slept with them all that way when he was asleep in bed. He could remember Garbo still, and Harlow. Yes, Harlow many times. Maybe it was like those dreams.

But he could still remember the time Garbo came to his bed the night before the attack at Pozoblanco and she was wearing a soft silky wool sweater when he put his arm around her and when she leaned forward her hair swept forward and over his face and she said why had he never told her that he loved her when she had loved him all this time? She was not shy, nor cold, nor distant. She was just lovely to hold and kind and lovely and like the old days with Jack Gilbert and it was as true as though it happened and he loved her much more than Harlow though Garbo was only there once while Harlow——maybe this was like those dreams.

Maybe it isn't too, he said to himself. Maybe I could reach over and touch that Maria now, he said to himself. Maybe you are afraid to he said to himself. Maybe you would find out that it never happened and it was not true and it was something you made up like those dreams about the people of the cinema or how all your old girls come back and sleep in that robe at night on all the bare floors, in the straw of the haybarns, the stables, the *corrales* and the *cortijos,* the woods, the garages, the trucks and all the hills of Spain. They all came to that robe when he was asleep and they were all much nicer than they ever had been in life. Maybe it was like that. Maybe you would be afraid to touch her to see if it was true. Maybe you would, and probably it is something that you made up or that you dreamed.

He took a step across the trail and put his hand on the girl's arm. Under his fingers he felt the smoothness of her arm in the worn khaki. She looked at him and smiled.

"Hello, Maria," he said.

"Hello, *Inglés,*" she answered and he saw her tawny brown face and the yellow-gray eyes and the full lips smiling and the cropped sun-burned hair and she lifted her face at him and smiled in his eyes. It was true all right.

Now they were in sight of El Sordo's camp in the last of the pines, where there was a rounded gulch-head shaped like an up-turned basin. All these limestone upper basins must be full of caves, he thought. There are two caves there ahead. The scrub pines growing in the rock hide them well. This is as good or a better place than Pablo's.

"How was this shooting of thy family?" Pilar was saying to Joaquín.

"Nothing, woman," Joaquín said. "They were of the left as many others in Valladolid. When the fascists purified the town they shot first the father. He had voted Socialist. Then they shot the mother. She had voted the same. It was the first time she had ever voted. After that they shot the husband of one of the sisters. He was a member of the syndicate of tramway drivers. Clearly he could not drive a tram without belonging to the syndicate. But he was without politics. I knew him well. He was even a little bit shameless. I do not think he was even a good comrade. Then the husband of the other girl, the other sister, who was also in the trams, had gone to the hills as I had. They thought she knew where he was. But she did not. So they shot her because she would not tell them where he was."

"What barbarians," said Pilar. "Where is El Sordo? I do not see him."

"He is here. He is probably inside," answered Joaquín and stopping now, and resting the rifle butt on the ground, said, "Pilar, listen to me. And thou, Maria. Forgive me if I have molested you speaking of things of the family. I know that all have the same troubles and it is more valuable not to speak of them."

"That you should speak," Pilar said. "For what are we born if not to aid one another? And to listen and say nothing is a cold enough aid."

"But it can molest the Maria. She has too many things of her own."

"*Qué va,*" Maria said. "Mine are such a big bucket that yours falling in will never fill it. I am sorry, Joaquín, and I hope thy sister is well."

"So far she's all right," Joaquín said. "They have her in prison and it seems they do not mistreat her much."

"Are there others in the family?" Robert Jordan asked.

"No," the boy said. "Me. Nothing more. Except the brother-in-law who went to the hills and I think he is dead."

"Maybe he is all right," Maria said. "Maybe he is with a band in other mountains."

"For me he is dead," Joaquín said. "He was never too good at getting about and he was conductor of a tram and that is not the best preparation for the hills. I doubt if he could last a year. He was somewhat weak in the chest too."

"But he may be all right," Maria put her arm on his shoulder.

"Certainly, girl. Why not?" said Joaquín.

As the boy stood there, Maria reached up, put her arms around his neck and kissed him. Joaquín turned his head away because he was crying.

"That is as a brother," Maria said to him. "I kiss thee as a brother."

The boy shook his head, crying without making any noise.

"I am thy sister," Maria said. "And I love thee and thou hast a family. We are all thy family."

"Including the *Inglés,*" boomed Pilar. "Isn't it true, *Inglés?*"

"Yes," Robert Jordan said to the boy, "we are all thy family, Joaquín."

"He's your brother," Pilar said. "Hey *Inglés?*"

Robert Jordan put his arm around the boy's shoulder. "We are all brothers," he said. The boy shook his head.

"I am ashamed to have spoken," he said. "To speak of such things makes it more difficult for all. I am ashamed of molesting you."

"I obscenity in the milk of my shame," Pilar said in her deep lovely voice. "And if the Maria kisses thee again I will commence kissing thee myself. It's years since I've kissed a bullfighter, even an unsuccessful one like thee, I would like to kiss an unsuccessful bullfighter turned Communist. Hold him, *Inglés,* till I get a good kiss at him."

"Deja," the boy said and turned away sharply. "Leave me alone. I am all right and I am ashamed."

He stood there, getting his face under control. Maria put her hand in Robert Jordan's. Pilar stood with her hands on her hips looking at the boy mockingly now.

"When I kiss thee," she said to him, "it will not be as any sister. This trick of kissing as a sister."

"It is not necessary to joke," the boy said. "I told you I am all right, I am sorry that I spoke."

"Well then let us go and see the old man," Pilar said. "I tire myself with such emotion."

The boy looked at her. From his eyes you could see he was suddenly very hurt.

"Not thy emotion," Pilar said to him. "Mine. What a tender thing thou art for a bullfighter."

"I was a failure," Joaquín said. "You don't have to keep insisting on it."

"But you are growing the pigtail another time."

"Yes, and why not? Fighting stock serves best for that purpose economically. It gives employment to many and the State will control it. And perhaps now I would not be afraid."

"Perhaps not," Pilar said. "Perhaps not."

"Why do you speak in such a brutal manner, Pilar?" Maria said to her. "I love thee very much but thou art acting very barbarous."

"It is possible that I am barbarous," Pilar said. "Listen, *Inglés.* Do you know what you are going to say to El Sordo?"

"Yes."

"Because he is a man of few words unlike me and thee and this sentimental menagerie."

"Why do you talk thus?" Maria asked again, angrily.

"I don't know," said Pilar as she strode along. "Why do you think?"

"I do not know."

"At times many things tire me," Pilar said angrily. "You understand? And one of them is to have forty-eight years. You hear me? Forty-eight years and an ugly face. And another is to see panic in the face of a failed bullfighter of Communist tendencies when I say, as a joke, I might kiss him."

"It's not true, Pilar," the boy said. "You did not see that."

"*Qué va,* it's not true. And I obscenity in the milk of all of you. Ah, there he is. *Hola,* Santiago! *Qué tal?*"

The man to whom Pilar spoke was short and heavy, brown-faced, with broad cheekbones; gray haired, with wide-set yellow-brown eyes, a thin-bridged, hooked nose like an Indian's, a long upper lip and a wide, thin mouth. He was clean shaven and he walked toward them from the mouth of the cave, moving with the bow-legged walk that went with his cattle herdsman's breeches and boots. The day was warm but he had on a sheep's-wool-lined short leather jacket buttoned up to the neck. He put out a big brown hand to Pilar. "*Hola,* woman," he said. "*Hola,*" he said to Robert Jordan and shook his hand and looked him keenly in the face. Robert Jordan saw his eyes were yellow as a cat's and flat as reptile's eyes are. "*Guapa,*" he said to Maria and patted her shoulder.

"Eaten?" he asked Pilar. She shook her head.

"Eat," he said and looked at Robert Jordan. "Drink?" he asked, making a motion with his hand decanting his thumb downward.

"Yes, thanks."

"Good," El Sordo said. "Whiskey?"

"You have whiskey?"

El Sordo nodded. "*Inglés?*" he asked. "Not *Ruso?*"

"*Americano.*"

"Few Americans here," he said.

"Now more."

"Less bad. North or South?"

"North."

"Same as *Inglés.* When blow bridge?"

"You know about the bridge?"

El Sordo nodded.

"Day after tomorrow morning."

"Good," said El Sordo.

"Pablo?" he asked Pilar.

She shook her head. El Sordo grinned.

"Go away," he said to Maria and grinned again. "Come back," he looked at a large watch he pulled out on a leather thong from inside his coat. "Half an hour."

He motioned to them to sit down on a flattened log that served as a bench and looking at Joaquín, jerked his thumb down the trail in the direction they had come from.

"I'll walk down with Joaquín and come back," Maria said.

El Sordo went into the cave and came out with a pinch bottle of Scotch whiskey and three glasses. The bottle was under one arm, and three glasses were in the hand of that arm, a finger in each glass, and his other hand was around the neck of an earthenware jar of water. He put the glasses and the bottle down on the log and set the jug on the ground.

"No ice," he said to Robert Jordan and handed him the bottle.

"I don't want any," Pilar said and covered her glass with her hand.

"Ice last night on ground," El Sordo said and grinned. "All melt. Ice up there," El Sordo said and pointed to the snow that showed on the bare crest of the mountains. "Too far."

Robert Jordan started to pour into El Sordo's glass but the deaf man shook his head and made a motion for the other to pour for himself.

Robert Jordan poured a big drink of Scotch into the glass and El Sordo watched him eagerly and when he had finished, handed him the water jug and Robert Jordan filled the glass with the cold water that ran in a stream from the earthenware spout as he tipped up the jug.

El Sordo poured himself half a glassful of whiskey and filled the glass with water.

"Wine?" he asked Pilar.

"No. Water."

"Take it," he said. "No good," he said to Robert Jordan and grinned. "Knew many English. Always much whiskey."

"Where?"

"Ranch," El Sordo said. "Friends of boss."

"Where do you get the whiskey?"

"What?" he could not hear.

"You have to shout," Pilar said. "Into the other ear."

El Sordo pointed to his better ear and grinned.

"Where do you get the whiskey?" Robert Jordan shouted.

"Make it," El Sordo said and watched Robert Jordan's hand check on its way to his mouth with the glass.

"No," El Sordo said and patted his shoulder. "Joke. Comes from La Granja. Heard last night comes English dynamiter. Good. Very happy. Get whiskey. For you. You like?"

"Very much," said Robert Jordan. "It's very good whiskey."

"Am contented," Sordo grinned. "Was bringing tonight with information."

"What information?"

"Much troop movement."

"Where?"

"Segovia. Planes you saw."

"Yes."

"Bad, eh?"

"Bad."

"Troop movement?"

"Much between Villacastín and Segovia. On Valladolid road. Much between Villacastín and San Rafael. Much. Much."

"What do you think?"

"We prepare something?"

"Possibly."

"They know. Prepare too."

"It is possible."

"Why not blow bridge tonight?"

"Orders."

"Whose orders?"

"General Staff."

"So."

"Is the time of the blowing important?" Pilar asked.

"Of all importance."

"But if they are moving up troops?"

"I will send Anselmo with a report of all movement and concentrations. He is checking the road."

"You have some one at road?" Sordo asked.

Robert Jordan did not know how much he had heard. You never know with a deaf man.

"Yes," he said.

"Me, too. Why not blow bridge now?"

"I have my orders."

"I don't like it," El Sordo said. "This I do not like."

"Nor I," said Robert Jordan.

El Sordo shook his head and took a sip of the whiskey. "You want of me?"

"How many men have you?"

"Eight."

"To cut the telephone, attack the post at the house of the road-menders, take it, and fall back on the bridge."

"It is easy."

"It will all be written out."

"Don't trouble. And Pablo?"

"Will cut the telephone below, attack the post at the sawmill, take it and fall back on the bridge."

"And afterwards for the retreat?" Pilar asked. "We are seven men, two women and five horses. You are," she shouted into Sordo's ear.

"Eight men and four horses. *Faltan caballos,*" he said. "Lacks horses."

"Seventeen people and nine horses," Pilar said. "Without accounting for transport."

Sordo said nothing.

"There is no way of getting horses?" Robert Jordan said into Sordo's best ear.

"In war a year," Sordo said. "Have four." He showed four fingers. "Now you want eight for tomorrow."

"Yes," said Robert Jordan. "Knowing you are leaving. Having no need to be careful as you have been in this neighborhood. Not having to be cautious here now. You could not cut out and steal eight head of horses?"

"Maybe," Sordo said. "Maybe none. Maybe more."

"You have an automatic rifle?" Robert Jordan asked.

Sordo nodded.

"Where?"

"Up the hill."

"What kind?"

"Don't know name. With pans."

"How many rounds?"

"Five pans."

"Does any one know how to use it?"

"Me. A little. Not shoot too much. Not want make noise here. Not want use cartridges."

"I will look at it afterwards," Robert Jordan said. "Have you hand grenades?"

"Plenty."

"How many rounds per rifle?"

"Plenty."

"How many?"

"One hundred fifty. More maybe."

"What about other people?"

"For what?"

"To have sufficient force to take the posts and cover the bridge while I am blowing it. We should have double what we have."

"Take posts don't worry. What time day?"

"Daylight."

"Don't worry."

"I could use twenty more men, to be sure," Robert Jordan said.

"Good ones do not exist. You want undependables?"

"No. How many good ones?"

"Maybe four."

"Why so few?"

"No trust."

"For horseholders?"

"Must trust much to be horseholders."

"I'd like ten more good men if I could get them."

"Four."

"Anselmo told me there were over a hundred here in these hills."

"No good."

"You said thirty," Robert Jordan said to Pilar. "Thirty of a certain degree of dependability."

"What about the people of Elias?" Pilar shouted to Sordo. He shook his head.

"No good."

"You can't get ten?" Robert Jordan asked. Sordo looked at him with his flat, yellow eyes and shook his head.

"Four," he said and held up four fingers.

"Yours are good?" Robert Jordan asked, regretting it as he said it.

Sordo nodded.

"*Dentro de la gravedad,*" he said in Spanish. "Within the limits of the danger." He grinned. "Will be bad, eh?"

"Possibly."

"Is the same to me," Sordo said simply and not boasting. "Better four good than much bad. In this war always much bad, very little good. Every day fewer good. And Pablo?" he looked at Pilar.

"As you know," Pilar said. "Worse every day."

Sordo shrugged his shoulders.

"Take drink," Sordo said to Robert Jordan. "I bring mine and four more. Makes twelve. Tonight we discuss all. I have sixty sticks dynamite. You want?"

"What per cent?"

"Don't know. Common dynamite. I bring."

"We'll blow the small bridge above with that," Robert Jordan said. "That is fine. You'll come down tonight? Bring that, will you? I've no orders for that but it should be blown."

"I come tonight. Then hunt horses."

"What chance for horses?"

"Maybe. Now eat."

Does he talk that way to every one? Robert Jordan thought. Or is that his idea of how to make foreigners understand?

"And where are we going to go when this is done?" Pilar shouted into Sordo's ear.

He shrugged his shoulders.

"All that must be arranged," the woman said.

"Of course," said Sordo. "Why not?"

"It is bad enough," Pilar said. "It must be planned very well."

"Yes, woman," Sordo said. "What has thee worried?"

"Everything," Pilar shouted.

Sordo grinned at her.

"You've been going about with Pablo," he said.

So he does only speak that pidgin Spanish for foreigners, Robert Jordan thought. Good. I'm glad to hear him talking straight.

"Where do you think we should go?" Pilar asked.

"Where?"

"Yes, where?"

"There are many places," Sordo said. "Many places. You know Gredos?"

"There are many people there. All these places will be cleaned up as soon as they have time."

"Yes. But it is a big country and very wild."

"It would be very difficult to get there," Pilar said.

"Everything is difficult," El Sordo said. "We can get to Gredos as well as to anywhere else. Travelling at night. Here it is very dangerous now. It is a miracle we have been here this long. Gredos is safer country than this."

"Do you know where I want to go?" Pilar asked him.

"Where? The Paramera? That's no good."

"No," Pilar said. "Not the Sierra de Paramera. I want to go to the Republic."

"That is possible."

"Would your people go?"

"Yes. If I say to."

"Of mine, I do not know," Pilar said. "Pablo would not want to although, truly, he might feel safer there. He is too old to have to go for a soldier unless they call more classes. The gypsy will not wish to go. I do not know about the others."

"Because nothing passes her for so long they do not realize the danger," El Sordo said.

"Since the planes today they will see it more," Robert Jordan said. "But I should think you could operate very well from the Gredos."

"What?" El Sordo said and looked at him with his eyes very flat. There was no friendliness in the way he asked the question.

"You could raid more effectively from there," Robert Jordan said.

"So," El Sordo said. "You know Gredos?"

"Yes. You could operate against the main line of the railway from there. You could keep cutting it as we are doing farther south in Estremadura. To operate from there would be better than returning to the Republic," Robert Jordan said. "You are more useful there."

They had both gotten sullen as he talked.

Sordo looked at Pilar and she looked back at him.

"You know Gredos?" Sordo asked. "Truly?"

"Sure," said Robert Jordan.

"Where would you go?"

"Above Barco de Avila. Better places than here. Raid against the main road and the railroad between Béjar and Plasencia."

"Very difficult," Sordo said.

"We have worked against that same railroad in much more dangerous country in Estremadura," Robert Jordan said.

"Who is we?"

"The *guerrilleros* group of Estremadura."

"You are many?"

"About forty."

"Was the one with the bad nerves and the strange name from there?" asked Pilar.

"Yes."

"Where is he now?"

"Dead, as I told you."

"You are from there, too?"

"Yes."

"You see what I mean?" Pilar said to him.

And I have made a mistake, Robert Jordan thought to himself. I have told Spaniards we can do something better than they can when the rule is never to speak of your own exploits or abilities. When I should have flattered them I have told them what I think they should do and now they are furious. Well, they will either get over it or they will not. They are certainly much more useful in the Gredos than here. The proof is that here they have done nothing since the train that Kashkin organized. It was not much of a show. It cost the fascists one engine and killed a few troops but they all talk as though it were the high point of the war. Maybe they will shame into going to the Gredos. Yes and maybe I will get thrown out of here too. Well, it is not a very rosy-looking dish anyway that you look into it.

"Listen *Inglés,*" Pilar said to him. "How are your nerves?"

"All right," said Robert Jordan. "O.K."

"Because the last dynamiter they sent to work with us, although a formidable technician, was very nervous."

"We have nervous ones," Robert Jordan said.

"I do not say that he was a coward because he comported himself very well," Pilar went on. "But he spoke in a very rare and windy way." She raised her voice. "Isn't it true, Santiago, that the last dynamiter, he of the train, was a little rare?"

"Algo raro," the deaf man nodded and his eyes went over Robert Jordan's face in a way that reminded him of the round opening at the end of the wand of a vacuum cleaner. *"Si, algo raro, pero bueno."*

"Murió," Robert Jordan said into the deaf man's ear. "He is dead."

"How was that?" the deaf man asked, dropping his eyes down from Robert Jordan's eyes to his lips.

"I shot him," Robert Jordan said. "He was too badly wounded to travel and I shot him."

"He was always talking of such a necessity," Pilar said. "It was his obsession."

"Yes," said Robert Jordan. "He was always talking of such a necessity and it was his obsession."

"Como fué?" the deaf man asked. "Was it a train?"

"It was returning from a train," Robert Jordan said. "The train was successful. Returning in the dark we encountered a fascist patrol and as we ran he was shot high in the back but without hitting any bone except the shoulder blade. He travelled quite a long way, but with the wound was unable to travel more. He was unwilling to be left behind and I shot him."

"Menos mal," said El Sordo. "Less bad."

"Are you sure your nerves are all right?" Pilar said to Robert Jordan.

"Yes," he told her. "I am sure that my nerves are all right and I think that when we terminate this of the bridge you would do well to go to the Gredos."

As he said that, the woman started to curse in a flood of obscene invective that rolled over and around him like the hot white water splashing down from the sudden eruption of a geyser.

The deaf man shook his head at Robert Jordan and grinned in

delight. He continued to shake his head happily as Pilar went on vilifying and Robert Jordan knew that it was all right again now. Finally she stopped cursing, reached for the water jug, tipped it up and took a drink and said, calmly, "Then just shut up about what we are to do afterwards, will you, *Inglés?* You go back to the Republic and you take your piece with you and leave us others alone here to decide what part of these hills we'll die in."

"Live in," El Sordo said. "Calm thyself, Pilar."

"Live in and die in," Pilar said. "I can see the end of it well enough. I like thee, *Inglés,* but keep thy mouth off of what we must do when thy business is finished."

"It is thy business," Robert Jordan said. "I do not put my hand in it."

"But you did," Pilar said. "Take thy little cropped-headed whore and go back to the Republic but do not shut the door on others who are not foreigners and who loved the Republic when thou wert wiping thy mother's milk off thy chin."

Maria had come up the trail while they were talking and she heard this last sentence which Pilar, raising her voice again, shouted at Robert Jordan. Maria shook her head at Robert Jordan violently and shook her finger warningly. Pilar saw Robert Jordan looking at the girl and saw him smile and she turned and said, "Yes. I said whore and I mean it. And I suppose that you'll go to Valencia together and we can eat goat crut in Gredos."

"I'm a whore if thee wishes, Pilar," Maria said. "I suppose I am in all case if you say so. But calm thyself. What passes with thee?"

"Nothing," Pilar said and sat down on the bench, her voice calm now and all the metallic rage gone out of it. "I do not call thee that. But I have such a desire to go to the Republic."

"We can all go," Maria said.

"Why not?" Robert Jordan said. "Since thou seemest not to love the Gredos."

Sordo grinned at him.

"We'll see," Pilar said, her rage gone now. "Give me a glass of that rare drink. I have worn my throat out with anger. We'll see. We'll see what happens."

"You see, Comrade," El Sordo explained. "It is the morning that is difficult." He was not talking the pidgin Spanish now and he was looking into Robert Jordan's eyes calmly and explainingly; not searchingly nor suspiciously, nor with the flat superiority of the old campaigner that had been in them before. "I understand your needs and I know the posts must be exterminated and the bridge covered while you do your work. This I understand perfectly. This is easy to do before daylight or at daylight."

"Yes," Robert Jordan said. "Run along a minute, will you?" he said to Maria without looking at her.

The girl walked away out of hearing and sat down, her hands clasped over her ankles.

"You see," Sordo said. "In that there is no problem. But to leave afterward and get out of this country in daylight presents a grave problem."

"Clearly," said Robert Jordan. "I have thought of it. It is daylight for me also."

"But you are one," El Sordo said. "We are various."

"There is the possibility of returning to the camps and leaving from there at dark," Pilar said, putting the glass to her lips and then lowering it.

"That is very dangerous, too," El Sordo explained. "That is perhaps even more dangerous."

"I can see how it would be," Robert Jordan said.

"To do the bridge in the night would be easy," El Sordo said. "Since you make the condition that it must be done at daylight, it brings grave consequences."

"I know it."

"You could not do it at night?"

"I would be shot for it."

"It is very possible we will all be shot for it if you do it in the daytime."

"For me myself that is less important once the bridge is blown," Robert Jordan said. "But I see your viewpoint. You cannot work out a retreat for daylight?"

"Certainly," El Sordo said. "We will work out such a retreat. But I explain to you why one is preoccupied and why one is irritated. You speak of going to Gredos as though it were a military manœuvre to be accomplished. To arrive at Gredos would be a miracle."

Robert Jordan said nothing.

"Listen to me," the deaf man said. "I am speaking much. But it is so we may understand one another. We exist here by a miracle. By a miracle of laziness and stupidity of the fascists which they will remedy in time. Of course we are very careful and we make no disturbance in these hills."

"I know."

"But now, with this, we must go. We must think much about the manner of our going."

"Clearly."

"Then," said El Sordo. "Let us eat now. I have talked much."

"Never have I heard thee talk so much," Pilar said. "Is it this?" she held up the glass.

"No," El Sordo shook his head. "It isn't whiskey. It is that never have I had so much to talk of."

"I appreciate your aid and your loyalty," Robert Jordan said. "I appreciate the difficulty caused by the timing of the blowing of the bridge."

"Don't talk of that," El Sordo said. "We are here to do what we can do. But this is complicated."

"And on paper very simple," Robert Jordan grinned. "On paper the bridge is blown at the moment the attack starts in order that nothing shall come up the road. It is very simple."

"That they should let us do something on paper," El Sordo said. "That we should conceive and execute something on paper."

"'Paper bleeds little,'" Robert Jordan quoted the proverb.

"But it is very useful," Pilar said. *"Es muy utíl.* What I would like to do is use thy orders for that purpose."

"Me too," said Robert Jordan. "But you could never win a war like that."

"No," the big woman said. "I suppose not. But do you know what I would like?"

"To go to the Republic," El Sordo said. He had put his good ear close to her as she spoke. *"Ya irás, mujer.* Let us win this and it will all be Republic."

"All right," Pilar said. "And now, for God's sake let us eat."

CHAPTER TWELVE

THEY left El Sordo's after eating and started down the trail. El Sordo had walked with them as far as the lower post.

"*Salud,*" he said. "Until tonight."

"*Salud, Camarada,*" Robert Jordan had said to him and the three of them had gone on down the trail, the deaf man standing looking after them. Maria had turned and waved her hand at him and El Sordo waved disparagingly with the abrupt, Spanish upward flick of the forearm as though something were being tossed away which seems the negation of all salutation which has not to do with business. Through the meal he had never unbuttoned his sheepskin coat and he had been carefully polite, careful to turn his head to hear and had returned to speaking his broken Spanish, asking Robert Jordan about conditions in the Republic politely; but it was obvious he wanted to be rid of them.

As they had left him, Pilar had said to him, "Well, Santiago?"

"Well, nothing, woman," the deaf man said. "It is all right. But I am thinking."

"Me, too," Pilar had said and now as they walked down the trail, the walking easy and pleasant down the steep trail through the pines that they had toiled up, Pilar said nothing. Neither Robert Jordan nor Maria spoke and the three of them travelled along fast until the trail rose steeply out of the wooded valley to come up through the timber, leave it, and come out into the high meadow.

It was hot in the late May afternoon and halfway up this last steep grade the woman stopped. Robert Jordan, stopping and looking back, saw the sweat beading on her forehead. He thought her brown face looked pallid and the skin sallow and that there were dark areas under her eyes.

"Let us rest a minute," he said. "We go too fast."

"No," she said. "Let us go on."

"Rest, Pilar," Maria said. "You look badly."

"Shut up," the woman said. "Nobody asked for thy advice."

She started on up the trail but at the top she was breathing heavily and her face was wet with perspiration and there was no doubt about her pallor now.

"Sit down, Pilar," Maria said. "Please, please sit down."

"All right," said Pilar and the three of them sat down under a pine tree and looked across the mountain meadow to where the tops of the peaks seemed to jut out from the roll of the high country with snow shining bright on them now in the early afternoon sun.

"What rotten stuff is the snow and how beautiful it looks," Pilar said. "What an illusion is the snow." She turned to Maria. "I am sorry I was rude to thee, *guapa*. I don't know what has held me today. I have an evil temper."

"I never mind what you say when you are angry," Maria told her. "And you are angry often."

"Nay, it is worse than anger," Pilar said, looking across at the peaks.

"Thou art not well," Maria said.

"Neither is it that," the woman said. "Come here, *guapa,* and put thy head in my lap."

Maria moved close to her, put her arms out and folded them as one does who goes to sleep without a pillow and lay with her head on her arms. She turned her face up at Pilar and smiled at her but the big woman looked on across the meadow at the mountains. She stroked the girl's head without looking down at her and ran a blunt finger across the girl's forehead and then around the line of her ear and down the line where the hair grew on her neck.

"You can have her in a little while, *Inglés,"* she said. Robert Jordan was sitting behind her.

"Do not talk like that," Maria said.

"Yes, he can have thee," Pilar said and looked at neither of them. "I have never wanted thee. But I am jealous."

"Pilar," Maria said. "Do not talk thus."

"He can have thee," Pilar said and ran her finger around the lobe of the girl's ear. "But I am very jealous."

"But Pilar," Maria said. "It was thee explained to me there was nothing like that between us."

"There is always something like that," the woman said. "There is always something like something that there should not be. But with me there is not. Truly there is not. I want thy happiness and nothing more."

Maria said nothing but lay there, trying to make her head rest lightly.

"Listen, *guapa*," said Pilar and ran her finger now absently but tracingly over the contours of her cheeks. "Listen, *guapa*, I love thee and he can have thee, I am no *tortillera* but a woman made for men. That is true. But now it gives me pleasure to say thus, in the daytime, that I care for thee."

"I love thee, too."

"*Qué va*. Do not talk nonsense. Thou dost not know even of what I speak."

"I know."

"*Qué va*, that you know. You are for the *Inglés*. That is seen and as it should be. That I would have. Anything else I would not have. I do not make perversions. I only tell you something true. Few people will ever talk to thee truly and no women. I am jealous and say it and it is there. And I say it."

"Do not say it," Maria said. "Do not say it, Pilar."

"*Por qué*, do not say it," the woman said, still not looking at either of them. "I will say it until it no longer pleases me to say it. And," she looked down at the girl now, "that time has come already. I do not say it more, you understand?"

"Pilar," Maria said. "Do not talk thus."

"Thou art a very pleasant little rabbit," Pilar said. "And lift thy head now because this silliness is over."

"It was not silly," said Maria. "And my head is well where it is."

"Nay. Lift it," Pilar told her and put her big hands under the girl's head and raised it. "And thou, *Inglés*?" she said, still holding the girl's head as she looked across at the mountains. "What cat has eaten thy tongue?"

"No cat," Robert Jordan said.

"What animal then?" She laid the girl's head down on the ground.

"No animal," Robert Jordan told her.

"You swallowed it yourself, eh?"

"I guess so," Robert Jordan said.

"And did you like the taste?" Pilar turned now and grinned at him.

"Not much."

"I thought not," Pilar said. "I *thought* not. But I give you back our rabbit. Nor ever did I try to take your rabbit. That's a good name for her. I heard you call her that this morning."

Robert Jordan felt his face redden.

"You are a very hard woman," he told her.

"No," Pilar said. "But so simple I am very complicated. Are you very complicated, *Inglés?*"

"No. Nor not so simple."

"You please me, *Inglés,*" Pilar said. Then she smiled and leaned forward and smiled and shook her head. "Now if I could take the rabbit from thee and take thee from the rabbit."

"You could not."

"I know it," Pilar said and smiled again. "Nor would I wish to. But when I was young I could have."

"I believe it."

"You believe it?"

"Surely," Robert Jordan said. "But such talk is nonsense."

"It is not like thee," Maria said.

"I am not much like myself today," Pilar said. "Very little like myself. Thy bridge has given me a headache, *Inglés.*"

"We can tell it the Headache Bridge," Robert Jordan said. "But I will drop it in that gorge like a broken bird cage."

"Good," said Pilar. "Keep on talking like that."

"I'll drop it as you break a banana from which you have removed the skin."

"I could eat a banana now," said Pilar. "Go on, *Inglés*. Keep on talking largely."

"There is no need," Robert Jordan said. "Let us get to camp."

"Thy duty," Pilar said. "It will come quickly enough. I said that I would leave the two of you."

"No. I have much to do."

"That is much too and does not take long."

"Shut thy mouth, Pilar," Maria said. "You speak grossly."

""I am gross," Pilar said. "But I am also very delicate. *Soy muy delicada*. I will leave the two of you. And the talk of jealousness is nonsense. I was angry at Joaquín because I saw from his look how ugly I am. I am only jealous that you are nineteen. It is not a jealousy which lasts. You will not be nineteen always. Now I go."

She stood up and with a hand on one hip looked at Robert Jordan, who was also standing. Maria sat on the ground under the tree, her head dropped forward.

"Let us all go to camp together," Robert Jordan said. "It is better and there is much to do."

Pilar nodded with her head toward Maria, who sat there, her head turned away from them, saying nothing.

Pilar smiled and shrugged her shoulders almost imperceptibly and said, "You know the way?"

"I know it," Maria said, not raising her head.

"Pues me voy," Pilar said. "Then I am going. We'll have something hearty for you to eat, *Inglés."*

She started to walk off into the heather of the meadow toward the stream that led down through it toward the camp.

"Wait," Robert Jordan called to her. "It is better that we should all go together."

Maria sat there and said nothing.

Pilar did not turn.

"Qué va, go together," she said. "I will see thee at the camp."

Robert Jordan stood there.

"Is she all right?" he asked Maria. "She looked ill before."

"Let her go," Maria said, her head still down.

"I think I should go with her."

"Let her go," said Maria. "Let her go!"

CHAPTER THIRTEEN

THEY were walking through the heather of the mountain meadow and Robert Jordan felt the brushing of the heather against his legs, felt the weight of his pistol in its holster against his thigh, felt the sun on his head, felt the breeze from the snow of the mountain peaks cool on his back and, in his hand, he felt the girl's hand firm and strong, the fingers locked in his. From it, from the palm of her hand against the palm of his, from their fingers locked together; and from her wrist across his wrist something came from her hand, her fingers and her wrist to his that was as fresh as the first light air that moving toward you over the sea barely wrinkles the glassy surface of a calm, as light as a feather moved across one's lip, or a leaf falling when there is no breeze; so light that it could be felt with the touch of their fingers alone, but that was so strengthened, so intensified, and made so urgent, so aching and so strong by the hard pressure of their fingers and the close pressed palm and wrist, that it was as though a current moved up his arm and filled his whole body with an aching hollowness of wanting. With the sun shining on her hair, tawny as wheat, and on her gold-brown smooth-lovely face and on the curve of her throat he bent her head back and held her to him and kissed her. He felt her trembling as he kissed her and he held the length of her body tight to him and felt her breasts against his chest through the two khaki shirts, he felt them small and firm and he reached and undid the buttons on her shirt and bent and kissed her and she stood shivering, holding her head back, his arm behind her. Then she dropped her chin to his head and then he felt her hands holding his head and rocking it against her. He straightened and with his two arms around her held her so tightly that she was lifted off the ground, tight against him, and he felt her trembling and then her lips were on his throat, and then he put her down and said, "Maria, oh, my Maria."

Then he said, "Where should we go?"

She did not say anything but slipped her hand inside of his shirt and he felt her undoing the shirt buttons and she said, "You, too. I want to kiss, too."

"No, little rabbit."

"Yes. Yes. Everything as you."

"Nay. That is an impossibility."

"Well, then. Oh, then. Oh, then. Oh."

Then there was the smell of heather crushed and the roughness of the bent stalks under her head and the sun bright on her closed eyes and all his life he would remember the curve of her throat with her head pushed back into the heather roots and her lips that moved smally and by themselves and the fluttering of the lashes on the eyes tight closed against the sun and against everything, and for her everything was red, orange, gold-red from the sun on the closed eyes, and it all was that color, all of it, the filling, the possessing, the having, all of that color, all in a blindness of that color. For him it was a dark passage which led to nowhere, then to nowhere, then again to nowhere, once again to nowhere, always and forever to nowhere, heavy on the elbows in the earth to nowhere, dark, never any end to nowhere, hung on all time always to unknowing nowhere, this time and again for always to nowhere, now not to be borne once again always and to nowhere, now beyond all bearing up, up, up and into nowhere, suddenly, scaldingly, holdingly all nowhere gone and time absolutely still and they were both there, time having stopped and he felt the earth move out and away from under them.

Then he was lying on his side, his head deep in the heather, smelling it and the smell of the roots and the earth and the sun came through it and it was scratchy on his bare shoulders and along his flanks and the girl was lying opposite him with her eyes still shut and then she opened them and smiled at him and he said very tiredly and from a great but friendly distance, "Hello, rabbit." And she smiled and from no distance said, "Hello, my *Inglés.*"

"I'm not an *Inglés,*" he said very lazily.

"Oh yes, you are," she said. "You're my *Inglés,*" and reached and took hold of both his ears and kissed him on the forehead.

"There," she said. "How is that? Do I kiss thee better?"

Then they were walking along the stream together and he said,

"Maria, I love thee and thou art so lovely and so wonderful and so beautiful and it does such things to me to be with thee that I feel as though I wanted to die when I am loving thee."

"Oh," she said. "I die each time. Do you not die?"

"No. Almost. But did thee feel the earth move?"

"Yes. As I died. Put thy arm around me, please."

"No. I have thy hand. Thy hand is enough."

He looked at her and across the meadow where a hawk was hunting and the big afternoon clouds were coming now over the mountains.

"And it is not thus for thee with others?" Maria asked him, they now walking hand in hand.

"No. Truly."

"Thou hast loved many others."

"Some. But not as thee."

"And it was not thus? Truly?"

"It was a pleasure but it was not thus."

"And then the earth moved. The earth never moved before?"

"Nay. Truly never."

"Ay," she said. "And this we have for one day."

He said nothing.

"But we have had it now at least," Maria said. "And do you like me too? Do I please thee? I will look better later."

"Thou art very beautiful now."

"Nay," she said. "But stroke thy hand across my head."

He did that feeling her cropped hair soft and flattening and then rising between his fingers and he put both hands on her head and turned her face up to his and kissed her.

"I like to kiss very much," she said. "But I do not do it well."

"Thou hast no need to kiss."

"Yes, I have. If I am to be thy woman I should please thee in all ways."

"You please me enough. I would not be more pleased. There is no thing I could do if I were more pleased."

"But you will see," she said very happily. "My hair amuses thee now because it is odd. But every day it is growing. It will be long and then I will not look ugly and perhaps you will love me very much."

"Thou hast a lovely body," he said. "The loveliest in the world."

"It is only young and thin."

"No. In a fine body there is magic. I do not know what makes it in one and not in another. But thou hast it."

"For thee," she said.

"Nay."

"Yes. For thee and for thee always and only for thee. But it is little to bring thee. I would learn to take good care of thee. But tell me truly. Did the earth never move for thee before?"

"Never," he said truly.

"Now am I happy," she said. "Now am I truly happy."

"You are thinking of something else now?" she asked him.

"Yes. My work."

"I wish we had horses to ride," Maria said. "In my happiness I would like to be on a good horse and ride fast with thee riding fast beside me and we would ride faster and faster, galloping, and never pass my happiness."

"We could take thy happiness in a plane," he said absently.

"And go over and over in the sky like the little pursuit planes shining in the sun," she said. "Rolling it in loops and in dives. *Qué bueno!*" she laughed. "My happiness would not even notice it."

"Thy happiness has a good stomach," he said half hearing what she said.

Because now he was not there. He was walking beside her but his mind was thinking of the problem of the bridge now and it was all clear and hard and sharp as when a camera lens is brought into focus. He saw the two posts and Anselmo and the gypsy watching. He saw the road empty and he saw movement on it. He saw where he would place the two automatic rifles to get the most level field of fire, and who will serve them, he thought, me at the end, but who at the start? He placed the charges, wedged and lashed them, sunk his caps and crimped them, ran his wires, hooked them up and got back to where he had placed the old box of the exploder and then he started to think of all the things that could have happened and that might go wrong. Stop it, he told himself. You have made love to this girl and now your head is clear, properly clear, and you start to worry. It is one thing to think you must do and it is another thing to worry. Don't worry. You mustn't worry. You know the things that you may have to do and you know what may happen. Certainly it may happen.

You went into it knowing what you were fighting for. You were fighting against exactly what you were doing and being forced into doing to have any chance of winning. So now he was compelled to use these people whom he liked as you should use troops toward whom you have no feeling at all if you were to be successful. Pablo was evidently the smartest. He knew how bad it was instantly. The woman was all for it, and still was; but the realization of what it really consisted in had overcome her steadily and it had done plenty to her already. Sordo recognized it instantly and would do it but he did not like it any more than he, Robert Jordan, liked it.

So you say that it is not that which will happen to yourself but that which may happen to the woman and the girl and to the others that you think of. All right. What would have happened to them if you had not come? What happened to them and what passed with them before you were ever here? You must not think in that way. You have no responsibility for them except in action. The orders do not come from you. They come from Golz. And who is Golz? A good general. The best you've ever served under. But should a man carry out impossible orders knowing what they lead to? Even though they come from Golz, who is the party as well as the army? Yes. He should carry them out because it is only in the performing of them that they can prove to be impossible. How do you know they are impossible until you have tried them? If every one said orders were impossible to carry out when they were received where would you be? Where would we all be if you just said, "Impossible," when orders came?

He had seen enough of commanders to whom all orders were impossible. That swine Gomez in Estremadura. He had seen enough attacks when the flanks did not advance because it was impossible. No, he would carry out the orders and it was bad luck that you liked the people you must do it with.

In all the work that they, the *partizans,* did, they brought added danger and bad luck to the people that sheltered them and worked with them. For what? So that, eventually, there should be no more danger and so that the country should be a good place to live in. That was true no matter how trite it sounded.

If the Republic lost it would be impossible for those who believed in it to live in Spain. But would it? Yes, he knew that it would be, from the things that happened in the parts the fascists had already taken.

Pablo was a swine but the others were fine people and was it not a betrayal of them all to get them to do this? Perhaps it was. But if they did not do it two squadrons of cavalry would come and hunt them out of these hills in a week.

No. There was nothing to be gained by leaving them alone. Except that all people should be left alone and you should interfere with no one. So he believed that, did he? Yes, he believed that. And what about a planned society and the rest of it? That was for the others to do. He had something else to do after this war. He fought now in this war because it had started in a country that he loved and he believed in the Republic and that if it were destroyed life would be unbearable for all those people who believed in it. He was under Communist discipline for the duration of the war. Here in Spain the Communists offered the best discipline and the soundest and sanest for the prosecution of the war. He accepted their discipline for the duration of the war because, in the conduct of the war, they were the only party whose program and whose discipline he could respect.

What were his politics then? He had none now, he told himself. But do not tell any one else that, he thought. Don't ever admit that. And what are you going to do afterwards? I am going back and earn my living teaching Spanish as before, and I am going to write a true book. I'll bet, he said. I'll bet that will be easy.

He would have to talk with Pablo about politics. It would certainly be interesting to see what his political development had been. The classical move from left to right, probably; like old Lerroux. Pablo was quite a lot like Lerroux. Prieto was as bad. Pablo and Prieto had about an equal faith in the ultimate victory. They all had the politics of horse thieves. He believed in the Republic as a form of government but the Republic would have to get rid of all of that bunch of horse thieves that brought it to the pass it was in when the rebellion started. Was there ever a people whose leaders were as truly their enemies as this one?

Enemies of the people. That was a phrase he might omit. That was a catch phrase he would skip. That was one thing that sleeping with Maria had done. He had gotten to be as bigoted and hide-bound about his politics as a hard-shelled Baptist and phrases like enemies of the people came into his mind without his much criticizing them in any way. Any sort of *clichés* both revolutionary and patriotic. His mind employed them without criticism. Of course they were true but it was too easy to be nimble about using them. But since last night and this afternoon his mind was much clearer and cleaner on that business. Bigotry is an odd thing. To be bigoted you have to be absolutely sure that you are right and nothing makes that surety and righteousness like continence. Continence is the foe of heresy.

How would that premise stand up if he examined it? That was probably why the Communists were always cracking down on Bohemianism. When you were drunk or when you committed either fornication or adultery you recognized your own personal fallibility of that so mutable substitute for the apostles' creed, the party line. Down with Bohemianism, the sin of Mayakovsky.

But Mayakovsky was a saint again. That was because he was safely dead. You'll be safely dead yourself, he told himself. Now stop thinking that sort of thing. Think about Maria.

Maria was very hard on his bigotry. So far she had not affected his resolution but he would much prefer not to die. He would abandon a hero's or a martyr's end gladly. He did not want to make a Thermopylæ, nor be Horatius at any bridge, nor be the Dutch boy with his finger in that dyke. No. He would like to spend some time with Maria. That was the simplest expression of it. He would like to spend a long, long time with her.

He did not believe there was ever going to be any such thing as a long time any more but if there ever was such a thing he would like to spend it with her. We could go into the hotel and register as Doctor and Mrs. Livingstone I presume, he thought.

Why not marry her? Sure, he thought. I will marry her. Then we will be Mr. and Mrs. Robert Jordan of Sun Valley, Idaho. Or Corpus Christi, Texas, or Butte, Montana.

Spanish girls make wonderful wives. I've never had one so I know. And when I get my job back at the university she can be an instructor's wife and when undergraduates who take Spanish IV come in to smoke pipes in the evening and have those so valuable informal discussions about Quevedo, Lope de Vega, Galdós and the other always admirable dead, Maria can tell them about how some of the blue-shirted crusaders for the true faith sat on her head while others twisted her arms and pulled her skirts up and stuffed them in her mouth.

I wonder how they will like Maria in Missoula, Montana? That is if I can get a job back in Missoula. I suppose that I am ticketed as a Red there now for good and will be on the general blacklist. Though you never know. You never can tell. They've no proof of what you do, and as a matter of fact they would never believe it if you told them, and my passport was valid for Spain before they issued the restrictions.

The time for getting back will not be until the fall of thirty-seven. I left in the summer of thirty-six and though the leave is for a year you do not need to be back until the fall term opens in the following year. There is a lot of time between now and the fall term. There is a lot of time between now and day after tomorrow if you want to put it that way. No. I think there is no need to worry about the university. Just you turn up there in the fall and it will be all right. Just try and turn up there.

But it has been a strange life for a long time now. Damned if it hasn't. Spain was your work and your job, so being in Spain was natural and sound. You had worked summers on engineering projects and in the forest service building roads and in the park and learned to handle powder, so the demolition was a sound and normal job too. Always a little hasty, but sound.

Once you accept the idea of demolition as a problem it is only a problem. But there was plenty that was not so good that went with it although God knows you took it easily enough. There was the constant attempt to approximate the conditions of successful assassination that accompanied the demolition. Did big words make it more defensible? Did they make killing any more palatable? You took to it a little too readily if you ask me, he told himself. And what you will be like or just exactly what you will be suited for when you leave the service of the Republic is, to me, he thought, extremely doubtful. But my guess is you will get rid of all that by writing about it, he said. Once you write it down it is all gone. It will be a good book if you can write it. Much better than the other.

But in the meantime all the life you have or ever will have is today, tonight, tomorrow, today, tonight, tomorrow, over and over again (I hope), he thought and so you had better take what time there is and be very thankful for it. If the bridge goes bad. It does not look too good just now.

But Maria has been good. Has she not? Oh, has she not, he thought. Maybe that is what I am to get now from life. Maybe that is my life and instead of it being threescore years and ten it is forty-eight hours or just threescore hours and ten or twelve rather. Twenty-four hours in a day would be threescore and twelve for the three full days.

I suppose it is possible to live as full a life in seventy hours as in seventy years; granted that your life has been full up to the time that the seventy hours start and that you have reached a certain age.

What nonsense, he thought. What rot you get to thinking by yourself. That is *really* nonsense. And maybe it isn't nonsense too. Well, we will see. The last time I slept with a girl was in Madrid. No it wasn't. It was in the Escorial and, except that I woke in the night and thought it was some one else and was excited until I realized who it really was, it was just dragging ashes; except that it was pleasant enough. And the time before that was in Madrid and except for some lying and pretending I did to myself as to identity while things were going on, it was the same or something less. So I am no romantic glorifier of the Spanish Woman nor did I ever think of a casual piece as anything much other than a casual piece in any country. But when I am with Maria I love her so that I feel, literally, as though I would die and I never believed in that nor thought that it could happen.

So if your life trades its seventy years for seventy hours I have that value now and I am lucky enough to know it. And if there is not any such thing as a long time, nor the rest of your lives, nor from now on, but there is only now, why then now is the thing to praise and I am very happy with it. Now, *ahora, maintenant, heute. Now,* it has a funny sound to be a whole world and your life. *Esta noche,* tonight, *ce soir, heute abend.* Life and wife, *Vie* and *Mari.* No it didn't work out. The French turned it into husband. There was now and *frau;* but that did not prove anything either. Take dead, *mort, muerto,* and *todt. Todt* was the deadest of them all. War, *guerre, guerra,* and *krieg. Krieg* was the most like war, or was it?

Or was it only that he knew German the least well? Sweetheart, *chérie*, *prenda*, and *schatz*. He would trade them all for Maria. There was a name.

Well, they would all be doing it together and it would not be long now. It certainly looked worse all the time. It was just something that you could not bring off in the morning. In an impossible situation you hang on until night to get away. You try to last out until night to get back in. You are all right, maybe, if you can stick it out until dark and then get in. So what if you start this sticking it out at daylight? How about that? And that poor bloody Sordo abandoning his pidgin Spanish to explain it to him so carefully. As though he had not thought about that whenever he had done any particularly bad thinking ever since Golz had first mentioned it. As though he hadn't been living with that like a lump of undigested dough in the pit of his stomach ever since the night before the night before last.

What a business. You go along your whole life and they seem as though they mean something and they always end up not meaning anything. There was never any of what this is. You think that is one thing that you will never have. And then, on a lousy show like this, co-ordinating two chicken-crut guerilla bands to help you blow a bridge under impossible conditions, to abort a counter-offensive that will probably already be started, you run into a girl like this Maria. Sure. That is what you would do. You ran into her rather late, that was all.

So a woman like that Pilar practically pushed this girl into your sleeping bag and what happens? Yes, what happens? What happens? You tell me what happens, please. Yes. That is just what happens. That is exactly what happens.

Don't lie to yourself about Pilar pushing her into your sleeping robe and try to make it nothing or to make it lousy. You were gone when you first saw her. When she first opened her mouth and spoke to you it was there already and you know it. Since you have it and you never thought you would have it, there is no sense throwing dirt at it, when you know what it is and you know it came the first time you looked at her as she came out bent over carrying that iron cooking platter.

It hit you then and you know it and so why lie about it? You went all strange inside every time you looked at her and every time she looked at you. So why don't you admit it? All right, I'll admit it. And as for Pilar pushing her onto you, all Pilar did was be an intelligent woman. She had taken good care of the girl and she saw what was coming the minute the girl came back into the cave with the cooking dish.

So she made things easier. She made things easier so that there was last night and this afternoon. She is a damned sight more civilized than you are and she knows what time is all about. Yes, he said to himself, I think we can admit that she has certain notions about the value of time. She took a beating and all because she did not want other people losing what she'd lost and then the idea of admitting it was lost was too big a thing to swallow. So she took a beating back there on the hill and I guess we did not make it any easier for her.

Well, so that is what happens and what has happened and you might as well admit it and now you will never have two whole nights with her. Not a lifetime, not to live together, not to have what people were always supposed to have, not at all. One night that is past, once one afternoon, one night to come; maybe. No, sir.

Not time, not happiness, not fun, not children, not a house, not a bathroom, not a clean pair of pajamas, not the morning paper, not to wake up together, not to wake and know she's there and that you're not alone. No. None of that. But why, when this is all you are going to get in life of what you want; when you have found it; why not just one night in a bed with sheets?

You ask for the impossible. You ask for the ruddy impossible. So if you love this girl as much as you say you do, you had better love her very hard and make up in intensity what the relation will lack in duration and in continuity. Do you hear that? In the old days people devoted a lifetime to it. And now when you have found it if you get two nights you wonder where all the luck came from. Two nights. Two nights to love, honor and cherish. For better and for worse. In sickness and in death. No that wasn't it. In sickness and in health. Till death do us part. In two nights. Much more than likely. Much more than likely and now lay off that sort of thinking. You can stop that now. That's not good for you. Do nothing that is not good for you. Sure that's it.

This was what Golz had talked about. The longer he was around, the smarter Golz seemed. So this was what he was asking about; the compensation of irregular service. Had Golz had this and was it the urgency and the lack of time and the circumstances that made it? Was this something that happened to every one given comparable circumstances? And did he only think it was something special because it was happening to him? Had Golz slept around in a hurry when he was commanding irregular cavalry in the Red Army and had the combination of the circumstances and the rest of it made the girls seem the way Maria was?

Probably Golz knew all about this too and wanted to make the point that you must make your whole life in the two nights that are given to you; that living as we do now you must concentrate all of that which you should always have into the short time that you can have it.

It was a good system of belief. But he did not believe that Maria had only been made by the circumstances. Unless, of course, she is a reaction from her own circumstance as well as his. Her one circumstance is not so good, he thought. No, not so good.

If this was how it was then this was how it was. But there was no law that made him say he liked it. I did not know that I could ever feel what I have felt, he thought. Nor that this could happen to me. I would like to have it for my whole life. You will, the other part of him said. You will. You have it *now* and that is all your whole life is; now. There is nothing else than now. There is neither yesterday, certainly, nor is there any tomorrow. How old must you be before you know that? There is only now, and if now is only two days, then two days is your life and everything in it will be in proportion. This is how you live a life in two days. And if you stop complaining and asking for what you never will get, you will have a good life. A good life is not measured by any biblical span.

So now do not worry, take what you have, and do your work and you will have a long life and a very merry one. Hasn't it been merry lately? What are you complaining about? That's the thing about this sort of work, he told himself, and was very pleased with the thought, it isn't so much what you learn as it is the people you meet. He was pleased then because he was joking and he came back to the girl.

"I love you, rabbit," he said to the girl. "What was it you were saying?"

"I was saying," she told him, "that you must not worry about your work because I will not bother you nor interfere. If there is anything I can do you will tell me."

"There's nothing," he said. "It is really very simple."

"I will learn from Pilar what I should do to take care of a man well and those things I will do," Maria said. "Then, as I learn, I will discover things for myself and other things you can tell me."

"There is nothing to do."

"*Qué va,* man, there is nothing! Thy sleeping robe, this morning, should have been shaken and aired and hung somewhere in the sun. Then, before the dew comes, it should be taken into shelter."

"Go on, rabbit."

"Thy socks should be washed and dried. I would see thee had two pair."

"What else?"

"If thou would show me I would clean and oil thy pistol."

"Kiss me," Robert Jordan said.

"Nay, this is serious. Wilt thou show me about the pistol? Pilar has rags and oil. There is a cleaning rod inside the cave that should fit it."

"Sure. I'll show you."

"Then," Maria said. "If you will teach me to shoot it either one of us could shoot the other and himself, or herself, if one were wounded and it were necessary to avoid capture."

"Very interesting," Robert Jordan said. "Do you have many ideas like that?"

"Not many," Maria said. "But it is a good one. Pilar gave me this and showed me how to use it," she opened the breast pocket of her shirt and took out a cut-down leather holder such as pocket combs are carried in and, removing a wide rubber band that closed both ends, took out a Gem type, single-edged razor blade. "I keep this always," she explained. "Pilar says you must make the cut here just below the ear and draw it toward here." She showed him with her finger. "She says there is a big artery there and that drawing the blade from there you cannot miss it. Also, she says there is no pain and you must simply press firmly below the ear and draw it downward. She says it is nothing and that they cannot stop it if it is done."

"That's right," said Robert Jordan. "That's the carotid artery."

So she goes around with that all the time, he thought, as a definitely accepted and properly organized possibility.

"But I would rather have thee shoot me," Maria said. "Promise if there is ever any need that thou wilt shoot me."

"Sure," Robert Jordan said. "I promise."

"Thank thee very much," Maria told him. "I know it is not easy to do."

"That's all right," Robert Jordan said.

You forget all this, he thought. You forget about the beauties of a civil war when you keep your mind too much on your work. You have forgotten this. Well, you are supposed to. Kashkin couldn't forget it and it spoiled his work. Or do you think the old boy had a hunch? It was very strange because he had experienced absolutely no emotion about the shooting of Kashkin. He expected that at some time he might have it. But so far there had been absolutely none.

"But there are other things I can do for thee," Maria told him, walking close beside him, now, very serious and womanly.

"Besides shoot me?"

"Yes. I can roll cigarettes for thee when thou hast no more of those with tubes. Pilar has taught me to roll them very well, tight and neat and not spilling."

"Excellent," said Robert Jordan. "Do you lick them yourself?"

"Yes," the girl said, "and when thou art wounded I will care for thee and dress thy wound and wash thee and feed thee—"

"Maybe I won't be wounded," Robert Jordan said.

"Then when you are sick I will care for thee and make thee soups and clean thee and do all for thee. And I will read to thee."

"Maybe I won't get sick."

"Then I will bring thee coffee in the morning when thou wakest——"

"Maybe I don't like coffee," Robert Jordan told her.

"Nay, but you do," the girl said happily. "This morning you took two cups."

"Suppose I get tired of coffee and there's no need to shoot me and

I'm neither wounded nor sick and I give up smoking and have only one pair of socks and hang up my robe myself. What then, rabbit?" he patted her on the back. "What then?"

"Then," said Maria, "I will borrow the scissors of Pilar and cut thy hair."

"I don't like to have my hair cut."

"Neither do I," said Maria. "And I like thy hair as it is. So. If there is nothing to do for thee, I will sit by thee and watch thee and in the nights we will make love."

"Good," Robert Jordan said. "The last project is very sensible."

"To me it seems the same," Maria smiled. "Oh, *Inglés,*" she said.

"My name is Roberto."

"Nay. But I call thee *Inglés* as Pilar does."

"Still it is Roberto."

"No," she told him. "Now for a whole day it is *Inglés*. And *Inglés,* can I help thee with thy work?"

"No. What I do now I do alone and very coldly in my head."

"Good," she said. "And when will it be finished?"

"Tonight, with luck."

"Good," she said.

Below them was the last woods that led to the camp.

"Who is that?" Robert Jordan asked and pointed.

"Pilar," the girl said, looking along his arm. "Surely it is Pilar."

At the lower edge of the meadow where the first trees grew the woman was sitting, her head on her arms. She looked like a dark bundle from where they stood; black against the brown of the tree trunk.

"Come on," Robert Jordan said and started to run toward her through the knee-high heather. It was heavy and hard to run in and when he had run a little way, he slowed and walked. He could see the woman's head was on her folded arms and she looked broad and black against the tree trunk. He came up to her and said, "Pilar!" sharply.

The woman raised her head and looked up at him.

"Oh," she said. "You have terminated already?"

"Art thou ill?" he asked and bent down by her.

"*Qué va,*" she said. "I was asleep."

"Pilar," Maria, who had come up, said and kneeled down by her. "How are you? Are you all right?"

"I'm magnificent," Pilar said but she did not get up. She looked at the two of them. "Well, *Inglés,*" she said. "You have been doing manly tricks again?"

"You are all right?" Robert Jordan asked, ignoring the words.

"Why not? I slept. Did you?"

"No."

"Well," Pilar said to the girl. "It seems to agree with you."

Maria blushed and said nothing.

"Leave her alone," Robert Jordan said.

"No one spoke to thee," Pilar told him. "Maria," she said and her voice was hard. The girl did not look up.

"Maria," the woman said again. "I said it seems to agree with thee."

"Oh, leave her alone," Robert Jordan said again.

"Shut up, you," Pilar said without looking at him. "Listen, Maria, tell me one thing."

"No," Maria said and shook her head.

"Maria," Pilar said, and her voice was as hard as her face and there was nothing friendly in her face. "Tell me one thing of thy own volition."

The girl shook her head.

Robert Jordan was thinking, if I did not have to work with this woman and her drunken man and her chicken-crut outfit, I would slap her so hard across the face that——

"Go ahead and tell me," Pilar said to the girl.

"No," Maria said. "No."

"Leave her alone," Robert Jordan said and his voice did not sound like his own voice. I'll slap her anyway and the hell with it, he thought.

Pilar did not even speak to him. It was not like a snake charming a bird, nor a cat with a bird. There was nothing predatory. Nor was there anything perverted about it. There was a spreading, though, as a cobra's hood spreads. He could feel this. He could feel the menace of the spreading. But the spreading was a domination, not of evil, but of searching. I wish I did not see this, Robert Jordan thought. But it is not a business for slapping.

"Maria," Pilar said. "I will not touch thee. Tell me now of thy own volition."

"De tu propia voluntad," the words were in Spanish.

The girl shook her head.

"Maria," Pilar said. "Now and of thy own volition. You hear me? Anything at all."

"No," the girl said softly. "No and no."

"Now you will tell me," Pilar told her. "Anything at all. You will see. Now you will tell me."

"The earth moved," Maria said, not looking at the woman. "Truly. It was a thing I cannot tell thee."

"So," Pilar said and her voice was warm and friendly and there was no compulsion in it. But Robert Jordan noticed there were small drops of perspiration on her forehead and her lips. "So there was that. So that was it."

"It is true," Maria said and bit her lip.

"Of course it is true," Pilar said kindly. "But do not tell it to your own people for they never will believe you. You have no *Cali* blood, *Inglés?"*

She got to her feet, Robert Jordan helping her up.

"No," he said. "Not that I know of."

"Nor has the Maria that she knows of," Pilar said, *"Pues es muy raro.* It is very strange."

"But it happened, Pilar," Maria said.

"Cómo que no, hija?" Pilar said. "Why not, daughter? When I was young the earth moved so that you could feel it all shift in space and were afraid it would go out from under you. It happened every night."

"You lie," Maria said.

"Yes," Pilar said. "I lie. It never moves more than three times in a lifetime. Did it *really* move?"

"Yes," the girl said. "Truly."

"For you, *Inglés?"* Pilar looked at Robert Jordan. "Don't lie."

"Yes," he said. "Truly."

"Good," said Pilar. "Good. That is something."

"What do you mean about the three times?" Maria asked. "Why do you say that?"

"Three times," said Pilar. "Now you've had one."

"Only three times?"

"For most people, never," Pilar told her. "You are sure it moved?"

"One could have fallen off," Maria said.

"I guess it moved, then," Pilar said. "Come, then, and let us get to camp."

"What's this nonsense about three times?" Robert Jordan said to the big woman as they walked through the pines together.

"Nonsense?" she looked at him wryly. "Don't talk to me of nonsense, little English."

"Is it a wizardry like the palms of the hands?"

"Nay, it is common and proven knowledge with *Gitanos.*"

"But we are not *Gitanos.*"

"Nay. But you have had a little luck. Non-gypsies have a little luck sometimes."

"You mean it truly about the three times?"

She looked at him again, oddly. "Leave me, *Inglés,*" she said. "Don't molest me. You are too young for me to speak to."

"But, Pilar," Maria said.

"Shut up," Pilar told her. "You have had one and there are two more in the world for thee."

"And you?" Robert Jordan asked her.

"Two," said Pilar and put up two fingers. "Two. And there will never be a third."

"Why not?" Maria asked.

"Oh, shut up," Pilar said. "Shut up. *Busnes* of thy age bore me."

"Why not a third?" Robert Jordan asked.

"Oh, shut up, will you?" Pilar said. "Shut up!"

All right, Robert Jordan said to himself. Only I am not having any. I've known a lot of gypsies and they are strange enough. But so are we. The difference is we have to make an honest living. Nobody knows what tribes we came from nor what our tribal inheritance is nor what the mysteries were in the woods where the people lived that we came from. All we know is that we do not know. We know nothing about what happens to us in the nights. When it happens in the day though, it *is* something. Whatever happened, happened and now this woman not only has to make the girl say it when she did not want to; but she has to take it over and make it her own. She has to make it into a gypsy thing. I thought she took a beating up the hill but she was certainly dominating just now back there. If it had been evil she should have been shot. But it wasn't evil. It was only wanting to keep her hold on life. To keep it through Maria.

When you get through with this war you might take up the study of women, he said to himself. You could start with Pilar. She has put in a pretty complicated day, if you ask me. She never brought in the gypsy stuff before. Except the hand, he thought. Yes, of course the hand. And I don't think she was faking about the hand. She wouldn't tell me what she saw, of course. Whatever she saw she believed in herself. But that proves nothing.

"Listen, Pilar," he said to the woman.

Pilar looked at him and smiled.

"What is it?" she asked.

"Don't be so mysterious," Robert Jordan said. "These mysteries tire me very much."

"So?" Pilar said.

"I do not believe in ogres, soothsayers, fortune tellers, or chicken-crut gypsy witchcraft."

"Oh," said Pilar.

"No. And you can leave the girl alone."

"I will leave the girl alone."

"And leave the mysteries," Robert Jordan said. "We have enough work and enough things that will be done without complicating it with chicken-crut. Fewer mysteries and more work."

"I see," said Pilar and nodded her head in agreement. "And listen, _Inglés_," she said and smiled at him. "Did the earth move?"

"Yes, God damn you. It moved."

Pilar laughed and laughed and stood looking at Robert Jordan laughing.

"Oh, _Inglés. Inglés,_" she said laughing. "You are very comical. You must do much work now to regain thy dignity."

The Hell with you, Robert Jordan thought. But he kept his mouth shut. While they had spoken the sun had clouded over and as he looked back up toward the mountains the sky was now heavy and gray.

"Sure," Pilar said to him, looking at the sky. "It will snow."

"Now? almost in June?"

"Why not? These mountains do not know the names of the months. We are in the moon of May."

"It can't be snow," he said. "It *can't* snow."

"Just the same, *Inglés,*" she said to him, "it will snow."

Robert Jordan looked up at the thick gray of the sky with the sun gone faintly yellow, and now as he watched gone completely and the gray becoming uniform so that it was soft and heavy; the gray now cutting off the tops of the mountains.

"Yes," he said. "I guess you are right."

CHAPTER FOURTEEN

By the time they reached the camp it was snowing and the flakes were dropping diagonally through the pines. They slanted through the trees, sparse at first and circling as they fell, and then, as the cold wind came driving down the mountain, they came whirling and thick and Robert Jordan stood in front of the cave in a rage and watched them.

"We will have much snow," Pablo said. His voice was thick and his eyes were red and bleary.

"Has the gypsy come in?" Robert Jordan asked him.

"No," Pablo said. "Neither him nor the old man."

"Will you come with me to the upper post on the road?"

"No," Pablo said. "I will take no part in this."

"I will find it myself."

"In this storm you might miss it," Pablo said. "I would not go now."

"It's just downhill to the road and then follow it up."

"You could find it. But thy two sentries will be coming up now with the snow and you would miss them on the way."

"The old man is waiting for me."

"Nay. He will come in now with the snow."

Pablo looked at the snow that was blowing fast now past the mouth of the cave and said, "You do not like the snow, *Inglés?*"

Robert Jordan swore and Pablo looked at him through his bleary eyes and laughed.

"With this thy offensive goes, *Inglés,*" he said. "Come into the cave and thy people will be in directly."

Inside the cave Maria was busy at the fire and Pilar at the kitchen table. The fire was smoking but, as the girl worked with it, poking in a stick of wood and then fanning it with a folded paper, there was a puff and then a flare and the wood was burning, drawing brightly as the wind sucked a draft out of the hole in the roof.

"And this snow," Robert Jordan said. "You think there will be much?"

"Much," Pablo said contentedly. Then called to Pilar, "You don't like it, woman, either? Now that you command you do not like this snow?"

"*A mi qué?*" Pilar said, over her shoulder. "If it snows it snows."

"Drink some wine, *Inglés,*" Pablo said. "I have been drinking all day waiting for the snow."

"Give me a cup," Robert Jordan said.

"To the snow," Pablo said and touched cups with him. Robert Jordan looked him in the eyes and clinked his cup. You bleary-eyed murderous sod, he thought. I'd like to clink this cup against your teeth. *Take it easy,* he told himself, *take it easy.*

"It is very beautiful the snow," Pablo said. "You won't want to sleep outside with the snow falling."

So *that's* on your mind too is it? Robert Jordan thought. You've a lot of troubles, haven't you, Pablo?

"No?" he said, politely.

"No. Very cold," Pablo said. "Very wet."

You don't know why those old eiderdowns cost sixty-five dollars, Robert Jordan thought. I'd like to have a dollar for every time I've slept in that thing in the snow.

"Then I should sleep in here?" he asked politely.

"Yes."

"Thanks," Robert Jordan said. "I'll be sleeping outside."

"In the snow?"

"Yes" (damn your bloody, red pig-eyes and your swine-bristly swines-end of a face). "In the snow." (In the utterly-damned, ruinous, unexpected, slutting, defeat-conniving, bastard-cessery of the snow.)

He went over to where Maria had just put another piece of pine on the fire.

"Very beautiful, the snow," he said to the girl.

"But it is bad for the work, isn't it?" she asked him. "Aren't you worried?"

"*Qué va,*" he said. "Worrying is no good. When will supper be ready?"

"I thought you would have an appetite," Pilar said. "Do you want a cut of cheese now?"

"Thanks," he said and she cut him a slice, reaching up to unhook the big cheese that hung in a net from the ceiling, drawing a knife across the open end and handing him the heavy slice. He stood, eating it. It was just a little too goaty to be enjoyable.

"Maria," Pablo said from the table where he was sitting.

"What?" the girl asked.

"Wipe the table clean, Maria," Pablo said and grinned at Robert Jordan.

"Wipe thine own spillings," Pilar said to him. "Wipe first thy chin and thy shirt and then the table."

"Maria," Pablo called.

"Pay no heed to him. He is drunk," Pilar said.

"Maria," Pablo called. "It is still snowing and the snow is beautiful."

He doesn't know about that robe, Robert Jordan thought. Good old pig-eyes doesn't know why I paid the Woods boys sixty-five dollars for that robe. I wish the gypsy would come in though. As soon as the gypsy comes I'll go after the old man. I should go now but it is very possible that I would miss them. I don't know where he is posted.

"Want to make snowballs?" he said to Pablo. "Want to have a snowball fight?"

"What?" Pablo asked. "What do you propose?"

"Nothing," Robert Jordan said. "Got your saddles covered up good?"

"Yes."

Then in English Robert Jordan said, "Going to grain those horses or peg them out and let them dig for it?"

"What?"

"Nothing. It's your problem, old pal. I'm going out of here on my feet."

"Why do you speak in English?" Pablo asked.

"I don't know," Robert Jordan said. "When I get very tired sometimes I speak English. Or when I get very disgusted. Or baffled, say. When I get highly baffled I just talk English to hear the sound of it. It's a reassuring noise. You ought to try it sometime."

"What do you say, *Inglés?*" Pilar said. "It sounds very interesting but I do not understand."

"Nothing," Robert Jordan said. "I said, 'nothing' in English."

"Well then, talk Spanish," Pilar said. "It's shorter and simpler in Spanish."

"Surely," Robert Jordan said. But oh boy, he thought, oh Pablo, oh Pilar, oh Maria, oh you two brothers in the corner whose names I've forgotten and must remember, but I get tired of it sometimes. Of it and of you and of me and of the war and why in all why did it have to snow now? That's too bloody much. No, it's not. Nothing is too bloody much. You just have to take it and fight out of it and now stop prima-donnaing and accept the fact that it is snowing as you did a moment ago and the next thing is to check with your gypsy and pick up your old man. But to snow! Now in this month. Cut it out, he said to himself. Cut it out and take it. It's that cup, you know. How did it go about that cup? He'd either have to improve his memory or else never think of quotations because when you missed one it hung in your mind like a name you had forgotten and you could not get rid of it. How did it go about that cup?

"Let me have a cup of wine, please," he said in Spanish. Then, "Lots of snow? Eh?" he said to Pablo. *"Mucha nieve."*

The drunken man looked up at him and grinned. He nodded his head and grinned again.

"No offensive. No *aviones*. No bridge. Just snow," Pablo said.

"You expect it to last a long time?" Robert Jordan sat down by him. "You think we're going to be snowed in all summer, Pablo, old boy?"

"All summer, no," Pablo said. "Tonight and tomorrow, yes."

"What makes you think so?"

"There are two kinds of storms," Pablo said, heavily and judiciously. "One comes from the Pyrenees. With this one there is great cold. It is too late for this one."

"Good," Robert Jordan said. "That's something."

"This storm comes from the Cantabrico," Pablo said. "It comes from the sea. With the wind in this direction there will be a great storm and much snow."

"Where did you learn all this, old timer?" Robert Jordan asked.

Now that his rage was gone he was excited by this storm as he was always by all storms. In a blizzard, a gale, a sudden line squall, a tropical storm, or a summer thunder shower in the mountains there was an excitement that came to him from no other thing. It was like the excitement of battle except that it was clean. There is a wind that blows through battle but that was a hot wind; hot and dry as your mouth; and it blew heavily; hot and dirtily; and it rose and died away with the fortunes of the day. He knew that wind well.

But a snowstorm was the opposite of all of that. In the snowstorm you came close to wild animals and they were not afraid. They travelled across country not knowing where they were and the deer stood sometimes in the lee of the cabin. In a snowstorm you rode up to a moose and he mistook your horse for another moose and trotted forward to meet you. In a snowstorm it always seemed, for a time, as though there were no enemies. In a snowstorm the wind could blow a gale; but it blew a white cleanness and the air was full of a driving whiteness and all things were changed and when the wind stopped there would be the stillness. This was a big storm and he might as well enjoy it. It was ruining everything, but you might as well enjoy it.

"I was an arroyero for many years," Pablo said. "We trucked freight across the mountains with the big carts before the camions came into use. In that business we learned the weather."

"And how did you get into the movement?"

"I was always of the left," Pablo said. "We had many contacts with the people of Asturias where they are much developed politically. I have always been for the Republic."

"But what were you doing before the movement?"

"I worked then for a horse contractor of Zaragoza. He furnished horses for the bull rings as well as remounts for the army. It was then that I met Pilar who was, as she told you, with the matador Finito de Palencia."

He said this with considerable pride.

"He wasn't much of a matador," one of the brothers at the table said looking at Pilar's back where she stood in front of the stove.

"No?" Pilar said, turning around and looking at the man. "He wasn't much of a matador?"

Standing there now in the cave by the cooking fire she could see him, short and brown and sober-faced, with the sad eyes, the cheeks sunken and the black hair curled wet on his forehead where the tight-fitting matador's hat had made a red line that no one else noticed. She saw him stand, now, facing the five-year-old bull, facing the horns that had lifted the horses high, the great neck thrusting the horse up, up, as that rider poked into that neck with the spiked pole, thrusting up and up until the horse went over with a crash and the rider fell against the wooden fence and, with the bull's legs thrusting him forward, the big neck swung the horns that searched the horse for the life that was in him. She saw him, Finito, the not-so-good matador, now standing in front of the bull and turning sideways toward him. She saw him now clearly as he furled the heavy flannel cloth around the stick; the flannel hanging blood-heavy from the passes where it had swept over the bull's head and shoulders and the wet streaming shine of his withers and on down and over his back as the bull raised into the air and the banderillas clattered. She saw Finito stand five paces from the bull's head, profiled, the bull standing still and heavy, and draw the sword slowly up until it was level with his shoulder and then sight along the dipping blade at a point he could not yet see because the bull's head was higher than his eyes. He would bring that head down with the sweep his left arm would make with the wet, heavy cloth; but now he rocked back a little on his heels and sighted along the blade, profiled in front of the splintered horn; the bull's chest heaving and his eyes watching the cloth.

She saw him very clearly now and she heard his thin, clear voice as he turned his head and looked toward the people in the first row of the ring above the red fence and said, "Let's see if we can kill him like this!"

She could hear the voice and then see the first bend of the knee as he started forward and watch his voyage in onto the horn that lowered now magically as the bull's muzzle followed the low swept cloth, the thin, brown wrist controlled, sweeping the horns down and past, as the sword entered the dusty height of the withers.

She saw its brightness going in slowly and steadily as though the bull's rush plucked it into himself and out from the man's hand and she watched it move in until the brown knuckles rested against the taut hide and the short, brown man whose eyes had never left the entry place of the sword now swung his sucked-in belly clear of the horn and rocked clear from the animal, to stand holding the cloth on the stick in his left hand, raising his right hand to watch the bull die.

She saw him standing, his eyes watching the bull trying to hold the ground, watching the bull sway like a tree before it falls, watching the bull fight to hold his feet to the earth, the short man's hand raised in a formal gesture of triumph. She saw him standing there in the sweated, hollow relief of it being over, feeling the relief that the bull was dying, feeling the relief that there had been no shock, no blow of the horn as he came clear from it and then, as he stood, the bull could hold to the earth no longer and crashed over, rolling dead with all four feet in the air, and she could see the short, brown man walking tired and unsmiling to the fence.

She knew he could not run across the ring if his life depended on it and she watched him walk slowly to the fence and wipe his mouth on a towel and look up at her and shake his head and then wipe his face on the towel and start his triumphant circling of the ring.

She saw him moving slowly, dragging around the ring, smiling, bowing, smiling, his assistants walking behind him, stooping, picking up cigars, tossing back hats; he circling the ring sad-eyed and smiling, to end the circle before her. Then she looked over and saw him sitting now on the step of the wooden fence, his mouth in a towel.

Pilar saw all this as she stood there over the fire and she said, "So he wasn't a good matador? With what class of people is my life passed now!"

"He was a good matador," Pablo said. "He was handicapped by his short stature."

"And clearly he was tubercular," Primitivo said.

"Tubercular?" Pilar said. "Who wouldn't be tubercular from the punishment he received? In this country where no poor man can ever hope to make money unless he is a criminal like Juan March, or a bull-fighter, or a tenor in the opera? Why wouldn't he be tubercular? In a country where the bourgeoisie over-eat so that their stomachs are all ruined and they cannot live without bicarbonate of soda and the poor are hungry from their birth till the day they die, why wouldn't he be tubercular? If you travelled under the seats in third-class carriages to ride free when you were following the fairs learning to fight as a boy, down there in the dust and dirt with the fresh spit and the dry spit, wouldn't you be tubercular if your chest was beaten out by horns?"

"Clearly," Primitivo said. "I only said he was tubercular."

"Of course he was tubercular," Pilar said, standing there with the big wooden stirring spoon in her hand. "He was short of stature and he had a thin voice and much fear of bulls. Never have I seen a man with more fear before the bullfight and never have I seen a man with less fear in the ring. "You," she said to Pablo. "You are afraid to die now. You think that is something of importance. But Finito was afraid all the time and in the ring he was like a lion."

"He had the fame of being very valiant," the second brother said.

"Never have I known a man with so much fear," Pilar said. "He would not even have a bull's head in the house. One time at the feria of Valladolid he killed a bull of Pablo Romero very well——"

"I remember," the first brother said. "I was at the ring. It was a soap-colored one with a curly forehead and with very high horns. It was a bull of over thirty arrobas. It was the last bull he killed in Valladolid."

"Exactly," Pilar said. "And afterwards the club of enthusiasts who met in the Café Colon and had taken his name for their club had the head of the bull mounted and presented it to him at a small banquet at the Café Colon. During the meal they had the head on the the wall, but it was covered with a cloth. I was at the table and others were there, Pastora, who is uglier than I am, and the Niña de los Peines, and other gypsies and whores of great category. It was a banquet, small but of great intensity and almost of a violence due to a dispute between Pastora and one of the most significant whores over a question of propriety. I, myself, was feeling more than happy and I was sitting by Finito and I noticed he would not look up at the bull's head, which was shrouded in a purple cloth as the images of the saints are covered in church duing the week of the passion of our former Lord.

"Finito did not eat much because he had received a *palotaxo*, a blow from the flat of the horn when he had gone in to kill in his last corrida of the year at Zaragoza, and it had rendered him unconscious for some time and even now he could not hold food on his stomach and he would put his handkerchief to his mouth and deposit a quantity of blood in it at intervals throughout the banquet. What was I going to tell you?"

"The bull's head," Primitivo said. "The stuffed head of the bull."

"Yes," Pilar said. "Yes. But I must tell certain details so that you will see it. Finito was never very merry, you know. He was essentially solemn and I had never known him when we were alone to laugh at anything. Not even at things which were very comic. He took everything with great seriousness. He was almost as serious as Fernando. But this was a banquet given him by a club of *aficionados* banded together into the *Club Finito* and it was necessary for him to give an appearance of gaiety and friendliness and merriment. So all during the meal he smiled and made friendly remarks and it was only I who noticed what he was doing with the handkerchief. He had three handkerchiefs with him and he filled the three of them and then he said to me in a very low voice, 'Pilar, I can support this no further. I think I must leave.'

"'Let us leave then,' I said. For I saw he was suffering much. There was great hilarity by this time at the banquet and the noise was tremendous.

"'No. I cannot leave,' Finito said to me. 'After all it is a club named for me and I have an obligation.'

"'If thou art ill let us go,' I said.

"'Nay,' he said. 'I will stay. Give me some of that manzanilla.'

"I did not think it was wise of him to drink, since he had eaten nothing, and since he had such a condition of the stomach; but he was evidently unable to support the merriment and the hilarity and the noise longer without taking something. So I watched him drink, very rapidly, almost a bottle of the manzanilla. Having exhausted his handkerchiefs he was now employing his napkin for the use he had previously made of his handkerchiefs.

"Now indeed the banquet had reached a stage of great enthusiasm and some of the least heavy of the whores were being paraded around the table on the shoulders of various of the club members. Pastora was prevailed upon to sing and El Niño Ricardo played the guitar and it was very moving and an occasion of true joy and drunken friendship of the highest order. Never have I seen a banquet at which a higher pitch of real *flamenco* enthusiasm was reached and yet we had not arrived at the unveiling of the bull's head which was, after all, the reason for the celebration of the banquet.

"I was enjoying myself to such an extent and I was so busy clapping my hands to the playing of Ricardo and aiding to make up a team to clap for the singing of the Niña de los Peines that I did not notice that Finito had filled his own napkin by now, and that he had taken mine. He was drinking more manzanilla now and his eyes were very bright, and he was nodding very happily to every one. He could not speak much because at any time, while speaking, he might have to resort to his napkin; but he was giving an appearance of great gayety and enjoyment which, after all, was what he was there for.

"So the banquet proceeded and the man who sat next to me had been the former manager of Rafael el Gallo and he was telling me a story, and the end of it was, 'So Rafael came to me and said, "You are the best friend I have in the world and the noblest. I love you like a brother and I wish to make you a present." So then he gave me a beautiful diamond stick pin and kissed me on both cheeks and we were both very moved. Then Rafael el Gallo, having given me the diamond stick pin, walked out of the café and I said to Retana who was sitting at the table, "That dirty gypsy had just signed a contract with another manager."'

"'"What do you mean?" Retana asked.'

"'I've managed him for ten years and he has never given me a present before,' the manager of El Gallo had said. 'That's the only thing it can mean.' And sure enough it was true and that was how El Gallo left him.

"But at this point, Pastora intervened in the conversation, not perhaps as much to defend the good name of Rafael, since no one had ever spoken harder against him than she had herself, but because the manager had spoken against the gypsies by employing the phrase, 'Dirty gypsy.' She intervened so forcibly and in such terms that the manager was reduced to silence. I intervened to quiet Pastora and another *Gitana* intervened to quiet me and the din was such that no one could distinguish any words which passed except the one great word 'whore' which roared out above all other words until quiet was restored and the three of us who had intervened sat looking down into our glasses and then I noticed that Finito was staring at the bull's head, still draped in the purple cloth, with a look of horror on his face.

"At this moment the president of the Club commenced the speech which was to precede the unveiling of the head and all through the speech which was applauded with shouts of *'Olé!'* and poundings on the table I was watching Finito who was making use of his, no, my, napkin and sinking further back in his chair and staring with horror and fascination at the shrouded bull's head on the wall opposite him.

"Toward the end of the speech, Finito began to shake his head and he got further back in the chair all the time.

"'How are you, little one?' I said to him but when he looked at me he did not recognize me and he only shook his head and said, 'No. No. No.'

"So the president of the Club reached the end of the speech and then, with everybody cheering him, he stood on a chair and reached up and untied the cord that bound the purple shroud over the head and slowly pulled it clear of the head and it stuck on one of the horns and he lifted it clear and pulled it off the sharp polished horns and there was that great yellow bull with black horns that swung way out and pointed forward, their white tips sharp as porcupine quills, and the head of the bull was as though he were alive; his forehead was curly as in life and his nostrils were open and his eyes were bright and he was there looking straight at Finito.

"Every one shouted and applauded and Finito sunk further back in the chair and then every one was quiet and looking at him and he said, 'No. No,' and looked at the bull and pulled further back and then he said, 'No!' very loudly and a big blob of blood came out and he didn't even put up the napkin and it slid down his chin and he was still looking at the bull and he said, 'All season, yes. To make money, yes. To eat, yes. But I can't eat. Hear me? My stomach's bad. But now with the season finished! No! No! No!' He looked around at the table and then he looked at the bull's head and said, 'No,' once more and then he put his head down and he put his napkin up to his mouth and then he just sat there like that and said nothing and the banquet, which had started so well, and promised to mark an epoch in hilarity and good fellowship was not a success."

"Then how long after that did he die?" Primitivo asked.

"That winter," Pilar said. "He never recovered from that last blow with the flat of the horn in Zaragoza. They are worse than a goring, for the injury is internal and it does not heal. He received one almost every time he went in to kill and it was for this reason he was not more successful. It was difficult for him to get out from over the horn because of his short stature. Nearly always the side of the horn struck him. But of course many were only glancing blows."

"If he was so short he should not have tried to be a matador," Primitivo said.

Pilar looked at Robert Jordan and shook her head. Then she bent over the big iron pot, still shaking her head.

What a people they are, she thought. What a people are the Spaniards, "and if he was so short he should not have tried to be a matador." And I hear it and say nothing. I have no rage for that and having made an explanation I am silent. How simple it is when one knows nothing. *Qué sencillo!* Knowing nothing one says, "He was not much of a matador." Knowing nothing another says, "He was tubercular." And another says, after one, knowing, has explained, "If he was so short he should not have tried to be a matador."

Now, bending over the fire, she saw on the bed again the naked brown body with the gnarled scars in both thighs, the deep, seared whorl below the ribs on the right side of the chest and the long white welt along the side that ended in the armpit. She saw the eyes closed and the solemn brown face and the curly black hair pushed back now from the forehead and she was sitting by him on the bed rubbing the legs, chafing the taut muscles of the calves, kneading them, loosening them, and then tapping them lightly with her folded hands, loosening the cramped muscles.

"How is it?" she said to him. "How are the legs, little one?"

"Very well, Pilar," he would say without opening his eyes.

"Do you want me to rub the chest?"

"Nay, Pilar. Please do not touch it."

"And the upper legs?"

"No. They hurt too badly."

"But if I rub them and put liniment on, it will warm them and they will be better."

"Nay, Pilar. Thank thee. I would rather they were not touched."

"I will wash thee with alcohol."

"Yes. Do it very lightly."

"You were enormous in the last bull," she would say to him and he would say, "Yes, I killed him very well."

Then, having washed him and covered him with a sheet, she would lie by him in the bed and he would put a brown hand out and touch her and say, "Thou art much woman, Pilar." It was the nearest to a joke he ever made and then, usually, after the fight, he would go to sleep and she would lie there, holding his hand in her two hands and listening to him breathe.

He was often frightened in his sleep and she would feel his hand grip tightly and see the sweat bead on his forehead and if he woke, she said, "It's nothing," and he slept again. She was with him thus five years and never was unfaithful to him, that is almost never, and then after the funeral, she took up with Pablo who led picador horses in the ring and was like all the bulls that Finito had spent his life killing. But neither bull force nor bull courage lasted, she knew now, and what did last? I last, she thought. Yes, I have lasted. But for what?

"Maria," she said. "Pay some attention to what you are doing. That is a fire to cook with. Not to burn down a city."

Just then the gypsy came in the door. He was covered with snow and he stood there holding his carbine and stamping the snow from his feet.

Robert Jordan stood up and went over to the door, "Well?" he said to the gypsy.

"Six-hour watches, two men at a time on the big bridge," the gypsy said. "There are eight men and a corporal at the road mender's hut. Here is thy chronometer."

"What about the sawmill post?"

"The old man is there. He can watch that and the road both."

"And the road?" Robert Jordan asked.

"The same movement as always," the gypsy said. "Nothing out of the usual. Several motor cars."

The gypsy looked cold, his dark face was drawn with the cold and his hands were red. Standing in the mouth of the cave he took off his jacket and shook it.

"I stayed until they changed the watch," he said. "It was changed at noon and at six. That is a long watch. I am glad I am not in their army."

"Let us go for the old man," Robert Jordan said, putting on his leather coat.

"Not me," the gypsy said. "I go now for the fire and the hot soup. I will tell one of these where he is and he can guide you. Hey, loafers," he called to the men who sat at the table. "Who wants to guide the *Inglés* to where the old man is watching the road?"

"I will go," Fernando rose. "Tell me where it is."

"Listen," the gypsy said. "It is here—" and he told him where the old man, Anselmo, was posted.

CHAPTER FIFTEEN

ANSELMO was crouched in the lee of the trunk of a big tree and the snow blew past on either side. He was pressed close against the tree and his hands were inside of the sleeves of his jacket, each hand shoved up into the opposite sleeve, and his head was pulled as far down into the jacket as it would go. If I stay here much longer I will freeze, he thought, and that will be of no value. The *Inglés* told me to stay until I was relieved but he did not know then about this storm. There has been no abnormal movement on the road and I know the dispositions and the habits of this post at the sawmill across the road. I should go now to the camp. Anybody with sense would be expecting me to return to the camp. I will stay a little longer, he thought, and then go to the camp. It is the fault of the orders, which are too rigid. There is no allowance for a change in circumstance. He rubbed his feet together and then took his hands out of the jacket sleeves and bent over and rubbed his legs with them and patted his feet together to keep the circulation going. It was less cold there, out of the wind in the shelter of the tree, but he would have to start walking shortly.

As he crouched, rubbing his feet, he heard a motorcar on the road. It had on chains and one link of chain was slapping and, as he watched, it came up the snow-covered road, green and brown painted, in broken patches of daubed color, the windows blued over so that you could not see in, with only a half circle left clear in the blue for the occupants to look out through. It was a two-year-old Rolls-Royce town car camouflaged for the use of the General Staff but Anselmo did not know that. He could not see into the car where three officers sat wrapped in their capes. Two were on the back seat and one sat on the folding chair. The officer on the folding chair was looking out of the slit in the blue of the window as the car passed but Anselmo did not know this. Neither of them saw the other.

The car passed in the snow directly below him. Anselmo saw the chauffeur, red-faced and steel-helmeted, his face and helmet projecting out of the blanket cape he wore and he saw the forward jut of the automatic rifle the orderly who sat beside the chauffeur carried. Then the car was gone up the road and Anselmo reached into the inside of his jacket and took out from his shirt pocket the two sheets torn from Robert Jordan's notebook and made a mark after the drawing of a motorcar. It was the tenth car up for the day. Six had come down. Four were still up. It was not an unusual amount of cars to move upon that road but Anselmo did not distinguish between the Fords, Fiats, Opels, Renaults, and Citroens of the staff of the Division that held the passes and the line of the mountain and the Rolls-Royces, Lancias, Mercedes, and Isottas of the General Staff. This was the sort of distinction that Robert Jordan should have made and, if he had been there instead of the old man, he would have appreciated the significance of these cars which had gone up. But he was not there and the old man simply made a mark for a motorcar going up the road, on the sheet of note paper.

Anselmo was now so cold that he decided he had best go to camp before it was dark. He had no fear of missing the way, but he thought it was useless to stay longer and the wind was blowing colder all the time and there was no lessening of the snow. But when he stood up and stamped his feet and looked through the driving snow at the road he did not start off up the hillside but stayed leaning against the sheltered side of the pine tree.

The _Inglés_ told me to stay, he thought. Even now he may be on the way here and, if I leave this place, he may lose himself in the snow searching for me. All through this war we have suffered from a lack of discipline and from the disobeying of orders and I will wait a while still for the _Inglés_. But if he does not come soon I must go in spite of all orders for I have a report to make now, and I have much to do in these days, and to freeze here is an exaggeration and without utility.

Across the road at the sawmill smoke was coming out of the chimney and Anselmo could smell it blown toward him through the snow. The fascists are warm, he thought, and they are comfortable, and tomorrow night we will kill them. It is a strange thing and I do not like to think of it. I have watched them all day and they are the same men that we are. I believe that I could walk up to the mill and knock on the door and I would be welcome except that they have orders to challenge all travellers and ask to see their papers. It is only orders that come between us. Those men are not fascists. I call them so, but they are not. They are poor men as we are. They should never be fighting against us and I do not like to think of the killing.

These at this post are Gallegos. I know that from hearing them talk this afternoon. They cannot desert because if they do their families will be shot. Gallegos are either very intelligent or very dumb and brutal. I have known both kinds. Lister is a Gallego from the same town as Franco. I wonder what these Gallegos think of this snow now at this time of year. They have no high mountains such as these and in their country it always rains and it is always green.

A light showed in the window of the sawmill and Anselmo shivered and thought, damn that *Inglés!* There are the Gallegos warm and in a house here in our country, and I am freezing behind a tree and we live in a hole in the rocks like beasts in the mountain. But tomorrow, he thought, the beasts will come out of their hole and these that are now so comfortable will die warm in their blankets. As those died in the night when we raided Otero, he thought. He did not like to remember Otero.

In Otero, that night, was when he first killed and he hoped he would not have to kill in this of the suppressing of these posts. It was in Otero that Pablo knifed the sentry when Anselmo pulled the blanket over his head and the sentry caught Anselmo's foot and held it, smothered as he was in the blanket, and made a crying noise in the blanket and Anselmo had to feel in the blanket and knife him until he let go of the foot and was still. He had his knee across the man's throat to keep him silent and he was knifing into the bundle when Pablo tossed the bomb through the window into the room where the men of the post were all sleeping. And when the flash came it was as though the whole world burst red and yellow before your eyes and two more bombs were in already. Pablo had pulled the pins and tossed them quickly through the window, and those who were not killed in their beds were killed as they rose from bed when the second bomb exploded. That was in the great days of Pablo when he scourged the country like a tartar and no fascist post was safe at night.

And now, he is as finished and as ended as a boar that has been altered, Anselmo thought, and, when the altering has been accomplished and the squealing is over you cast the two stones away and the boar, that is a boar no longer, goes snouting and rooting up to them and eats them. No, he is not that bad, Anselmo grinned, one can think too badly even of Pablo. But he is ugly enough and changed enough.

It is too cold, he thought. That the *Inglés* should come and that I should not have to kill in this of the posts. These four Gallegos and their corporal are for those who like the killing. The *Inglés* said that. I will do it if it is my duty but the *Inglés* said that I would be with him at the bridge and that this would be left to others. At the bridge there will be a battle and, if I am able to endure the battle, then I will have done all that an old man may do in this war. But let the *Inglés* come now, for I am cold and to see the light in the mill where I know that the Gallegos are warm makes me colder still. I wish that I were in my own house again and that this war were over. But you have no house now, he thought. We must win this war before you can ever return to your house.

Inside the sawmill one of the soldiers was sitting on his bunk and greasing his boots. Another lay in his bunk sleeping. The third was cooking and the corporal was reading a paper. Their helmets hung on nails driven into the wall and their rifles leaned against the plank wall.

"What kind of country is this where it snows when it is almost June?" the soldier who was sitting on the bunk said.

"It is a phenomenon," the corporal said.

"We are in the moon of May," the soldier who was cooking said. "The moon of May has not yet terminated."

"What kind of a country is it where it snows in May?" the soldier on the bunk insisted.

"In May snow is no rarity in these mountains," the corporal said. "I have been colder in Madrid in the month of May than in any other month."

"And hotter, too," the soldier who was cooking said.

"May is a month of great contrasts in temperature," the corporal said. "Here, in Castile, May is a month of great heat but it can have much cold."

"Or rain," the soldier on the bunk said. "In this past May it rained almost every day."

"It did not," the soldier who was cooking said. "And anyway this past May was the moon of April."

"One could go crazy listening to thee and thy moons," the corporal said. "Leave this of the moons alone."

"Any one who lives either by the sea or by the land knows that it is the moon and not the month which counts," the soldier who was cooking said. "Now for example, we have just started the moon of May. Yet it is coming on June."

"Why then do we not get definitely behind in the seasons?" the corporal said. "The whole proposition gives me a headache."

"You are from a town," the soldier who was cooking said. "You are from Lugo. What would you know of the sea or of the land?"

"One learns more in a town than you *analfabetos* learn in thy sea or thy land."

"In this moon the first of the big schools of sardines come," the soldier who was cooking said. "In this moon the sardine boats will be outfitting and the mackerel will have gone north."

"Why are you not in the navy if you come from Noya?" the corporal asked.

"Because I am not inscribed from Noya but from Negreira, where I was born. And from Negreira, which is up the river Tambre, they take you for the army."

"Worse luck," said the corporal.

"Do not think the navy is without peril," the soldier who was sitting on the bunk said. "Even without the possibility of combat that is a dangerous coast in the winter."

"Nothing can be worse than the army," the corporal said.

"And you a corporal," the soldier who was cooking said. "What a way of speaking is that?"

"Nay," the corporal said. "I mean for dangers. I mean the endurance of bombardments, the necessity to attack, the life of the parapet."

"Here we have little of that," the soldier on the bunk said.

"By the Grace of God," the corporal said. "But who knows when we will be subject to it again? Certainly we will not have something as easy as this forever!"

"How much longer do you think we will have this detail?"

"I don't know," the corporal said. "But I wish we could have it for all of the war."

"Six hours is too long to be on guard," the soldier who was cooking said.

"We will have three-hour watches as long as this storm holds," the corporal said. "That is only normal."

"What about all those staff cars?" the soldier on the bunk asked. "I did not like the look of all those staff cars."

"Nor I," the corporal said. "All such things are of evil omen."

"And aviation," the soldier who was cooking said. "Aviation is another bad sign."

"But we have formidable aviation," the corporal said. "The Reds have no aviation such as we have. Those planes this morning were something to make any man happy."

"I have seen the Red planes when they were something serious," the soldier on the bunk said. "I have seen those two motor bombers when they were a horror to endure."

"Yes. But they are not as formidable as our aviation," the corporal said. "We have an aviation that is insuperable."

This was how they were talking in the sawmill while Anselmo waited in the snow watching the road and the light in the sawmill window.

I hope I am not for the killing, Anselmo was thinking. I think that after the war there will have to be some great penance done for the killing. If we no longer have religion after the war then I think there must be some form of civic penance organized that all may be cleansed from the killing or else we will never have a true and human basis for living. The killing is necessary, I know, but still the doing of it is very bad for a man and I think that, after all this is over and we have won the war, there must be a penance of some kind for the cleansing of us all.

Anselmo was a very good man and whenever he was alone for long, and he was alone much of the time, this problem of the killing returned to him.

I wonder about the *Inglés,* he thought. He told me that he did not mind it. Yet he seems to be both sensitive and kind. It may be that in the younger people it does not have an importance. It may be that in foreigners, or in those who have not had our religion, there is not the same attitude. But I think any one doing it will be brutalized in time and I think that even though necessary, it is a great sin and that afterwards we must do something very strong to atone for it.

It was dark now and he looked at the light across the road and shook his arms against his chest to warm them. Now, he thought, he would certainly leave for the camp; but something kept him there beside the tree above the road. It was snowing harder and Anselmo thought: if only we could blow the bridge tonight. On a night like this it would be nothing to take the posts and blow the bridge and it would all be over and done with. On a night like this you could do anything.

Then he stood there against the tree stamping his feet softly and he did not think any more about the bridge. The coming of the dark always made him feel lonely and tonight he felt so lonely that there was a hollowness in him as of hunger. In the old days he could help this loneliness by the saying of prayers and often coming home from hunting he would repeat a great number of the same prayer and it made him feel better. But he had not prayed once since the movement. He missed the prayers but he thought it would be unfair and hypocritical to say them and he did not wish to ask any favors or for any different treatment than all the men were receiving.

No, he thought, I am lonely. But so are all the soldiers and the wives of all the soldiers and all those who have lost families or parents. I have no wife, but I am glad that she died before the movement. She would not have understood it. I have no children and I never will have any children. I am lonely in the day when I am not working but when the dark comes it is a time of great loneliness. But one thing I have that no man nor any God can take from me and that is that I have worked well for the Republic. I have worked hard for the good that we will all share later. I have worked my best from the first of the movement and I have done nothing that I am ashamed of.

All that I am sorry for is the killing. But surely there will be an opportunity to atone for that because for a sin of that sort that so many bear, certainly some just relief will be devised. I would like to talk with the *Inglés* about it but, being young, it is possible that he might not understand. He mentioned the killing before. Or was it I that mentioned it? He must have killed much, but he shows no signs of liking it. In those who like it there is always a rottenness.

It must really be a great sin, he thought. Because certainly it is the one thing we have no right to do even though, as I know, it is necessary. But in Spain it is done too lightly and often without true necessity and there is much quick injustice which, afterward, can never be repaired. I wish I did not think about it so much, he thought. I wish there were a penance for it that one could commence now because it is the only thing that I have done in all my life that makes me feel badly when I am alone. All the other things are forgiven or one had a chance to atone for them by kindness or in some decent way. But I think this of the killing must be a very great sin and I would like to fix it up. Later on there may be certain days that one can work for the state or something that one can do that will remove it. It will probably be something that one pays as in the days of the Church, he thought, and smiled. The Church was well organized for sin. That pleased him and he was smiling in the dark when Robert Jordan came up to him. He came silently and the old man did not see him until he was there.

"*Hola, viejo,*" Robert Jordan whispered and clapped him on the back. "How's the old one?"

"Very cold," Anselmo said. Fernando was standing a little apart, his back turned against the driving snow.

"Come on," Robert Jordan whispered. "Get on up to camp and get warm. It was a crime to leave you here so long."

"That is their light," Anselmo pointed.

"Where's the sentry?"

"You do not see him from here. He is around the bend."

"The hell with them," Robert Jordan said. "You tell me at camp. Come on, let's go."

"Let me show you," Anselmo said.

"I'm going to look at it in the morning," Robert Jordan said. "Here, take a swallow of this."

He handed the old man his flask. Anselmo tipped it up and swallowed.

"*Ayee,*" he said and rubbed his mouth. "It is fire."

"Come on," Robert Jordan said in the dark. "Let us go."

It was so dark now you could only see the flakes blowing past and the rigid dark of the pine trunks. Fernando was standing a little way up the hill. Look at that cigar store Indian, Robert Jordan thought. I suppose I have to offer him a drink.

"Hey, Fernando," he said as he came up to him. "A swallow?"

"No," said Fernando. "Thank you."

Thank *you,* I mean, Robert Jordan thought. I'm glad cigar store Indians don't drink. There isn't too much of that left. Boy, I'm glad to see this old man, Robert Jordan thought. He looked at Anselmo and then clapped him on the back again as they started up the hill.

"I'm glad to see you, *viejo,*" he said to Anselmo. "If I ever get gloomy, when I see you it cheers me up. Come on, let's get up there."

They were going up the hill in the snow.

"Back to the palace of Pablo," Robert Jordan said to Anselmo. It sounded wonderful in Spanish.

"El Palacio del Miedo," Anselmo said. "The Palace of Fear."

"La cueva de los huevos perdidos," Robert Jordan capped the other happily. "The cave of the lost eggs."

"What eggs?" Fernando asked.

"A joke," Robert Jordan said. "Just a joke. Not eggs, you know. The others."

"But why are they lost?" Fernando asked.

"I don't know," said Robert Jordan. "Take a book to tell you. Ask Pilar," then he put his arm around Anselmo's shoulder and held him tight as they walked and shook him. "Listen," he said. "I'm glad to see you, hear? You don't know what it means to find somebody in this country in the same place they were left."

It showed what confidence and intimacy he had that he could say anything against the country.

"I am glad to see thee," Anselmo said. "But I was just about to leave."

"Like hell you would have," Robert Jordan said happily. "You'd have frozen first."

"How was it up above?" Anselmo asked.

"Fine," said Robert Jordan. "Everything is fine."

He was very happy with that sudden, rare happiness that can come to any one with a command in a revolutionary arm; the happiness of finding that even one of your flanks holds. If both flanks ever held I suppose it would be too much to take, he thought. I don't know who is prepared to stand that. And if you extend along a flank, any flank, it eventually becomes one man. Yes, one man. This was not the axiom he wanted. But this was a good man. One good man. You are going to be the left flank when we have the battle, he thought. I better not tell you that yet. It's going to be an awfully small battle, he thought. But it's going to be an awfully good one. Well, I always wanted to fight one on my own. I always had an opinion on what was wrong with everybody else's, from Agincourt down. I will have to make this a good one. It is going to be small but very select. If I have to do what I think I will have to do it will be very select indeed.

"Listen," he said to Anselmo. "I'm awfully glad to see you."

"And me to see thee," the old man said.

As they went up the hill in the dark, the wind at their backs, the storm blowing past them as they climbed, Anselmo did not feel lonely. He had not been lonely since the *Inglés* had clapped him on the shoulder. The *Inglés* was pleased and happy and they joked together. The *Inglés* said it all went well and he was not worried. The drink in his stomach warmed him and his feet were warming now climbing.

"Not much on the road," he said to the *Inglés*.

"Good," the *Inglés* told him. "You will show me when we get there."

Anselmo was happy now and he was very pleased that he had stayed there at the post of observation.

If he had come in to camp it would have been all right. It would have been the intelligent and correct thing to have done under the circumstances, Robert Jordan was thinking. But he stayed as he was told, Robert Jordan thought. That's the rarest thing that can happen in Spain. To stay in a storm, in a way, corresponds to a lot of things. It's not for nothing that the Germans call an attack a storm. I could certainly use a couple more who would stay. I most certainly could. I wonder if that Fernando would stay. It's just possible. After all, he is the one who suggested coming out just now. Do you suppose he would stay? Wouldn't that be good? He's just about stubborn enough. I'll have to make some inquiries. Wonder what the old cigar store Indian is thinking about now.

"What are you thinking about, Fernando?" Robert Jordan asked.

"Why do you ask?"

"Curiosity," Robert Jordan said. "I am a man of great curiosity."

"I was thinking of supper," Fernando said.

"Do you like to eat?"

"Yes. Very much."

"How's Pilar's cooking?"

"Average," Fernando answered.

He's a second Coolidge, Robert Jordan thought. But, you know, I have just a hunch that he would stay.

The three of them plodded up the hill in the snow.

CHAPTER SIXTEEN

"EL SORDO was here," Pilar said to Robert Jordan. They had come in out of the storm to the smoky warmth of the cave and the woman had motioned Robert Jordan over to her with a nod of her head. "He's gone to look for horses."

"Good. Did he leave any word for me?"

"Only that he had gone for horses."

"And we?"

"*No sé,*" she said. "Look at him."

Robert Jordan had seen Pablo when he came in and Pablo had grinned at him. Now he looked over at him sitting at the board table and grinned and waved his hand.

"*Inglés,*" Pablo called. "It's still falling, *Inglés.*"

Robert Jordan nodded at him.

"Let me take thy shoes and dry them," Maria said. "I will hang them here in the smoke of the fire."

"Watch out you don't burn them," Robert Jordan told her. "I don't want to go around here barefoot. What's the matter?" he turned to Pilar. "Is this a meeting? Haven't you any sentries out?"

"In this storm? *Qué va.*"

There were six men sitting at the table and leaning back against the wall. Anselmo and Fernando were still shaking the snow from their jackets, beating their trousers and rapping their feet against the wall by the entrance.

"Let me take thy jacket," Maria said. "Do not let the snow melt on it."

Robert Jordan slipped out of his jacket, beat the snow from his trousers, and untied his shoes.

"You will get everything wet here," Pilar said.

"It was thee who called me."

"Still there is no impediment to returning to the door for thy brushing."

"Excuse me," Robert Jordan said, standing in his bare feet on the dirt floor. "Hunt me a pair of socks, Maria."

"The Lord and Master," Pilar said and poked a piece of wood into the fire.

"Hay que aprovechar el tiempo," Robert Jordan told her. "You have to take advantage of what time there is."

"It is locked," Maria said.

"Here is the key," and he tossed it over.

"It does not fit this sack."

"It is the other sack. They are on top and at the side."

The girl found the pair of socks, closed the sack, locked it and brought them over with the key.

"Sit down and put them on and rub thy feet well," she said. Robert Jordan grinned at her.

"Thou canst not dry them with thy hair?" he said for Pilar to hear.

"What a swine," she said. "First he is the Lord of the Manor. Now he is our ex-Lord Himself. Hit him with a chunk of wood, Maria."

"Nay," Robert Jordan said to her. "I am joking because I am happy."

"You are happy?"

"Yes," he said. "I think everything goes very well."

"Roberto," Maria said. "Go sit down and dry thy feet and let me bring thee something to drink to warm thee."

"You would think that man had never dampened foot before," Pilar said. "Nor that a flake of snow had ever fallen."

Maria brought him a sheepskin and put it on the dirt floor of the cave.

"There," she said. "Keep that under thee until thy shoes are dry."

The sheepskin was fresh dried and not tanned and as Robert Jordan rested his stocking feet on it he could feel it crackle like parchment.

The fire was smoking and Pilar called to Maria, "Blow up the fire, worthless one. This is no smokehouse."

"Blow it thyself," Maria said. "I am searching for the bottle that El Sordo left."

"It is behind his packs," Pilar told her. "Must you care for him as a sucking child?"

"No," Maria said. "As a man who is cold and wet. And a man who has just come to his house. Here it is." She brought the bottle to where Robert Jordan sat. "It is the bottle of this noon. With this bottle one could make a beautiful lamp. When we have electricity again, what a lamp we can make of this bottle." She looked at the pinch-bottle admiringly. "How do you take this, Roberto?"

"I thought I was *Inglés*," Robert Jordan said to her.

"I call thee Roberto before the others," she said in a low voice and blushed. "How do you want it, Roberto?"

"Roberto," Pablo said thickly and nodded his head at Robert Jordan. "How do you want it, Don Roberto?"

"Do you want some?" Robert Jordan asked him.

Pablo shook his head. "I am making myself drunk with wine," he said with dignity.

"Go with Bacchus," Robert Jordan said in Spanish.

"Who is Bacchus?" Pablo asked.

"A comrade of thine," Robert Jordan said.

"Never have I heard of him," Pablo said heavily. "Never in these mountains."

"Give a cup to Anselmo," Robert Jordan said to Maria. "It is he who is cold." He was putting on the dry pair of socks and the whiskey and water in the cup tasted clean and thinly warming. But it does not curl around inside of you the way the absinthe does, he thought. There is nothing like absinthe.

Who would imagine they would have whiskey up here, he thought. But La Granja was the most likely place in Spain to find it when you thought it over. Imagine Sordo getting a bottle for the visiting dynamiter and then remembering to bring it down and leave it. It wasn't just manners that they had. Manners would have been producing the bottle and having a formal drink. That was what the French would have done and then they would have saved what was left for another occasion. No, the true thoughtfulness of thinking the visitor would like it and then bringing it down for him to enjoy when you yourself were engaged in something where there was every reason to think of no one else but yourself and of nothing but the matter in hand—that was Spanish. One kind of Spanish, he thought. Remembering to bring the whiskey was one of the reasons you loved these people. Don't go romanticizing them, he thought.

There are as many sorts of Spanish as there are Americans. But still, bringing the whiskey was very handsome.

"How do you like it?" he asked Anselmo.

The old man was sitting by the fire with a smile on his face, his big hands holding the cup. He shook his head.

"No?" Robert Jordan asked him.

"The child put water in it," Anselmo said.

"Exactly as Roberto takes it," Maria said. "Art thou something special?"

"No," Anselmo told her. "Nothing special at all. But I like to feel it burn as it goes down."

"Give me that," Robert Jordan told the girl, "and pour him some of that which burns."

He tipped the contents of the cup into his own and handed it back empty to the girl, who poured carefully into it from the bottle.

"Ah," Anselmo took the cup, put his head back and let it run down his throat. He looked at Maria standing holding the bottle and winked at her, tears coming from both eyes. "That," he said. "That." Then he licked his lips. "*That* is what kills the worm that haunts us."

"Roberto," Maria said and came over to him, still holding the bottle. "Are you ready to eat?"

"Is it ready?"

"It is ready when you wish it."

"Have the others eaten?"

"All except you, Anselmo and Fernando."

"Let us eat then," he told her. "And thou?"

"Afterwards with Pilar."

"Eat now with us."

"No. It would not be well."

"Come on and eat. In my country a man does not eat before his woman."

"That is thy country. Here it is better to eat after."

"Eat with him," Pablo said, looking up from the table. "Eat with him. Drink with him. Sleep with him. Die with him. Follow the customs of his country."

"Are you drunk?" Robert Jordan said, standing in front of Pablo. The dirty, stubble-faced man looked at him happily.

"Yes," Pablo said. "Where is thy country, *Inglés,* where the women eat with the men?"

"In *Estados Unidos* in the state of Montana."

"Is it there that the men wear skirts as do the women?"

"No. That is in Scotland."

"But listen," Pablo said. "When you wear skirts like that, *Inglés*——"

"I don't wear them," Robert Jordan said.

"When you are wearing those skirts," Pablo went on, "what do you wear under them?"

"I don't know what the Scotch wear," Robert Jordan said. "I've wondered myself."

"Not the *Escoceses,*" Pablo said. "Who cares about the *Escoceses?* Who cares about anything with a name as rare as that? Not me. I don't care. You, I say, *Inglés.* You. What do you wear under your skirts in your country?"

"Twice I have told you that we do not wear skirts," Robert Jordan said. "Neither drunk nor in joke."

"But under your skirts," Pablo insisted. "Since it is well known that you wear skirts. Even the soldiers. I have seen photographs and also I have seen them in the Circus of Price. What do you wear under your skirts, *Inglés?*"

"*Los cojones,*" Robert Jordan said.

Anselmo laughed and so did the others who were listening; all except Fernando. The sound of the word, of the gross word spoken before the women, was offensive to him.

"Well, that is normal," Pablo said. "But it seems to me that with enough *cojones* you would not wear skirts."

"Don't let him get started again, *Inglés,*" the flat-faced man with the broken nose who was called Primitivo said. "He is drunk. Tell me, what do they raise in your country?"

"Cattle and sheep," Robert Jordan said. "Much grain also and beans. And also much beets for sugar."

The three were at the table now and the others sat close by except Pablo, who sat by himself in front of a bowl of the wine. It was the same stew as the night before and Robert Jordan ate it hungrily.

"In your country there are mountains? With that name surely there are mountains," Primitivo asked politely to make conversation. He was embarrassed at the drunkenness of Pablo.

"Many mountains and very high."

"And are there good pastures?"

"Excellent; high pasture in the summer in forests controlled by the government. Then in the fall the cattle are brought down to the lower ranges."

"Is the land there owned by the peasants?"

"Most land is owned by those who farm it. Originally the land was owned by the state and by living on it and declaring the intention of improving it, a man could obtain a title to a hundred and fifty hectares."

"Tell me how this is done," Agustín asked. "That is an agrarian reform which means something."

Robert Jordan explained the process of homesteading. He had never thought of it before as an agrarian reform.

"That is magnificent," Primitivo said. "Then you have a communism in your country?"

"No. That is done under the Republic."

"For me," Agustín said, "everything can be done under the Republic. I see no need for other form of government."

"Do you have no big proprietors?" Andrés asked.

"Many."

"Then there must be abuses."

"Certainly. There are many abuses."

"But you will do away with them?"

"We try to more and more. But there are many abuses still."

"But there are not great estates that must be broken up?"

"Yes. But there are those who believe that taxes will break them up."

"How?"

Robert Jordan, wiping out the stew bowl with bread, explained how the income tax and inheritance tax worked. "But the big estates remain. Also there are taxes on the land," he said.

"But surely the big proprietors and the rich will make a revolution against such taxes. Such taxes appear to me to be revolutionary. They will revolt against the government when they see that they are threatened, exactly as the fascists have done here," Primitivo said.

"It is possible."

"Then you will have to fight in your country as we fight here."

"Yes, we will have to fight."

"But are there not many fascists in your country?"

"There are many who do not know they are fascists but will find it out when the time comes."

"But you cannot destroy them until they rebel?"

"No," Robert Jordan said. "We cannot destroy them. But we can educate the people so that they will fear fascism and recognize it as it appears and combat it."

"Do you know where there are no fascists?" Andrés asked.

"Where?"

"In the town of Pablo," Andrés said and grinned.

"You know what was done in that village?" Primitivo asked Robert Jordan.

"Yes. I have heard the story."

"From Pilar?"

"Yes."

"You could not hear all of it from the woman," Pablo said heavily. "Because she did not see the end of it because she fell from a chair outside of the window."

"You tell him what happened then," Pilar said. "Since I know not the story, let you tell it."

"Nay," Pablo said. "I have never told it."

"No," Pilar said. "And you will not tell it. And now you wish it had not happened."

"No," Pablo said. "That is not true. And if all had killed the fascists as I did we would not have this war. But I would not have had it happen as it happened."

"Why do you say that?" Primitivo asked him. "Are you changing your politics?"

"No. But it was barbarous," Pablo said. "In those days I was very barbarous."

"And now you are drunk," Pilar said.

"Yes," Pablo said. "With your permission."

"I liked you better when you were barbarous," the woman said. "Of all men the drunkard is the foulest. The thief when he is not stealing is like another. The extortioner does not practise in the home. The murderer when he is at home can wash his hands. But the drunkard stinks and vomits in his own bed and dissolves his organs in alcohol."

"You are a woman and you do not understand," Pablo said equably. "I am drunk on wine and I would be happy except for those people I have killed. All of them fill me with sorrow." He shook his head lugubriously.

"Give him some of that which Sordo brought," Pilar said. "Give him something to animate him. He is becoming too sad to bear."

"If I could restore them to life, I would," Pablo said.

"Go and obscenity thyself," Agustín said to him. "What sort of place is this?"

"I would bring them all back to life," Pablo said sadly. "Every one."

"Thy mother," Agustín shouted at him. "Stop talking like this or get out. Those were fascists you killed."

"You heard me," Pablo said. "I would restore them all to life."

"And then you would walk on the water," Pilar said. "In my life I have never seen such a man. Up until yesterday you preserved some remnants of manhood. And today there is not enough of you left to make a sick kitten. Yet you are happy in your soddenness."

"We should have killed all or none," Pablo nodded his head. "All or none."

"Listen, *Inglés*," Agustín said. "How did you happen to come to Spain? Pay no attention to Pablo. He is drunk."

"I came first twelve years ago to study the country and the language," Robert Jordan said. "I teach Spanish in a university."

"You look very little like a professor," Primitivo said.

"He has no beard," Pablo said. "Look at him. He has no beard."

"Are you truly a professor?"

"An instructor."

"But you teach?"

"Yes."

"But why Spanish?" Andrés asked. "Would it not be easier to teach English since you are English?"

"He speaks Spanish as we do," Anselmo said. "Why should he not teach Spanish?"

"Yes. But it is, in a way, presumptuous for a foreigner to teach Spanish," Fernando said. "I mean nothing against you, Don Roberto."

"He's a false professor," Pablo said, very pleased with himself. "He hasn't got a beard."

"Surely you know English better," Fernando said. "Would it not be better and easier and clearer to teach English?"

"He doesn't teach it to Spaniards—" Pilar started to intervene.

"I should hope not," Fernando said.

"Let me finish, you mule," Pilar said to him. "He teaches Spanish to Americans. North Americans."

"Can they not speak Spanish?" Fernando asked. "South Americans can."

"Mule," Pilar said. "He teaches Spanish to North Americans who speak English."

"Still and all I think it would be easier for him to teach English if that is what he speaks," Fernando said.

"Can't you hear he speaks Spanish?" Pilar shook her head hopelessly at Robert Jordan.

"Yes. But with an accent."

"Of where?" Robert Jordan asked.

"Of Estremadura," Fernando said primly.

"Oh my mother," Pilar said. "What a people!"

"It is possible," Robert Jordan said. "I have come here from there."

"As he well knows," Pilar said. "You old maid," she turned to Fernando. "Have you had enough to eat?"

"I could eat more if there is a sufficient quantity," Fernando told her. "And do not think that I wish to say anything against you, Don Roberto——"

"Milk," Agustín said simply. "And milk again. Do we make the revolution in order to say Don Roberto to a comrade?"

"For me the revolution is so that all will say Don to all," Fernando said. "Thus should it be under the Republic."

"Milk," Agustín said. "Black milk."

"And I still think it would be easier and clearer for Don Roberto to teach English."

"Don Roberto has no beard," Pablo said. "He is a false professor."

"What do you mean, I have no beard?" Robert Jordan said. "What's this?" He stroked his chin and his cheeks where the three-day growth made a blond stubble.

"Not a beard," Pablo said. He shook his head. "That's not a beard." He was almost jovial now. "He's a false professor."

"I obscenity in the milk of all," Agustín said, "if it does not seem like a lunatic asylum here."

"You should drink," Pablo said to him. "To me everything appears normal. Except the lack of beard of Don Roberto."

Maria ran her hand over Robert Jordan's cheek.

"He has a beard," she said to Pablo.

"You should know," Pablo said and Robert Jordan looked at him.

I don't think he is so drunk, Robert Jordan thought. No, not so drunk. And I think I had better watch myself.

"Thou," he said to Pablo. "Do you think this snow will last?"

"What do you think?"

"I asked you."

"Ask another," Pablo told him. "I am not thy service of information. You have a paper from thy service of information. Ask the woman. She commands."

"I asked thee."

"Go and obscenity thyself," Pablo told him. "Thee and the woman and the girl."

"He is drunk," Primitivo said. "Pay him no heed, *Inglés.*"

"I do not think he is so drunk," Robert Jordan said.

Maria was standing behind him and Robert Jordan saw Pablo watching her over his shoulder. The small eyes, like a boar's, were watching her out of the round, stubble-covered head and Robert Jordan thought: I have known many killers in this war and some before and they were all different; there is no common trait nor feature; nor any such thing as the criminal type; but Pablo is certainly not handsome.

"I don't believe you can drink," he said to Pablo. "Nor that you're drunk."

"I am drunk," Pablo said with dignity. "To drink is nothing. It is to be drunk that is important. *Estoy muy borracho.*"

"I doubt it," Robert Jordan told him. "Cowardly, yes."

It was so quiet in the cave, suddenly, that he could hear the hissing noise the wood made burning on the hearth where Pilar cooked. He heard the sheepskin crackle as he rested his weight on his feet.

He thought he could almost hear the snow falling outside. He could not, but he could hear the silence where it fell.

I'd like to kill him and have it over with, Robert Jordan was thinking. I don't know what he is going to do, but it is nothing good. Day after tomorrow is the bridge and this man is bad and he constitutes a danger to the success of the whole enterprise. Come on. Let us get it over with.

Pablo grinned at him and put one finger up and wiped it across his throat. He shook his head that turned only a little each way on his thick, short neck.

"Nay, *Inglés,*" he said. "Do not provoke me." He looked at Pilar and said to her, "It is not thus that you get rid of me."

"*Sinverguenza,*" Robert Jordan said to him, committed now in his own mind to the action. "*Cobarde.*"

"It is very possible," Pablo said. "But I am not to be provoked. Take something to drink, *Inglés,* and signal to the woman it was not successful."

"Shut thy mouth," Robert Jordan said. "I provoke thee for myself."

"It is not worth the trouble," Pablo told him. "I do not provoke."

"Thou art a *bicho raro,*" Robert Jordan said, not wanting to let it go; not wanting to have it fail for the second time; knowing as he spoke that this had all been gone through before; having that feeling that he was playing a part from memory of something that he had read or had dreamed, feeling it all moving in a circle.

"Very rare, yes," Pablo said. "Very rare and very drunk. To your health, *Inglés.*" He dipped a cup in the wine bowl and held it up. "*Salud y cojones.*"

He's rare, all right, Robert Jordan thought, and smart, and very complicated. He could no longer hear the fire for the sound of his own breathing.

"Here's to you," Robert Jordan said, and dipped a cup into the wine. Betrayal wouldn't amount to anything without all these pledges, he thought. Pledge up. "*Salud,*" he said. "*Salud* and *Salud* again," you *salud,* he thought. *Salud,* you *salud.*

"Don Roberto," Pablo said heavily.

"Don Pablo," Robert Jordan said.

"You're no professor," Pablo said, "because you haven't got a beard.

And also to do away with me you have to assassinate me and, for this, you have not *cojones*."

He was looking at Robert Jordan with his mouth closed so that his lips made a tight line, like the mouth of a fish, Robert Jordan thought. With that head it is like one of those porcupine fish that swallow air and swell up after they are caught.

"*Salud*, Pablo," Robert Jordan said and raised the cup up and drank from it. "I am learning much from thee."

"I am teaching the professor," Pablo nodded his head. "Come on, Don Roberto, we will be friends."

"We are friends already," Robert Jordan said.

"But now we will be good friends."

"We are good friends already."

"I'm going to get out of here," Agustín said. "Truly, it is said that we must eat a ton of it in this life but I have twenty-five pounds of it stuck in each of my ears this minute."

"What is the matter, *negro?*" Pablo said to him. "Do you not like to see friendship between Don Roberto and me?"

"Watch your mouth about calling me *negro*." Agustín went over to him and stood in front of Pablo holding his hands low.

"So you are called," Pablo said.

"Not by thee."

"Well, then, *blanco*——"

"Nor that, either."

"What are you then, Red?"

"Yes. Red. *Rojo*. With the Red star of the army and in favor of the Republic. And my name is Agustín."

"What a patriotic man," Pablo said. "Look, *Inglés*, what an exemplary patriot."

Agustín hit him hard across the mouth with his left hand, bringing it forward in a slapping, backhand sweep. Pablo sat there. The corners of his mouth were wine-stained and his expression did not change, but Robert Jordan watched his eyes narrow, as a cat's pupils close to vertical slits in a strong light.

"Nor this," Pablo said. "Do not count on this, woman." He turned his head toward Pilar. "I am not provoked."

Agustín hit him again. This time he hit him on the mouth with his closed fist. Robert Jordan was holding his pistol in his hand under the table. He had shoved the safety catch off and he pushed Maria away with his left hand. She moved a little way and he pushed her hard in the ribs with his left hand again to make her get really away. She was gone now and he saw her from the corner of his eye, slipping along the side of the cave toward the fire and now Robert Jordan watched Pablo's face.

The round-headed man sat staring at Agustín from his flat little eyes. The pupils were even smaller now. He licked his lips then, put up an arm and wiped his mouth with the back of his hand, looked down and saw the blood on his hand. He ran his tongue over his lips, then spat.

"Nor that," he said. "I am not a fool. I do not provoke."

"*Cabrón,*" Agustín said.

"You should know," Pablo said. "You know the woman."

Agustín hit him again hard in the mouth and Pablo laughed at him, showing the yellow, bad, broken teeth in the reddened line of his mouth.

"Leave it alone," Pablo said and reached with a cup to scoop some wine from the bowl. "Nobody here has *cojones* to kill me and this of the hands is silly."

"*Cobarde,*" Agustín said.

"Nor words either," Pablo said and made a swishing noise rinsing the wine in his mouth. He spat on the floor. "I am far past words."

Agustín stood there looking down at him and cursed him, speaking slowly, clearly, bitterly and contemptuously and cursing as steadily as though he were dumping manure on a field, lifting it with a dung fork out of a wagon.

"Nor of those," Pablo said. "Leave it, Agustín. And do not hit me more. Thou wilt injure thy hands."

Agustín turned from him and went to the door.

"Do not go out," Pablo said. "It is snowing outside. Make thyself comfortable in here."

"And thou! Thou!" Agustín turned from the door and spoke to him, putting all his contempt in the single, "*Tu.*"

"Yes, me," said Pablo. "I will be alive when you are dead."

He dipped up another cup of wine and raised it to Robert Jordan. "To the professor," he said. Then turned to Pilar. "To the Señora Commander." Then toasted them all, "To all the illusioned ones."

Agustín walked over to him and, striking quickly with the side of his hand, knocked the cup out of his hand.

"That is a waste," Pablo said. "That is silly."

Agustín said something vile to him.

"No," Pablo said, dipping up another cup. "I am drunk, seest thou? When I am not drunk I do not talk. You have never heard me talk much. But an intelligent man is sometimes forced to be drunk to spend his time with fools."

"Go and obscenity in the milk of thy cowardice," Pilar said to him. "I know too much about thee and thy cowardice."

"How the woman talks," Pablo said. "I will be going out to see the horses."

"Go and befoul them," Agustín said. "Is not that one of thy customs?"

"No," Pablo said and shook his head. He was taking down his big blanket cape from the wall and he looked at Agustín. "Thou," he said, "and thy violence."

"What do you go to do with the horses?" Agustín said.

"Look to them," Pablo said.

"Befoul them," Agustín said. "Horse lover."

"I care for them very much," Pablo said. "Even from behind they are handsomer and have more sense than these people. Divert yourselves," he said and grinned. "Speak to them of the bridge, *Inglés*. Explain their duties in the attack. Tell them how to conduct the retreat. Where will you take them, *Inglés,* after the bridge? Where will you take your patriots? I have thought of it all day while I have been drinking."

"What have you thought?" Agustín asked.

"What have I thought?" Pablo said and moved his tongue around exploringly inside his lips. *"Qué te importa,* what have I thought."

"Say it," Agustín said to him.

"Much," Pablo said. He pulled the blanket coat over his head, the roundness of his head protruding now from the dirty yellow folds of the blanket. "I have thought much."

"What?" Agustín said. "What?"

"I have thought you are a group of illusioned people," Pablo said. "Led by a woman with her brains between her thighs and a foreigner who comes to destroy you."

"Get out," Pilar shouted at him. "Get out and fist yourself into the snow. Take your bad milk out of here, you horse exhausted *maricón.*"

"Thus one talks," Agustín said admiringly, but absent-mindedly. He was worried.

"I go," said Pablo. "But I will be back shortly." He lifted the blanket over the door of the cave and stepped out. Then from the door he called, "It's still falling, *Inglés.*"

CHAPTER SEVENTEEN

THE ONLY noise in the cave now was the hissing from the hearth where snow was falling through the hole in the roof onto the coals of the fire.

"Pilar," Fernando said. "Is there more of the stew?"

"Oh, shut up," the woman said. But Maria took Fernando's bowl over to the big pot set back from the edge of the fire and ladled into it. She brought it over to the table and set it down and then patted Fernando on the shoulder as he bent to eat. She stood for a moment beside him, her hand on his shoulder. But Fernando did not look up. He was devoting himself to the stew.

Agustín stood beside the fire. The others were seated. Pilar sat at the table opposite Robert Jordan.

"Now, *Inglés,*" she said, "you have seen how he is."

"What will he do?" Robert Jordan asked.

"Anything," the woman looked down at the table. "Anything. He is capable of doing anything."

"Where is the automatic rifle?" Robert Jordan asked.

"There in the corner wrapped in the blanket," Primitivo said. "Do you want it?"

"Later," Robert Jordan said. "I wished to know where it is."

"It is there," Primitivo said. "I brought it in and I have wrapped it in my blanket to keep the action dry. The pans are in that sack."

"He would not do that," Pilar said. "He would not do anything with the *máquina.*"

"I thought you said he would do anything."

"He might," she said. "But he has no practice with the *máquina.* He could toss in a bomb. That is more his style."

"It is an idiocy and a weakness not to have killed him," the gypsy said. He had taken no part in any of the talk all evening. "Last night Roberto should have killed him."

"Kill him," Pilar said. Her big face was dark and tired looking. "I am for it now."

"I was against it," Agustín said. He stood in front of the fire, his long arms hanging by his sides, his cheeks, stubble-shadowed below the cheekbones, hollow in the firelight. "Now I am for it," he said. "He is poisonous now and he would like to see us all destroyed."

"Let all speak," Pilar said and her voice was tired. "Thou, Andrés?"

"*Matarlo,*" the brother with the dark hair growing far down in the point on his forehead said and nodded his head.

"Eladio?"

"Equally," the other brother said. "To me he seems to constitute a great danger. And he serves for nothing."

"Primitivo?"

"Equally."

"Fernando?"

"Could we not hold him as a prisoner?" Fernando asked.

"Who would look after a prisoner?" Primitivo said. "It would take two men to look after a prisoner and what would we do with him in the end?"

"We could sell him to the fascists," the gypsy said.

"None of that," Agustín said. "None of that filthiness."

"It was only an idea," Rafael, the gypsy, said. "It seems to me that the *facciosos* would be happy to have him."

"Leave it alone," Agustín said. "That is filthy."

"No filthier than Pablo," the gypsy justified himself.

"One filthiness does not justify another," Agustín said. "Well, that is all. Except for the old man and the *Inglés.*"

"They are not in it," Pilar said. "He has not been their leader."

"One moment," Fernando said. "I have not finished."

"Go ahead," Pilar said. "Talk until he comes back. Talk until he rolls a hand grenade under that blanket and blows this all up. Dynamite and all."

"I think that you exaggerate, Pilar," Fernando said. "I do not think that he has any such conception."

"I do not think so either," Agustín said. "Because that would blow the wine up too and he will be back in a little while to the wine."

"Why not turn him over to El Sordo and let El Sordo sell him to the fascists?" Rafael suggested. "You could blind him and he would be easy to handle."

"Shut up," Pilar said. "I feel something very justified against thee too when thou talkest."

"The fascists would pay nothing for him anyway," Primitivo said. "Such things have been tried by others and they pay nothing. They will shoot thee too."

"I believe that blinded he could be sold for something," Rafael said.

"Shut up," Pilar said. "Speak of blinding again and you can go with the other."

"But, he, Pablo, blinded the *guardia civil* who was wounded," the gypsy insisted. "You have forgotten that?"

"Close thy mouth," Pilar said to him. She was embarrassed before Robert Jordan by this talk of blinding.

"I have not been allowed to finish," Fernando interrupted.

"Finish," Pilar told him. "Go on. Finish."

"Since it is impractical to hold Pablo as a prisoner," Fernando commenced, "and since it is repugnant to offer him——"

"Finish," Pilar said. "For the love of God, finish."

"——in any class of negotiation," Fernando proceeded calmly, "I am agreed that it is perhaps best that he should be eliminated in order that the operations projected should be insured of the maximum possibility of success."

Pilar looked at the little man, shook her head, bit her lips and said nothing.

"That is my opinion," Fernando said. "I believe we are justified in believing that he constitutes a danger to the Republic——"

"Mother of God," Pilar said. "Even here one man can make a bureaucracy with his mouth."

"Both from his own words and his recent actions," Fernando continued. "And while he is deserving of gratitude for his actions in the early part of the movement and up until the most recent time——"

Pilar had walked over to the fire. Now she came up to the table.

"Fernando," Pilar said quietly and handed a bowl to him. "Take this stew please in all formality and fill thy mouth with it and talk no more. We are in possession of thy opinion."

"But, how then—" Primitivo asked and paused without completing the sentence.

"*Estoy listo,*" Robert Jordan said. "I am ready to do it. Since you are all decided that it should be done it is a service that I can do."

What's the matter? he thought. From listening to him I am beginning to talk like Fernando. That language must be infectious. French, the language of diplomacy. Spanish, the language of bureaucracy.

"No," Maria said. "No."

"This is none of thy business," Pilar said to the girl. "Keep thy mouth shut."

"I will do it tonight," Robert Jordan said.

He saw Pilar looking at him, her fingers on her lips. She was looking toward the door.

The blanket fastened across the opening of the cave was lifted and Pablo put his head in. He grinned at them all, pushed under the blanket and then turned and fastened it again. He turned around and stood there, then pulled the blanket cape over his head and shook the snow from it.

"You were speaking of me?" he addressed them all. "I am interrupting?"

No one answered him and he hung the cape on a peg in the wall and walked over to the table.

"*Qué tal?*" he asked and picked up his cup which had stood empty on the table and dipped it into the wine bowl. "There is no wine," he said to Maria. "Go draw some from the skin."

Maria picked up the bowl and went over to the dusty, heavily distended, black-tarred wineskin that hung neck down from the wall and unscrewed the plug from one of the legs enough so that the wine squirted from the edge of the plug into the bowl. Pablo watched her kneeling, holding the bowl up and watched the light red wine flooding into the bowl so fast that it made a whirling motion as it filled it.

"Be careful," he said to her. "The wine's below the chest now."

No one said anything.

"I drank from the belly-button to the chest today," Pablo said. "It's a day's work. What's the matter with you all? Have you lost your tongues?"

No one said anything at all.

"Screw it up, Maria," Pablo said. "Don't let it spill."

"There'll be plenty of wine," Agustín said. "You'll be able to be drunk."

"One has encountered his tongue," Pablo said and nodded to Agustín. "Felicitations. I thought you'd been struck dumb."

"By what?" Agustín asked.

"By my entry."

"Thinkest thou that thy entry carries importance?"

He's working himself up to it, maybe, Robert Jordan thought. Maybe Agustín is going to do it. He certainly hates him enough. I don't hate him, he thought. No, I don't hate him. He is disgusting but I do not hate him. Though that blinding business puts him in a special class. Still this is their war. But he is certainly nothing to have around for the next two days. I am going to keep away out of it, he thought. I made a fool of myself with him once tonight and I am perfectly willing to liquidate him. But I am not going to fool with him beforehand. And there are not going to be any shooting matches or monkey business in here with that dynamite around either. Pablo thought of that, of course. And did you think of it, he said to himself? No, you did not and neither did Agustín. You deserve whatever happens to you, he thought.

"Agustín," he said.

"What?" Agustín looked up sullenly and turned his head away from Pablo.

"I wish to speak to thee," Robert Jordan said.

"Later."

"Now," Robert Jordan said. *"Por favor."*

Robert Jordan had walked to the opening of the cave and Pablo followed him with his eyes. Agustín, tall and sunken cheeked, stood up and came over to him. He moved reluctantly and contemptuously.

"Thou hast forgotten what is in the sacks?" Robert Jordan said to him, speaking so low that it could not be heard.

"Milk!" Agustín said. "One becomes accustomed and one forgets."

"I, too, forgot."

"Milk!" Agustín said. *"Leche!* What fools we are." He swung back loose-jointedly to the table and sat down. "Have a drink, Pablo, old boy," he said. "How were the horses?"

"Very good," Pablo said. "And it is snowing less."

"Do you think it will stop?"

"Yes," Pablo said. "It is thinning now and there are small, hard pellets. The wind will blow but the snow is going. The wind has changed."

"Do you think it will clear tomorrow?" Robert Jordan asked him.

"Yes," Pablo said. "I believe it will be cold and clear. This wind is shifting."

Look at him, Robert Jordan thought. Now he is friendly. He has shifted like the wind. He has the face and the body of a pig and I know he is many times a murderer and yet he has the sensitivity of a good aneroid. Yes, he thought, and the pig is a very intelligent animal, too. Pablo has hatred for us, or perhaps it is only for our projects, and pushes his hatred with insults to the point where you are ready to do away with him and when he sees that this point has been reached he drops it and starts all new and clean again.

"We will have good weather for it, *Inglés*," Pablo said to Robert Jordan.

"We," Pilar said. *"We?"*

"Yes, we," Pablo grinned at her and drank some of the wine. "Why not? I thought it over while I was outside. Why should we not agree?"

"In what?" the woman asked. "In what now?"

"In all," Pablo said to her. "In this of the bridge. I am with thee now."

"You are with us now?" Agustín said to him. "After what you have said?"

"Yes," Pablo told him. "With the change of the weather I am with thee."

Agustín shook his head. "The weather," he said and shook his head again. "And after me hitting thee in the face?"

"Yes," Pablo grinned at him and ran his fingers over his lips. "After that too."

Robert Jordan was watching Pilar. She was looking at Pablo as at some strange animal. On her face there was still a shadow of the expression the mention of the blinding had put there. She shook her head as though to be rid of that, then tossed it back. "Listen," she said to Pablo.

"Yes, woman."

"What passes with thee?"

"Nothing," Pablo said. "I have changed my opinion. Nothing more."

"You were listening at the door," she told him.

"Yes," he said. "But I could hear nothing."

"You fear that we will kill thee."

"No," he told her and looked at her over the wine cup. "I do not fear that. You know that."

"Well, what passes with thee?" Agustín said. "One moment you are drunk and putting your mouth on all of us and disassociating yourself from the work in hand and speaking of our death in a dirty manner and insulting the women and opposing that which should be done——"

"I was drunk," Pablo told him.

"And now——"

"I am not drunk," Pablo said. "And I have changed my mind."

"Let the others trust thee. I do not," Agustín said.

"Trust me or not," Pablo said. "But there is no one who can take thee to Gredos as I can."

"Gredos?"

"It is the only place to go after this of the bridge."

Robert Jordan, looking at Pilar, raised his hand on the side away from Pablo and tapped his right ear questioningly.

The woman nodded. Then nodded again. She said something to Maria and the girl came over to Robert Jordan's side.

"She says, 'Of course he heard,'" Maria said in Robert Jordan's ear.

"Then Pablo," Fernando said judicially. "Thou art with us now and in favor of this of the bridge?"

"Yes, man," Pablo said. He looked Fernando squarely in the eye and nodded.

"In truth?" Primitivo asked.

"*De veras,*" Pablo told him.

"And you think it can be successful?" Fernando asked. "You now have confidence?"

"Why not?" Pablo said. "Haven't you confidence?"

"Yes," Fernando said. "But I always have confidence."

"I'm going to get out of here," Agustín said.

"It is cold outside," Pablo told him in a friendly tone.

"Maybe," Agustín said. "But I can't stay any longer in this *manicomio*."

"Do not call this cave an insane asylum," Fernando said.

"A *manicomio* for criminal lunatics," Agustín said. "And I'm getting out before I'm crazy, too."

CHAPTER EIGHTEEN

IT IS LIKE a merry-go-round, Robert Jordan thought. Not a merry-go-round that travels fast, and with a calliope for music, and the children ride on cows with gilded horns, and there are rings to catch with sticks, and there is the blue, gas-flare-lit early dark of the Avenue du Maine, with fried fish sold from the next stall, and a wheel of fortune turning with the leather flaps slapping against the posts of the numbered compartments, and the packages of lump sugar piled in pyramids for prizes. No, it is not that kind of a merry-go-round; although the people are waiting, like the men in caps and the women in knitted sweaters, their heads bare in the gaslight and their hair shining, who stand in front of the wheel of fortune as it spins. Yes, those are the people. But this is another wheel. This is like a wheel that goes up and around.

It has been around twice now. It is a vast wheel, set at an angle, and each time it goes around and then is back to where it starts. One side is higher than the other and the sweep it makes lifts you back and down to where you started. There are no prizes either, he thought, and no one would choose to ride this wheel. You ride it each time and make the turn with no intention ever to have mounted. There is only one turn; one large, elliptical, rising and falling turn and you are back where you have started. We are back again now, he thought, and nothing is settled.

It was warm in the cave and the wind had dropped outside. Now he was sitting at the table with his notebook in front of him figuring all the technical part of the bridge-blowing. He drew three sketches, figured his formulas, marked the method of blowing with two drawings as clearly as a kindergarten project so that Anselmo could complete it in case anything should happen to himself during the process of the demolition. He finished these sketches and studied them.

Maria sat beside him and looked over his shoulder while he worked. He was conscious of Pablo across the table and of the others talking and playing cards and he smelled the odors of the cave which had changed now from those of the meal and the cooking to the fire smoke and man smell, the tobacco, red-wine and brassy, stale body smell, and when Maria, watching him finishing a drawing, put her hand on the table he picked it up with his left hand and lifted it to his face and smelled the coarse soap and water freshness from her washing of the dishes. He laid her hand down without looking at her and went on working and he could not see her blush. She let her hand lie there, close to his, but he did not lift it again.

Now he had finished the demolition project and he took a new page of the notebook and commenced to write out the operation orders. He was thinking clearly and well on these and what he wrote pleased him. He wrote two pages in the notebook and read them over carefully.

I think that is all, he said to himself. It is perfectly clear and I do not think there are any holes in it. The two posts will be destroyed and the bridge will be blown according to Golz's orders and that is all of my responsibility. All of this business of Pablo is something with which I should never have been saddled and it will be solved one way or another. There will be Pablo or there will be no Pablo. I care nothing about it either way. But I am not going to get on that wheel again. Twice I have been on that wheel and twice it has gone around and come back to where it started and I am taking no more rides on it.

He shut the notebook and looked up at Maria. *"Hola, guapa,"* he said to her. "Did you make anything out of all that?"

"No, Roberto," the girl said and put her hand on his hand that still held the pencil. "Have you finished?"

"Yes. Now it is all written out and ordered."

"What have you been doing, *Inglés?"* Pablo asked from across the table. His eyes were bleary again.

Robert Jordan looked at him closely. Stay off that wheel, he said to himself. Don't step on that wheel. I think it is going to start to swing again.

"Working on the problem of the bridge," he said civilly.

"How is it?" asked Pablo.

"Very good," Robert Jordan said. "All very good."

"I have been working on the problem of the retreat," Pablo

said and Robert Jordan looked at his drunken pig eyes and at the wine bowl. The wine bowl was nearly empty.

Keep off the wheel, he told himself. He is drinking again. Sure. But don't you get on that wheel now. Wasn't Grant supposed to be drunk a good part of the time during the Civil War? Certainly he was. I'll bet Grant would be furious at the comparison if he could see Pablo. Grant was a cigar smoker, too. Well, he would have to see about getting Pablo a cigar. That was what that face really needed to complete it; a half chewed cigar. Where could he get Pablo a cigar?

"How does it go?" Robert Jordan asked politely.

"Very well," Pablo said and nodded his head heavily and judiciously. *"Muy bien."*

"You've thought up something?" Agustín asked from where they were playing cards.

"Yes," Pablo said. "Various things."

"Where did you find them? In that bowl?" Agustín demanded.

"Perhaps," Pablo said. "Who knows? Maria, fill the bowl, will you, please?"

"In the wineskin itself there should be some fine ideas," Agustín turned back to the card game. "Why don't you crawl in and look for them inside the skin?"

"Nay," said Pablo equably. "I search for them in the bowl."

He is not getting on the wheel either, Robert Jordan thought. It must be revolving by itself. I suppose you cannot ride that wheel too long. That is probably quite a deadly wheel. I'm glad we are off of it. It was making me dizzy there a couple of times. But it is the thing that drunkards and those who are truly mean or cruel ride until they die. It goes around and up and the swing is never quite the same and then it comes around down. Let it swing, he thought. They will not get me onto it again. No sir, General Grant, I am off that wheel.

Pilar was sitting by the fire, her chair turned so that she could see over the shoulders of the two card players who had their backs to her. She was watching the game.

Here it is the shift from deadliness to normal family life that is the strangest, Robert Jordan thought. It is when the damned wheel comes down that it gets you. But I am off that wheel, he thought. And nobody is going to get me onto it again.

Two days ago I never knew that Pilar, Pablo nor the rest existed, he thought. There was no such thing as Maria in the world. It was certainly a much simpler world. I had instructions from Golz that were perfectly clear and seemed perfectly possible to carry out although they presented certain difficulties and involved certain consequences. After we blew the bridge I expected either to get back to the lines or not get back and if we got back I was going to ask for some time in Madrid. No one has any leave in this war but I am sure I could get two or three days in Madrid.

In Madrid I wanted to buy some books, to go to the Florida Hotel and get a room and to have a hot bath, he thought. I was going to send Luis the porter out for a bottle of absinthe if he could locate one at the Mantequerías Leonesas or at any of the places off the Gran Via and I was going to lie in bed and read after the bath and drink a couple of absinthes and then I was going to call up Gaylord's and see if I could come up there and eat.

He did not want to eat at the Gran Via because the food was no good really and you had to get there on time or whatever there was of it would be gone. Also there were too many newspaper men there he knew and he did not want to have to keep his mouth shut. He wanted to drink the absinthes and to feel like talking and then go up to Gaylord's and eat with Karkov, where they had good food and real beer, and find out what was going on in the war.

He had not liked Gaylord's, the hotel in Madrid the Russians had taken over, when he first went there because it seemed too luxurious and the food was too good for a besieged city and the talk too cynical for a war. But I corrupted very easily, he thought. Why should you not have as good food as could be organized when you came back from something like this? And the talk that he had thought of as cynicism when he had first heard it had turned out to be much too true. This will be something to tell at Gaylord's, he thought, when this is over. Yes, when this is over.

Could you take Maria to Gaylord's? No. You couldn't. But you could leave her in the hotel and she could take a hot bath and be there when you came back from Gaylord's. Yes, you could do that and after you had told Karkov about her, you could bring her later because they would be curious about her and want to see her.

Maybe you wouldn't go to Gaylord's at all. You could eat early at the Gran Via and hurry back to the Florida. But you knew you would go to Gaylord's because you wanted to see all that again; you wanted to eat that food again and you wanted to see all the comfort of it and the luxury of it after this. Then you would come back to the Florida and there Maria would be. Sure, she would be there after this was over. After this was over. Yes, after this was over. If he did this well he would rate a meal at Gaylord's.

Gaylord's was the place where you met famous peasant and worker Spanish commanders who had sprung to arms from the people at the start of the war without any previous military training and found that many of them spoke Russian. That had been the first big disillusion to him a few months back and he had started to be cynical to himself about it. But when he realized how it happened it was all right. They *were* peasants and workers. They had been active in the 1934 revolution and had to flee the country when it failed and in Russia they had sent them to the military academy and to the Lenin Institute the Comintern maintained so they would be ready to fight the next time and have the necessary military education to command.

The Comintern had educated them there. In a revolution you could not admit to outsiders who helped you nor that any one knew more than he was supposed to know. He had learned that. If a thing was right fundamentally the lying was not supposed to matter. There was a lot of lying though. He did not care for the lying at first. He hated it. Then later he had come to like it. It was part of being an insider but it was a very corrupting business.

It was at Gaylord's that you learned that Valentín Gonzalez, called El Campesino or The Peasant, had never been a peasant but was an ex-sergeant in the Spanish Foreign Legion who had deserted and fought with Abd el Krim. That was all right, too. Why shouldn't he be? You had to have these peasant leaders quickly in this sort of war and a real peasant leader might be a little too much like Pablo. You couldn't wait for the real Peasant Leader to arrive and he might have too many peasant characteristics when he did. So you had to manufacture one. At that, from what he had seen of Campesino, with his black beard, his thick negroid lips, and his feverish, staring eyes, he thought he might give almost as much trouble as a real peasant leader. The last time he had seen him he seemed to have gotten to believe his own publicity and think he was a peasant. He was a brave, tough man; no braver in the world. But God, how he talked too much. And when he was excited he would say anything no matter what the consequences of his indiscretion. And those consequences had been many already. He was a wonderful Brigade Commander though in a situation where it looked as though everything was lost. He never knew when everything was lost and if it was, he would fight out of it.

At Gaylord's, too, you met the simple stonemason, Enrique Lister from Galicia, who now commanded a division and who talked Russian, too. And you met the cabinet worker, Juan Modesto from Andalucía who had just been given an Army Corps. He never learned his Russian in Puerto de Santa Maria although he might have if they had a Berlitz School there that the cabinet makers went to. He was the most trusted of the young soldiers by the Russians because he was a true party man, "a hundred per cent" they said, proud to use the Americanism. He was much more intelligent than Lister or El Campesino.

Sure, Gaylord's was the place you needed to complete your education. It was there you learned how it was all really done instead of how it was supposed to be done. He had only started his education, he thought. He wondered whether he would continue with it long. Gaylord's was good and sound and what he needed. At the start when he had still believed all the nonsense it had come as a shock to him. But now he knew enough to accept the necessity for all the deception and what he learned at Gaylord's only strengthened him in his belief in the things that he did hold to be true. He liked to know how it really was; not how it was supposed to be. There was always lying in a war. But the truth of Lister, Modesto, and El Campesino was much better than the lies and legends. Well, some day they would tell the truth to every one and meantime he was glad there was a Gaylord's for his own learning of it.

Yes, that was where he would go in Madrid after he had bought the books and after he had lain in the hot bath and had a couple of drinks and had read awhile. But that was before Maria had come into all this that he had that plan. All right. They would have two rooms and she could do what she liked while he went up there and he'd come back from Gaylord's to her. She had waited up in the hills all this time. She could wait a little while at the Hotel Florida. They would have three days in Madrid. Three days could be a long time. He'd take her to see the Marx Brothers at the Opera. That had been running for three months now and would certainly be good for three months more. She'd like the Marx Brothers at the Opera, he thought. She'd like that very much.

It was a long way from Gaylord's to this cave though. No, that was not the long way. The long way was going to be from this cave to Gaylord's. Kashkin had taken him there first and he had not liked it. Kashkin had said he should meet Karkov because Karkov wanted to know Americans and because he was the greatest lover of Lope de Vega in the world and thought "Fuente Ovejuna" was the greatest play ever written. Maybe it was at that, but he, Robert Jordan, did not think so.

He had liked Karkov but not the place. Karkov was the most intelligent man he had ever met. Wearing black riding boots, gray breeches, and a gray tunic, with tiny hands and feet, puffily fragile of face and body, with a spitting way of talking through his bad teeth, he looked comic when Robert Jordan first saw him. But he had more brains and more inner dignity and outer insolence and humor than any man that he had ever known.

Gaylord's itself had seemed indecently luxurious and corrupt. But why shouldn't the representatives of a power that governed a sixth of the world have a few comforts? Well, they had them and Robert Jordan had at first been repelled by the whole business and then had accepted it and enjoyed it. Kashkin had made him out to be a hell of a fellow and Karkov had at first been insultingly polite and then, when Robert Jordan had not played at being a hero but had told a story that was really funny and obscenely discreditable to himself, Karkov had shifted from the politeness to a relieved rudeness and then to insolence and they had become friends.

Kashkin had only been tolerated there. There was something

wrong with Kashkin evidently and he was working it out in Spain. They would not tell him what it was but maybe they would now that he was dead. Anyway, he and Karkov had become friends and he had become friends too with the incredibly thin, drawn, dark, loving, nervous, deprived and unbitter woman with a lean, neglected body and dark, gray-streaked hair cut short who was Karkov's wife and who served as an interpreter with the tank corps. He was a friend too of Karkov's mistress, who had cat-eyes, reddish gold hair (sometimes more red; sometimes more gold, depending on the coiffeurs), a lazy sensual body (made to fit well against other bodies), a mouth made to fit other mouths, and a stupid, ambitious and utterly loyal mind. This mistress loved gossip and enjoyed a periodically controlled promiscuity which seemed only to amuse Karkov. Karkov was supposed to have another wife somewhere besides the tank-corps one, maybe two more, but nobody was very sure about that. Robert Jordan liked both the wife he knew and the mistress. He thought he would probably like the other wife, too, if he knew her, if there was one. Karkov had good taste in women.

There were sentries with bayonets downstairs outside the porte-cochere at Gaylord's and tonight it would be the pleasantest and most comfortable place in all of besieged Madrid. He would like to be there tonight instead of here. Though it was all right here, now they had stopped that wheel. And the snow was stopping too.

He would like to show his Maria to Karkov but he could not take her there unless he asked first and he would have to see how he was received after this trip. Golz would be there after this attack was over and if he had done well they would all know it from Golz. Golz would make fun of him, too, about Maria. After what he'd said to him about no girls.

He reached over to the bowl in front of Pablo and dipped up a cup of wine. "With your permission," he said.

Pablo nodded. He is engaged in his military studies, I imagine, Robert Jordan thought. Not seeking the bubble reputation in the cannon's mouth but seeking the solution to the problem in yonder bowl. But you know the bastard must be fairly able to have run this band successfully for as long as he did. Looking at Pablo he wondered what sort of guerilla leader he would have been in the

American Civil War. There were lots of them, he thought. But we know very little about them. Not the Quantrills, nor the Mosbys, nor his own grandfather, but the little ones, the bushwhackers. And about the drinking. Do you suppose Grant really was a drunk? His grandfather always claimed he was. That he was always a little drunk by four o'clock in the afternoon and that before Vicksburg sometimes during the siege he was very drunk for a couple of days. But grandfather claimed that he functioned perfectly normally no matter how much he drank except that sometimes it was very hard to wake him. But if you *could* wake him he was normal.

There wasn't any Grant, nor any Sherman nor any Stonewall Jackson on either side so far in this war. No. Nor any Jeb Stuart either. Nor any Sheridan. It was overrun with McClellans though. The fascists had plenty of McClellans and we had at least three of them.

He had certainly not seen any military geniuses in this war. Not a one. Nor anything resembling one. Kleber, Lucasz, and Hans had done a fine job of their share in the defense of Madrid with the International Brigades and then the old bald, spectacled, conceited, stupid-as-an-owl, unintelligent-in-conversation, brave-and-as-dumb-as-a-bull, propaganda-build-up defender of Madrid, Miaja, had been so jealous of the publicity Kleber received that he had forced the Russians to relieve Kleber of his command and send him to Valencia. Kleber was a good soldier; but limited and he *did* talk too much for the job he had. Golz was a good general and a fine soldier but they always kept him in a subordinate position and never gave him a free hand. This attack was going to be his biggest show so far and Robert Jordan did not like too much what he had heard about the attack. Then there was Gall, the Hungarian, who ought to be shot if you could believe half you heard at Gaylord's. Make it if you can believe ten per cent of what you hear at Gaylord's, Robert Jordan thought.

He wished that he had seen the fighting on the plateau beyond Guadalajara when they beat the Italians. But he had been down in Estremadura then. Hans had told him about it one night in Gaylord's two weeks ago and made him see it all. There was one moment when it was really lost when the Italians had broken the

line near Trijueque and the Twelfth Brigade would have been cut
off if the Torija-Brihuega road had been cut. "But knowing they
were Italians," Hans had said, "we attempted to manœuvre which
would have been unjustifiable against other troops. And it was
successful."

Hans had shown it all to him on his maps of the battle. Hans
carried them around with him in his map case all the time and
still seemed marvelled and happy at the miracle of it. Hans was a
fine soldier and a good companion. Lister's and Modesto's and
Campesino's Spanish troops had all fought well in that battle,
Hans had told him, and that was to be credited to their leaders
and to the discipline they enforced. But Lister and Campesino and
Modesto had been told many of the moves they should make by
their Russian military advisers. They were like students flying a
machine with dual controls which the pilot could take over whenever they made a mistake. Well, this year would show how much
and how well they learned. After a while there would not be dual
controls and then we would see how well they handled divisions
and army corps alone.

They were Communists and they were disciplinarians. The discipline that they would enforce would make good troops. Lister
was murderous in discipline. He was a true fanatic and he had the
complete Spanish lack of respect for life. In a few armies since the
Tartar's first invasion of the West were men executed summarily
for as little reason as they were under his command. But he knew
how to forge a division into a fighting unit. It is one thing to hold
positions. It is another to attack positions and take them and it is
something very different to manœuvre an army in the field,
Robert Jordan thought as he sat there at the table. From what I
have seen of him, I wonder how Lister will be at that once the
dual controls are gone? But maybe they won't go, he thought. I
wonder if they will go? Or whether they will strengthen? I wonder what the Russian stand is on the whole business? Gaylord's is
the place, he thought. There is much that I need to know now
that I can learn only at Gaylord's.

At one time he had thought Gaylord's had been bad for him. It
was the opposite of the puritanical, religious communism of
Velazquez 63, the Madrid palace that had been turned into the

International Brigade headquarters in the capital. At Velazquez 63 it was like being a member of a religious order—and Gaylord's was a long way away from the feeling you had at the headquarters of the Fifth Regiment before it had been broken up into the brigades of the new army.

At either of those places you felt that you were taking part in a crusade. That was the only word for it although it was a word that had been so worn and abused that it no longer gave its true meaning. You felt, in spite of all bureaucracy and inefficiency and party strife, something that was like the feeling you expected to have and did not have when you made your first communion. It was a feeling of consecration to a duty toward all of the oppressed of the world which would be as difficult and embarrassing to speak about as religious experience and yet it was authentic as the feeling you had when you heard Bach, or stood in Chartres Cathedral or the Cathedral at León and saw the light coming through the great windows; or when you saw Mantegna and Greco and Brueghel in the Prado. It gave you a part in something that you could believe in wholly and completely and in which you felt an absolute brotherhood with the others who were engaged in it. It was something that you had never known before but that you had experienced now and you gave such importance to it and the reasons for it that your own death seemed of complete unimportance; only a thing to be avoided because it would interfere with the performance of your duty. But the best thing was that there was something you could do about this feeling and this necessity too. You could fight.

So you fought, he thought. And in the fighting soon there was no purity of feeling for those who survived the fighting and were good at it. Not after the first six months.

The defense of a position or of a city is a part of war in which you can feel that first sort of feeling. The fighting in the Sierras had been that way. They had fought there with the true comradeship of the revolution. Up there when there had been the first necessity for the enforcement of discipline he had approved and understood it. Under the shelling men had been cowards and had run. He had seen them shot and left to swell beside the road, nobody bothering to do more than strip them of their cartridges and their valuables.

Taking their cartridges, their boots and their leather coats was right. Taking the valuables was only realistic. It only kept the anarchists from getting them.

It had seemed just and right and necessary that the men who ran were shot. There was nothing wrong about it. Their running was a selfishness. The fascists had attacked and we had stopped them on that slope in the gray rocks, the scrub pines and the gorse of the Guadarrama hillsides. We had held along the road under the bombing from the planes and the shelling when they brought their artillery up and those who were left at the end of that day had counterattacked and driven them back. Later, when they had tried to come down on the left, sifting down between the rocks and through the trees, we had held out in the Sanitarium firing from the windows and the roof although they had passed it on both sides, and we lived through knowing what it was to be surrounded until the counterattack had cleared them back behind the road again.

In all that, in the fear that dries your mouth and your throat, in the smashed plaster dust and the sudden panic of a wall falling, collapsing in the flash and roar of a shellburst, clearing the gun, dragging those away who had been serving it, lying face downward and covered with rubble, your head behind the shield working on a stoppage, getting the broken case out, straightening the belt again, you now lying straight behind the shield, the gun searching the roadside again; you did the thing there was to do and knew that you were right. You learned the dry-mouthed, fear-purged, purging ecstasy of battle and you fought that summer and that fall for all the poor in the world, against all tyranny, for all the things that you believed and for the new world you had been educated into. You learned that fall, he thought, how to endure and how to ignore suffering in the long time of cold and wetness, of mud and of digging and fortifying. And the feeling of the summer and the fall was buried deep under tiredness, sleepiness, and nervousness and discomfort. But it was still there and all that you went through only served to validate it. It was in those days, he thought, that you had a deep and sound and selfless pride—that would have made you a bloody bore at Gaylord's, he thought suddenly.

No, you would not have been so good at Gaylord's then, he thought. You were too naïve. You were in a sort of state of grace. But Gaylord's might not have been the way it was now at that time, either. No, as a matter of fact, it was not that way, he told himself. It was not that way at all. There was not any Gaylord's then.

Karkov had told him about those days. At that time what Russians there were had lived at the Palace Hotel. Robert Jordan had known none of them then. That was before the first *partizan* groups had been formed; before he had met Kashkin or any of the others. Kashkin had been in the north at Irun, at San Sebastian and in the abortive fighting toward Vitoria. He had not arrived in Madrid until January and while Robert Jordan had fought at Carabanchel and at Usera in those three days when they stopped the right wing of the fascist attack on Madrid and drove the Moors and the *Tercio* back from house to house to clear that battered suburb on the edge of the gray, sun-baked plateau and establish a line of defense along the heights that would protect that corner of the city, Karkov had been in Madrid.

Karkov was not cynical about those times either when he talked. Those were the days they all shared when everything looked lost and each man retained now, better than any citation or decoration, the knowledge of just how he would act when everything looked lost. The government had abandoned the city, taking all the motor cars from the ministry of war in their flight and old Miaja had to ride down to inspect his defensive positions on a bicycle. Robert Jordan did not believe that one. He could not see Miaja on a bicycle even in his most patriotic imagination, but Karkov said it was true. But then he had written it for Russian papers so he probably wanted to believe it was true after writing it.

But there was another story that Karkov had not written. He had three wounded Russians in the Palace Hotel for whom he was responsible. They were two tank drivers and a flyer who were too bad to be moved, and since, at that time, it was of the greatest importance that there should be no evidence of any Russian intervention to justify an open intervention by the fascists, it was Karkov's responsibility that these wounded should not fall into the hands of the fascists in case the city should be abandoned.

In the event the city should be abandoned, Karkov was to poison them to destroy all evidence of their identity before leaving the Palace Hotel. No one could prove from the bodies of three wounded men, one with three bullet wounds in his abdomen, one with his jaw shot away and his vocal cords exposed, one with his femur smashed to bits by a bullet and his hands and face so badly burned that his face was just an eyelashless, eyebrowless, hairless blister that they were Russians. No one could tell from the bodies of these wounded men he would leave in beds at the Palace, that they were Russians. Nothing proved a naked dead man was a Russian. Your nationality and your politics did not show when you were dead.

Robert Jordan had asked Karkov how he felt about the necessity of performing this act and Karkov had said that he had not looked forward to it. "How were you going to do it?" Robert Jordan had asked him and had added, "You know it isn't so simple just suddenly to poison people." And Karkov had said, "Oh, yes, it is when you carry it always for your own use." Then he had opened his cigarette case and showed Robert Jordan what he carried in one side of it.

"But the first thing anybody would do if they took you prisoner would be to take your cigarette case," Robert Jordan had objected. "They would have your hands up."

"But I have a little more here," Karkov had grinned and showed the lapel of his jacket. "You simply put the lapel in your mouth like this and bite it and swallow."

"That's much better," Robert Jordan had said. "Tell me, does it smell like bitter almonds the way it always does in detective stories?"

"I don't know," Karkov said delightedly. "I have never smelled it. Should we break a little tube and smell it?"

"Better keep it."

"Yes," Karkov said and put the cigarette case away. "I am not a defeatist, you understand, but it is always possible that such serious times might come again and you cannot get this anywhere. Have you seen the communiqué from the Córdoba front? It is very beautiful. It is now my favorite among all the communiqués."

"What did it say?" Robert Jordan had come to Madrid from the Córdoban Front and he had the sudden stiffening that comes when some one jokes about a thing which you yourself may joke about but which they may not. "Tell me?"

"Nuestra gloriosa tropa siga avanzando sin perder ni una sola palma de terreno," Karkov said in his strange Spanish.

"It didn't really say that," Robert Jordan doubted.

"Our glorious troops continue to advance without losing a foot of ground," Karkov repeated in English. "It is in the communiqué. I will find it for you."

You could remember the men you knew who died in the fighting around Pozoblanco; but it was a joke at Gaylord's.

So that was the way it was at Gaylord's now. Still there had not always been Gaylord's and if the situation was now one which produced such a thing as Gaylord's out of the survivors of the early days, he was glad to see Gaylord's and to know about it. You are a long way from how you felt in the Sierra and at Carabanchel and at Usera, he thought. You corrupt very easily, he thought. But was it corruption or was it merely that you lost the naïveté that you started with? Would it not be the same in anything? Who else kept that first chastity of mind about their work that young doctors, young priests, and young soldiers usually started with? The priests certainly kept it, or they got out. I suppose the Nazis keep it, he thought, and the Communists who have a severe enough self-discipline. But look at Karkov.

He never tired of considering the case of Karkov. The last time he had been at Gaylord's Karkov had been wonderful about a certain British economist who had spent much time in Spain. Robert Jordan had read this man's writing for years and he had always respected him without knowing anything about him. He had not cared very much for what this man had written about Spain. It was too clear and simple and too open and shut and many of the statistics he knew were faked by wishful thinking. But he thought you rarely cared for journalism written about a country you really knew about and he respected the man for his intentions.

Then he had seen the man, finally, on the afternoon when they had attacked at Carabanchel. They were sitting in the lee of the bull ring and there was shooting down the two streets and every one was nervous waiting for the attack. A tank had been promised and it had not come up and Montero was sitting with his head in his hand saying, "The tank has not come. The tank has not come."

It was a cold day and the yellow dust was blowing down the street and Montero had been hit in the left arm and the arm was stiffening. "We have to have a tank," he said. "We must wait for the tank, but we cannot wait." His wound was making him sound petulant.

Robert Jordan had gone back to look for the tank which Montero said he thought might have stopped behind the apartment building on the corner of the tram-line. It was there all right. But it was not a tank. Spaniards called anything a tank in those days. It was an old armored car. The driver did not want to leave the angle of the apartment house and bring it up to the bull ring. He was standing behind it with his arms folded against the metal of the car and his head in the leather-padded helmet on his arms. He shook his head when Robert Jordan spoke to him and kept it pressed against his arms. Then he turned his head without looking at Robert Jordan.

"I have no orders to go there," he said sullenly.

Robert Jordan had taken his pistol out of the holster and pushed the muzzle of the pistol against the leather coat of the armored car driver.

"Here are your orders," he had told him. The man shook his head with the big padded-leather helmet like a football player's on it and said, "There is no ammunition for the machine gun."

"We have ammunition at the bull ring," Robert Jordan had told him. "Come on, let's go. We will fill the belts there. Come on."

"There is no one to work the gun," the driver said.

"Where is he? Where is your mate?"

"Dead," the driver had said. "Inside there."

"Get him out," Robert Jordan had said. "Get him out of there."

"I do not like to touch him," the driver had said. "And he is bent over between the gun and the wheel and I cannot get past him."

"Come on," Robert Jordan had said. "We will get him out together."

He had banged his head as he climbed into the armored car and it had made a small cut over his eyebrow that bled down onto his face. The dead man was heavy and so stiff you could not bend him and he had to hammer at his head to get it out from where it had wedged, face down, between his seat and the wheel. Finally he got it up by pushing with his knee up under the dead man's head and then, pulling back on the man's waist now that the head was loose, he pulled the dead man out himself toward the door.

"Give me a hand with him," he had said to the driver.

"I do not want to touch him," the driver had said and Robert Jordan had seen that he was crying. The tears ran straight down on each side of his nose on the powder-grimed slope of his face and his nose was running, too.

Standing beside the door he had swung the dead man out and the dead man fell onto the sidewalk beside the tram-line still in that hunched-over, doubled-up position. He lay there, his face waxy gray against the cement sidewalk, his hands bent under him as they had been in the car.

"Get in, God damn it," Robert Jordan had said, motioning now with his pistol to the driver. "Get in there now."

Just then he had seen this man who had come out from the lee of the apartment house building. He had on a long overcoat and he was bareheaded and his hair was gray, his cheekbones broad and his eyes were deep and set close together. He had a package of Chesterfields in his hand and he took one out and handed it toward Robert Jordan who was pushing the driver into the armored car with his pistol.

"Just a minute, Comrade," he had said to Robert Jordan in Spanish. "Can you explain to me something about the fighting?"

Robert Jordan took the cigarette and put it in the breast pocket of his blue mechanic jumper. He had recognized this comrade from his pictures. It was the British economist.

"Go muck yourself," he said in English and then, in Spanish, to the armored car driver. "Down there. The bull ring. See?" And he had pulled the heavy side door to with a slam and locked it and they had started down that long slope in the car and the bullets had commenced to hit against the car, sounding like pebbles tossed against an iron boiler. Then when the machine gun opened on them, they were like sharp hammer tappings. They had pulled up behind the shelter of the bull ring with the last October posters still pasted up beside the ticket window and the ammunition boxes knocked open and the comrades with the rifles, the grenades on their

belts and in their pockets, waiting there in the lee and Montero
had said, "Good. Here is the tank. Now we can attack."

Later that night when they had the last houses on the hill, he
lay comfortable behind a brick wall with a hole knocked in the
bricks for a loophole and looked across the beautiful level field of
fire they had between them and the ridge the fascists had retired
to and thought, with a comfort that was almost voluptuous, of the
rise of the hill with the smashed villa that protected the left flank.
He had lain in a pile of straw in his sweat-soaked clothes and
wound a blanket around him while he dried. Lying there he
thought of the economist and laughed, and then felt sorry he had
been rude. But at the moment, when the man had handed him
the cigarette, pushing it out almost like offering a tip for information, the combatant's hatred for the noncombatant had been too
much for him.

Now he remembered Gaylord's and Karkov speaking of this
same man. "So it was there you met him," Karkov had said. "I
did not get farther than the Puente de Toledo myself on that day.
He was very far toward the front. That was the last day of his
bravery I believe. He left Madrid the next day. Toledo was where
he was the bravest, I believe. At Toledo he was enormous. He was
one of the architects of our capture of the Alcazar. You should
have seen him at Toledo. I believe it was largely through his ef-
forts and his advice that our siege was successful. That was the sil-
liest part of the war. It reached an ultimate in silliness but tell me,
what is thought of him in America?"

"In America," Robert Jordan said, "he is supposed to be very
close to Moscow."

"He is not," said Karkov. "But he has a wonderful face and his
face and his manners are very successful. Now with my face I could
do nothing. What little I have accomplished was all done in spite
of my face which does not either inspire people nor move them
to love me and to trust me. But this man Mitchell has a face he
makes his fortune with. It is the face of a conspirator. All who have
read of conspirators in books trust him instantly. Also he has the
true manner of the conspirator. Any one seeing him enter a room
knows that he is instantly in the presence of a conspirator of the
first mark. All of your rich compatriots who wish sentimentally to

aid the Soviet Union as they believe or to insure themselves a little against any eventual success of the party see instantly in the face of this man, and in his manner that he can be none other than a trusted agent of the Comintern."

"Has he no connections in Moscow?"

"None. Listen, Comrade Jordan. Do you know about the two kinds of fools?"

"Plain and damn?"

"No. The two kinds of fools we have in Russia," Karkov grinned and began. "First there is the winter fool. The winter fool comes to the door of your house and he knocks loudly. You go to the door and you see him there and you have never seen him before. He is an impressive sight. He is a very big man and he has on high boots and a fur coat and a fur hat and he is all covered with snow. First he stamps his boots and snow falls from them. Then he takes off his fur coat and shakes it and more snow falls. Then he takes off his fur hat and knocks it against the door. More snow falls from his fur hat. Then he stamps his boots again and advances into the room. Then you look at him and you see he is a fool. That is the winter fool.

"Now in the summer you see a fool going down the street and he is waving his arms and jerking his head from side to side and everybody from two hundred yards away can tell he is a fool. That is a summer fool. This economist is a winter fool."

"But why do people trust him here?" Robert Jordan asked.

"His face," Karkov said. "His beautiful *gueule de conspirateur.* And his invaluable trick of just having come from somewhere else where he is very trusted and important. Of course," he smiled, "he must travel very much to keep the trick working. You know the Spanish are very strange," Karkov went on. "This government has had much money. Much gold. They will give nothing to their friends. You are a friend. All right. You will do it for nothing and should not be rewarded. But to people representing an important firm or a country which is not friendly but must be influenced— to such people they give much. It is very interesting when you follow it closely."

"I do not like it. Also that money belongs to the Spanish workers."

"You are not supposed to like things. Only to understand," Karkov had told him. "I teach you a little each time I see you and eventually you will acquire an education. It would be very interesting for a professor to be educated."

"I don't know whether I'll be able to be a professor when I get back. They will probably run me out as a Red."

"Well, perhaps you will be able to come to the Soviet Union and continue your studies there. That might be the best thing for you to do."

"But Spanish is my field."

"There are many countries where Spanish is spoken," Karkov had said. "They cannot all be as difficult to do anything with as Spain is. Then you must remember that you have not been a professor now for almost nine months. In nine months you may have learned a new trade. How much dialectics have you read?"

"I have read the Handbook of Marxism that Emil Burns edited. That is all."

"If you have read it all that is quite a little. There are fifteen hundred pages and you could spend some time on each page. But there are some other things you should read."

"There is no time to read now."

"I know," Karkov had said. "I mean eventually. There are many things to read which will make you understand some of these things that happen. But out of this will come a book which is very necessary; which will explain many things which it is necessary to know. Perhaps I will write it. I hope that it will be me who will write it."

"I don't know who could write it better."

"Do not flatter," Karkov had said. "I am a journalist. But like all journalists I wish to write literature. Just now, I am very busy on a study of Calvo Sotelo. He was a very good fascist; a true Spanish fascist. Franco and these other people are not. I have been studying all of Sotelo's writing and speeches. He was very intelligent and it was very intelligent that he was killed."

"I thought that you did not believe in political assassination."

"It is practised very extensively," Karkov said. "Very, very extensively."

"But——"

"We do not believe in acts of terrorism by individuals," Karkov had smiled. "Not of course by criminal terrorist and counter-revolutionary organizations. We detest with horror the duplicity and villainy of the murderous hyenas of Bukharinite wreckers and such dregs of humanity as Zinoviev, Kamenev, Rykov and their henchmen. We hate and loathe these veritable fiends," he smiled again. "But I still believe that political assassination can be said to be practised very extensively."

"You mean——"

"I mean nothing. But certainly we execute and destroy such veritable fiends and dregs of humanity and the treacherous dogs of generals and the revolting spectacle of admirals unfaithful to their trust. These are destroyed. They are not assassinated. You see the difference?"

"I see," Robert Jordan had said.

"And because I make jokes sometime: and you know how dangerous it is to make jokes even in joke? Good. Because I make jokes, do not think that the Spanish people will not live to regret that they have not shot certain generals that even now hold commands. I do not like the shootings, you understand."

"I don't mind them," Robert Jordan said. "I do not like them but I do not mind them any more."

"I know that," Karkov had said. "I have been told that."

"Is it important?" Robert Jordan said. "I was only trying to be truthful about it."

"It is regretful," Karkov had said. "But it is one of the things that makes people be treated as reliable who would ordinarily have to spend much more time before attaining that category."

"Am I supposed to be reliable?"

"In your work you are supposed to be very reliable. I must talk to you sometime to see how you are in your mind. It is regrettable that we never speak seriously."

"My mind is in suspension until we win the war," Robert Jordan had said.

"Then perhaps you will not need it for a long time. But you should be careful to exercise it a little."

"I read *Mundo Obrero*," Robert Jordan had told him and Karkov had said, "All right. Good. I can take a joke too. But there are very intelligent things in *Mundo Obrero*. The only intelligent things written on this war."

"Yes," Robert Jordan had said. "I agree with you. But to get a full picture of what is happening you cannot read only the party organ."

"No," Karkov had said. "But you will not find any such picture if you read twenty papers and then, if you had it, I do not know what you would do with it. I have such a picture almost constantly and what I do is try to forget it."

"You think it is that bad?"

"It is better now than it was. We are getting rid of some of the worst. But it is very rotten. We are building a huge army now and some of the elements, those of Modesto, of El Campesino, of Lister and of Durán, are reliable. They are more than reliable. They are magnificent. You will see that. Also we still have the Brigades although their role is changing. But an army that is made up of good and bad elements cannot win a war. All must be brought to a certain level of political development; all must know why they are fighting, and its importance. All must believe in the fight they are to make and all must accept discipline. We are making a huge conscript army without the time to implant the discipline that a conscript army must have, to behave properly under fire. We call it a people's army but it will not have the assets of a true people's army and it will not have the iron discipline that a conscript army needs. You will see. It is a very dangerous procedure."

"You are not very cheerful today."

"No," Karkov had said. "I have just come back from Valencia where I have seen many people. No one comes back very cheerful from Valencia. In Madrid you feel good and clean and with no possibility of anything but winning. Valencia is something else. The cowards who fled from Madrid still govern there. They have settled happily into the sloth and bureaucracy of governing. They have only contempt for those of Madrid. Their obsession now is the weakening of the commissariat for war. And Barcelona. You should see Barcelona."

"How is it?"

"It is all still comic opera. First it was the paradise of the crack-

pots and the romantic revolutionists. Now it is the paradise of the
fake soldier. The soldiers who like to wear uniforms, who like to
strut and swagger and wear red-and-black scarves. Who like
everything about war except to fight. Valencia makes you sick and
Barcelona makes you laugh."

"What about the P. O. U. M. putsch?"

"The P. O. U. M. was never serious. It was a heresy of crack-
pots and wild men and it was really just an infantilism. There
were some honest misguided people. There was one fairly good
brain and there was a little fascist money. Not much. The poor
P. O. U. M. They were very silly people."

"But were many killed in the putsch?"

"Not so many as were shot afterwards or will be shot. The
P. O. U. M. It is like the name. Not serious. They should have
called it the M. U. M. P. S. or the M. E. A. S. L. E. S. But no. The
Measles is much more dangerous. It can affect both sight and
hearing. But they made one plot you know to kill me, to kill Wal-
ter, to kill Modesto and to kill Prieto. You see how badly mixed
up they were? We are not at all alike. Poor P. O. U. M. They
never did kill anybody. Not at the front nor anywhere else. A few
in Barcelona, yes."

"Were you there?"

"Yes. I have sent a cable describing the wickedness of that infa-
mous organization of Trotskyite murderers and their fascist
machinations all beneath contempt but, between us, it is not very
serious, the P. O. U. M. Nin was their only man. We had him but
he escaped from our hands."

"Where is he now?"

"In Paris. We say he is in Paris. He was a very pleasant fellow
but with bad political aberrations."

"But they were in communication with the fascists, weren't
they?"

"Who is not?"

"We are not."

"Who knows? I hope we are not. You go often behind their
lines," he grinned. "But the brother of one of the secretaries of the
Republican Embassy at Paris made a trip to St. Jean de Luz last
week to meet people from Burgos."

"I like it better at the front," Robert Jordan had said. "The closer to the front the better the people."

"How do you like it behind the fascist lines?"

"Very much. We have fine people there."

"Well, you see they must have their fine people behind our lines the same way. We find them and shoot them and they find ours and shoot them. When you are in their country you must always think of how many people they must send over to us."

"I have thought about them."

"Well," Karkov had said. "You have probably enough to think about for today, so drink that beer that is left in the pitcher and run along now because I have to go upstairs to see people. Upstairs people. Come again to see me soon."

Yes, Robert Jordan thought. You learned a lot at Gaylord's. Karkov had read the one and only book he had published. The book had not been a success. It was only two hundred pages long and he doubted if two thousand people had ever read it. He had put in it what he had discovered about Spain in ten years of travelling in it, on foot, in third-class carriages, by bus, on horse- and mule-back and in trucks. He knew the Basque country, Navarre, Aragon, Galicia, the two Castiles and Estremadura well. There had been such good books written by Borrow and Ford and the rest that he had been able to add very little. But Karkov said it was a good book.

"It is why I bother with you," he said. "I think you write absolutely truly and that is very rare. So I would like you to know some things."

All right. He would write a book when he got through with this. But only about the things he knew, truly, and about what he knew. But I will have to be a much better writer than I am now to handle them, he thought. The things he had come to know in this war were not so simple.

CHAPTER NINETEEN

"What do you do sitting there?" Maria asked him. She was standing close beside him and he turned his head and smiled at her.

"Nothing," he said. "I have been thinking."

"What of? The bridge?"

"No. The bridge is terminated. Of thee and of a hotel in Madrid where I know some Russians, and of a book I will write some time."

"Are there many Russians in Madrid?"

"No. Very few."

"But in the fascist periodicals it says there are hundreds of thousands."

"Those are lies. There are very few."

"Do you like the Russians? The one who was here was a Russian."

"Did you like him?"

"Yes. I was sick then but I thought he was very beautiful and very brave."

"What nonsense, beautiful," Pilar said. "His nose was flat as my hand and he had cheekbones as wide as a sheep's buttocks."

"He was a good friend and comrade of mine," Robert Jordan said to Maria. "I cared for him very much."

"Sure," Pilar said. "But you shot him."

When she said this the card players looked up from the table and Pablo stared at Robert Jordan. Nobody said anything and then the gypsy, Rafael, asked, "Is it true, Roberto?"

"Yes," Robert Jordan said. He wished Pilar had not brought this up and he wished he had not told it at El Sordo's. "At his request. He was badly wounded."

"*Qué cosa mas rara,*" the gypsy said. "All the time he was with us he talked of such a possibility. I don't know how many times I have promised him to perform such an act. What a rare thing," he said again and shook his head.

"He was a very rare man," Primitivo said. "Very singular."

"Look," Andrés, one of the brothers, said. "You who are Professor and all. Do you believe in the possibility of a man seeing ahead what is to happen to him?"

"I believe he cannot see it," Robert Jordan said. Pablo was staring at him curiously and Pilar was watching him with no expression on her face. "In the case of this Russian comrade he was very nervous from being too much time at the front. He had fought at Irun which, you know, was bad. Very bad. He had fought later in the north. And since the first groups who did this work behind the lines were formed he had worked here, in Estremadura and in Andalucía. I think he was very tired and nervous and he imagined ugly things."

"He would undoubtedly have seen many evil things," Fernando said.

"Like all the world," Andrés said. "But listen to me, *Inglés*. Do you think there is such a thing as a man knowing in advance what will befall him?"

"No," Robert Jordan said. "That is ignorance and superstition."

"Go on," Pilar said. "Let us hear the viewpoint of the professor." She spoke as though she were talking to a precocious child.

"I believe that fear produces evil visions," Robert Jordan said. "Seeing bad signs——"

"Such as the airplanes today," Primitivo said.

"Such as thy arrival," Pablo said softly and Robert Jordan looked across the table at him, saw it was not a provocation but only an expressed thought, then went on. "Seeing bad signs, one, with fear, imagines an end for himself and one thinks that imagining comes by divination," Robert Jordan concluded. "I believe there is nothing more to it than that. I do not believe in ogres, nor soothsayers, nor in the supernatural things."

"But this one with the rare name saw his fate clearly," the gypsy said. "And that was how it happened."

"He did not see it," Robert Jordan said. "He had a fear of such a possibility and it became an obsession. No one can tell me that he saw anything."

"Not I?" Pilar asked him and picked some dust up from the

fire and blew it off the palm of her hand. "I cannot tell thee either?"

"No. With all wizardry, gypsy and all, thou canst not tell me either."

"Because thou art a miracle of deafness," Pilar said, her big face harsh and broad in the candlelight. "It is not that thou art stupid. Thou art simply deaf. One who is deaf cannot hear music. Neither can he hear the radio. So he might say, never having heard them, that such things do not exist. *Qué va, Inglés*. I saw the death of that one with the rare name in his face as though it were burned there with a branding iron."

"You did not," Robert Jordan insisted. "You saw fear and apprehension. The fear was made by what he had been through. The apprehension was for the possibility of evil he imagined."

"*Qué va*," Pilar said. "I saw death there as plainly as though it were sitting on his shoulder. And what is more he smelt of death."

"He smelt of death," Robert Jordan jeered. "Of fear maybe. There is a smell to fear."

"*De la muerte*," Pilar said. "Listen. When Blanquet, who was the greatest *peon de brega* who ever lived, worked under the orders of Granero he told me that on the day of Manolo Granero's death, when they stopped in the chapel on the way to the ring, the odor of death was so strong on Manolo that it almost made Blanquet sick. And he had been with Manolo when he had bathed and dressed at the hotel before setting out for the ring. The odor was not present in the motorcar when they had sat packed tight together riding to the bull ring. Nor was it distinguishable to any one else but Juan Luis de la Rosa in the chapel. Neither Marcial nor Chicuelo smelled it neither then nor when the four of them lined up for the paseo. But Juan Luis was dead white, Blanquet told me, and he, Blanquet, spoke to him saying, 'Thou also?'

" 'So that I cannot breathe,' Juan Luis said to him. 'And from thy matador.'

" '*Pues nada*,' Blanquet said. 'There is nothing to do. Let us hope we are mistaken.'

" 'And the others?' Juan Luis asked Blanquet.

" '*Nada*,' Blanquet said. 'Nothing. But this one stinks worse than José at Talavera.'

"And it was on that afternoon that the bull *Pocapena* of the ranch of Veragua destroyed Manolo Granero against the planks of the barrier in front of *tendido* two in the Plaza de Toros of Madrid. I was there with Finito and I saw it. The horn entirely destroyed the cranium, the head of Manolo being wedged under the *estribo* at the base of the *barrera* where the bull had tossed him."

"But did you smell anything?" Fernando asked.

"Nay," Pilar said. "I was too far away. We were in the seventh row of the *tendido* three. It was thus, being at an angle, that I could see all that happened. But that same night Blanquet who had been under the orders of Joselito when he too was killed told Finito about it at Fornos, and Finito asked Juan Luis de la Rosa and he would say nothing. But he nodded his head that it was true. I was present when this happened. So, *Inglés,* it may be that thou art deaf to some things as Chicuelo and Marcial Lalanda and all of their *banderilleros* and picadors and all of the *gente* of Juan Luis and Manolo Granero were deaf to this thing on this day. But Juan Luis and Blanquet were not deaf. Nor am I deaf to such things."

"Why do you say deaf when it is a thing of the nose?" Fernando asked.

"*Leche!*" Pilar said. "Thou shouldst be the professor in place of the *Inglés.* But I could tell thee of other things, *Inglés,* and do not doubt what thou simply cannot see nor cannot hear. Thou canst not hear what a dog hears. Nor canst thou smell what a dog smells. But already thou hast experienced a little of what can happen to man."

Maria put her hand on Robert Jordan's shoulder and let it rest there and he thought suddenly, let us finish all this nonsense and take advantage of what time we have. But it is too early yet. We have to kill this part of the evening. So he said to Pablo, "Thou, believest thou in this wizardry?"

"I do not know," Pablo said. "I am more of thy opinion. No supernatural thing has ever happened to me. But fear, yes certainly. Plenty. But I believe that the Pilar can divine events from the hand. If she does not lie perhaps it is true that she has smelt such a thing."

"*Qué va* that I should lie," Pilar said. "This is not a thing of my invention. This man Blanquet was a man of extreme seriousness and furthermore very devout. He was no gypsy but a bourgeois from Valencia. Hast thou never seen him?"

"Yes," Robert Jordan said. "I have seen him many times. He was small, gray-faced and no one handled a cape better. He was quick on his feet as a rabbit."

"Exactly," Pilar said. "He had a gray face from heart trouble and gypsies said that he carried death with him but that he could flick it away with a cape as you might dust a table. Yet he, who was no gypsy, smelled death on Joselito when he fought at Talavera. Although I do not see how he could smell it above the smell of manzanilla. Blanquet spoke of this afterwards with much diffidence but those to whom he spoke said that it was a fantasy and that what he had smelled was the life that José led at that time coming out in sweat from his armpits. But then, later, came this of Manolo Granero in which Juan Luis de la Rosa also participated. Clearly Juan Luis was a man of very little honor, but of much sensitiveness in his work and he was also a great layer of women. But Blanquet was serious and very quiet and completely incapable of telling an untruth. And I tell you that I smelled death on your colleague who was here."

"I do not believe it," Robert Jordan said. "Also you said that Blanquet smelled this just before the paseo. Just before the bullfight started. Now this was a successful action here of you and Kashkin and the train. He was not killed in that. How could you smell it then?"

"That has nothing to do with it," Pilar explained. "In the last season of Ignacio Sanchez Mejias he smelled so strongly of death that many refused to sit with him in the café. All gypsies knew of this."

"After the death such things are invented," Robert Jordan argued. "Every one knew that Sanchez Mejias was on the road to a *cornada* because he had been too long out of training, because his style was heavy and dangerous, and because his strength and the agility in his legs were gone and his reflexes no longer as they had been."

"Certainly," Pilar told him. "All of that is true. But all the gypsies knew also that he smelled of death and when he would come into the Villa Rosa you would see such people as Ricardo and Felipe Gonzalez leaving by the small door behind the bar."

"They probably owed him money," Robert Jordan said.

"It is possible," Pilar said. "Very possible. But they also smelled the thing and all knew of it."

"What she says is true, *Inglés,*" the gypsy, Rafael, said. "It is a well-known thing among us."

"I believe nothing of it," Robert Jordan said.

"Listen, *Inglés,*" Anselmo began. "I am against all such wizardry. But this Pilar has the fame of being very advanced in such things."

"But what does it smell like?" Fernando asked. "What odor has it? If there be an odor it must be a definite odor."

"You want to know, Fernandito?" Pilar smiled at him. "You think that you could smell it?"

"If it actually exists why should I not smell it as well as another?"

"Why not?" Pilar was making fun of him, her big hands folded across her knees. "Hast thou ever been aboard a ship, Fernando?"

"Nay. And I would not wish to."

"Then thou might not recognize it. For part of it is the smell that comes when, on a ship, there is a storm and the portholes are closed up. Put your nose against the brass handle of a screwed-tight porthole on a rolling ship that is swaying under you so that you are faint and hollow in the stomach and you have a part of that smell."

"It would be impossible for me to recognize because I will go on no ship," Fernando said.

"I have been on ships several times," Pilar said. "Both to go to Mexico and to Venezuela."

"What's the rest of it?" Robert Jordan asked. Pilar looked at him mockingly, remembering now, proudly, her voyages.

"All right, *Inglés.* Learn. That's the thing. Learn. All right. After that of the ship you must go down the hill in Madrid to the Puente de Toledo early in the morning to the *matadero* and stand there on the wet paving when there is a fog from the Manzanares and wait for the old women who go before daylight to drink the blood of the beasts that are slaughtered. When such an old woman comes out of the *matadero,* holding her shawl around her, with her face gray and her eyes hollow, and the whiskers of age on her chin, and on her cheeks, set in the waxen white of her face as the sprouts grow from the seed of the bean, not bristles, but pale sprouts in the death of her face; put your arms tight around her, *Inglés,* and hold her to you and kiss her on the mouth and you will know the second part that odor is made of."

"That one has taken my appetite," the gypsy said. "That of the sprouts was too much."

"Do you want to hear some more?" Pilar asked Robert Jordan.

"Surely," he said. "If it is necessary for one to learn let us learn."

"That of the sprouts in the face of the old women sickens me," the gypsy said. "Why should that occur in old women, Pilar? With us it is not so."

"Nay," Pilar mocked at him. "With us the old woman, who was so slender in her youth, except of course for the perpetual bulge that is the mark of her husband's favor, that every gypsy pushes always before her——"

"Do not speak thus," Rafael said. "It is ignoble."

"So thou art hurt," Pilar said. "Hast thou ever seen a *gitana* who was not about to have, or just to have had, a child?"

"Thou."

"Leave it," Pilar said. "There is no one who cannot be hurt. What I was saying is that age brings its own form of ugliness to all. There is no need to detail it. But if the *Inglés* must learn that odor that he covets to recognize he must go to the *matadero* early in the morning."

"I will go," Robert Jordan said. "But I will get the odor as they pass without kissing one. I fear the sprouts, too, as Rafael does."

"Kiss one," Pilar said. "Kiss one, *Inglés,* for thy knowledge's sake and then, with this in thy nostrils, walk back up into the city and when thou seest a refuse pail with dead flowers in it plunge thy nose deep into it and inhale so that scent mixes with those thou hast already in thy nasal passages."

"Now have I done it," Robert Jordan said. "What flowers were they?"

"Chrysanthemums."

"Continue," Robert Jordan said. "I smell them."

"Then," Pilar went on, "it is important that the day be in autumn with rain, or at least some fog, or early winter even and now thou shouldst continue to walk through the city and down the Calle de Salud smelling what thou wilt smell where they are sweeping out the *casas de putas* and emptying the slop jars into the drains and, with this odor of love's labor lost mixed sweetly with soapy water and cigarette butts only faintly reaching thy nostrils, thou shouldst go on to the Jardín Botánico where at night those girls who can no longer work in the houses do their work against the iron gates of the park and the iron picketed fences and upon the sidewalks. It is there in the shadow of the trees against the iron railings that they will perform all that a man wishes; from the simplest requests at a remuneration of ten centimos up to a peseta for that great act that we are born to and there, on a dead flower bed that has not yet been plucked out and replanted, and so serves to soften the earth that is so much softer than the sidewalk, thou wilt find an abandoned gunny sack with the odor of the wet earth, the dead flowers, and the doings of that night. In this sack will be contained the essence of it all, both the dead earth and the dead stalks of the flowers and their rotted blooms and the smell that is both the death and birth of man. Thou wilt wrap this sack around thy head and try to breathe through it."

"No."

"Yes," Pilar said. "Thou wilt wrap this sack around thy head and try to breathe and then, if thou hast not lost any of the previous odors, when thou inhalest deeply, thou wilt smell the odor of death-to-come as we know it."

"All right," Robert Jordan said. "And you say Kashkin smelt like that when he was here?"

"Yes."

"Well," said Robert Jordan gravely. "If that is true it is a good thing that I shot him."

"*Olé,*" the gypsy said. The others laughed.

"Very good," Primitivo approved. "That should hold her for a while."

"But Pilar," Fernando said. "Surely you could not expect one of Don Roberto's education to do such vile things."

"No," Pilar agreed.

"All of that is of the utmost repugnance."

"Yes," Pilar agreed.

"You would not expect him actually to perform those degrading acts?"

"No," Pilar said. "Go to bed, will you?"

"But, Pilar—" Fernando went on.

"Shut up, will you?" Pilar said to him suddenly and viciously. "Do not make a fool of thyself and I will try not to make a fool of myself talking with people who cannot understand what one speaks of."

"I confess I do not understand," Fernando began.

"Don't confess and don't try to understand," Pilar said. "Is it still snowing outside?"

Robert Jordan went to the mouth of the cave, lifted the blanket and looked out. It was clear and cold in the night outside and no snow was falling. He looked through the tree trunks where the whiteness lay and up through the trees to where the sky was now clear. The air came into his lungs sharp and cold as he breathed.

"El Sordo will leave plenty of tracks if he has stolen horses tonight," he thought.

He dropped the blanket and came back into the smoky cave. "It is clear," he said. "The storm is over."

CHAPTER TWENTY

NOW IN the night he lay and waited for the girl to come to him. There was no wind now and the pines were still in the night. The trunks of the pines projected from the snow that covered all the ground, and he lay in the robe feeling the suppleness of the bed under him that he had made, his legs stretched long against the warmth of the robe, the air sharp and cold on his head and in his nostrils as he breathed. Under his head, as he lay on his side, was the bulge of the trousers and the coat that he had wrapped around his shoes to make a pillow and against his side was the cold metal of the big automatic pistol he had taken from the holster when he undressed and fastened by its lanyard to his right wrist. He pushed the pistol away and settled deeper into the robe as he watched, across the snow, the dark break in the rocks that was the entrance to the cave. The sky was clear and there was enough light reflected from the snow to see the trunks of the trees and the bulk of the rocks where the cave was.

Earlier in the evening he had taken the ax and gone outside of the cave and walked through the new snow to the edge of the clearing and cut down a small spruce tree. In the dark he had dragged it, butt first, to the lee of the rock wall. There close to the rock, he had held the tree upright, holding the trunk firm with one hand, and, holding the ax-haft close to the head had lopped off all the boughs until he had a pile of them. Then, leaving the pile of boughs, he had laid the bare pole of the trunk down in the snow and gone into the cave to get a slap of wood he had seen against the wall. With this slab he scraped the ground clear of the snow along the rock wall and then picked up his boughs and shaking them clean of snow laid them in rows, like over-lapping plumes, until he had a bed. He put the pole across the foot of the bough bed to hold the branches in place and pegged it firm with two pointed pieces of wood he split from the edge of the slab.

Then he carried the slab and the ax back into the cave, ducking under the blanket as he came in, and leaned them both against the wall.

"What do you do outside?" Pilar had asked.

"I made a bed."

"Don't cut pieces from my new shelf for thy bed."

"I am sorry."

"It has no importance," she said. "There are more slabs at the sawmill. What sort of bed hast thou made?"

"As in my country."

"Then sleep well on it," she had said and Robert Jordan had opened one of the packs and pulled the robe out and replaced those things wrapped in it back in the pack and carried the robe out, ducking under the blanket again, and spread it over the boughs so that the closed end of the robe was against the pole that was pegged cross-wise at the foot of the bed. The open head of the robe was protected by the rock wall of the cliff. Then he went back into the cave for his packs but Pilar said, "They can sleep with me as last night."

"Will you not have sentries?" he asked. "The night is clear and the storm is over."

"Fernando goes," Pilar said.

Maria was in the back of the cave and Robert Jordan could not see her.

"Good night to every one," he had said. "I am going to sleep."

Of the others, who were laying out blankets and bedrolls on the floor in front of the cooking fire, pushing back the slab tables and the rawhide-covered stools to make sleeping space, Primitivo and Andrés looked up and said, *"Buenas noches."*

Anselmo was already asleep in a corner, rolled in his blanket and his cape, not even his nose showing. Pablo was asleep in his chair.

"Do you want a sheep hide for thy bed?" Pilar asked Robert Jordan softly.

"Nay," he said. "Thank thee. I do not need it."

"Sleep well," she said. "I will respond for thy material."

Fernando had gone out with him and stood a moment where Robert Jordan had spread the sleeping robe.

"You have a curious idea to sleep in the open, Don Roberto," he said standing there in the dark, muffled in his blanket cape, his carbine slung over his shoulder.

"I am accustomed to it. Good night."

"Since you are accustomed to it."

"When are you relieved?"

"At four."

"There is much cold between now and then."

"I am accustomed to it," Fernando said.

"Since, then, you are accustomed to it—" Robert Jordan said politely.

"Yes," Fernando agreed. "Now I must get up there. Good night, Don Roberto."

"Good night, Fernando."

Then he had made a pillow of the things he took off and gotten into the robe and then lain and waited, feeling the spring of the boughs under the flannelly, feathered lightness of the robe warmth, watching the mouth of the cave across the snow; feeling his heart beat as he waited.

The night was clear and his head felt as clear and cold as the air. He smelled the odor of the pine boughs under him, the piney smell of the crushed needles and the sharper odor of the resinous sap from the cut limbs. Pilar, he thought. Pilar and the smell of death. This is the smell I love. This and fresh-cut clover, the crushed sage as you ride after cattle, wood-smoke and the burning leaves of autumn. That must be the odor of nostalgia, the smell of the smoke from the piles of raked leaves burning in the streets in the fall in Missoula. Which would you rather smell? Sweet grass the Indians used in their baskets? Smoked leather? The odor of the ground in the spring after rain? The smell of the sea as you walk through the gorse on a headland in Galicia? Or the wind from the land as you come in toward Cuba in the dark? That was the odor of the cactus flowers, mimosa and the sea-grape shrubs. Or would you rather smell frying bacon in the morning when you are hungry? Or coffee in the morning? Or a Jonathan apple as you bit into it? Or a cider mill in the grinding, or bread fresh from the oven? You must be hungry, he thought, and he lay on his side and watched the entrance of the cave in the light that the stars reflected from the snow.

Some one came out from under the blanket and he could see whoever it was standing by the break in the rock that made the entrance. Then he heard a slithering sound in the snow and then whoever it was ducked down and went back in.

I suppose she won't come until they are all asleep, he thought. It is a waste of time. The night is half gone. Oh, Maria. Come now quickly, Maria, for there is little time. He heard the soft sound of snow falling from a branch onto the snow on the ground. A little wind was rising. He felt it on his face. Suddenly he felt a panic that she might not come. The wind rising now reminded him how soon it would be morning. More snow fell from the branches as he heard the wind now moving the pine tops.

Come now, Maria. Please come here now quickly, he thought. Oh, come here now. Do not wait. There is no importance any more to your waiting until they are asleep.

Then he saw her coming out from under the blanket that covered the cave mouth. She stood there a moment and he knew it was she but he could not see what she was doing. He whistled a low whistle and she was still at the cave mouth doing something in the darkness of the rock shadow. Then she came running, carrying something in her hands and he saw her running long-legged through the snow. Then she was kneeling by the robe, her head pushed hard against him, slapping snow from her feet. She kissed him and handed him her bundle.

"Put it with thy pillow," she said. "I took these off there to save time."

"You came barefoot through the snow?"

"Yes," she said, "and wearing only my wedding shirt."

He held her close and tight in his arms and she rubbed her head against his chin.

"Avoid the feet," she said. "They are very cold, Roberto."

"Put them here and warm them."

"Nay," she said. "They will warm quickly. But say quickly now that you love me."

"I love thee."

"Good. Good. Good."

"I love thee, little rabbit."

"Do you love my wedding shirt?"

"It is the same one as always."

"Yes. As last night. It is my wedding shirt."

"Put thy feet here."

"Nay, that would be abusive. They will warm of themselves. They are warm to me. It is only that the snow has made them cold toward thee. Say it again."

"I love thee, my little rabbit."

"I love thee, too, and I am thy wife."

"Were they asleep?"

"No," she said. "But I could support it no longer. And what importance has it?"

"None," he said, and felt her against him, slim and long and warmly lovely. "No other thing has importance."

"Put thy hand on my head," she said, "and then let me see if I can kiss thee."

"Was it well?" she asked.

"Yes," he said. "Take off thy wedding shirt."

"You think I should?"

"Yes, if thou wilt not be cold."

"*Qué va,* cold. I am on fire."

"I, too. But afterwards thou wilt not be cold?"

"No. Afterwards we will be as one animal of the forest and be so close that neither one can tell that one of us is one and not the other. Can you not feel my heart be your heart?"

"Yes. There is no difference."

"Now, feel. I am thee and thou art me and all of one is the other. And I love thee, oh, I love thee so. Are you not truly one? Canst thou not feel it?"

"Yes," he said. "It is true."

"And feel now. Thou hast no heart but mine."

"Nor any other legs, nor feet, nor of the body."

"But we are different," she said. "I would have us exactly the same."

"You do not mean that."

"Yes I do. I do. That is a thing I had to tell thee."

"You do not mean that."

"Perhaps I do not," she said speaking softly with her lips against his shoulder. "But I wished to say it. Since we are different I am glad that thou art Roberto and I Maria. But if thou should ever wish to change I would be glad to change. I would be thee because I love thee so."

"I do not wish to change. It is better to be one and each one to be the one he is."

"But we will be one now and there will never be a separate one." Then she said, "I will be thee when thou are not there. Oh, I love thee so and I must care well for thee."

"Maria."

"Yes."

"Maria."

"Yes."

"Maria."

"Oh, yes. Please."

"Art thou not cold?"

"Oh, no. Pull the robe over thy shoulders."

"Maria."

"I cannot speak."

"Oh, Maria. Maria. Maria."

Then afterwards, close, with the night cold outside, in the long warmth of the robe, her head touching his cheek, she lay quiet and happy against him and then said softly, "And thou?"

"Como tu," he said.

"Yes," she said. "But it was not as this afternoon."

"No."

"But I loved it more. One does not need to die."

"Ojala no," he said. "I hope not."

"I did not mean that."

"I know. I know what thou meanest. We mean the same."

"Then why did you say that instead of what I meant?"

"With a man there is a difference."

"Then I am glad that we are different."

"And so am I," he said. "But I understood about the dying. I only spoke thus, as a man, from habit. I feel the same as thee."

"However thou art and however thou speakest is how I would have thee be."

"And I love thee and I love thy name, Maria."

"It is a common name."

"No," he said. "It is not common."

"Now should we sleep?" she said. "I could sleep easily."

"Let us sleep," he said, and he felt the long light body, warm against him, comforting against him, abolishing loneliness against him, magically, by a simple touching of flanks, of shoulders and of feet, making an alliance against death with him, and he said, "Sleep well, little long rabbit."

She said, "I am asleep already."

"I am going to sleep," he said. "Sleep well, beloved." Then he was asleep and happy as he slept.

But in the night he woke and held her tight as though she were all of life and it was being taken from him. He held her feeling she was all of life there was and it was true. But she was sleeping well and soundly and she did not wake. So he rolled away onto his side and pulled the robe over her head and kissed her once on her neck under the robe and then pulled the pistol lanyard up and put the pistol by his side where he could reach it handily and then he lay there in the night thinking.

CHAPTER TWENTY-ONE

A WARM wind came with daylight and he could hear the snow melting in the trees and the heavy sound of its falling. It was a late spring morning. He knew with the first breath he drew that the snow had been only a freak storm in the mountains and it would be gone by noon. Then he heard a horse coming, the hoofs balled with the wet snow thumping dully as the horseman trotted. He heard the noise of a carbine scabbard slapping loosely and the creak of leather.

"Maria," he said, and shook the girl's shoulder to waken her. "Keep thyself under the robe," and he buttoned his shirt with one hand and held the automatic pistol in the other, loosening the safety catch with his thumb. He saw the girl's cropped head disappear with a jerk under the robe and then he saw the horseman coming through the trees. He crouched now in the robe and holding the pistol in both hands aimed it at the man as he rode toward him. He had never seen this man before.

The horseman was almost opposite him now. He was riding a big gray gelding and he wore a khaki beret, a blanket cape like a poncho, and heavy black boots. From the scabbard on the right of his saddle projected the stock and the long oblong clip of a short automatic rifle. He had a young, hard face and at this moment he saw Robert Jordan.

He reached his hand down toward the scabbard and as he swung low, turning and jerking at the scabbard, Robert Jordan saw the scarlet of the formalized device he wore on the left breast of his khaki blanket cape.

Aiming at the center of his chest, a little lower than the device, Robert Jordan fired.

The pistol roared in the snowy woods.

The horse plunged as though he had been spurred and the young man, still tugging at the scabbard, slid over toward the ground, his right foot caught in the stirrup. The horse broke off through the trees dragging him, bumping, face downward, and Robert Jordan stood up holding the pistol now in one hand.

The big gray horse was galloping through the pines. There was a broad swath in the snow where the man dragged with a scarlet streak along one side of it. People were coming out of the mouth of the cave. Robert Jordan reached down and unrolled his trousers from the pillow and began to put them on.

"Get thee dressed," he said to Maria.

Overhead he heard the noise of a plane flying very high. Through the trees he saw where the gray horse had stopped and was standing, his rider still hanging face down from the stirrup.

"Go catch that horse," he called to Primitivo who had started over toward him. Then, "Who was on guard at the top?"

"Rafael," Pilar said from the cave. She stood there, her hair still down her back in two braids.

"There's cavalry out," Robert Jordan said. "Get your damned gun up there."

He heard Pilar call, "Agustín," into the cave. Then she went into the cave and then two men came running out, one with the automatic rifle with its tripod swung on his shoulder; the other with a sackful of the pans.

"Get up there with them," Robert Jordan said to Anselmo. "You lie beside the gun and hold the legs still," he said.

The three of them went up the trail through the woods at a run.

The sun had not yet come up over the tops of the mountains and Robert Jordan stood straight buttoning his trousers and tightening his belt, the big pistol hanging from the lanyard on his wrist. He put the pistol in its holster on his belt and slipped the knot down on the lanyard and passed the loop over his head.

Somebody will choke you with that sometime, he thought. Well, this has done it. He took the pistol out of the holster, removed the clip, inserted one of the cartridges from the row alongside of the holster and shoved the clip back into the butt of the pistol.

He looked through the trees to where Primitivo, holding the reins of the horse, was twisting the rider's foot out of the stirrup. The body lay face down in the snow and as he watched Primitivo was going through the pockets.

"Come on," he called. "Bring the horse."

As he knelt to put on his rope-soled shoes, Robert Jordan could feel Maria against his knees, dressing herself under the robe. She had no place in his life now.

That cavalryman did not expect anything, he was thinking. He was not following horse tracks and he was not even properly alert, let alone alarmed. He was not even following the tracks up to the post. He must have been one of a patrol scattered out in these hills. But when the patrol misses him they will follow his tracks here. Unless the snow melts first, he thought. Unless something happens to the patrol.

"You better get down below," he said to Pablo.

They were all out of the cave now, standing there with the carbines and with grenades on their belts. Pilar held a leather bag of grenades toward Robert Jordan and he took three and put them in his pocket. He ducked into the cave, found his two packs, opened the one with the submachine gun in it and took out the barrel and stock, slipped the stock onto the forward assembly and put one clip into the gun and three in his pockets. He locked the pack and started for the door. I've got two pockets full of hardware, he thought. I hope the seams hold. He came out of the cave and said to Pablo, "I'm going up above. Can Agustín shoot that gun?"

"Yes," Pablo said. He was watching Primitivo leading up the horse.

"*Mira qué caballo,*" he said. "Look, what a horse."

The big gray was sweating and shivering a little and Robert Jordan patted him on the withers.

"I will put him with the others," Pablo said.

"No," Robert Jordan said. "He has made tracks into here. He must make them out."

"True," agreed Pablo. "I will ride him out and will hide him and bring him in when the snow is melted. Thou hast much head today, *Inglés.*"

"Send some one below," Robert Jordan said. "We've got to get up there."

"It is not necessary," Pablo said. "Horsemen cannot come that way. But we can get out, by there and by two other places. It is better not to make tracks if there are planes coming. Give me the *bota* with wine, Pilar."

"To go off and get drunk," Pilar said. "Here, take these instead." He reached over and put two of the grenades in his pockets.

"*Qué va,* to get drunk," Pablo said. "There is gravity in the situation. But give me the *bota*. I do not like to do all this on water."

He reached his arms up, took the reins and swung up into the saddle. He grinned and patted the nervous horse. Robert Jordan saw him rub his leg along the horse's flank affectionately.

"*Qué caballo más bonito,*" he said and patted the big gray again. "*Qué caballo más hermoso.* Come on. The faster this gets out of here the better."

He reached down and pulled the light automatic rifle with its ventilated barrel, really a submachine gun built to take the 9 mm. pistol cartridge, from the scabbard, and looked at it. "Look how they are armed," he said. "Look at modern cavalry."

"There's modern cavalry over there on his face," Robert Jordan said. "*Vamonos.*"

"Do you, Andrés, saddle and hold the horses in readiness. If you hear firing bring them up to the woods behind the gap. Come with thy arms and leave the women to hold the horses. Fernando, see that my sacks are brought also. Above all, that my sacks are brought carefully. Thou to look after my sacks, too," he said to Pilar. "Thou to verify that they come with the horses. *Vamonos,*" he said. "Let us go."

"The Maria and I will prepare all for leaving," Pilar said. Then to Robert Jordan, "Look at him," nodding at Pablo on the gray horse, sitting him in the heavy-thighed herdsman manner, the horse's nostrils widening as Pablo replaced the clip in the automatic rifle. "See what a horse has done for him."

"That I should have two horses," Robert Jordan said fervently.

"Danger is thy horse."

"Then give me a mule," Robert Jordan grinned.

"Strip me that," he said to Pilar and jerked his head toward where the man lay face down in the snow. "And bring everything, all the letters and papers, and put them in the outside pocket of my sack. Everything, understand?"

"Yes."

"*Vamonos,*" he said.

Pablo rode ahead and the two men followed in a single file in order not to track up the snow. Robert Jordan carried the submachine gun muzzle down, carrying it by its forward hand grip. I wish it took the same ammunition that saddle gun takes, he thought. But it doesn't. This is a German gun. This was old Kashkin's gun.

The sun was coming over the mountains now. A warm wind was blowing and the snow was melting. It was a lovely late spring morning.

Robert Jordan looked back and saw Maria now standing with Pilar. Then she came running up the trail. He dropped behind Primitivo to speak to her.

"Thou," she said. "Can I go with thee?"

"No. Help Pilar."

She was walking behind him and put her hand on his arm.

"I'm coming."

"Nay."

She kept on walking close behind him.

"I could hold the legs of the gun in the way thou told Anselmo."

"Thou wilt hold no legs. Neither of guns nor of nothing."

Walking beside him she reached forward and put her hand in his pocket.

"No," he said. "But take good care of thy wedding shirt."

"Kiss me," she said, "if thou goest."

"Thou art shameless," he said.

"Yes," she said. "Totally."

"Get thee back now. There is much work to do. We may fight here if they follow these horse tracks."

"Thou," she said. "Didst thee see what he wore on his chest?"

"Yes. Why not?"

"It was the Sacred Heart."

"Yes. All the people of Navarre wear it."

"And thou shot for that?"

"No. Below it. Get thee back now."

"Thou," she said. "I saw all."

"Thou saw nothing. One man. One man from a horse. *Vete.* Get thee back."

"Say that you love me."

"No. Not now."

"Not love me now?"

"*Déjamos*. Get thee back. One does not do that and love all at the same moment."

"I want to go to hold the legs of the gun and while it speaks love thee all in the same moment."

"Thou art crazy. Get thee back now."

"I am crazy," she said. "I love thee."

"Then get thee back."

"Good. I go. And if thou dost not love me, I love thee enough for both."

He looked at her and smiled through his thinking.

"When you hear firing," he said, "come with the horses. Aid the Pilar with my sacks. It is possible there will be nothing. I hope so."

"I go," she said. "Look what a horse Pablo rides."

The big gray was moving ahead up the trail.

"Yes. But go."

"I go."

Her fist, clenched tight in his pocket, beat hard against his thigh. He looked at her and saw there were tears in her eyes. She pulled her fist out of his pocket and put both arms tight around his neck and kissed him.

"I go," she said. "*Me voy.* I go."

He looked back and saw her standing there, the first morning sunlight on her brown face and the cropped, tawny, burned-gold hair. She lifted her fist at him and turned and walked back down the trail, her head down.

Primitivo turned around and looked after her.

"If she did not have her hair cut so short she would be a pretty girl," he said.

"Yes," Robert Jordan said. He was thinking of something else.

"How is she in the bed?" Primitivo asked.

"What?"

"In the bed."

"Watch thy mouth."

"One should not be offended when——"

"Leave it," Robert Jordan said. He was looking at the position.

CHAPTER TWENTY-TWO

"CUT ME pine branches," Robert Jordan said to Primitivo, "and bring them quickly."

"I do not like the gun there," he said to Agustín.

"Why?"

"Place it over there," Robert Jordan pointed, "and later I will tell thee."

"Here, thus. Let me help thee. Here," he said, then squatted down.

He looked out across the narrow oblong, noting the height of the rocks on either side.

"It must be farther," he said, "farther out. Good. Here. That will do until it can be done properly. There. Put the stones there. Here is one. Put another there at the side. Leave room for the muzzle to swing. The stone must be farther to this side. Anselmo. Get thee down to the cave and bring me an ax. Quickly."

"Have you never had a proper emplacement for the gun?" he said to Agustín.

"We always placed it here."

"Kashkin never said to put it there?"

"No. The gun was brought after he left."

"Did no one bring it who knew how to use it?"

"No. It was brought by porters."

"What a way to do things," Robert Jordan said. "It was just given to you without instruction?"

"Yes, as a gift might be given. One for us and one for El Sordo. Four men brought them. Anselmo guided them."

"It was a wonder they did not lose them with four men to cross the lines."

"I thought so, too," Agustín said. "I thought those who sent them meant for them to be lost. But Anselmo brought them well."

"You know how to handle it?"

"Yes. I have experimented. I know. Pablo knows. Primitivo knows. So does Fernando. We have made a study of taking it apart and putting it together on the table in the cave. Once we had it apart and could not get it together for two days. Since then we have not had it apart."

"Does it shoot now?"

"Yes. But we do not let the gypsy nor others frig with it."

"You see? From there it was useless," he said. "Look. Those rocks which should protect your flanks give cover to those who will attack you. With such a gun you must seek a flatness over which to fire. Also you must take them sideways. See? Look now. All that is dominated."

"I see," said Agustín. "But we have never fought in defense except when our town was taken. At the train there were soldiers with the *máquina*."

"Then we will all learn together," Robert Jordan said. "There are a few things to observe. Where is the gypsy who should be here?"

"I do not know."

"Where is it possible for him to be?"

"I do not know."

Pablo had ridden out through the pass and turned once and ridden in a circle across the level space at the top that was the field of fire for the automatic rifle. Now Robert Jordan watched him riding down the slope alongside the tracks the horse had left when he was ridden in. He disappeared in the trees turning to the left.

"I hope he doesn't run right into cavalry," Robert Jordan thought. "I'm afraid we'd have him right here in our laps."

Primitivo brought the pine branches and Robert Jordan stuck them through the snow into the unfrozen earth, arching them over the gun from either side.

"Bring more," he said. "There must be cover for the two men who serve it. This is not good but it will serve until the ax comes. Listen," he said, "if you hear a plane lie flat wherever thou art in the shadows of the rocks. I am here with the gun."

Now with the sun up and the warm wind blowing it was pleasant on the side of the rocks where the sun shone. Four horses, Robert Jordan thought. The two women and me, Anselmo, Primitivo, Fernando, Agustín, what the hell is the name of the other brother? That's eight. Not counting the gypsy. Makes nine. Plus Pablo gone with one horse makes ten. Andrés is his name. The other brother.

Plus the other, Eladio. Makes ten. That's not one-half a horse apiece. Three men can hold this and four can get away. Five with Pablo. That's two left over. Three with Eladio. Where the hell is he?

God knows what will happen to Sordo today if they picked up the trail of those horses in the snow. That was tough; the snow stopping that way. But it melting today will even things up. But not for Sordo. I'm afraid it's too late to even it up for Sordo.

If we can last through today and not have to fight we can swing the whole show tomorrow with what we have. I know we can. Not well, maybe. Not as it should be, to be foolproof, not as we would have done; but using everybody we can swing it. *If we don't have to fight today.* God help us if we have to fight today.

I don't know any place better to lay up in the meantime than this. If we move now we only leave tracks. This is as good a place as any and if the worst gets to be the worst there are three ways out of this place. There is the dark then to come and from wherever we are in these hills, I can reach and do the bridge at daylight. I don't know why I worried about it before. It seems easy enough now. I hope they get the planes up on time for once. I certainly hope that. Tomorrow is going to be a day with dust on the road.

Well, today will be very interesting or very dull. Thank God we've got that cavalry mount out and away from here. I don't think even if they ride right up here they will go in the way those tracks are now. They'll think he stopped and circled and they'll pick up Pablo's tracks. I wonder where the old swine will go. He'll probably leave tracks like an old bull elk spooking out of the country and work way up and then when the snow melts circle back below. That horse certainly did things for him. Of course he may have just mucked off with him too. Well, he should be able to take care of himself. He's been doing this a long time. I wouldn't trust him farther than you can throw Mount Everest, though.

I suppose it's smarter to use these rocks and build a good blind for this gun than to make a proper emplacement for it. You'd be digging and get caught with your pants down if they come or if the planes come. She will hold this, the way she is, as long as it is any use to hold it, and anyway I can't stay to fight. I have to get out of here with that stuff and I'm going to take

Anselmo with me. Who would stay to cover us while we got away if we have to fight here?

Just then, while he was watching all of the country that was visible, he saw the gypsy coming through the rocks to the left. He was walking with a loose, high-hipped, sloppy swing, his carbine was slung on his back, his brown face was grinning and he carried two big hares, one in each hand. He carried them by the legs, heads swinging.

"Hola, Roberto," he called cheerfully.

Robert Jordan put his hand to his mouth, and the gypsy looked startled. He slid over behind the rocks to where Robert Jordan was crouched beside the brush-shielded automatic rifle. He crouched down and laid the hares in the snow. Robert Jordan looked up at him.

"You *hijo de la gran puta!"* he said softly. "Where the obscenity have you been?"

"I tracked them," the gypsy said. "I got them both. They had made love in the snow."

"And thy post?"

"It was not for long," the gypsy whispered. "What passes? Is there an alarm?"

"There is cavalry out."

"Rediós!" the gypsy said. "Hast thou seen them?"

"There is one at the camp now," Robert Jordan said. "He came for breakfast."

"I thought I heard a shot or something like one," the gypsy said. "I obscenity in the milk! Did he come through here?"

"Here. *Thy* post."

"Ay, mi madre!" the gypsy said. "I am a poor, unlucky man."

"If thou wert not a gypsy, I would shoot thee."

"No, Roberto. Don't say that. I am sorry. It was the hares. Before daylight I heard the male thumping in the snow. You cannot imagine what a debauch they were engaged in. I went toward the noise but they were gone. I followed the tracks in the snow and high up I found them together and slew them both. Feel the fatness of the two for this time of year. Think what the Pilar will do with those two. I am sorry, Roberto, as sorry as thee. Was the cavalryman killed?"

"Yes."

"By thee?"

"Yes."

"*Qué tio!*" the gypsy said in open flattery. "Thou art a veritable phenomenon."

"Thy mother!" Robert Jordan said. He could not help grinning at the gypsy. "Take thy hares to camp and bring us up some breakfast."

He put a hand out and felt of the hares that lay limp, long, heavy, thick-furred, big-footed and long-eared in the snow, their round dark eyes open.

"They *are* fat," he said.

"Fat!" the gypsy said. "There's a tub of lard on the ribs of each one. In my life have I never dreamed of such hares."

"Go then," Robert Jordan said, "and come quickly with the breakfast and bring to me the documentation of that *requeté*. Ask Pilar for it."

"You are not angry with me, Roberto?"

"Not angry. Disgusted that you should leave your post. Suppose it had been a troop of cavalry?"

"*Rediós,*" the gypsy said. "How reasonable you are."

"Listen to me. You cannot leave a post again like that. Never. I do not speak of shooting lightly."

"Of course not. And another thing. Never would such an opportunity as the two hares present itself again. Not in the life of one man."

"*Anda!*" Robert Jordan said. "And hurry back."

The gypsy picked up the two hares and slipped back through the rocks and Robert Jordan looked out across the flat opening and the slopes of the hill below. Two crows circled overhead and then lit in a pine tree below. Another crow joined them and Robert Jordan, watching them, thought: those are my sentinels. As long as those are quiet there is no one coming through the trees.

The gypsy, he thought. He is truly worthless. He has no political development, nor any discipline, and you could not rely on him for anything. But I need him for tomorrow. I have a use for him tomorrow. It's odd to see a gypsy in a war. They should be exempted like conscientious objectors. Or as the physically and mentally unfit. They are worthless. But conscientious objectors weren't exempted in this war. No one was exempted. It came to one and all alike. Well, it had come here now to this lazy outfit. They had it now.

Agustín and Primitivo came up with the brush and Robert Jordan built a good blind for the automatic rifle, a blind that would conceal the gun from the air and that would look natural from the forest. He showed them where to place a man high in the rocks to the right where he could see all the country below and to the right, and another where he could command the only stretch where the left wall might be climbed.

"Do not fire if you see any one from there," Robert Jordan said. "Roll a rock down as a warning, a small rock, and signal to us with thy rifle, thus," he lifted the rifle and held it over his head as though guarding it. "Thus for numbers," he lifted the rifle up and down. "If they are dismounted point thy rifle muzzle at the ground. Thus. Do not fire from there until thou hearest the *máquina* fire. Shoot at a man's knees when you shoot from that height. If you hear me whistle twice on this whistle get down, keeping behind cover, and come to these rocks where the *máquina* is."

Primitivo raised the rifle.

"I understand," he said. "It is very simple."

"Send first the small rock as a warning and indicate the direction and the number. See that you are not seen."

"Yes," Primitivo said. "If I can throw a grenade?"

"Not until the *máquina* has spoken. It may be that cavalry will come searching for their comrade and still not try to enter. They may follow the tracks of Pablo. We do not want combat if it can be avoided. Above all that we should avoid it. Now get up there."

"Me voy," Primitivo said, and climbed up into the high rocks with his carbine.

"Thou, Agustín," Robert Jordan said. "What do you know of the gun?"

Agustín squatted there, tall, black, stubbly-joweled, with his sunken eyes and thin mouth and his big work-worn hands.

"*Pues,* to load it. To aim it. To shoot it. Nothing more."

"You must not fire until they are within fifty meters and only when you are sure they will be coming into the pass which leads to the cave," Robert Jordan said.

"Yes. How far is that?"

"That rock."

"If there is an officer shoot him first. Then move the gun onto the others. Move very slowly. It takes little movement. I will teach Fernando to tap it. Hold it tight so that it does not jump and sight carefully and do not fire more than six shots at a time if you can help it. For the fire of the gun jumps upward. But each time fire at one man and then move from him to another. At a man on a horse, shoot at his belly."

"Yes."

"One man should hold the tripod still so that the gun does not jump. Thus. He will load the gun for thee."

"And where will you be?"

"I will be here on the left. Above, where I can see all and I will cover thy left with this small *máquina.* Here. If they should come it would be possible to make a massacre. But you must not fire until they are that close."

"I believe that we could make a massacre. *Menuda matanza!*"

"But I hope they do not come."

"If it were not for thy bridge we could make a massacre here and get out."

"It would avail nothing. That would serve no purpose. The bridge is a part of a plan to win the war. This would be nothing. This would be an incident. A nothing."

"*Qué va,* nothing. Every fascist dead is a fascist less."

"Yes. But with this of the bridge we can take Segovia. The Capital of a Province. Think of that. It will be the first one we will take."

"Thou believest in this seriously? That we can take Segovia?"

"Yes. It is possible with the bridge blown correctly."

"I would like to have the massacre here and the bridge, too."

"Thou hast much appetite," Robert Jordan told him.

All this time he had been watching the crows. Now he saw one was watching something. The bird cawed and flew up. But the other crow still stayed in the tree. Robert Jordan looked up toward Primitivo's place high in the rocks. He saw him watching out over the country below but he made no signal. Robert Jordan leaned forward and worked the lock on the automatic rifle, saw the round in the chamber and let the lock down. The crow was still there in the tree. The other circled wide over the snow and then settled again. In the sun and the warm wind the snow was falling from the laden branches of the pines.

"I have a massacre for thee for tomorrow morning," Robert Jordan said. "It is necessary to exterminate the post at the sawmill."

"I am ready," Agustín said, *"Estoy listo."*

"Also the post at the road mender's hut below the bridge."

"For the one or for the other," Agustín said. "Or for both."

"Not for both. They will be done at the same time," Robert Jordan said.

"Then for either one," Agustín said. "Now for a long time have I wished for action in this war. Pablo has rotted us here with inaction."

Anselmo came up with the ax.

"Do you wish more branches?" he asked. "To me it seems well hidden."

"Not branches," Robert Jordan said. "Two small trees that we can plant here and there to make it look more natural. There are not enough trees here for it to be truly natural."

"I will bring them."

"Cut them well back, so the stumps cannot be seen."

Robert Jordan heard the ax sounding in the woods behind him. He looked up at Primitivo above in the rocks and he looked down at the pines across the clearing. The one crow was still there. Then he heard the first high, throbbing murmur of a plane coming. He looked up and saw it high and tiny and silver in the sun, seeming hardly to move in the high sky.

"They cannot see us," he said to Agustín. "But it is well to keep down. That is the second observation plane today."

"And those of yesterday?" Agustín asked.

"They are like a bad dream now," Robert Jordan said.

"They must be at Segovia. The bad dream waits there to become a reality."

The plane was out of sight now over the mountains but the sound of its motors still persisted.

As Robert Jordan looked, he saw the crow fly up. He flew straight away through the trees without cawing.

CHAPTER TWENTY-THREE

"GET THEE down," Robert Jordan whispered to Agustín, and he turned his head and flicked his hand *Down, Down,* to Anselmo who was coming through the gap with a pine tree, carrying it over his shoulder like a Christmas tree. He saw the old man drop his pine tree behind a rock and then he was out of sight in the rocks and Robert Jordan was looking ahead across the open space toward the timber. He saw nothing and heard nothing but he could feel his heart pounding and then he heard the clack of stone on stone and the leaping, dropping clicks of a small rock falling. He turned his head to the right and looking up saw Primitivo's rifle raised and lowered four times horizontally. Then there was nothing more to see but the white stretch in front of him with the circle of horse tracks and the timber beyond.

"Cavalry," he said softly to Agustín.

Agustín looked at him and his dark, sunken cheeks widened at their base as he grinned. Robert Jordan noticed he was sweating. He reached over and put his hand on his shoulder. His hand was still there as they saw the four horsemen ride out of the timber and he felt the muscles in Agustín's back twitch under his hand.

One horseman was ahead and three rode behind. The one ahead was following the horse tracks. He looked down as he rode. The other three came behind him, fanned out through the timber. They were all watching carefully. Robert Jordan felt his heart beating against the snowy ground as he lay, his elbows spread wide and watched them over the sights of the automatic rifle.

The man who was leading rode along the trail to where Pablo had circled and stopped. The others rode up to him and they all stopped.

Robert Jordan saw them clearly over the blued steel barrel of the automatic rifle. He saw the faces of the men, the sabers hanging, the sweat-darkened flanks of the horses, and the cone-like slope of the khaki capes, and the Navarrese slant of the khaki berets. The leader turned his horse directly toward the opening in the rocks where the gun was placed and Robert Jordan saw his young, sun- and wind-darkened face, his close-set eyes, hawk nose and the over-long wedge-shaped chin.

Sitting his horse there, the horse's chest toward Robert Jordan, the horse's head high, the butt of the light automatic rifle projecting forward from the scabbard at the right of the saddle, the leader pointed toward the opening where the gun was.

Robert Jordan sunk his elbows into the ground and looked along the barrel at the four riders stopped there in the snow. Three of them had their automatic rifles out. Two carried them across the pommels of their saddles. The other sat his' horse with the rifle swung out to the right, the butt resting against his hip.

You hardly ever see them at such range, he thought. Not along the barrel of one of these do you see them like this. Usually the rear sight is raised and they seem miniatures of men and you have hell to make it carry up there; or they come running, flopping, running, and you beat a slope with fire or bar a certain street, or keep it on the windows; or far away you see them marching on a road. Only at the trains do you see them like this. Only then are they like now, and with four of these you can make them scatter. Over the gun sights, at this range, it makes them twice the size of men.

Thou, he thought, looking at the wedge of the front sight placed now firm in the slot of the rear sight, the top of the wedge against the center of the leader's chest, a little to the right of the scarlet device that showed bright in the morning sun against the khaki cape. Though, he thought, thinking in Spanish now and pressing his fingers forward against the trigger guard to keep it away from where it would bring the quick, shocking, hurtling rush from the automatic rifle. Thou, he thought again, thou art dead now in thy youth. And thou, he thought, and thou, and thou. But let it not happen. Do not let it happen.

He felt Agustín beside him start to cough, felt him hold it, choke and swallow. Then as he looked along the oiled blue of the barrel out through the opening between the branches, his finger still pressed forward against the trigger guard, he saw the leader turn his horse and point into the timber where Pablo's trail led. The four of them trotted into the timber and Agustín said softly, *"Cabrones!"*

Robert Jordan looked behind him at the rocks where Anselmo had dropped the tree.

The gypsy, Rafael, was coming toward them through the rocks, carrying a pair of cloth saddlebags, his rifle slung on his back. Robert Jordan waved him down and the gypsy ducked out of sight.

"We could have killed all four," Agustín said quietly. He was still wet with sweat.

"Yes," Robert Jordan whispered. "But with the firing who knows what might have come?"

Just then he heard the noise of another rock falling and he looked around quickly. But both the gypsy and Anselmo were out of sight. He looked at his wrist watch and then up to where Primitivo was raising and lowering his rifle in what seemed an infinity of short jerks. Pablo has forty-five minutes' start, Robert Jordan thought, and then he heard the noise of a body of cavalry coming.

"No te apures," he whispered to Agustín. "Do not worry. They will pass as the others."

They came into sight trotting along the edge of the timber in column of twos, twenty mounted men, armed and uniformed as the others had been, their sabers swinging, their carbines in their holsters; and then they went down into the timber as the others had.

"Tu ves?" Robert Jordan said to Agustín. "Thou seest?"

"There were many," Agustín said.

"These would we have had to deal with if we had destroyed the others," Robert Jordan said very softly. His heart had quieted now and his shirt felt wet on his chest from the melting snow. There was a hollow feeling in his chest.

The sun was bright on the snow and it was melting fast. He could see it hollowing away from the tree trunks and just ahead of the gun, before his eyes, the snow surface was damp and lacily fragile as the heat of the sun melted the top and the warmth of the earth breathed warmly up at the snow that lay upon it.

Robert Jordan looked up at Primitivo's post and saw him signal, "Nothing," crossing his two hands, palms down.

Anselmo's head showed above a rock and Robert Jordan motioned him up. The old man slipped from rock to rock until he crept up and lay down flat beside the gun.

"Many," he said. "Many!"

"I do not need the trees," Robert Jordan said to him. "There is no need for further forestal improvement."

Both Anselmo and Agustín grinned.

"This has stood scrutiny well and it would be dangerous to plant trees now because those people will return and perhaps they are not stupid."

He felt the need to talk that, with him, was the sign that there had just been much danger. He could always tell how bad it had been by the strength of the desire to talk that came after.

"It was a good blind, eh?" he said.

"Good," said Agustín. "To obscenity with all fascism good. We could have killed the four of them. Didst thou see?" he said to Anselmo.

"I saw."

"Thou," Robert Jordan said to Anselmo. "Thou must go to the post of yesterday or another good post of thy selection to watch the road and report on all movement as of yesterday. Already we are late in that. Stay until dark. Then come in and we will send another."

"But the tracks that I will make?"

"Go from below as soon as the snow is gone. The road will be muddied by the snow. Note if there has been much traffic of trucks or if there are tank tracks in the softness on the road. That is all we can tell until you are there to observe."

"With your permission?" the old man asked.

"Surely."

"With your permission, would it not be better for me to go into La Granja and inquire there what passed last night and arrange for one to observe today thus in the manner you have taught me? Such a one could report tonight or, better, I could go again to La Granja for the report."

"Have you no fear of encountering cavalry?"

"Not when the snow is gone."

"Is there some one in La Granja capable of this?"

"Yes. Of this, yes. It would be a woman. There are various women of trust in La Granja."

"I believe it," Agustín said. "More, I know it, and several who serve for other purposes. You do not wish me to go?"

"Let the old man go. You understand this gun and the day is not over."

"I will go when the snow melts," Anselmo said. "And the snow is melting fast."

"What think you of their chance of catching Pablo?" Robert Jordan asked Agustín.

"Pablo is smart," Agustín said. "Do men catch a wise stag without hounds?"

"Sometimes," Robert Jordan said.

"Not Pablo," Agustín said. "Clearly, he is only a garbage of what he once was. But it is not for nothing that he is alive and comfortable in these hills and able to drink himself to death while there are so many others that have died against a wall."

"Is he as smart as they say?"

"He is much smarter."

"He has not seemed of great ability here."

"*Cómo qúe no?* If he were not of great ability he would have died last night. It seems to me you do not understand politics, *Inglés,* nor guerilla warfare. In politics and this other the first thing is to continue to exist. Look how he continued to exist last night. And the quantity of dung he ate both from me and from thee."

Now that Pablo was back in the movements of the unit, Robert Jordan did not wish to talk against him and as soon as he had uttered it he regretted saying the thing about his ability. He knew himself how smart Pablo was. It was Pablo who had seen instantly all that was wrong with the orders for the destruction of the bridge. He had made the remark only from dislike and he knew as he made it that it was wrong. It was part of the talking too much after a strain. So now he dropped the matter and said to Anselmo, "And to go into La Granja in daylight?"

"It is not bad," the old man said. "I will not go with a military band."

"Nor with a bell around his neck," Agustín said. "Nor carrying a banner."

"How will you go?"

"Above and down through the forest."

"But if they pick you up."

"I have papers."

"So have we all but thou must eat the wrong ones quickly."

Anselmo shook his head and tapped the breast pocket of his smock.

"How many times have I contemplated that," he said. "And never did I like to swallow paper."

"I have thought we should carry a little mustard on them all," Robert Jordan said. "In my left breast pocket I carry our papers. In my right the fascist papers. Thus one does not make a mistake in an emergency."

It must have been bad enough when the leader of the first patrol of cavalry had pointed toward the entry because they were all talking very much. Too much, Robert Jordan thought.

"But look, Roberto," Agustín said. "They say the government moves further to the right each day. That in the Republic they no longer say Comrade but Señor and Señora. Canst shift thy pockets?"

"When it moves far enough to the right I will carry them in my hip pocket," Robert Jordan said, "and sew it in the center."

"That they should stay in thy shirt," Agustín said. "Are we to win this war and lose the revolution?"

"Nay," Robert Jordan said. "But if we do not win this war there will be no revolution nor any Republic nor any thou nor any me nor anything but the most grand *carajo.*"

"So say I," Anselmo said. "That we should win the war."

"And afterwards shoot the anarchists and the Communists and all this *canalla* except the good Republicans," Agustín said.

"That we should win this war and shoot nobody," Anselmo said. "That we should govern justly and that all should participate in the benefits according as they have striven for them. And that those who have fought against us should be educated to see their error."

"We will have to shoot many," Agustín said. "Many, many, many."

He thumped his closed right fist against the palm of his left hand.

"That we should shoot none. Not even the leaders. That they should be reformed by work."

"I know the work I'd put them at," Agustín said, and he picked up some snow and put it in his mouth.

"What, bad one?" Robert Jordan asked.

"Two trades of the utmost brilliance."

"They are?"

Agustín put some more snow in his mouth and looked across the clearing where the cavalry had ridden. Then he spat the melted snow out. "*Vaya*. What a breakfast," he said. "Where is the filthy gypsy?"

"What trades?" Robert Jordan asked him. "Speak, bad mouth."

"Jumping from planes without parachutes," Agustín said, and his eyes shone. "That for those that we care for. And being nailed to the tops of fence posts to be pushed over backwards for the others."

"That way of speaking is ignoble," Anselmo said. "Thus we will never have a Republic."

"I would like to swim ten leagues in a strong soup made from the *cojones* of all of them," Agustín said. "And when I saw those four there and thought that we might kill them I was like a mare in the corral waiting for the stallion."

"You know why we did not kill them, though?" Robert Jordan said quietly.

"Yes," Agustín said. "Yes. But the necessity was on me as it is on a mare in heat. You cannot know what it is if you have not felt it."

"You sweated enough," Robert Jordan said. "I thought it was fear."

"Fear, yes," Agustín said. "Fear and the other. And in this life there is no stronger thing than the other."

Yes, Robert Jordan thought. We do it coldly but they do not, nor ever have. It is their extra sacrament. Their old one that they had before the new religion came from the far end of the Mediterranean, the one they have never abandoned but only suppressed and hidden to bring it out again in wars and inquisitions. They are the people of the Auto de Fé; the act of faith. Killing is something one must do, but ours are different from theirs. And you, he thought, you have never been corrupted by it? You never had it in the Sierra? Nor at Usera? Nor through all the time in Estremadura? Nor at any time? *Qué va,* he told himself. At every train.

Stop making dubious literature about the Berbers and the old Iberians and admit that you have liked to kill as all who are soldiers by choice have enjoyed it at some time whether they lie about it or not. Anselmo does not like to because he is a hunter, not a soldier. Don't idealize him, either. Hunters kill animals and soldiers kill men. Don't lie to yourself, he thought. Nor make up literature about it. You have been tainted with it for a long time now. And do not think against Anselmo either. He is a Christian. Something very rare in Catholic countries.

But with Agustín I had thought it was fear, he thought. That natural fear before action. So it was the other, too. Of course, he may be bragging now. There was plenty of fear. I felt the fear under my hand. Well, it was time to stop talking.

"See if the gypsy brought food," he said to Anselmo. "Do not let him come up. He is a fool. Bring it yourself. And however much he brought, send back for more. I am hungry."

CHAPTER TWENTY-FOUR

NOW THE morning was late May, the sky was high and clear and the wind blew warm on Robert Jordan's shoulders. The snow was going fast and they were eating breakfast. There were two big sandwiches of meat and the goaty cheese apiece, and Robert Jordan had cut thick slices of onion with his clasp knife and put them on each side of the meat and cheese between the chunks of bread.

"You will have a breath that will carry through the forest to the fascists," Agustín said, his own mouth full.

"Give me the wineskin and I will rinse the mouth," Robert Jordan said, his mouth full of meat, cheese, onion and chewed bread.

He had never been hungrier and he filled his mouth with wine, faintly tarry-tasting from the leather bag, and swallowed. Then he took another big mouthful of wine, lifting the bag up to let the jet of wine spurt into the back of his mouth, the wineskin touching the needles of the blind of pine branches that covered the automatic rifle as he lifted his hand, his head leaning against the pine branches as he bent it back to let the wine run down.

"Dost thou want this other sandwich?" Agustín asked him, handing it toward him across the gun.

"No. Thank you. Eat it."

"I cannot. I am not accustomed to eat in the morning."

"You do not want it, truly?"

"Nay. Take it."

Robert Jordan took it and laid it on his lap while he got the onion out of his side jacket pocket where the grenades were and opened his knife to slice it. He cut off a thin sliver of the surface that had dirtied in his pocket, then cut a thick slice. An outer segment fell and he picked it up and bent the circle together and put it into the sandwich.

"Eatest thou always onions for breakfast?" Agustín asked.

"When there are any."

"Do all in thy country do this?"

"Nay," Robert Jordan said. "It is looked on badly there."

"I am glad," Agustín said. "I had always considered America a civilized country."

"What hast thou against the onion?"

"The odor. Nothing more. Otherwise it is like the rose."

Robert Jordan grinned at him with his mouth full.

"Like the rose," he said. "Mighty like the rose. A rose is a rose is an onion."

"Thy onions are affecting thy brain," Agustín said. "Take care."

"An onion is an onion is an onion," Robert Jordan said cheerily and, he thought, a stone is a stein is a rock is a boulder is a pebble.

"Rinse thy mouth with wine," Agustín said. "Thou art very rare, *Inglés*. There is great difference between thee and the last dynamiter who worked with us."

"There is one great difference."

"Tell it to me."

"I am alive and he is dead," Robert Jordan said. Then: what's the matter with you? he thought. Is that the way to talk? Does food make you that slap happy? What are you, drunk on onions? Is that all it means to you, now? It never meant much, he told himself truly. You tried to make it mean something, but it never did. There is no need to lie in the time that is left.

"No," he said, seriously now. "That one was a man who had suffered greatly."

"And thou? Hast thou not suffered?"

"No," said Robert Jordan. "I am of those who suffer little."

"Me also," Agustín told him. "There are those who suffer and those who do not. I suffer very little."

"Less bad," Robert Jordan tipped up the wineskin again. "And with this, less."

"I suffer for others."

"As all good men should."

"But for myself very little."

"Hast thou a wife?"

"No."

"Me neither."

"But now you have the Maria."

"Yes."

"There is a rare thing," Agustín said. "Since she came to us at the train the Pilar has kept her away from all as fiercely as though she were in a convent of Carmelites. You cannot imagine with what fierceness she guarded her. You come, and she gives her to thee as a present. How does that seem to thee?"

"It was not thus."

"How was it, then?"

"She has put her in my care."

"And thy care is to *joder* with her all night?"

"With luck."

"What a manner to care for one."

"You do not understand that one can take good care of one thus?"

"Yes, but such care could have been furnished by any one of us."

"Let us not talk of it any more," Robert Jordan said. "I care for her seriously."

"Seriously?"

"As there can be nothing more serious in this world."

"And afterwards? After this of the bridge?"

"She goes with me."

"Then," Agustín said. "That no one speaks of it further and that the two of you go with all luck."

He lifted the leather wine bag and took a long pull, then handed it to Robert Jordan.

"One thing more, *Inglés*," he said.

"Of course."

"I have cared much for her, too."

Robert Jordan put his hand on his shoulder.

"Much," Agustín said. "Much. More than one is able to imagine."

"I can imagine."

"She has made an impression on me that does not dissipate."

"I can imagine."

"Look. I say this to thee in all seriousness."

"Say it."

"I have never touched her nor had anything to do with her but I care for her greatly. *Inglés,* do not treat her lightly. Because she sleeps with thee she is no whore."

"I will care for her."

"I believe thee. But more. You do not understand how such a girl would be if there had been no revolution. You have much responsibility. This one, truly, has suffered much. She is not as we are."

"I will marry her."

"Nay. Not that. There is no need for that under the revolution. But—" he nodded his head—"it would be better."

"I will marry her," Robert Jordan said and could feel his throat swelling as he said it. "I care for her greatly."

"Later," Agustín said. "When it is convenient. The important thing is to have the intention."

"I have it."

"Listen," Agustín said. "I am speaking too much of a matter in which I have no right to intervene, but hast thou known many girls of this country?"

"A few."

"Whores?"

"Some who were not."

"How many?"

"Several."

"And did you sleep with them?"

"No."

"You see?"

"Yes."

"What I mean is that this Maria does not do this lightly."

"Nor I."

"If I thought you did I would have shot you last night as you lay with her. For this we kill much here."

"Listen, old one," Robert Jordan said. "It is because of the lack of time that there has been informality. What we do not have is time. Tomorrow we must fight. To me that is nothing. But for the Maria and me it means that we must live all of our life in this time."

"And a day and a night is little time," Agustín said.

"Yes. But there has been yesterday and the night before and last night."

"Look," Agustín said. "If I can aid thee."

"No. We are all right."

"If I could do anything for thee or for the cropped head——"

"No."

"Truly, there is little one man can do for another."

"No. There is much."

"What?"

"No matter what passes today and tomorrow in respect to combat, give me thy confidence and obey even though the orders may appear wrong."

"You have my confidence. Since this of the cavalry and the sending away of the horse."

"That was nothing. You see that we are working for one thing. To win the war. Unless we win, all other things are futile. Tomorrow we have a thing of great importance. Of true importance. Also we will have combat. In combat there must be discipline. For many things are not as they appear. Discipline must come from trust and confidence."

Agustín spat on the ground.

"The Maria and all such things are apart," he said. "That you and the Maria should make use of what time there is as two human beings. If I can aid thee I am at thy orders. But for the thing of tomorrow I will obey thee blindly. If it is necessary that one should die for the thing of tomorrow one goes gladly and with the heart light."

"Thus do I feel," Robert Jordan said. "But to hear it from thee brings pleasure."

"And more," Agustín said. "That one above," he pointed toward Primitivo, "is a dependable value. The Pilar is much, much more than thou canst imagine. The old man Anselmo, also. Andrés also. Eladio also. Very quiet, but a dependable element. And Fernando. I do not know how thou hast appreciated him. It is true he is heavier than mercury. He is fuller of boredom than a steer draw-ing a cart on the highroad. But to fight and to do as he is told. *Es muy hombre!* Thou wilt see."

"We are lucky."

"No. We have two weak elements. The gypsy and Pablo. But the band of Sordo are as much better than we are as we are better than goat manure."

"All is well then."

"Yes," Agustín said. "But I wish it was for today."

"Me, too. To finish with it. But it is not."

"Do you think it will be bad?"

"It can be."

"But thou are very cheerful now, *Inglés.*"

"Yes."

"Me also. In spite of this of the Maria and all."

"Do you know why?"

"No."

"Me neither. Perhaps it is the day. The day is good."

"Who knows? Perhaps it is that we will have action."

"I think it is that," Robert Jordan said. "But not today. Of all things; of all importance we must avoid it today."

As he spoke he heard something. It was a noise far off that came above the sound of the warm wind in the trees. He could not be sure and he held his mouth open and listened, glancing up at Primitivo as he did so. He thought he heard it but then it was gone. The wind was blowing in the pines and now Robert Jordan strained all of himself to listen. Then he heard it faintly coming down the wind.

"It is nothing tragic with me," he heard Agustín say. "That I should never have the Maria is nothing. I will go with the whores as always."

"Shut up," he said, not listening, and lying beside him, his head having been turned away. Agustín looked over at him suddenly.

"Qué pasa?" he asked.

Robert Jordan put his hand over his own mouth and went on listening. There it came again. It came faint, muted, dry and far away. But there was no mistaking it now. It was the precise, crack-ling, curling roll of automatic rifle fire. It sounded as though pack after pack of miniature firecrackers were going off at a distance that was almost out of hearing.

Robert Jordan looked up at Primitivo who had his head up now, his face looking toward them, his hand cupped to his ear. As he looked Primitivo pointed up the mountain toward the highest country.

"They are fighting at El Sordo's," Robert Jordan said.

"Then let us go to aid them," Agustín said. "Collect the people. *Vamonos.*"

"No," Robert Jordan said. "We stay here."

CHAPTER TWENTY-FIVE

ROBERT JORDAN looked up at where Primitivo stood now in his lookout post, holding his rifle and pointing. He nodded his head but the man kept pointing, putting his hand to his ear and then pointing insistently and as though he could not possibly have been understood.

"Do you stay with this gun and unless it is sure, sure, sure that they are coming in do not fire. And then not until they reach that shrub," Robert Jordan pointed. "Do you understand?"

"Yes. But——"

"No but. I will explain to thee later. I go to Primitivo."

Anselmo was by him and he said to the old man:

"*Viejo,* stay there with Agustín with the gun." He spoke slowly and unhurriedly. "He must not fire unless cavalry is actually entering. If they merely present themselves he must let them alone as we did before. If he must fire, hold the legs of the tripod firm for him and hand him the pans when they are empty."

"Good," the old man said. "And La Granja?"

"Later."

Robert Jordan climbed up, over and around the gray boulders that were wet now under his hands as he pulled himself up. The sun was melting the snow on them fast. The tops of the boulders were drying and as he climbed he looked across the country and saw the pine woods and the long open glade and the dip of the country before the high mountains beyond. Then he stood beside Primitivo in a hollow behind two boulders and the short, brown-faced man said to him, "They are attacking Sordo. What is it that we do?"

"Nothing," Robert Jordan said.

He heard the firing clearly here and as he looked across the country, he saw, far off, across the distant valley where the country rose steeply again, a troop of cavalry ride out of the timber and cross the snowy slope riding uphill in the direction of the firing. He saw the oblong double line of men and horses dark against the snow as they forced at an angle up the hill. He watched the double line top the ridge and go into the farther timber.

"We have to aid them," Primitivo said. His voice was dry and flat.

"It is impossible," Robert Jordan told him. "I have expected this all morning."

"How?"

"They went to steal horses last night. The snow stopped and they tracked them up there."

"But we have to aid them," Primitivo said. "We cannot leave them alone to this. Those are our comrades."

Robert Jordan put his hand on the other man's shoulder.

"We can do nothing," he said. "If we could I would do it."

"There is a way to reach there from above. We can take that way with the horses and the two guns. This one below and thine. We can aid them thus."

"Listen—" Robert Jordan said.

"That is what I listen to," Primitivo said.

The firing was rolling in overlapping waves. Then they heard the noise of hand grenades heavy and sodden in the dry rolling of the automatic rifle fire.

"They are lost," Robert Jordan said. "They were lost when the snow stopped. If we go there we are lost, too. It is impossible to divide what force we have."

There was a gray stubble of beard stippled over Primitivo's jaws, his lip and his neck. The rest of his face was flat brown with a broken, flattened nose and deep-set gray eyes, and watching him Robert Jordan saw the stubble twitching at the corners of his mouth and over the cord of his throat.

"Listen to it," he said. "It is a massacre."

"If they have surrounded the hollow it is that," Robert Jordan said. "Some may have gotten out."

"Coming on them now we could take them from behind," Primitivo said. "Let four of us go with the horses."

"And then what? What happens after you take them from behind?"

"We join with Sordo."

"To die there? Look at the sun. The day is long."

The sky was high and cloudless and the sun was hot on their backs. There were big bare patches now on the southern slope of the open glade below them and the snow was all dropped from the pine trees. The boulders below them that had been wet as the snow melted were steaming faintly now in the hot sun.

"You have to stand it," Robert Jordan said. *"Hay que aguantarse.* There are things like this in a war."

"But there is nothing we can do? Truly?" Primitivo looked at him and Robert Jordan knew he trusted him. "Thou couldst not send me and another with the small machine gun?"

"It would be useless," Robert Jordan said.

He thought he saw something that he was looking for but it was a hawk that slid down into the wind and then rose above the line of the farthest pine woods. "It would be useless if we all went," he said.

Just then the firing doubled in intensity and in it was the heavy bumping of the hand grenades.

"Oh, obscenity them," Primitivo said with an absolute devoutness of blasphemy, tears in his eyes and his cheeks twitching. "Oh, God and the Virgin, obscenity them in the milk of their filth."

"Calm thyself," Robert Jordan said. "You will be fighting them soon enough. Here comes the woman."

Pilar was climbing up to them, making heavy going of it in the boulders.

Primitivo kept saying. "Obscenity them. Oh, God and the Virgin, befoul them," each time for firing rolled down the wind, and Robert Jordan climbed down to help Pilar up.

"Qué tal, woman," he said, taking hold of both her wrists and hoisting as she climbed heavily over the last boulder.

"Thy binoculars," she said and lifted their strap over her head. "So it has come to Sordo?"

"Yes."

"Pobre," she said in commiseration. "Poor Sordo."

She was breathing heavily from the climb and she took hold of Robert Jordan's hand and gripped it tight in hers as she looked out over the country.

"How does the combat seem?"

"Bad. Very bad."

"He's *jodido?*"

"I believe so."

"Pobre," she said. "Doubtless because of the horses?"

"Probably."

"Pobre," Pilar said. Then, "Rafael recounted me all of an entire novel of dung about cavalry. What came?"

"A patrol and part of a squadron."

"Up to what point?"

Robert Jordan pointed out where the patrol had stopped and showed her where the gun was hidden. From where they stood they could just see one of Agustín's boots protruding from the rear of the blind.

"The gypsy said they rode to where the gun muzzle pressed against the chest of the horse of the leader," Pilar said. "What a race! Thy glasses were in the cave."

"Have you packed?"

"All that can be taken. Is there news of Pablo?"

"He was forty minutes ahead of the cavalry. They took his trail."

Pilar grinned at him. She still held his hand. Now she dropped it. "They'll never see him," she said. "Now for Sordo. Can we do anything?"

"Nothing."

"Pobre," she said. "I was fond of Sordo. Thou art sure, *sure* that he is *jodido?*"

"Yes. I have seen much cavalry."

"More than were here?"

"Another full troop on their way up there."

"Listen to it," Pilar said. *"Pobre, pobre Sordo."*

They listened to the firing.

"Primitivo wanted to go up there," Robert Jordan said.

"Art thou crazy?" Pilar said to the flat-faced man. "What kind of *locos* are we producing here?"

"I wish to aid them."

"Qué va," Pilar said. "Another romantic. Dost thou not believe thou wilt die quick enough here without useless voyages?"

Robert Jordan looked at her, at the heavy brown face with the high Indian cheekbones, the wide-set dark eyes and the laughing mouth with the heavy, bitter upper lip.

"Thou must act like a man," she said to Primitivo. "A grown man. You with your gray hairs and all."

"Don't joke at me," Primitivo said sullenly. "If a man has a little heart and a little imagination——"

"He should learn to control them," Pilar said. "Thou wilt die soon enough with us. There is no need to seek that with strangers. As for thy imagination. The gypsy has enough for all. What a novel he told me."

"If thou hadst seen it thou wouldst not call it a novel," Primitivo said. "There was a moment of great gravity."

"*Qué va,*" Pilar said. "Some cavalry rode here and they rode away. And you all make yourselves a heroism. It is to this we have come with so much inaction."

"And this of Sordo is not grave?" Primitivo said contemptuously now. He suffered visibly each time the firing came down the wind and he wanted either to go to the combat or have Pilar go and leave him alone.

"*Total, qué?*" Pilar said. "It has come so it has come. Don't lose thy *cojones* for the misfortune of another."

"Go defile thyself," Primitivo said. "There are women of a stupidity and brutality that is insupportable."

"In order to support and aid those men poorly equipped for procreation," Pilar said, "if there is nothing to see I am going."

Just then Robert Jordan heard the plane high overhead. He looked up and in the high sky it looked to be the same observation plane that he had seen earlier in the morning. Now it was returning from the direction of the lines and it was moving in the direction of the high country where El Sordo was being attacked.

"There is the bad luck bird," Pilar said. "Will it see what goes on there?"

"Surely," Robert Jordan said. "If they are not blind."

They watched the plane moving high and silvery and steady in the sunlight. It was coming from the left and they could see the round disks of light the two propellers made.

"Keep down," Robert Jordan said.

Then the plane was overhead, its shadows passing over the open glade, the throbbing reaching its maximum of portent. Then it was past and headed toward the top of the valley. They watched it go steadily on its course until it was just out of sight and then they saw it coming back in a wide dipping circle, to circle twice over the high country and then disappear in the direction of Segovia.

Robert Jordan looked at Pilar. There was perspiration on her forehead and she shook her head. She had been holding her lower lip between her teeth.

"For each one there is something," she said. "For me it is those."

"Thou hast not caught my fear?" Primitivo said sarcastically.

"Nay," she put her hand on his shoulder. "Thou hast no fear to catch. I know that. I am sorry I joked too roughly with thee. We are all in the same caldron." Then she spoke to Robert Jordan. "I will send up food and wine. Dost need anything more?"

"Not in this moment. Where are the others?"

"Thy reserve is intact below with the horses," she grinned. "Everything is out of sight. Everything to go is ready. Maria is with thy material."

"If by any chance we *should* have aviation keep her in the cave."

"Yes, my Lord *Inglés*," Pilar said. *"Thy* gypsy (I give him to thee) I have sent to gather mushrooms to cook with the hares. There are many mushrooms now and it seemed to me we might as well eat the hares although they would be better tomorrow or the day after."

"I think it is best to eat them," Robert Jordan said, and Pilar put her big hand on his shoulder where the strap of the submachine gun crossed his chest, then reached up and mussed his hair with her fingers. "What an *Inglés*," Pilar said. "I will send the Maria with the *puchero* when they are cooked."

The firing from far away and above had almost died out and now there was only an occasional shot.

"You think it is over?" Pilar asked.

"No," Robert Jordan said. "From the sound that we have heard they have attacked and been beaten off. Now I would say the attackers have them surrounded. They have taken cover and they wait for the planes."

Pilar spoke to Primitivo, "Thou. Dost understand there was no intent to insult thee?"

"Ya lo sé," said Primitivo. "I have put up with worse than that from thee. Thou hast a vile tongue. But watch thy mouth, woman. Sordo was a good comrade of mine."

"And not of mine?" Pilar asked him. "Listen, flat face. In war one cannot say what one feels. We have enough of our own without taking Sordo's."

Primitivo was still sullen.

"You should take a physic," Pilar told him. "Now I go to prepare the meal."

"Did you bring the documentation of the *requeté?*" Robert Jordan asked her.

"How stupid I am," she said. "I forgot it. I will send the Maria."

CHAPTER TWENTY-SIX

IT WAS three o'clock in the afternoon before the planes came. The snow had all been gone by noon and the rocks were hot now in the sun. There were no clouds in the sky and Robert Jordan sat in the rocks with his shirt off browning his back in the sun and reading the letters that had been in the pockets of the dead cavalryman. From time to time he would stop reading to look across the open slope to the line of the timber, look over the high country above and then return to the letters. No more cavalry had appeared. At intervals there would be the sound of a shot from the direction of El Sordo's camp. But the firing was desultory.

From examining his military papers he knew the boy was from Tafalla in Navarra, twenty-one years old, unmarried, and the son of a blacksmith. His regiment was the Nth cavalry, which surprised Robert Jordan, for he had believed that regiment to be in the North. He was a Carlist, and he had been wounded at the fighting for Irun at the start of the war.

I've probably seen him run through the streets ahead of the bulls at the Feria in Pamplona, Robert Jordan thought. You never kill any one that you want to kill in a war, he said to himself. Well, hardly ever, he amended and went on reading the letters.

The first letters he read were very formal, very carefully written and dealt almost entirely with local happenings. They were from his sister and Robert Jordan learned that everything was all right in Tafalla, that father was well, that mother was the same as always but with certain complaints about her back, that she hoped he was well and not in too great danger and she was happy he was doing away with the Reds to liberate Spain from the domination of the Marxist hordes. Then there was a list of those boys from Tafalla who had been killed or badly wounded since she wrote last. She mentioned ten who were killed. That is a great many for a town the size of Tafalla, Robert Jordan thought.

There was quite a lot of religion in the letter and she prayed to Saint Anthony, to the Blessed Virgin of Pilar, and to other Virgins to protect him and she wanted him never to forget that he was also protected by the Sacred Heart of Jesus that he wore still, she trusted, at all times over his own heart where it had been proven innumerable—this was underlined—times to have the power of stopping bullets. She was as always his loving sister Concha.

This letter was a little stained around the edges and Robert Jordan put it carefully back with the military papers and opened a letter with a less severe handwriting. It was from the boy's *novia,* his fiancée, and it was quietly, formally, and completely hysterical with concern for his safety. Robert Jordan read it through and then put all the letters together with the papers into his hip pocket. He did not want to read the other letters.

I guess I've done my good deed for today, he said to himself. I guess you have all right, he repeated.

"What are those you were reading?" Primitivo asked him.

"The documentation and the letters of that *requeté* we shot this morning. Do you want to see it?"

"I can't read," Primitivo said. "Was there anything interesting?"

"No," Robert Jordan told him. "They are personal letters."

"How are things going where he came from? Can you tell from the letters?"

"They seem to be going all right," Robert Jordan said. "There are many losses in his town." He looked down to where the blind for the automatic rifle had been changed a little and improved after the snow melted. It looked convincing enough. He looked off across the country.

"From what town is he?" Primitivo asked.

"Tafalla," Robert Jordan told him.

All right, he said to himself. I'm sorry, if that does any good.

It doesn't, he said to himself.

All right then, drop it, he said to himself.

All right, it's dropped.

But it would not drop that easily. How many is that you have killed? he asked himself. I don't know. Do you think you have a right to kill any one? No. But I have to. How many of those you have killed have been real fascists? Very few. But they are all the enemy to whose force we are opposing force. But you like the people of Navarra better than those of any other part of Spain. Yes. And you kill them. Yes. If you don't believe it go down there to the camp. Don't you know it is wrong to kill? Yes. But you do it? Yes. And you still believe absolutely that your cause is right? Yes.

It is right, he told himself, not reassuringly, but proudly. I believe in the people and their right to govern themselves as they wish. But you mustn't believe in killing, he told himself. You must do it as a necessity but you must not believe in it. If you believe in it the whole thing is wrong.

But how many do you suppose you have killed? I don't know because I won't keep track. But do you know? Yes. How many? You can't be sure how many. Blowing the trains you kill many. Very many. But you can't be sure. But of those you are sure of? More than twenty. And of those how many were real fascists? Two that I am sure of. Because I had to shoot them when we took them prisoners at Usera. And you did not mind that? No. Nor did you like it? No. I decided never to do it again. I have avoided it. I have avoided killing those who are unarmed.

Listen, he told himself. You better cut this out. This is very bad for you and for your work. Then himself said back to him, You listen, see? Because you are doing something very serious and I have to see you understand it all the time. I have to keep you straight in your head. Because if you are not absolutely straight in your head you have no right to do the things you do for all of them are crimes and no man has a right to take another man's life unless it is to prevent something worse happening to other people. So get it straight and do not lie to yourself.

But I won't keep a count of people I have killed as though it were a trophy record or a disgusting business like notches in a gun, he told himself. I have a right to not keep count and I have a right to forget them.

No, himself said. You have no right to forget anything. You have no right to shut your eyes to any of it nor any right to forget any of it nor to soften it nor to change it.

Shut up, he told himself. You're getting awfully pompous.

Nor ever to deceive yourself about it, himself went on.

All right, he told himself. Thanks for all the good advice and is it all right for me to love Maria?

Yes, himself said.

Even if there isn't supposed to be any such thing as love in a purely materialistic conception of society?

Since when did you ever have any such conception? himself asked. Never. And you never could have. You're not a real Marxist and you know it. You believe in Liberty, Equality and Fraternity. You believe in Life, Liberty and the Pursuit of Happiness. Don't ever kid yourself with too much dialectics. They are for some but not for you. You have to know them in order not to be a sucker. You have put many things in abeyance to win a war. If this war is lost all of those things are lost.

But afterwards you can discard what you do not believe in. There is plenty you do not believe in and plenty that you do believe in.

And another thing. Don't ever kid yourself about loving some one. It is just that most people are not lucky enough ever to have it. You never had it before and now you have it. What you have with Maria, whether it lasts just through today and a part of tomorrow, or whether it lasts for a long life is the most important thing that can happen to a human being. There will always be people who say it does not exist because they cannot have it. But I tell you it is true and that you have it and that you are lucky even if you die tomorrow.

Cut out the dying stuff, he said to himself. That's not the way we talk. That's the way our friends the anarchists talk. Whenever things get really bad they want to set fire to something and to die. It's a very odd kind of mind they have. Very odd. Well, we're getting through today, old timer, he told himself. It's nearly three o'clock now and there is going to be some food sooner or later. They are still shooting up at Sordo's, which means that they have him surrounded and are waiting to bring up more people, probably. Though they have to make it before dark.

I wonder what it is like up at Sordo's. That's what we all have to expect, given enough time. I imagine it is not too jovial up at Sordo's. We certainly got Sordo into a fine jam with that horse business. How does it go in Spanish? *Un callejón sin salida.* A passageway with no exit. I suppose I could go through with it all right. You only have to do it once and it is soon over with. But wouldn't it be luxury to fight in a war some time where, when you were surrounded, you could surrender? *Estamos copados.* We are surrounded. That was the great panic cry of this war. Then the next thing was that you were shot; with nothing bad before if you were lucky. Sordo wouldn't be lucky that way. Neither would they when the time ever came.

It was three o'clock. Then he heard the far-off, distant throbbing and, looking up, he saw the planes.

CHAPTER TWENTY-SEVEN

EL SORDO was making his fight on a hilltop. He did not like this hill and when he saw it he thought it had the shape of a chancre. But he had had no choice except this hill and he had picked it as far away as he could see it and galloped for it, the automatic rifle heavy on his back, the horse laboring, barrel heaving between his thighs, the sack of grenades swinging against one side, the sack of automatic rifle pans banging against the other, and Joaquín and Ignacio halting and firing, halting and firing to give him time to get the gun in place.

There had still been snow then, the snow that had ruined them, and when his horse was hit so that he wheezed in a slow, jerking, climbing stagger up the last part of the crest, splattering the snow with a bright, pulsing jet, Sordo had hauled him along by the bridle, the reins over his shoulder as he climbed. He climbed as hard as he could with the bullets spatting on the rocks, with the two sacks heavy on his shoulders, and then, holding the horse by the mane, had shot him quickly, expertly, and tenderly just where he had needed him, so that the horse pitched, head forward down to plug a gap between two rocks. He had gotten the gun to firing over the horse's back and he fired two pans, the gun clattering, the empty shells pitching into the snow, the smell of burnt hair from the burnt hide where the hot muzzle rested, him firing at what came up to the hill, forcing them to scatter for cover, while all the time there was a chill in his back from not knowing what was behind him. Once the last of the five men had reached the hilltop the chill went out of his back and he had saved the pans he had left until he would need them.

There were two more horses dead along the slope and three more were dead here on the hilltop. He had only succeeded in stealing three horses last night and one had bolted when they tried to mount him bareback in the corral at the camp when the first shooting had started.

Of the five men who had reached the hilltop three were wounded.

Sordo was wounded in the calf of his leg and in two places in his left arm. He was very thirsty, his wounds had stiffened, and one of the wounds in his left arm was very painful. He also had a bad headache and as he lay waiting for the planes to come he thought of a joke in Spanish. It was, *"Hay que tomar la muerte como si fuera aspirina,"* which means, "You will have to take death as an aspirin." But he did not make the joke aloud. He grinned somewhere inside the pain in his head and inside the nausea that came whenever he moved his arm and looked around at what there was left of his band.

The five men were spread out like the points of a five-pointed star. They had dug with their knees and hands and made mounds in front of their heads and shoulders with the dirt and piles of stones. Using this cover, they were linking the individual mounds up with stones and dirt. Joaquín, who was eighteen years old, had a steel helmet that he dug with and he passed dirt in it.

He had gotten this helmet at the blowing up of the train. It had a bullet hole through it and every one had always joked at him for keeping it. But he had hammered the jagged edges of the bullet hole smooth and driven a wooden plug into it and then cut the plug off and smoothed it even with the metal inside the helmet.

When the shooting started he had clapped this helmet on his head so hard it banged his head as though he had been hit with a casserole and, in the last lung-aching, leg-dead, mouth-dry, bullet-spatting, bullet-cracking, bullet-singing run up the final slope of the hill after his horse was killed, the helmet had seemed to weigh a great amount and to ring his bursting forehead with an iron band. But he had kept it. Now he dug with it in a steady, almost machinelike desperation. He had not yet been hit.

"It serves for something finally," Sordo said to him in his deep, throaty voice.

"Resistir y fortificar es vencer," Joaquín said, his mouth stiff with the dryness of fear which surpassed the normal thirst of battle. It was one of the slogans of the Communist party and it meant, "Hold out and fortify, and you will win."

Sordo looked away and down the slope at where a cavalryman was sniping from behind a boulder. He was very fond of this boy and he was in no mood for slogans.

"What did you say?"

One of the men turned from the building that he was doing. This man was lying flat on his face, reaching carefully up with his hands to put a rock in place while keeping his chin flat against the ground.

Joaquín repeated the slogan in his dried-up boy's voice without checking his digging for a moment.

"What was the last word?" the man with his chin on the ground asked.

"Vencer," the boy said. "Win."

"Mierda," the man with his chin on the ground said.

"There is another that applies to here," Joaquín said, bringing them out as though they were talismans, "Pasionaria says it is better to die on your feet than to live on your knees."

"Mierda again," the man said and another man said, over his shoulder, "We're on our bellies, not our knees."

"Thou. Communist. Do you know your Pasionaria has a son thy age in Russia since the start of the movement?"

"It's a lie," Joaquín said.

"Qué va, it's a lie," the other said. "The dynamiter with the rare name told me. He was of thy party, too. Why should he lie?"

"It's a lie," Joaquín said. "She would not do such a thing as keep a son hidden in Russia out of the war."

"I wish I were in Russia," another of Sordo's men said. "Will not thy Pasionaria send me now from here to Russia, Communist?"

"If thou believest so much in thy Pasionaria, get her to get us off this hill," one of the men who had a bandaged thigh said.

"The fascists will do that," the man with his chin in the dirt said.

"Do not speak thus," Joaquín said to him.

"Wipe the pap of your mother's breasts off thy lips and give me a hatful of that dirt," the man with his chin on the ground said. "No one of us will see the sun go down this night."

El Sordo was thinking: It is shaped like a chancre. Or the breast of a young girl with no nipple. Or the top cone of a volcano. You have never seen a volcano, he thought. Nor will you ever see one. And this hill is like a chancre. Let the volcanos alone. It's late now for the volcanos.

He looked very carefully around the withers of the dead horse and there was a quick hammering of firing from behind a boulder well down the slope and he heard the bullets from the submachine gun thud into the horse. He crawled along behind the horse and looked out of the angle between the horse's hindquarters and the rock. There were three bodies on the slope just below him where they had fallen when the fascists had rushed the crest under cover of the automatic rifle and submachine gunfire and he and the others had broken down the attack by throwing and rolling down hand grenades. There were other bodies that he could not see on the other sides of the hill crest. There was no dead ground by which attackers could approach the summit and Sordo knew that as long as his ammunition and grenades held out and he had as many as four men they could not get him out of there unless they brought up a trench mortar. He did not know whether they had sent to La Granja for a trench mortar. Perhaps they had not, because surely, soon, the planes would come. It had been four hours since the observation plane had flown over them.

This hill is truly like a chancre, Sordo thought, and we are the very pus of it. But we killed many when they made that stupidness. How could they think that they would take us thus? They have such modern armament that they lose all their sense with overconfidence. He had killed the young officer who had led the assault with a grenade that had gone bouncing and rolling down the slope as they came up it, running, bent half over. In the yellow flash and gray roar of smoke he had seen the officer dive forward to where he lay now like a heavy, broken bundle of old clothing marking the farthest point that the assault had reached. Sordo looked at this body and then, down the hill, at the others.

They are brave but stupid people, he thought. But they have sense enough now not to attack us again until the planes come. Unless, of course, they have a mortar coming. It would be easy with a mortar. The mortar was the normal thing and he knew that they would die as soon as a mortar came up, but when he thought of the planes coming up he felt as naked on that hilltop as though all of his clothing and even his skin had been removed. There is no nakeder thing than I feel, he thought. A flayed rabbit is as well covered as a bear in comparison. But why should they bring planes? They could get us out of here with a trench mortar easily. They are proud of their planes, though, and they will probably bring them. Just as they were so proud of their automatic weapons that they made that stupidness. But undoubtedly they must have sent for a mortar, too.

One of the men fired. Then jerked the bolt and fired again, quickly.

"Save thy cartridges," Sordo said.

"One of the sons of the great whore tried to reach that boulder," the man pointed.

"Did you hit him?" Sordo asked, turning his head with difficulty.

"Nay," the man said. "The fornicator ducked back."

"Who is a whore of whores is Pilar," the man with his chin in the dirt said. "That whore knows we are dying here."

"She could do no good," Sordo said. The man had spoken on the side of his good ear and he had heard him without turning his head. "What could she do?"

"Take these sluts from the rear."

"*Qué va,*" Sordo said. "They are spread around a hillside. How would she come on them? There are a hundred and fifty of them. Maybe more now."

"But if we hold out until dark," Joaquín said.

"And if Christmas comes on Easter," the man with his chin on the ground said.

"And if thy aunt had *cojones* she would be thy uncle," another said to him. "Send for thy Pasionaria. She alone can help us."

"I do not believe that about the son," Joaquín said. "Or if he is there he is training to be an aviator or something of that sort."

"He is hidden there for safety," the man told him.

"He is studying dialectics. Thy Pasionaria has been there. So have Lister and Modesto and others. The one with the rare name told me."

"That they should go to study and return to aid us," Joaquín said.

"That they should aid us now," another man said. "That all the cruts of Russian sucking swindlers should aid us now." He fired and said, *"Me cago en tal;* I missed him again."

"Save thy cartridges and do not talk so much or thou wilt be very thirsty," Sordo said. "There is no water on this hill."

"Take this," the man said and rolling on his side he pulled a wineskin that he wore slung from his shoulder over his head and handed it to Sordo. "Wash thy mouth out, old one. Thou must have much thirst with thy wounds."

"Let all take it," Sordo said.

"Then I will have some first," the owner said and squirted a long stream into his mouth before he handed the leather bottle around.

"Sordo, when thinkest thou the planes will come?" the man with his chin in the dirt asked.

"Any time," said Sordo. "They should have come before."

"Do you think these sons of the great whore will attack again?"

"Only if the planes do not come."

He did not think there was any need to speak about the mortar. They would know it soon enough when the mortar came.

"God knows they've enough planes with what we saw yesterday."

"Too many," Sordo said.

His head hurt very much and his arm was stiffening so that the pain of moving it was almost unbearable. He looked up at the bright, high, blue early summer sky as he raised the leather wine bottle with his good arm. He was fifty-two years old and he was sure this was the last time he would see that sky.

He was not at all afraid of dying but he was angry at being trapped on this hill which was only utilizable as a place to die. If we could have gotten clear, he thought. If we could have made them come up the long valley or if we could have broken loose across the road it would have been all right. But this chancre of a hill. We must use it as well as we can and we have used it very well so far.

If he had known how many men in history have had to use a hill to die on it would not have cheered him any for, in the moment he was passing through, men are not impressed by what has happened to other men in similar circumstances any more than a widow of one day is helped by the knowledge that other loved husbands have died. Whether one has fear of it or not, one's death is difficult to accept. Sordo had accepted it but there was no sweetness in its acceptance even at fifty-two, with three wounds and him surrounded on a hill.

He joked about it to himself but he looked at the sky and at the far mountains and he swallowed the wine and he did not want it. If one must die, he thought, and clearly one must, I can die. But I hate it.

Dying was nothing and he had no picture of it nor fear of it in his mind. But living was a field of grain blowing in the wind on the side of a hill. Living was a hawk in the sky. Living was an earthen jar of water in the dust of the threshing with the grain flailed out and the chaff blowing. Living was a horse between your legs and a carbine under one leg and a hill and a valley and a stream with trees along it and the far side of the valley and the hills beyond.

Sordo passed the wine bottle back and nodded his head in thanks. He leaned forward and patted the dead horse on the shoulder where the muzzle of the automatic rifle had burned the hide. He could still smell the burnt hair. He thought how he had held the horse there, trembling, with the fire around them, whispering and cracking, over and around them like a curtain, and had carefully shot him just at the intersection of the cross-lines between the two eyes and the ears. Then as the horse pitched down he had dropped down behind his warm, wet back to get the gun to going as they came up the hill.

"Eras mucho caballo," he said, meaning. "Thou wert plenty of horse."

El Sordo lay now on his good side and looked up at the sky. He was lying on a heap of empty cartridge hulls but his head was protected by the rock and his body lay in the lee of the horse. His wounds had stiffened badly and he had much pain and he felt too tired to move.

"What passes with thee, old one?" the man next to him asked.

"Nothing. I am taking a little rest."

"Sleep," the other said. *"They* will wake us when they come."

Just then some one shouted from down the slope.

"Listen, bandits!" the voice came from behind the rocks where the closest automatic rifle was placed. "Surrender now before the planes blow you to pieces."

"What is it he says?" Sordo asked.

Joaquín told him. Sordo rolled to one side and pulled himself up so that he was crouched behind the gun again.

"Maybe the planes aren't coming," he said. "Don't answer them and do not fire. Maybe we can get them to attack again."

"If we should insult them a little?" the man who had spoken to Joaquín about La Pasionaria's son in Russia asked.

"No," Sordo said. "Give me thy big pistol. Who has a big pistol?"

"Here."

"Give it to me." Crouched on his knees he took the big 9 mm.

Star and fired one shot into the ground beside the dead horse, waited, then fired again four times at irregular intervals. Then he waited while he counted sixty and then fired a final shot directly into the body of the dead horse. He grinned and handed back the pistol.

"Reload it," he whispered, "and that every one should keep his mouth shut and no one shoot."

"Bandidos!" the voice shouted from behind the rocks.

No one spoke on the hill.

"Bandidos! Surrender now before we blow thee to little pieces."

"They're biting," Sordo whispered happily.

As he watched, a man showed his head over the top of the rocks. There was no shot from the hilltop and the head went down again. El Sordo waited, watching, but nothing more happened. He turned his head and looked at the others who were all watching down their sectors of the slope. As he looked at them the others shook their heads.

"Let no one move," he whispered.

"Sons of the great whore," the voice came now from behind the rocks again.

"Red swine. Mother rapers. Eaters of the milk of thy fathers."

Sordo grinned. He could just hear the bellowed insults by turning his good ear. This is better than the aspirin, he thought. How many will we get? Can they be that foolish?

The voice had stopped again and for three minutes they heard nothing and saw no movement. Then the sniper behind the boulder a hundred yards down the slope exposed himself and fired. The bullet hit a rock and ricocheted with a sharp whine. Then Sordo saw a man, bent double, run from the shelter of the rocks where the automatic rifle was across the open ground to the big boulder behind which the sniper was hidden. He almost dove behind the boulder.

Sordo looked around. They signalled to him that there was no movement on the other slopes. El Sordo grinned happily and shook his head. This is ten times better than the aspirin, he thought, and he waited, as happy as only a hunter can be happy.

Below on the slope the man who had run from the pile of stones to the shelter of the boulder was speaking to the sniper.

"Do you believe it?"

"I don't know," the sniper said.

"It would be logical," the man, who was the officer in command, said. "They are surrounded. They have nothing to expect but to die."

The sniper said nothing.

"What do you think?" the officer asked.

"Nothing," the sniper said.

"Have you seen any movement since the shots?"

"None at all."

The officer looked at his wrist watch. It was ten minutes to three o'clock.

"The planes should have come an hour ago," he said. Just then another officer flopped in behind the boulder. The sniper moved over to make room for him.

"Thou, Paco," the first officer said. "How does it seem to thee?"

The second officer was breathing heavily from his sprint up and across the hillside from the automatic rifle position.

"For me it is a trick," he said.

"But if it is not? What a ridicule we make waiting here and laying siege to dead men."

"We have done something worse than ridiculous already," the second officer said. "Look at that slope."

He looked up the slope to where the dead were scattered close to the top. From where he looked the line of the hilltop showed the scattered rocks, the belly, projecting legs, shod hooves jutting out, of Sordo's horse, and the fresh dirt thrown up by the digging.

"What about the mortars?" asked the second officer.

"They should be here in an hour. If not before."

"Then wait for them. There has been enough stupidity already."

"*Bandidos!*" the first officer shouted suddenly, getting to his feet and putting his head well up above the boulder so that the crest of the hill looked much closer as he stood upright. "Red swine! Cowards!"

The second officer looked at the sniper and shook his head. The sniper looked away but his lips tightened.

The first officer stood there, his head all clear of the rock and with his hand on his pistol butt. He cursed and vilified the hilltop. Nothing happened. Then he stepped clear of the boulder and stood there looking up the hill.

"Fire, cowards, if you are alive," he shouted. "Fire on one who has no fear of any Red that ever came out of the belly of the great whore."

This last was quite a long sentence to shout and the officer's face was red and congested as he finished.

The second officer, who was a thin sunburned man with quiet eyes, a thin, long-lipped mouth and a stubble of beard over his hollow cheeks, shook his head again. It was this officer who was shouting who had ordered the first assault. The young lieutenant who was dead up the slope had been the best friend of this other lieutenant who was named Paco Berrendo and who was listening to the shouting of the captain, who was obviously in a state of exaltation.

"Those are the swine who shot my sister and my mother," the captain said. He had a red face and a blond, British-looking moustache and there was something wrong about his eyes. They were a light blue and the lashes were light, too. As you looked at them they seemed to focus slowly. Then "Reds," he shouted. "Cowards!" and commenced cursing again.

He stood absolutely clear now and, sighting carefully, fired his pistol at the only target that the hilltop presented: the dead horse that had belonged to Sordo. The bullet threw up a puff of dirt fifteen yards below the horse. The captain fired again. The bullet hit a rock and sung off.

The captain stood there looking at the hilltop. The Lieutenant Berrendo was looking at the body of the other lieutenant just below the summit. The sniper was looking at the ground under his eyes. Then he looked up at the captain.

"There is no one alive up there," the captain said. "Thou," he said to the sniper, "go up there and see."

The sniper looked down. He said nothing.

"Don't you hear me?" the captain shouted at him.

"Yes, my captain," the sniper said, not looking at him.

"Then get up and go." The captain still had his pistol out. "Do you hear me?"

"Yes, my captain."

"Why don't you go, then?"

"I don't want to, my captain."

"You don't *want* to?" The captain pushed the pistol against the small of the man's back. "You don't *want* to?"

"I am afraid, my captain," the soldier said with dignity.

Lieutenant Berrendo, watching the captain's face and his odd eyes, thought he was going to shoot the man then.

"Captain Mora," he said.

"Lieutenant Berrendo?"

"It is possible the soldier is right."

"That he is right to say he is afraid? That he is right to say he does not *want* to obey an order?"

"No. That he is right that it is a trick."

"They are all dead," the captain said. "Don't you hear me say they are all dead?'

"You mean our comrades on the slope?" Berrendo asked him. "I agree with you."

"Paco," the captain said, "don't be a fool. Do you think you are the only one who cared for Julián? I tell you the Reds are dead. Look!"

He stood up, then put both hands on top of the boulder and pulled himself up, kneeing-up awkwardly, then getting on his feet.

"Shoot," he shouted, standing on the gray granite boulder and waved both his arms. "Shoot me! Kill me!"

On the hilltop El Sordo lay behind the dead horse and grinned.

What a people, he thought. He laughed, trying to hold it in because the shaking hurt his arm.

"Reds," came the shout from below. "Red canaille. Shoot me! Kill me!"

Sordo, his chest shaking, barely peeped past the horse's crupper and saw the captain on top of the boulder waving his arms. Another officer stood by the boulder. The sniper was standing at the other side. Sordo kept his eye where it was and shook his head happily.

"Shoot me," he said softly to himself. "Kill me!" Then his shoulders shook again. The laughing hurt his arm and each time he laughed his head felt as though it would burst. But the laughter shook him again like a spasm.

Captain Mora got down from the boulder.

"Now do you believe me, Paco?" he questioned Lieutenant Berrendo.

"No," said Lieutenant Berrendo.

"*Cojones!*" the captain said. "Here there is nothing but idiots and cowards."

The sniper had gotten carefully behind the boulder again and Lieutenant Berrendo was squatting beside him.

The captain, standing in the open beside the boulder, commenced to shout filth at the hilltop. There is no language so filthy as Spanish. There are words for all the vile words in English and there are other words and expressions that are used only in countries where blasphemy keeps pace with the austerity of religion. Lieutenant Berrendo was a very devout Catholic. So was the sniper. They were Carlists from Navarra and while both of them cursed and blasphemed when they were angry they regarded it as a sin which they regularly confessed.

As they crouched now behind the boulder watching the captain and listening to what he was shouting, they both disassociated themselves from him and what he was saying. They did not want to have that sort of talk on their consciences on a day in which they might die. Talking thus will not bring luck, the sniper thought. Speaking thus of the *Virgen* is bad luck. This one speaks worse than the Reds.

Julián is dead, Lieutenant Berrendo was thinking. Dead there on the slope on such a day as this is. And this foul mouth stands there bringing more ill fortune with his blasphemies.

Now the captain stopped shouting and turned to Lieutenant Berrendo. His eyes looked stranger than ever.

"Paco," he said, happily, "you and I will go up there."

"Not me."

"What?" The captain had his pistol out again.

I hate these pistol brandishers, Berrendo was thinking. They cannot give an order without jerking a gun out. They probably pull out their pistols when they go to the toilet and order the move they will make.

"I will go if you order me to. But under protest," Lieutenant Berrendo told the captain.

"Then I will go alone," the captain said. "The smell of cowardice is too strong here."

Holding his pistol in his right hand, he strode steadily up the slope. Berrendo and the sniper watched him. He was making no attempt to take any cover and he was looking straight ahead of him at the rocks, the dead horse, and the fresh-dug dirt of the hilltop.

El Sordo lay behind the horse at the corner of the rock, watching the captain come striding up the hill.

Only one, he thought. We get only one. But from his manner of speaking he is *caza mayor*. Look at him walking. Look what an animal. Look at him stride forward. This one is for me. This one I take with me on the trip. This one coming now makes the same voyage I do. Come on, Comrade Voyager. Come striding. Come right along. Come along to meet it. Come on. Keep on walking. Don't slow up. Come right along. Come as thou art coming. Don't stop and look at those. That's right. Don't even look down. Keep on coming with your eyes forward. Look, he has a moustache. What do you think of that? He runs to a moustache, the Comrade Voyager. He is a captain. Look at his sleeves. I said he was *caza mayor*. He has the face of an *Inglés*. Look. With a red face and blond hair and blue eyes. With no cap on and his moustache is yellow. With blue eyes. With pale blue eyes. With pale blue eyes with something wrong with them. With pale blue eyes that don't focus. Close enough. Too close. Yes, Comrade Voyager. Take it, Comrade Voyager.

He squeezed the trigger of the automatic rifle gently and it pounded back three times against his shoulder with the slippery jolt the recoil of a tripoded automatic weapon gives.

The captain lay on his face on the hillside. His left arm was under him. His right arm that had held the pistol was stretched forward of his head. From all down the slope they were firing on the hill crest again.

Crouched behind the boulder, thinking that now he would have to sprint across that open space under fire, Lieutenant Berrendo heard the deep hoarse voice of Sordo from the hilltop.

"*Bandidos!*" the voice came. "*Bandidos!* Shoot me! Kill me!"

On the top of the hill El Sordo lay behind the automatic rifle laughing so that his chest ached, so that he thought the top of his head would burst.

"*Bandidos,*" he shouted again happily. "Kill me, *bandidos!*" Then he shook his head happily. We have lots of company for the Voyage, he thought.

He was going to try for the other officer with the automatic rifle when he would leave the shelter of the boulder. Sooner or later he would have to leave it. Sordo knew that he could never command from there and he thought he had a very good chance to get him.

Just then the others on the hill heard the first sound of the coming of the planes.

El Sordo did not hear them. He was covering the down-slope edge of the boulder with his automatic rifle and he was thinking: when I see him he will be running already and I will miss him if I am not careful. I could shoot behind him all across that stretch. I should swing the gun with him and ahead of him. Or let him start and then get on him and ahead of him. I will try to pick him up there at the edge of the rock and swing just ahead of him. Then he felt a touch on his shoulder and he turned and saw the gray, fear-drained face of Joaquín and he looked where the boy was pointing and saw the three planes coming.

At this moment Lieutenant Berrendo broke from behind the boulder and, with his head bent and his legs plunging, ran down and across the slope to the shelter of the rocks where the automatic rifle was placed.

Watching the planes, Sordo never saw him go.

"Help me to pull this out," he said to Joaquín and the boy dragged the automatic rifle clear from between the horse and the rock.

The planes were coming on steadily. They were in echelon and each second they grew larger and their noise was greater.

"Lie on your backs to fire at them," Sordo said. "Fire ahead of them as they come."

He was watching them all the time. *"Cabrones! Hijos de puta!"* he said rapidly.

"Ignacio!" he said. "Put the gun on the shoulder of the boy. Thou!" to Joaquín, "Sit there and do not move. Crouch over. More. No. More."

He lay back and sighted with the automatic rifle as the planes came on steadily.

"Thou, Ignacio, hold me the three legs of that tripod." They were dangling down the boy's back and the muzzle of the gun was shaking from the jerking of his body that Joaquín could not control as he crouched with bent head hearing the droning roar of their coming.

Lying flat on his belly and looking up into the sky watching them come, Ignacio gathered the legs of the tripod into his two hands and steadied the gun.

"Keep thy head down," he said to Joaquín. "Keep thy head forward."

"Pasionaria says 'Better to die on thy—'" Joaquín was saying to himself as the drone came nearer them. Then he shifted suddenly into "Hail Mary, full of grace, the Lord is with thee; Blessed art thou among women and Blessed is the fruit of thy womb, Jesus. Holy Mary, Mother of God, pray for us sinners now and at the hour of our death. Amen. Holy Mary, Mother of God," he started, then he remembered quickly as the roar came now unbearably and started an act of contrition racing in it, "Oh my God, I am heartily sorry for having offended thee who art worthy of all my love——"

Then there were the hammering explosions past his ears and the gun barrel hot against his shoulder. It was hammering now again and his ears were deafened by the muzzle blast. Ignacio was pulling down hard on the tripod and the barrel was burning his back. It was hammering now in the roar and he could not remember the act of contrition.

All he could remember was at the hour of our death. Amen. At the hour of our death. Amen. At the hour. At the hour. Amen. The others all were firing. Now and at the hour of our death. Amen.

Then, through the hammering of the gun, there was the whistle of the air splitting apart and then in the red black roar the earth rolled under his knees and then waved up to hit him in the face and then dirt and bits of rock were falling all over and Ignacio was lying on him and the gun was lying on him. But he was not dead because the whistle came again and the earth rolled under him with the roar. Then it came again and the earth lurched under his belly and one side of the hilltop rose into the air and then fell slowly over them where they lay.

The planes came back three times and bombed the hilltop but no one on the hilltop knew it. Then the planes machine-gunned the hilltop and went away. As they dove on the hill for the last time with their machine guns hammering, the first plane pulled up and winged over and then each plane did the same and they moved from echelon to V-formation and went away into the sky in the direction of Segovia.

Keeping a heavy fire on the hilltop, Lieutenant Berrendo pushed a patrol up to one of the bomb craters from where they could throw grenades onto the crest. He was taking no chances of any one being alive and waiting for them in the mess that was up there and he threw four grenades into the confusion of dead horses, broken and split rocks, and torn yellow-stained explosive-stinking earth before he climbed out of the bomb crater and walked over to have a look.

No one was alive on the hilltop except the boy Joaquín, who was unconscious under the dead body of Ignacio. Joaquín was bleeding from the nose and from the ears. He had known nothing and had no feeling since he had suddenly been in the very heart of the thunder and the breath had been wrenched from his body when the one bomb struck so close and Lieutenant Berrendo made the sign of the cross and then shot him in the back of the head, as quickly and as gently, if such an abrupt movement can be gentle, as Sordo had shot the wounded horse.

Lieutenant Berrendo stood on the hilltop and looked down the slope at his own dead and then across the country seeing where they had galloped before Sordo had turned at bay here. He noticed all the dispositions that had been made of the troops and then he ordered the dead men's horses to be brought up and the bodies tied across the saddles so that they might be packed in to La Granja.

"Take that one, too," he said. "The one with his hands on the automatic rifle. That should be Sordo. He is the oldest and it was he with the gun. No. Cut the head off and wrap it in a poncho." He considered a minute. "You might as well take all the heads. And of the others below on the slope and where we first found them. Collect the rifles and pistols and pack that gun on a horse."

Then he walked down to where the lieutenant lay who had been killed in the first assault. He looked down at him but did not touch him.

"Qué cosa más mala es la guerra," he said to himself, which meant, "What a bad thing war is."

Then he made the sign of the cross again and as he walked down the hill he said five Our Fathers and five Hail Marys for the repose of the soul of his dead comrade. He did not wish to stay to see his orders being carried out.

CHAPTER TWENTY-EIGHT

AFTER the planes went away Robert Jordan and Primitivo heard the firing start and his heart seemed to start again with it. A cloud of smoke drifted over the last ridge that he could see in the high country and the planes were three steadily receding specks in the sky.

"They've probably bombed hell out of their own cavalry and never touched Sordo and Company," Robert Jordan said to himself. "The damned planes scare you to death but they don't kill you."

"The combat goes on," Primitivo said, listening to the heavy firing. He had winced at each bomb thud and now he licked his dry lips.

"Why not?" Robert Jordan said. "Those things never kill anybody."

Then the firing stopped absolutely and he did not hear another shot. Lieutenant Berrendo's pistol shot did not carry that far.

When the firing first stopped it did not affect him. Then as the quiet kept on a hollow feeling came in his chest. Then he heard the grenades burst and for a moment his heart rose. Then everything was quiet again and the quiet kept on and he knew that it was over.

Maria came up from the camp with a tin bucket of stewed hare with mushrooms sunken in the rich gravy and a sack with bread, a leather wine bottle, four tin plates, two cups and four spoons. She stopped at the gun and ladled out two plates for Agustín and Eladio, who had replaced Anselmo at the gun, and gave them bread and unscrewed the horn tip of the wine bottle and poured two cups of wine.

Robert Jordan watched her climbing lithely up to his lookout post, the sack over her shoulder, the bucket in one hand, her cropped head bright in the sun. He climbed down and took the bucket and helped her up the last boulder.

"What did the aviation do?" she asked, her eyes frightened.

"Bombed Sordo."

He had the bucket open and was ladling out stew onto a plate.

"Are they still fighting?"

"No. It is over."

"Oh," she said and bit her lip and looked out across the country.

"I have no appetite," Primitivo said.

"Eat anyway," Robert Jordan told him.

"I could not swallow food."

"Take a drink of this, man," Robert Jordan said and handed him the wine bottle. "Then eat."

"This of Sordo has taken away desire," Primitivo said. "Eat, thou. I have no desire."

Maria went over to him and put her arms around his neck and kissed him.

"Eat, old one," she said. "Each one should take care of his strength."

Primitivo turned away from her. He took the wine bottle and tipping his head back swallowed steadily while he squirted a jet of wine into the back of his mouth. Then he filled his plate from the bucket and commenced to eat.

Robert Jordan looked at Maria and shook his head. She sat down by him and put her arm around his shoulder. Each knew how the other felt and they sat there and Robert Jordan ate the stew, taking time to appreciate the mushrooms completely, and he drank the wine and they said nothing.

"You may stay here, *guapa,* if you want," he said after a while when the food was all eaten.

"Nay," she said. "I must go to Pilar."

"It is all right to stay here. I do not think that anything will happen now."

"Nay. I must go to Pilar. She is giving me instruction."

"What does she give thee?"

"Instruction." She smiled at him and then kissed him. "Did you never hear of religious instruction?" She blushed. "It is something like that." She blushed again. "But different."

"Go to thy instruction," he said and patted her on the head. She smiled at him again, then said to Primitivo, "Do you want anything from below?"

"No, daughter," he said. They both saw that he was still not yet recovered.

"*Salud,* old one," she said to him.

"Listen," Primitivo said. "I have no fear to die but to leave them alone thus——" his voice broke.

"There was no choice," Robert Jordan told him.

"I know. But all the same."

"There was no choice," Robert Jordan repeated. "And now it is better not to speak of it."

"Yes. But there alone with no aid from us——"

"Much better not to speak of it," Robert Jordan said. "And thou, *guapa,* get thee to thy instruction."

He watched her climb down through the rocks. Then he sat there for a long time thinking and watching the high country.

Primitivo spoke to him but he did not answer. It was hot in the sun but he did not notice the heat while he sat watching the hill slopes and the long patches of pine trees that stretched up the highest slope. An hour passed and the sun was far to his left now when he saw them coming over the crest of the slope and he picked up his glasses.

The horses showed small and minute as the first two riders came into sight on the long green slope of the high hill. Then there were four more horsemen coming down, spread out across the wide hill and then through his glasses he saw the double column of men and horses ride into the sharp clarity of his vision. As he watched them he felt sweat come from his armpits and run down his flanks. One man rode at the head of the column. Then came more horsemen. Then came the riderless horses with their burdens tied across the saddles. Then there were two riders. Then came the wounded with men walking by them as they rode. Then came more cavalry to close the column.

Robert Jordan watched them ride down the slope and out of sight into the timber. He could not see at that distance the load one saddle bore of a long rolled poncho tied at each end and at intervals so that it bulged between each lashing as a pod bulges with peas. This was tied across the saddle and at each end it was lashed to the stirrup leathers. Alongside this on the top of the saddle the automatic rifle Sordo had served was lashed arrogantly.

Lieutenant Berrendo, who was riding at the head of the column, his flankers out, his point pushed well forward, felt no arrogance. He felt only the hollowness that comes after action. He was thinking: taking the heads is barbarous. But proof and identification is necessary. I will have trouble enough about this as it is and who knows? This of the heads may appeal to them. There are those of them who like such things. It is possible they will send them all to Burgos. It is a barbarous business. The planes were *muchos*. Much. Much. But we could have done it all, and almost without losses, with a Stokes mortar. Two mules to carry the shells and a mule with a mortar on each side of the pack saddle. What an army we would be then! With the fire power of all these automatic weapons. And another mule. No, two mules to carry ammunition. Leave it alone, he told himself. It is no longer cavalry. Leave it alone. You're building yourself an army. Next you will want a mountain gun.

Then he thought of Julián, dead on the hill, dead now, tied across a horse there in the first troop, and as he rode down into the dark pine forest, leaving the sunlight behind him on the hill, riding now in the quiet dark of the forest, he started to say a prayer for him again.

"Hail, holy queen mother of mercy," he started. "Our life, our sweetness and our hope. To thee do we send up our sighs, mournings and weepings in this valley of tears——"

He went on with the prayer, the horses' hooves soft on the fallen pine needles, the light coming through the tree trunks in patches as it comes through the columns of a cathedral, and as he prayed he looked ahead to see his flankers riding through the trees.

He rode out of the forest onto the yellow road that led into La Granja and the horses' hooves raised a dust that hung over them as they rode. It powdered the dead who were tied face down across the saddles and the wounded, and those who walked beside them, were in thick dust.

It was here that Anselmo saw them ride past in their dust.

He counted the dead and the wounded and he recognized Sordo's automatic rifle. He did not know what the poncho-wrapped bundle was which flapped against the led horse's flanks as the stirrup leathers swung but when, on his way home, he came in the dark onto the hill where Sordo had fought, he knew at once what the long poncho roll contained. In the dark he could not tell who had been up on the hill. But he counted those that lay there and then made off across the hills for Pablo's camp.

Walking alone in the dark, with a fear like a freezing of his heart from the feeling the holes of the bomb craters had given him, from them and from what he had found on the hill, he put all thought of the next day out of his mind. He simply walked as fast as he could to bring the news. And as he walked he prayed for the souls of Sordo and of all his band. It was the first time he had prayed since the start of the movement.

"Most kind, most sweet, most clement Virgin," he prayed.

But he could not keep from thinking of the next day finally. So he thought: I will do exactly as the *Inglés* says and as he says to do it. But let me be close to him, O Lord, and may his instructions be exact for I do not think that I could control myself under the bombardment of the planes. Help me, O Lord, tomorrow to comport myself as a man should in his last hours. Help me, O Lord, to understand clearly the needs of the day. Help me, O Lord, to dominate the movement of my legs that I should not run when the bad moment comes. Help me, O Lord, to comport myself as a man tomorrow in the day of battle. Since I have asked this aid of thee, please grant it, knowing I would not ask it if it were not serious, and I will ask nothing more of thee again.

Walking in the dark alone he felt much better from having prayed and he was sure, now, that he would comport himself well. Walking now down from the high country, he went back to praying for the people of Sordo and in a short time he had reached the upper post where Fernando challenged him.

"It is I," he answered, "Anselmo."

"Good," Fernando said.

"You know of this of Sordo, old one?" Anselmo asked Fernando, the two of them standing at the entrance of the big rocks in the dark.

"Why not?" Fernando said. "Pablo has told us."

"He was up there?"

"Why not?" Fernando said stolidly. "He visited the hill as soon as the cavalry left."

"He told you——"

"He told us all," Fernando said. "What barbarians these fascists are! We must do away with all such barbarians in Spain." He stopped, then said bitterly, "In them is lacking all conception of dignity."

Anselmo grinned in the dark. An hour ago he could not have imagined that he would ever smile again. What a marvel, that Fernando, he thought.

"Yes," he said to Fernando. "We must teach them. We must take away their planes, their automatic weapons, their tanks, their artillery and teach them dignity."

"Exactly," Fernando said. "I am glad that you agree."

Anselmo left him standing there alone with his dignity and went on down to the cave.

CHAPTER TWENTY-NINE

ANSELMO found Robert Jordan sitting at the plank table inside the cave with Pablo opposite him. They had a bowl poured full of wine between them and each had a cup of wine on the table. Robert Jordan had his notebook out and he was holding a pencil. Pilar and Maria were in the back of the cave out of sight. There was no way for Anselmo to know that the woman was keeping the girl back there to keep her from hearing the conversation and he thought that it was odd that Pilar was not at the table.

Robert Jordan looked up as Anselmo came in under the blanket that hung over the opening. Pablo stared straight at the table. His eyes were focused on the wine bowl but he was not seeing it.

"I come from above," Anselmo said to Robert Jordan.

"Pablo has told us," Robert Jordan said.

"There were six dead on the hill and they had taken the heads," Anselmo said. "I was there in the dark."

Robert Jordan nodded. Pablo sat there looking at the wine bowl and saying nothing. There was no expression on his face and his small pig-eyes were looking at the wine bowl as though he had never seen one before.

"Sit down," Robert Jordan said to Anselmo.

The old man sat down at the table on one of the hide-covered stools and Robert Jordan reached under the table and brought up the pinch-bottle of whiskey that had been the gift of Sordo. It was about half-full. Robert Jordan reached down the table for a cup and poured a drink of whiskey into it and shoved it along the table to Anselmo.

"Drink that, old one," he said.

Pablo looked from the wine bowl to Anselmo's face as he drank and then he looked back at the wine bowl.

As Anselmo swallowed the whiskey he felt a burning in his nose, his eyes and his mouth, and then a happy, comforting warmth in his stomach. He wiped his mouth with the back of his hand.

Then he looked at Robert Jordan and said, "Can I have another?"

"Why not?" Robert Jordan said and poured another drink from the bottle and handed it this time instead of pushing it.

This time there was not the burning when he swallowed but the warm comfort doubled. It was as good a thing for his spirit as a saline injection is for a man who has suffered a great hemorrhage.

The old man looked toward the bottle again.

"The rest is for tomorrow," Robert Jordan said. "What passed on the road, old one?"

"There was much movement," Anselmo said. "I have it all noted down as you showed me. I have one watching for me and noting now. Later I will go for her report."

"Did you see anti-tank guns? Those on rubber tires with the long barrels?"

"Yes," Anselmo said. "There were four camions which passed on the road. In each of them there was such a gun with pine branches spread across the barrels. In the trucks rode six men with each gun."

"Four guns, you say?" Robert Jordan asked him.

"Four," Anselmo said. He did not look at his papers.

"Tell me what else went up the road."

While Robert Jordan noted Anselmo told him everything he had seen move past him on the road. He told it from the beginning and in order with the wonderful memory of those who cannot read or write, and twice, while he was talking, Pablo reached out for more wine from the bowl.

"There was also the cavalry which entered La Granja from the high country where El Sordo fought," Anselmo went on.

Then he told the number of the wounded he had seen and the number of the dead across the saddles.

"There was a bundle packed across one saddle that I did not understand," he said. "But now I know it was the heads." He went on without pausing. "It was a squadron of cavalry. They had only one officer left. He was not the one who was here in the early morning when you were by the gun. He must have been one of the dead. Two of the dead were officers by their sleeves. They were lashed face down over the saddles, their arms hanging. Also they had the *máquina* of El Sordo tied to the saddle that bore the heads. The barrel was bent. That is all," he finished.

"It is enough," Robert Jordan said and dipped his cup into the wine bowl. "Who beside you has been through the lines to the side of the Republic?"

"Andrés and Eladio."

"Which is the better of those two?"

"Andrés."

"How long would it take him to get to Navacerrada from here?"

"Carrying no pack and taking his precautions, in three hours with luck. We came by a longer, safer route because of the material."

"He can surely make it?"

"*No sé,* there is no such thing as surely."

"Not for thee either?"

"Nay."

That decides that, Robert Jordan thought to himself. If he had said that he could make it surely, surely I would have sent him.

"Andrés can get there as well as thee?"

"As well or better. He is younger."

"But this must absolutely get there."

"If nothing happens he will get there. If anything happens it could happen to any one."

"I will write a dispatch and send it by him," Robert Jordan said. "I will explain to him where he can find the General. He will be at the Estado Mayor of the Division."

"He will not understand all this of divisions and all," Anselmo said. "Always has it confused me. He should have the name of the General and where he can be found."

"But it is at the Estado Mayor of the Division that he will be found."

"But is that not a place?"

"Certainly it is a place, old one," Robert Jordan explained patiently. "But it is a place the General will have selected. It is where he will make his headquarters for the battle."

"Where is it then?" Anselmo was tired and the tiredness was making him stupid. Also words like Brigades, Divisions, Army Corps confused him. First there had been columns, then there were regiments, then there were brigades. Now there were brigades and divisions, both. He did not understand. A place was a place.

"Take it slowly, old one," Robert Jordan said. He knew that if he could not make Anselmo understand he could never explain it clearly to Andrés either. "The Estado Mayor of the Division is a place the General will have picked to set up his organization to command. He commands a division, which is two brigades. I do not know where it is because I was not there when it was picked. It will probably be a cave or dugout, a refuge, and wires will run to it. Andrés must ask for the General and for the Estado Mayor of the Division. He must give this to the General or to the Chief of his Estado Mayor or to another whose name I will write. One of them will surely be there even if the others are out inspecting the preparations for the attack. Do you understand now?"

"Yes."

"Then get Andrés and I will write it now and seal it with this seal." He showed him the small, round, wooden-backed rubber stamp with the seal of the S.I.M. and the round, tin-covered inking pad no bigger than a fifty-cent piece he carried in his pocket. "That seal they will honor. Get Andrés now and I will explain to him. He must go quickly but first he must understand."

"He will understand if I do. But you must make it very clear. This of staffs and divisions is a mystery to me. Always have I gone to such things as definite places such as a house. In Navacerrada it is in the old hotel where the place of command is. In Guadarrama it is in a house with a garden."

"With this General," Robert Jordan said, "it will be some place very close to the lines. It will be underground to protect from the planes. Andrés will find it easily by asking, if he knows what to ask for. He will only need to show what I have written. But fetch him now for this should get there quickly."

Anselmo went out, ducking under the hanging blanket. Robert Jordan commenced writing in his notebook.

"Listen, *Inglés,*" Pablo said, still looking at the wine bowl.

"I am writing," Robert Jordan said without looking up.

"Listen, *Inglés,*" Pablo spoke directly to the wine bowl. "There is no need to be disheartened in this. Without Sordo we have plenty of people to take the posts and blow thy bridge."

"Good," Robert Jordan said without stopping writing.

"Plenty," Pablo said. "I have admired thy judgment much today, *Inglés,*" Pablo told the wine bowl. "I think thou hast much *picardia.*

That thou art smarter than I am. I have confidence in thee."

Concentrating on his report to Golz, trying to put it in the fewest words and still make it absolutely convincing, trying to put it so the attack would be cancelled, absolutely, yet convince them he wasn't trying to have it called off because of any fears he might have about the danger of his own mission, but wished only to put them in possession of all the facts, Robert Jordan was hardly half listening.

"*Inglés,*" Pablo said.

"I am writing," Robert Jordan told him without looking up.

I probably should send two copies, he thought. But if I do we will not have enough people to blow it if I have to blow it. What do I know about why this attack is made? Maybe it is only a holding attack. Maybe they want to draw those troops from somewhere else. Perhaps they make it to draw those planes from the North. Maybe that is what it is about. Perhaps it is not expected to succeed. What do I know about it? This is my report to Golz. I do not blow the bridge until the attack starts. My orders are clear and if the attack is called off I blow nothing. But I've got to keep enough people here for the bare minimum necessary to carry the orders out.

"What did you say?" he asked Pablo.

"That I have confidence, *Inglés.*" Pablo was still addressing the wine bowl.

Man, I wish I had, Robert Jordan thought. He went on writing.

CHAPTER THIRTY

So NOW everything had been done that there was to do that night. All orders had been given. Every one knew exactly what he was to do in the morning. Andrés had been gone three hours. Either it would come now with the coming of the daylight or it would not come. I believe that it will come, Robert Jordan told himself, walking back down from the upper post where he had gone to speak to Primitivo.

Golz makes the attack but he has not the power to cancel it. Permission to cancel it will have to come from Madrid. The chances are they won't be able to wake anybody up there and if they do wake up they will be too sleepy to think. I should have gotten word to Golz sooner of the preparations they have made to meet the attack, but how could I send word about something until it happened? They did not move up that stuff until just at dark. They did not want to have any movement on the road spotted by planes. But what about all their planes? What about those fascist planes?

Surely our people must have been warned by them. But perhaps the fascists were faking for another offensive down through Guadalajara with them. There were supposed to be Italian troops concentrated in Soria, and at Siguenza again besides those operating in the North. They haven't enough troops or material to run two major offensives at the same time though. That is impossible; so it must be just a bluff.

But we know how many troops the Italians have landed all last month and the month before at Cádiz. It is always possible they will try again at Guadalajara, not stupidly as before, but with three main fingers coming down to broaden it out and carry it along the railway to the west of the plateau. There was a way that they could do it all right. Hans had shown him. They made many mistakes the first time. The whole conception was unsound. They had not used any of the same troops in the Arganda offensive against the Madrid-Valencia road that they used at Guadalajara. Why had they not made those same drives simultaneously? Why? Why? When would we know why?

Yet we had stopped them both times with the very same troops. We never could have stopped them if they had pulled both drives at once. Don't worry, he told himself. Look at the miracles that have happened before this. Either you will have to blow that bridge in the morning or you will not have to. But do not start deceiving yourself into thinking you won't have to blow it. You will blow it one day or you will blow it another. Or if it is not this bridge it will be some other bridge. It is not you who decides what shall be done. You follow orders. Follow them and do not try to think beyond them.

The orders on this are very clear. Too very clear. But you must not worry nor must you be frightened. For if you allow yourself the luxury of normal fear that fear will infect those who must work with you.

But that heads business was quite a thing all the same, he told himself. And the old man running onto them on the hilltop alone. How would you have liked to run onto them like that? That impressed you, didn't it? Yes, that impressed you, Jordan. You have been quite impressed more than once today. But you have behaved O.K. So far you have behaved all right.

You do very well for an instructor in Spanish at the University of Montana, he joked at himself. You do all right for that. But do not start to thinking that you are anything very special. You haven't gotten very far in this business. Just remember Durán, who never had any military training and who was a composer and lad about town before the movement and is now a damned good general commanding a brigade. It was all as simple and easy to learn and understand to Durán as chess to a child chess prodigy. You had read on and studied the art of war ever since you were a boy and your grandfather had started you on the American Civil War. Except that Grandfather always called it the War of the Rebellion. But compared with Durán you were like a good sound chess player against a boy prodigy. Old Durán. It would be good to see Durán again. He would see him at Gaylord's after this was over. Yes. After this was over. See how well he was behaving?

I'll see him at Gaylord's, he said to himself again, after this is over. Don't kid yourself, he said. You do it all perfectly O.K. Cold. Without kidding yourself. You aren't going to see Durán any more and it is of no importance. Don't be that way either, he told himself. Don't go in for any of those luxuries.

Nor for heroic resignation either. We do not want any citizens full of heroic resignation in these hills. Your grandfather fought four years in our Civil War and you are just finishing your first year in this war. You have a long time to go yet and you are very well fitted for the work. And now you have Maria, too. Why, you've got everything. You shouldn't worry. What is a little brush between a guerilla band and a squadron of cavalry? That isn't anything. What if they took the heads? Does that make any difference? None at all.

The Indians always took the scalps when Grandfather was at Fort Kearny after the war. Do you remember the cabinet in your father's office with the arrowheads spread out on a shelf, and the eagle feathers of the war bonnets that hung on the wall, their plumes slanting, the smoked buckskin smell of the leggings and the shirts and the feel of the beaded moccasins? Do you remember the great stave of the buffalo bow that leaned in a corner of the cabinet and the two quivers of hunting and war arrows, and how the bundle of shafts felt when you closed your hand around them?

Remember something like that. Remember something concrete and practical. Remember Grandfather's saber, bright and well oiled in its dented scabbard and Grandfather showed you how the blade had been thinned from the many times it had been to the grinder's. Remember Grandfather's Smith and Wesson. It was a single action, officer's model .32 caliber and there was no trigger guard. It had the softest, sweetest trigger pull you had ever felt and it was always well oiled and the bore was clean although the finish was all worn off and the brown metal of the barrel and the cylinder was worn smooth from the leather of the holster. It was kept in the holster with a U.S. on the flap in a drawer in the cabinet with its cleaning equipment and two hundred rounds of cartridges. Their cardboard boxes were wrapped and tied neatly with waxed twine.

You could take the pistol out of the drawer and hold it. "Handle it freely," was Grandfather's expression. But you could not play with it because it was "a serious weapon."

You asked Grandfather once if he had ever killed any one with it and he said, "Yes."

Then you said, "When, Grandfather?" and he said, "In the War of the Rebellion and afterwards."

You said, "Will you tell me about it, Grandfather?"

And he said, "I do not care to speak about it, Robert."

Then after your father had shot himself with this pistol, and you had come home from school and they'd had the funeral, the coroner had returned it after the inquest saying, "Bob, I guess you might want to keep the gun. I'm supposed to hold it, but I know your dad set a lot of store by it because his dad packed it all through the War, besides out here when he first came out with the Cavalry, and it's still a hell of a good gun. I had her out trying her this afternoon. She don't throw much of a slug but you can hit things with her."

He had put the gun back in the drawer in the cabinet where it belonged, but the next day he took it out and he had ridden up to the top of the high country above Red Lodge, with Chub, where they had built the road to Cooke City now over the pass and across the Bear Tooth plateau, and up there where the wind was thin and there was snow all summer on the hills they had stopped by the lake which was supposed to be eight hundred feet deep and was a deep green color, and Chub held the two horses and he climbed out on a rock and leaned over and saw his face in the still water, and saw himself holding the gun, and then he dropped it, holding it by the muzzle, and saw it go down making bubbles until it was just as big as a watch charm in that clear water, and then it was out of sight. Then he came back off the rock and when he swung up into the saddle he gave old Bess such a clout with the spurs she started to buck like an old rocking horse. He bucked her out along the shore of the lake and as soon as she was reasonable they went on back along the trail.

"I know why you did that with the old gun, Bob," Chub said.

"Well, then we don't have to talk about it," he had said.

They never talked about it and that was the end of Grandfather's side arms except for the saber. He still had the saber in his trunk with the rest of his things at Missoula.

I wonder what Grandfather would think of this situation, he thought. Grandfather was a hell of a good soldier, everybody said. They said if he had been with Custer that day he never would have let him be sucked in that way. How could he ever not have seen the smoke nor the dust of all those lodges down there in the draw along the Little Big Horn unless there must have been a heavy morning mist? But there wasn't any mist.

I wish Grandfather were here instead of me. Well, maybe we will all be together by tomorrow night. If there should be any such damn fool business as a hereafter, and I'm sure there isn't, he thought, I would certainly like to talk to him. Because there are a lot of things I would like to know. I have a right to ask him now because I have had to do the same sort of things myself. I don't think he'd mind my asking now. I had no right to ask before. I understand him not telling me because he didn't know me. But now I think that we would get along all right. I'd like to be able to talk to him now and get his advice. Hell, if I didn't get advice I'd just like to talk to him. It's a shame there is such a jump in time between ones like us.

Then, as he thought, he realized that if there was any such thing as ever meeting, both he and his grandfather would be acutely embarrassed by the presence of his father. Any one has a right to do it, he thought. But it isn't a good thing to do. I understand it, but I do not approve of it. *Lache* was the word. But you *do* understand it? Sure, I understand it but. Yes, but. You have to be awfully occupied with yourself to do a thing like that.

Aw hell, I wish Grandfather was here, he thought. For about an hour anyway. Maybe he sent me what little I have through that other one that misused the gun. Maybe that is the only communication that we have. But, damn it. Truly damn it, but I wish the time-lag wasn't so long so that I could have learned from him what the other one never had to teach me. But suppose the fear he had to go through and dominate and just get rid of finally in four years of that and then in the Indian fighting, although in that, mostly, there couldn't have been so much fear, had made a *cobarde* out of the other one the way second generation bullfighters almost always are? Suppose that? And maybe the good juice only came through straight again after passing through that one?

I'll never forget how sick it made me the first time I knew he was a *cobarde*. Go on, say it in English. Coward. It's easier when you have it said and there is never any point in referring to a son of a bitch by some foreign term. He wasn't any son of a bitch, though.

He was just a coward and that was the worst luck any man could have. Because if he wasn't a coward he would have stood up to that woman and not let her bully him. I wonder what I would have been like if he had married a different woman? That's something you'll never know, he thought, and grinned. Maybe the bully in her helped to supply what was missing in the other. And you. Take it a little easy. Don't get to referring to the good juice and such other things until you are through tomorrow. Don't be snotty too soon. And then don't be snotty at all. We'll see what sort of juice you have tomorrow.

But he started thinking about Grandfather again.

"George Custer was not an intelligent leader of cavalry, Robert," his grandfather had said. "He was not even an intelligent man."

He remembered that when his grandfather said that he felt resentment that any one should speak against that figure in the buckskin shirt, the yellow curls blowing, that stood on that hill holding a service revolver as the Sioux closed in around him in the old Anheuser-Busch lithograph that hung on the poolroom wall in Red Lodge.

"He just had great ability to get himself in and out of trouble," his grandfather went on, "and on the Little Big Horn he got into it but he couldn't get out.

"Now Phil Sheridan was an intelligent man and so was Jeb Stuart. But John Mosby was the finest cavalry leader that ever lived."

He had a letter in his things in the trunk at Missoula from General Phil Sheridan to old Killy-the-Horse Kilpatrick that said his grandfather was a finer leader of irregular cavalry than John Mosby.

I ought to tell Golz about my grandfather, he thought. He wouldn't ever have heard of him though. He probably never even heard of John Mosby. The British all had heard of them though because they had to study our Civil War much more than people did on the Continent. Karkov said after this was over I could go to the Lenin Institute in Moscow if I wanted to. He said I could go to the military academy of the Red Army if I wanted to do that. I wonder what Grandfather would think of that? Grandfather, who never knowingly sat at table with a Democrat in his life.

Well, I don't want to be a soldier, he thought. I know that. So that's out. I just want us to win this war. I guess really good soldiers are really good at very little else, he thought. That's obviously untrue. Look at Napoleon and Wellington. You're very stupid this evening, he thought.

Usually his mind was very good company and tonight it had been when he thought about his grandfather. Then thinking of his father had thrown him off. He understood his father and he forgave him everything and he pitied him but he was ashamed of him.

You better not think at all, he told himself. Soon you will be with Maria and you won't have to think. That's the best way now that everything is worked out. When you have been concentrating so hard on something you can't stop and your brain gets to racing like a flywheel with the weight gone. You better just not think.

But just suppose, he thought. Just suppose that when the planes unload they smash those anti-tank guns and just blow hell out of the positions and the old tanks roll good up whatever hill it is for once and old Golz boots that bunch of drunks, *clochards,* bums, fanatics and heroes that make up the Quatorzième Brigade ahead of him, and I *know* how good Durán's people are in Golz's other brigade, and we are in Segovia tomorrow night.

Yes. Just suppose, he said to himself. I'll settle for La Granja, he told himself. But you are going to have to blow that bridge, he suddenly knew absolutely. There won't be any calling off. Because the way you have just been supposing there for a minute is how the possibilities of that attack look to those who have ordered it. Yes, you will have to blow the bridge, he knew truly. Whatever happens to Andrés doesn't matter.

Coming down the trail there in the dark, alone with the good feeling that everything that had to be done was over for the next four hours, and with the confidence that had come from thinking back to concrete things, the knowledge that he would surely have to blow the bridge came to him almost with comfort.

The uncertainty, the enlargement of the feeling of being uncertain, as when, through a misunderstanding of possible dates, one does not know whether the guests are really coming to a party, that had been with him ever since he had dispatched Andrés with the report to Golz, had all dropped from him now. He was sure now that the festival would not be cancelled. It's much better to be sure, he thought. It's always much better to be sure.

CHAPTER THIRTY-ONE

So now they were in the robe again together and it was late in the last night. Maria lay close against him and he felt the long smoothness of her thighs against his and her breasts like two small hills that rise out of the long plain where there is a well, and the far country beyond the hills was the valley of her throat where his lips were. He lay very quiet and did not think and she stroked his head with her hand.

"Roberto," Maria said very softly and kissed him. "I am ashamed. I do not wish to disappoint thee but there is a great soreness and much pain. I do not think I would be any good to thee."

"There is always a great soreness and much pain," he said. "Nay, rabbit. That is nothing. We will do nothing that makes pain."

"It is not that. It is that I am not good to receive thee as I wish to."

"That is of no importance. That is a passing thing. We are together when we lie together."

"Yes, but I am ashamed. I think it was from when things were done to me that it comes. Not from thee and me."

"Let us not talk of that."

"Nor do I wish to. I meant I could not bear to fail thee now on this night and so I sought to excuse myself."

"Listen, rabbit," he said. "All such things pass and then there is no problem." But he thought; it was not good luck for the last night.

Then he was ashamed and said, "Lie close against me, rabbit. I love thee as much feeling thee against me in here in the dark as I love thee making love."

"I am deeply ashamed because I thought it might be again tonight as it was in the high country when we came down from El Sordo's."

"*Qué va,*" he said to her. "That is not for every day. I like it thus as well as the other." He lied, putting aside disappointment. "We will be here together quietly and we will sleep. Let us talk together. I know thee very little from talking."

"Should we speak of tomorrow and of thy work? I would like to be intelligent about thy work."

"No," he said and relaxed completely into the length of the robe and lay now quietly with his cheek against her shoulder, his left arm under her head. "The most intelligent is not to talk about tomorrow nor what happened today. In this we do not discuss the losses and what we must do tomorrow we will do. Thou art not afraid?"

"*Qué va*," she said. "I am always afraid. But now I am afraid for thee so much I do not think of me."

"Thou must not, rabbit. I have been in many things. And worse than this," he lied.

Then suddenly surrendering to something, to the luxury of going into unreality, he said, "Let us talk of Madrid and of us in Madrid."

"Good," she said. Then, "Oh, Roberto, I am sorry I have failed thee. Is there not some other thing that I can do for thee?"

He stroked her head and kissed her and then lay close and relaxed beside her, listening to the quiet of the night.

"Thou canst talk with me of Madrid," he said and thought: I'll keep any oversupply of that for tomorrow. I'll need all of that there is tomorrow. There are no pine needles that need that now as I will need it tomorrow. Who was it cast his seed upon the ground in the Bible? Onan. How did Onan turn out? he thought. I don't remember ever hearing any more about Onan. He smiled in the dark.

Then he surrendered again and let himself slip into it, feeling a voluptuousness of surrender into unreality that was like a sexual acceptance of something that could come in the night when there was no understanding, only the delight of acceptance.

"My beloved," he said, and kissed her. "Listen. The other night I was thinking about Madrid and I thought how I would get there and leave thee at the hotel while I went up to see people at the hotel of the Russians. But that was false. I would not leave thee at any hotel."

"Why not?"

"Because I will take care of thee. I will not ever leave thee. I will go with thee to the Seguridad to get papers. Then I will go with thee to buy those clothes that are needed."

"They are few, and I can buy them."

"Nay, they are many and we will go together and buy good ones and thou wilt be beautiful in them."

"I would rather we stayed in the room in the hotel and sent out for the clothes. Where is the hotel?"

"It is on the Plaza del Callao. We will be much in that room in that hotel. There is a wide bed with clean sheets and there is hot running water in the bathtub and there are two closets and I will keep my things in one and thou wilt take the other. And there are tall, wide windows that open, and outside, in the streets, there is the spring. Also I know good places to eat that are illegal but with good food, and I know shops where there is still wine and whiskey. And we will keep things to eat in the room for when we are hungry and also whiskey for when I wish a drink and I will buy thee manzanilla."

"I would like to try the whiskey."

"But since it is difficult to obtain and if thou likest manzanilla."

"Keep thy whiskey, Roberto," she said "Oh, I love thee very much. Thou and thy whiskey that I could not have. What a pig thou art."

"Nay, you shall try it. But it is not good for a woman."

"And I have only had things that were good for a woman," Maria said. "Then there in bed I will still wear my wedding shirt?"

"Nay. I will buy thee various nightgowns and pajamas too if you should prefer them."

"I will buy seven wedding shirts," she said. "One for each day of the week. And I will buy a clean wedding shirt for thee. Dost ever wash thy shirt?"

"Sometimes."

"I will keep everything clean and I will pour thy whiskey and put the water in it as it was done at Sordo's. I will obtain olives and salted codfish and hazel nuts for thee to eat while thou drinkest and we will stay in the room for a month and never leave it. If I am fit to receive thee," she said, suddenly unhappy.

"That is nothing," Robert Jordan told her. "Truly it is nothing. It is possible thou wert hurt there once and now there is a scar that makes a further hurting. Such a thing is possible. All such things pass. And also there are good doctors in Madrid if there is truly anything."

"But all was good before," she said pleadingly.

"That is the promise that all will be good again."

"Then let us talk again about Madrid." She curled her legs between his and rubbed the top of her head against his shoulder. "But will I not be so ugly there with this cropped head that thou wilt be ashamed of me?"

"Nay. Thou art lovely. Thou hast a lovely face and a beautiful body, long and light, and thy skin is smooth and the color of burnt gold and every one will try to take thee from me."

"*Qué va,* take me from thee," she said. "No other man will ever touch me till I die. Take me from thee! *Qué va.*"

"But many will try. Thou wilt see."

"They will see I love thee so that they will know it would be as unsafe as putting their hands into a caldron of melted lead to touch me. But thou? When thou seest beautiful women of the same culture as thee? Thou wilt not be ashamed of me?"

"Never. And I will marry thee."

"If you wish," she said. "But since we no longer have the Church I do not think it carries importance."

"I would like us to be married."

"If you wish. But listen. If we were ever in another country where there still was the Church perhaps we could be married in it there."

"In my country they still have the Church," he told her. "There we can be married in it if it means aught to thee. I have never been married. There is no problem."

"I am glad thou hast never been married," she said. "But I am glad thou knowest about such things as you have told me for that means thou hast been with many women and the Pilar told me that it is only such men who are possible for husbands. But thou wilt not run with other women now? Because it would kill me."

"I have never run with many women," he said, truly. "Until thee I did not think that I could love one deeply."

She stroked his cheeks and then held her hands clasped behind his head. "Thou must have known very many."

"Not to love them."

"Listen. The Pilar told me something——"

"Say it."

"No. It is better not to. Let us talk again about Madrid."

"What was it you were going to say?"

"I do not wish to say it."

"Perhaps it would be better to say it if it could be important."

"You think it is important?"

"Yes."

"But how can you know when you do not know what it is?"

"From thy manner."

"I will not keep it from you then. The Pilar told me that we would all die tomorrow and that you know it as well as she does and that you give it no importance. She said this not in criticism but in admiration."

"She said that?" he said. The crazy bitch, he thought, and he said, "That is more of her gypsy manure. That is the way old market women and café cowards talk. That is manuring obscenity." He felt the sweat that came from under his armpits and slid down between his arm and his side and he said to himself, "So you are scared, eh?" and aloud he said, "She is a manure-mouthed superstitious bitch. Let us talk again of Madrid."

"Then you know no such thing?"

"Of course not. Do not talk such manure," he said, using a stronger, ugly word.

But this time when he talked about Madrid there was no slipping into make-believe again. Now he was just lying to his girl and to himself to pass the night before battle and he knew it. He liked to do it, but all the luxury of the acceptance was gone. But he started again.

"I have thought about thy hair," he said. "And what we can do about it. You see it grows now all over thy head the same length like the fur of an animal and it is lovely to feel and I love it very much and it is beautiful and it flattens and rises like a wheatfield in the wind when I pass my hand over it."

"Pass thy hand over it."

He did and left his hand there and went on talking to her throat, as he felt his own throat swell. "But in Madrid I thought we could go together to the coiffeur's and they could cut it neatly on the sides and in the back as they cut mine and that way it would look better in the town while it is growing out."

"I would look like thee," she said and held him close to her. "And then I never would want to change it."

"Nay. It will grow all the time and that will only be to keep it neat at the start while it is growing long. How long will it take it to grow long?"

"Really long?"

"No. I mean to thy shoulders. It is thus I would have thee wear it."

"As Garbo in the cinema?"

"Yes," he said thickly.

Now the making believe was coming back in a great rush and he would take it all to him. It had him now, and again he surrendered and went on. "So it will hang straight to thy shoulders and curl at the ends as a wave of the sea curls, and it will be the color of ripe wheat and thy face the color of burnt gold and thine eyes the only color they could be with thy hair and thy skin, gold with the dark flecks in them, and I will push thy head back and look in thy eyes and hold thee tight against me——"

"Where?"

"Anywhere. Wherever it is that we are. How long will it take for thy hair to grow?"

"I do not know because it never had been cut before. But I think in six months it should be long enough to hang well below my ears and in a year as long as thou couldst ever wish. But do you know what will happen first?"

"Tell me."

"We will be in the big clean bed in thy famous room in our famous hotel and we will sit in the famous bed together and look into the mirror of the *armoire* and there will be thee and there will be me in the glass and then I will turn to thee thus, and put my arms around thee thus, and then I will kiss thee thus."

Then they lay quiet and close together in the night, hot-aching, rigid, close together and holding her, Robert Jordan held closely too all those things that he knew could never happen, and he went on with it deliberately and said, "Rabbit, we will not always live in that hotel."

"Why not?"

"We can get an apartment in Madrid on that street that runs along the Parque of the Buen Retiro. I know an American woman who furnished apartments and rented them before the movement and I know how to get such an apartment for only the rent that was paid before the movement. There are apartments there that face on the park and you can see all of the park from the windows; the iron fence, the gardens, and the gravel walks and the green of the lawns where they touch the gravel, and the trees deep with shadows and the many fountains, and now the chestnut trees will be in bloom. In Madrid we can walk in the park and row on the lake if the water is back in it now."

"Why would the water be out?"

"They drained it in November because it made a mark to sight from when the planes came over for bombing. But I think that the water is back in it now. I am not sure. But even if there is no water in it we can walk through all the park away from the lake and there is a part that is like a forest with trees from all parts of the world with their names on them, with placards that tell what trees they are and where they came from."

"I would almost as soon go the cinema," Maria said. "But the trees sound very interesting and I will learn them all with thee if I can remember them."

"They are not as in a museum," Robert Jordan said. "They grow naturally and there are hills in the park and part of the park is like a jungle. Then below it there is the book fair where along the sidewalks there are hundreds of booths with second-hand books in them and now, since the movement, there are many books, stolen in the looting of the houses which have been bombed and from the houses of the fascists, and brought to the book fair by those who stole them. I could spend all day every day at the stalls of the book fair as I once did in the days before the movement, if I ever could have any time in Madrid."

"While thou art visiting the book fair I will occupy myself with the apartment," Maria said. "Will we have enough money for a servant?"

"Surely. I can get Petra who is at the hotel if she pleases thee. She cooks well and is clean. I have eaten there with newspapermen that she cooks for. They have electric stoves in their rooms."

"If you wish her," Maria said. "Or I can find some one. But wilt thou not be away much with thy work? They would not let me go with thee on such work as this."

"Perhaps I can get work in Madrid. I have done this work now for a long time and I have fought since the start of the movement. It is possible that they would give me work now in Madrid. I have never asked for it. I have always been at the front or in such work as this.

"Do you know that until I met thee I have never asked for anything? Nor wanted anything? Nor thought of anything except the movement and the winning of this war? Truly I have been very pure in my ambitions. I have worked much and now I love thee and," he said it now in a complete embracing of all that would not be, "I love thee as I love all that we have fought for. I love thee as I love liberty and dignity and the rights of all men to work and not be hungry. I love thee as I love Madrid that we have defended and as I love all my comrades that have died. And many have died. Many. Many. Thou canst not think how many. But I love thee as I love what I love most in the world and I love thee more. I love thee very much, rabbit. More than I can tell thee. But I say this now to tell thee a little. I have never had a wife and now I have thee for a wife and I am happy."

"I will make thee as good a wife as I can," Maria said. "Clearly I am not well trained but I will try to make up for that. If we live in Madrid; good. If we must live in any other place; good. If we live nowhere and I can go with thee; better. If we go to thy country I will learn to talk *Inglés* like the most *Inglés* that there is. I will study all their manners and as they do so will I do."

"Thou wilt be very comic."

"Surely. I will make mistakes but you will tell me and I will never make them twice, or maybe only twice. Then in thy country if thou art lonesome for our food I can cook for thee. And I will go to a school to learn to be a wife, if there is such a school, and study at it."

"There are such schools but thou dost not need that schooling."

"Pilar told me that she thought they existed in your country. She had read of them in a periodical. And she told me also that I must learn to speak *Inglés* and to speak it well so thou wouldst never be ashamed of me."

"When did she tell you this?"

"Today while we were packing. Constantly she talked to me about what I should do to be thy wife."

I guess she was going to Madrid too, Robert Jordan thought, and said, "What else did she say?"

"She said I must take care of my body and guard the line of my figure as though I were a bullfighter. She said this was of great importance."

"It is," Robert Jordan said. "But thou hast not to worry about that for many years."

"No. She said those of our race must watch that always as it can come suddenly. She told me she was once as slender as I but that in those days women did not take exercise. She told me what exercises I should take and that I must not eat too much. She told me which things not to eat. But I have forgotten and must ask her again."

"Potatoes," he said.

"Yes," she went on. "It was potatoes and things that are fried. Also when I told her about this of the soreness she said I must not tell thee but must support the pain and not let thee know. But I told thee because I do not wish to lie to thee ever and also I feared that thou might think we did not have the joy in common any longer and that other, as it was in the high country, had not truly happened."

"It was right to tell me."

"Truly? For I am ashamed and I will do anything for thee that thou should wish. Pilar has told me of things one can do for a husband."

"There is no need to do anything. What we have we have together and we will keep it and guard it. I love thee thus lying beside thee and touching thee and knowing thou art truly there and when thou art ready again we will have all."

"But hast thou not necessities that I can care for? She explained that to me."

"Nay. We will have our necessities together. I have no necessities apart from thee."

"That seems much better to me. But understand always that I will do what you wish. But thou must tell me for I have great ignorance and much of what she told me I did not understand clearly. For I was ashamed to ask and she is of such great and varied wisdom."

"Rabbit," he said. "Thou art very wonderful."

"*Qué va,*" she said. "But to try to learn all of that which goes into wifehood in a day while we are breaking camp and packing for a battle with another battle passing in the country above is a rare thing and if I make serious mistakes thou must tell me for I love thee. It could be possible for me to remember things incorrectly and much that she told me was very complicated."

"What else did she tell thee?"

"*Pues* so many things I cannot remember them. She said I could tell thee of what was done to me if I ever began to think of it again because thou art a good man and already have understood it all. But that it were better never to speak of it unless it came on me as a black thing as it had been before and then that telling it to thee might rid me of it."

"Does it weigh on thee now?"

"No. It is as though it had never happened since we were first together. There is the sorrow for my parents always. But that there will be always. But I would have thee know that which you should know for thy own pride if I am to be thy wife. Never did I submit to any one. Always I fought and always it took two of them or more to do me the harm. One would sit on my head and hold me. I tell thee this for thy pride."

"My pride is in thee. Do not tell it."

"Nay, I speak of thy own pride which it is necessary to have in thy wife. And another thing. My father was the mayor of the village and an honorable man. My mother was an honorable woman and a good Catholic and they shot her with my father because of the politics of my father who was a Republican. I saw both of them shot and my father said, '*Viva la República,*' when they shot him standing against the wall of the slaughterhouse of our village.

"My mother standing against the same wall said, 'Viva my husband who was the Mayor of this village,' and I hoped they would shoot me too and I was going to say '*Viva la República y vivan mis padres,*' but instead there was no shooting but instead the doing of the things.

"Listen. I will tell thee of one thing since it affects us. After the shooting at the *matadero* they took us, those relatives who had seen it but were not shot, back from the *matadero* up the steep hill into the main square of the town. Nearly all were weeping but some were numb with what they had seen and the tears had dried in them. I myself could not cry. I did not notice anything that passed for I could only see my father and my mother at the moment of the shooting and my mother saying, 'Long live my husband who was Mayor of this village,' and this was in my head like a scream that would not die but kept on and on. For my mother was not a Republican and she would not say, 'Viva la República,' but only Viva my father who lay there, on his face, by her feet.

"But what she had said, she had said very loud, like a shriek and then they shot and she fell and I tried to leave the line to go to her but we were all tied. The shooting was done by the *guardia civil* and they were still there waiting to shoot more when the Falangists herded us away and up the hill leaving the *guardias civiles* leaning on their rifles and leaving all the bodies there against the wall. We were tied by the wrists in a long line of girls and women and they herded us up by the hill and through the streets to the square and in the square they stopped in front of the barbershop which was across the square from the city hall.

"Then the two men looked at us and one said, 'That is the daughter of the Mayor,' and the other said, 'Commence with her.'

"Then they cut the rope that was on each of my wrists, one saying to others of them, 'Tie up the line,' and these two took me by the arms and into the barbershop and lifted me up and put me in the barber's chair and held me there.

"I saw my face in the mirror of the barbershop and the faces of those who were holding me and the faces of three others who were leaning over me and I knew none of their faces but in the glass I saw myself and them, but they saw only me. And it was as though one were in the dentist's chair and there were many dentists and they were all insane. My own face I could hardly recognize because my grief had changed it but I looked at it and knew that it was me. But my grief was so great that I had no fear nor any feeling but my grief.

"At that time I wore my hair in two braids and as I watched in the mirror one of them lifted one of the braids and pulled on it so it hurt me suddenly through my grief and then cut it off close to my head with a razor. And I saw myself with one braid and a slash where the other had been. Then he cut off the other braid but without pulling on it and the razor made a small cut on my ear and I saw blood come from it. Canst thou feel the scar with thy finger?"

"Yes. But would it be better not to talk of this?"

"This is nothing. I will not talk of that which is bad. So he had cut both braids close to my head with a razor and the others laughed and I did not even feel the cut on my ear and then he stood in front of me and struck me across the face with the braids while the other two held me and he said, 'This is how we make Red nuns. This will show thee how to unite with thy proletarian brothers. Bride of the Red Christ!'

"And he struck me again and again across the face with the braids which had been mine and then he put the two of them in my mouth and tied them tight around my neck, knotting them in the back to make a gag and the two holding me laughed.

"And all of them who saw it laughed and when I saw them laugh in the mirror I commenced to cry because until then I had been too frozen in myself from the shooting to be able to cry.

"Then the one who had gagged me ran a clippers all over my head; first from the forehead all the way to the back of the neck and then across the top and then all over my head and close behind my ears and they held me so I could see into the glass of the barber's mirror all the time that they did this and I could not believe it as I saw it done and I cried and I cried but I could not look away from the horror that my face made with the mouth open and the braids tied in it and my head coming naked under the clippers.

"And when the one with the clippers was finsihed he took a bottle of iodine from the shelf of the barber (they had shot the barber too for he belonged to a syndicate, and he lay in the doorway of the shop and they had lifted me over him as they brought me in) and with the glass wand that is in the iodine bottle he touched me on the ear where it had been cut and the small pain of that came through my grief and through my horror.

"Then he stood in front of me and wrote U. H. P. on my forehead with the iodine, lettering it slowly and carefully as though he were an artist and I saw all of this as it happened in the mirror and I no longer cried for my heart was frozen in me for my father and my mother and what happened to me now was nothing and I knew it.

"Then when he had finished the lettering, the Falangist stepped back and looked at me to examine his work and then he put down the iodine bottle and picked up the clippers and said, 'Next,' and they took me out of the barbershop holding me tight by each arm and I stumbled over the barber lying there still in the doorway on his back with his gray face up, and we nearly collided with Concepción Gracía, my best friend, that two of them were bringing in and when she saw me she did not recognize me, and then she recognized me, and she screamed, and I could hear her screaming all the time they were shoving me across the square, and into the doorway, and up the stairs of the city hall and into the office of my father where they laid me onto the couch. And it was there that the bad things were done."

"My rabbit," Robert Jordan said and held her as close and as gently as he could. But he was as full of hate as any man could be. "Do not talk more about it. Do not tell me any more for I cannot bear my hatred now."

She was stiff and cold in his arms and she said, "Nay. I will never talk more of it. But they are bad people and I would like to kill some of them with thee if I could. But I have told thee this only for thy pride if I am to be thy wife. So thou wouldst understand."

"I am glad you told me," he said. "For tomorrow, with luck, we will kill plenty."

"But will we kill Falangists? It was they who did it."

"They do not fight," he said gloomily. "They kill at the rear. It is not them we fight in battle."

"But can we not kill them in some way? I would like to kill some very much."

"I have killed them," he said. "And we will kill them again. At the trains we have killed them."

"I would like to go for a train with thee," Maria said. "The time of the train that Pilar brought me back from I was somewhat crazy. Did she tell thee how I was?"

"Yes. Do not talk of it."

"I was dead in my head with a numbness and all I could do was cry. But there is another thing that I must tell thee. This I must. Then perhaps thou wilt not marry me. But, Roberto, if thou should not wish to marry me, can we not, then, just be always together?"

"I will marry thee."

"Nay. I had forgotten this. Perhaps you should not. It is possible that I can never bear thee either a son or a daughter for the Pilar says that if I could it would have happened to me with the things which were done. I must tell thee that. Oh, I do not know why I had forgotten that."

"It is of no importance, rabbit," he said. "First it may not be true. That is for a doctor to say. Then I would not wish to bring either a son or a daughter into this world as this world is. And also you take all the love I have to give."

"I would like to bear thy son and thy daughter," she told him. "And how can the world be made better if there are no children of us who fight against the fascists?"

"Thou," he said. "I love thee. Hearest thou? And now we must sleep, rabbit. For I must be up long before daylight and the dawn comes early in this month."

"Then it is all right about the last thing I said? We can still be married?"

"We are married, now. I marry thee now. Thou art my wife. But go to sleep, my rabbit, for there is little time now."

"And we will truly be married? Not just a talking?"

"Truly."

"Then I will sleep and think of that if I wake."

"I, too."

"Good night, my husband."

"Good night," he said. "Good night, wife."

He heard her breathing steadily and regularly now and he knew she was asleep and he lay awake and very still not wanting to waken her by moving. He thought of all the part she had not told him and he lay there hating and he was pleased there would be killing in the morning. But I must not take any of it personally, he thought.

Though how can I keep from it? I know that we did dreadful things to them too. But it was because we were uneducated and knew no better. But they did that on purpose and deliberately. Those who did that are the last flowering of what their education has produced. Those are the flowers of Spanish chivalry. What a people they have been. What sons of bitches from Cortez, Pizarro, Menéndez de Avila all down through Enrique Lister to Pablo. And what wonderful people. There is no finer and no worse people in the world. No kinder people and no crueler. And who understands them? Not me, because if I did I would forgive it all. To understand is to forgive. That's not true. Forgiveness has been exaggerated. Forgiveness is a Christian idea and Spain has never been a Christian country. It has always had its own special idol worship within the Church. *Otra Virgen más.* I suppose that was why they had to destroy the virgins of their enemies. Surely it was deeper with them, with the Spanish religion fanatics, than it was with the people. The people had grown away from the Church because the Church was in the government and the government had always been rotten. This was the only country that the reformation never reached. They were paying for the Inquisition now, all right.

Well, it was something to think about. Something to keep your mind from worrying about your work. It was sounder than pretending. God, he had done a lot of pretending tonight. And Pilar had been pretending all day. Sure. What if they were killed tomorrow? What did it matter as long as they did the bridge properly? That was all they had to do tomorrow.

It didn't. You couldn't do these things indefinitely. But you weren't supposed to live forever. Maybe I have had all my life in three days, he thought. If that's true I wish we would have spent the last night differently. But last nights are never any good. Last nothings are any good. Yes, last words were good sometimes. "*Viva* my husband who was Mayor of this town" was good.

He knew it was good because it made a tingle run all over him when he said it to himself. He leaned over and kissed Maria who did not wake. In English he whispered very quietly, "I'd like to marry you, rabbit. I'm very proud of your family."

CHAPTER THIRTY-TWO

ON THAT same night in Madrid there were many people at the Hotel Gaylord. A car pulled up under the porte-cochere of the hotel, its headlights painted over with blue calcimine and a little man in black riding boots, gray riding breeches and a short, gray high-buttoned jacket stepped out and returned the salute of the two sentries as he opened the door, nodded to the secret police-man who sat at the concierge's desk and stepped into the elevator. There were two sentries seated on chairs inside the door, one on each side of the marble entrance hall, and these only looked up as the little man passed them at the door of the elevator. It was their business to feel every one they did not know along the flanks, under the armpits, and over the hip pockets to see if the person entering carried a pistol and, if he did, have him check it with the concierge. But they knew the short man in riding boots very well and they hardly looked up as he passed.

The apartment where he lived in Gaylord's was crowded as he entered. People were sitting and standing about and talking to-gether as in any drawing room and the men and the women were drinking vodka, whiskey and soda, and beer from small glasses filled from great pitchers. Four of the men were in uniform. The others wore windbreakers or leather jackets and three of the four women were dressed in ordinary street dresses while the fourth, who was haggardly thin and dark, wore a sort of severely cut militiawoman's uniform with a skirt with high boots under it.

When he came into the room, Karkov went at once to the woman in the uniform and bowed to her and shook hands. She was his wife and he said something to her in Russian that no one could hear and for a moment the insolence that had been in his eyes as he entered the room was gone. Then it lighted again as he saw the mahogany-colored head and the love-lazy face of the well-constructed girl who was his mistress and he strode with short, precise steps over to her and bowed and shook her hand in such a way that no one could tell it was not a mimicry of his greeting to his wife. His wife had not looked after him as he walked across the room. She was standing with a tall, good-looking Spanish officer and they were talking Russian now.

"Your great love is getting a little fat," Karkov was saying to the girl. "All of our heroes are fattening now as we approach the second year." He did not look at the man he was speaking of.

"You are so ugly you would be jealous of a toad," the girl told him cheerfully. She spoke in German. "Can I go with thee to the offensive tomorrow?"

"No. Nor is there one."

"Every one knows about it," the girl said. "Don't be so mysterious. Dolores is going. I will go with her or Carmen. Many people are going."

"Go with whoever will take you," Karkov said. "I will not."

Then he turned to the girl and asked seriously, "Who told thee of it? Be exact."

"Richard," she said as seriously.

Karkov shrugged his shoulders and left her standing.

"Karkov," a man of middle height with a gray, heavy, sagging face, puffed eye pouches and a pendulous under-lip called to him in a dyspeptic voice. "Have you heard the good news?"

Karkov went over to him and the man said, "I only have it now. Not ten minutes ago. It is wonderful. All day the fascists have been fighting among themselves near Segovia. They have been forced to quell the mutinies with automatic rifle and machine gun fire. In the afternoon they were bombing their own troops with planes."

"Yes?" asked Karkov.

"That is true," the puffy-eyed man said. "Dolores brought the news herself. She was here with the news and was in such a state of radiant exultation as I have never seen. The truth of the news shone from her face. That great face—" he said happily.

"That great face," Karkov said with no tone in his voice at all.

"If you could have heard her," the puffy-eyed man said. "The news itself shone from her with a light that was not of this world. In her voice you could tell the truth of what she said. I am putting it in an article for *Izvestia*. It was one of the greatest moments of the war to me when I heard the report in that great voice where pity, compassion and truth are blended. Goodness and truth shine from her as from a true saint of the people. Not for nothing is she called La Pasionaria."

"Not for nothing," Karkov said in a dull voice. "You better write it for *Izvestia* now, before you forget that last beautiful lead."

"That is a woman that is not to joke about. Not even by a cynic like you," the puffy-eyed man said. "If you could have been here to hear her and to see her face."

"That great voice," Karkov said. "That great face. Write it," he said. "Don't tell it to me. Don't waste whole paragraphs on me. Go and write it now."

"Not just now."

"I think you'd better," Karkov said and looked at him, and then looked away. The puffy-eyed man stood there a couple of minutes more holding his glass of vodka, his eyes, puffy as they were, absorbed in the beauty of what he had seen and heard and then he left the room to write it.

Karkov went over to another man of about forty-eight, who was short, chunky, jovial-looking with pale blue eyes, thinning blond hair and a gay mouth under a bristly yellow moustache. This man was in uniform. He was a divisional commander and he was a Hungarian.

"Were you here when the Dolores was here?" Karkov asked the man.

"Yes."

"What was the stuff?"

"Something about the fascists fighting among themselves. Beautiful if true."

"You hear much talk of tomorrow."

"Scandalous. All the journalists should be shot as well as most of the people in this room and certainly the intriguing German unmentionable of a Richard. Whoever gave that Sunday *függler* command of a brigade should be shot. Perhaps you and me should be shot too. It is possible," the General laughed. "Don't suggest it though."

"That is a thing I never like to talk about," Karkov said. "That American who comes here sometimes is over there. You know the one, Jordan, who is with the *partizan* group. He is there where this business they spoke of is supposed to happen."

"Well, he should have a report through on it tonight then," the

General said. "They don't like me down there or I'd go down and find out for you. He works with Golz on this, doesn't he? You'll see Golz tomorrow."

"Early tomorrow."

"Keep out of his way until it's going well," the General said. "He hates you bastards as much as I do. Though he has a much better temper."

"But about this――"

"It was probably the fascists having manœuvres," the General grinned. "Well, we'll see if Golz can manœuvre them a little. Let Golz try his hand at it. We manœuvred them at Guadalajara."

"I hear you are travelling too," Karkov said, showing his bad teeth as he smiled. The General was suddenly angry.

"And me too. Now is the mouth on me. And on all of us always. This filthy sewing circle of gossip. One man who could keep his mouth shut could save the country if he believed he could."

"Your friend Prieto can keep his mouth shut."

"But he doesn't believe he can win. How can you win without belief in the people?"

"You decide that," Karkov said. "I am going to get a little sleep."

He left the smoky, gossip-filled room and went into the back bedroom and sat down on the bed and pulled his boots off. He could still hear them talking so he shut the door and opened the window. He did not bother to undress because at two o'clock he would be starting for the drive by Colmenar, Cerceda, and Navacerrada up to the front where Golz would be attacking in the morning.

CHAPTER THIRTY-THREE

IT WAS two o'clock in the morning when Pilar waked him. As her hand touched him he thought, at first, it was Maria and he rolled toward her and said, "Rabbit." Then the woman's big hand shook his shoulder and he was suddenly, completely and absolutely awake and his hand was around the butt of the pistol that lay alongside of his bare right leg and all of him was as cocked as the pistol with its safety catch slipped off.

In the dark he saw it was Pilar and he looked at the dial of his wrist watch with the two hands shining in the short angle close to the top and seeing it was only two, he said, "What passes with thee, woman?"

"Pablo is gone," the big woman said to him.

Robert Jordan put on his trousers and shoes. Maria had not waked.

"When?" he asked.

"It must be an hour."

"And?"

"He has taken something of thine," the woman said miserably.

"So. What?"

"I do not know," she told him. "Come and see."

In the dark they walked over to the entrance of the cave, ducked under the blanket and went in. Robert Jordan followed her in the dead-ashes, bad-air and sleeping-men smell of the cave, shining his electric torch so that he would not step on any of those who were sleeping on the floor. Anselmo woke and said, "Is it time?"

"No," Robert Jordan whispered. "Sleep, old one."

The two sacks were at the head of Pilar's bed which was screened off with a hanging blanket from the rest of the cave. The bed smelt stale and sweat-dried and sickly-sweet the way an Indian's bed does as Robert Jordan knelt on it and shone the torch on the two sacks. There was a long slit from top to bottom in each one. Holding the torch in his left hand, Robert Jordan felt in the first sack with his right hand. This was the one that he carried his robe in and it should not be very full. It was not very full. There was some wire in it still but the square wooden box of the exploder was gone. So was the cigar box with the carefully wrapped and packed detonators. So was the screw-top tin with the fuse and the caps.

Robert Jordan felt in the other sack. It was still full of explosive. There might be one packet missing.

He stood up and turned to the woman. There is a hollow empty feeling that a man can have when he is waked too early in the morning that is almost like the feeling of disaster and he had this multiplied a thousand times.

"And this is what you call guarding one's materials," he said.

"I slept with my head against them and one arm touching them," Pilar told him.

"You slept well."

"Listen," the woman said. "He got up in the night and I said, 'Where do you go, Pablo?' 'To urinate, woman,' he told me and I slept again. When I woke again I did not know what time had passed but I thought, when he was not there, that he had gone down to look at the horses as was his custom. Then," she finished miserably, "when he did not come I worried and when I worried I felt of the sacks to be sure all was well and there were the slit places and I came to thee."

"Come on," Robert Jordan said.

They were outside now and it was still so near the middle of the night that you could not feel the morning coming.

"Can he get out with the horses other ways than by the sentry?"

"Two ways."

"Who's at the top?"

"Eladio."

Robert Jordan said nothing more until they reached the meadow where the horses were staked out to feed. There were three horses feeding in the meadow. The big bay and the gray were gone.

"How long ago do you think it was he left you?"

"It must have been an hour."

"Then that is that," Robert Jordan said. "I go to get what is left of my sacks and go back to bed."

"I will guard them."

"*Qué va,* you will guard them. You've guarded them once already."

"*Inglés,*" the woman said, "I feel in regard to this as you do. There is nothing I would not do to bring back thy property. You have no need to hurt me. We have both been betrayed by Pablo."

As she said this Robert Jordan realized that he could not afford the luxury of being bitter, that he could not quarrel with this woman. He had to work with this woman on that day that was already two hours and more gone.

He put his hand on her shoulder. "It is nothing, Pilar," he told her. "What is gone is of small importance. We shall improvise something that will do as well."

"But what did he take?"

"Nothing, woman. Some luxuries that one permits oneself."

"Was it part of thy mechanism for the exploding?"

"Yes. But there are other ways to do the exploding. Tell me, did Pablo not have caps and fuse? Surely they would have equipped him with those?"

"He has taken them," she said miserably. "I looked at once for them. They are gone, too."

They walked back through the woods to the entrance of the cave.

"Get some sleep," he said. "We are better off with Pablo gone."

"I go to see Eladio."

"He will have gone another way."

"I go anyway. I have betrayed thee with my lack of smartness."

"Nay," he said. "Get some sleep, woman. We must be under way at four."

He went into the cave with her and brought out the two sacks, carrying them held together in both arms so that nothing could spill from the slits.

"Let me sew them up."

"Before we start," he said softly. "I take them not against you but so that I can sleep."

"I must have them early to sew them."

"You shall have them early," he told her. "Get some sleep, woman."

"Nay," she said. "I have failed thee and I have failed the Republic."

"Get thee some sleep, woman," he told her gently. "Get thee some sleep."

CHAPTER THIRTY-FOUR

THE fascists held the crests of the hills here. Then there was a valley that no one held except for a fascist post in a farmhouse with its outbuildings and its barn that they had fortified. Andrés, on his way to Golz with the message from Robert Jordan, made a wide circle around this post in the dark. He knew where there was a trip wire laid that fired a set-gun and he located it in the dark, stepped over it, and started along the small stream bordered with poplars whose leaves were moving with the night wind. A cock crowed at the farmhouse that was the fascist post and as he walked along the stream he looked back and saw, through the trunks of the poplars, a light showing at the lower edge of one of the windows of the farmhouse. The night was quiet and clear and Andrés left the stream and struck across the meadow.

There were four haycocks in the meadow that had stood there ever since the fighting in July of the year before. No one had ever carried the hay away and the four seasons that had passed had flattened the cocks and made the hay worthless.

Andrés thought what a waste it was as he stepped over a trip wire that ran between two of the haycocks. But the Republicans would have had to carry the hay up the steep Guadarrama slope that rose beyond the meadow and the fascists did not need it, I suppose, he thought.

They have all the hay they need and all the grain. They have much, he thought. But we will give them a blow tomorrow morning. Tomorrow morning we will give them something for Sordo. What barbarians they are! But in the morning there will be dust on the road.

He wanted to get this message-taking over and be back for the attack on the posts in the morning. Did he really want to get back though or did he only pretend he wanted to be back? He knew the reprieved feeling he had felt when the *Inglés* had told him he was to go with the message. He had faced the prospect of the morn-

ing calmly. It was what was to be done. He had voted for it and
would do it. The wiping out of Sordo had impressed him deeply.
But, after all, that was Sordo. That was not them. What they had
to do they would do.

But when the *Inglés* had spoken to him of the message he had
felt the way he used to feel when he was a boy and he had wakened in the morning of the festival of his village and heard it rain-
ing hard so that he knew that it would be too wet and that the
bullbaiting in the square would be cancelled.

He loved the bullbaiting when he was a boy and he looked forward to it and to the moment when he would be in the square in
the hot sun and the dust with the carts ranged all around to close
the exits and to make a closed place into which the bull would
come, sliding down out of his box, braking with all four feet,
when they pulled the end-gate up. He looked forward with excitement, delight and sweating fear to the moment when, in the
square, he would hear the clatter of the bull's horns knocking
against the wood of his travelling box, and then the sight of him
as he came, sliding, braking out into the square, his head up, his
nostrils wide, his ears twitching, dust in the sheen of his black
hide, dried crut splashed on his flanks, watching his eyes set wide
apart, unblinking eyes under the widespread horns as smooth and
solid as driftwood polished by the sand, the sharp tips uptilted so
that to see them did something to your heart.

He looked forward all the year to that moment when the bull
would come out into the square on that day when you watched his
eyes while he made his choice of whom in the square he would attack
in that sudden head-lowering, horn-reaching, quick cat-gallop that
stopped your heart dead when it started. He had looked forward to
that moment all the year when he was a boy; but the feeling when the
Inglés gave the order about the message was the same as when you
woke to hear the reprieve of the rain falling on the slate roof, against
the stone wall and into the puddles on the dirt street of the village.

He had always been very brave with the bull in those village *capeas,*
as brave as any in the village or of the other near-by villages, and
not for anything would he have missed it any year although he did
not go to the *capeas* of other villages. He was able to wait still when
the bull charged and only jumped aside at the last moment. He

waved a sack under his muzzle to draw him off when the bull had some one down and many times he had held and pulled on the horns when the bull had some one on the ground and pulled sideways on the horn, had slapped and kicked him in the face until he left the man to charge some one else.

He had held the bull's tail to pull him away from a fallen man, bracing hard and pulling and twisting. Once he had pulled the tail around with one hand until he could reach a horn with the other and when the bull had lifted his head to charge him he had run backwards, circling with the bull, holding the tail in one hand and the horn in the other until the crowd had swarmed onto the bull with their knives and stabbed him. In the dust and the heat, the shouting, the bull and man and wine smell, he had been in the first of the crowd that threw themselves onto the bull and he knew the feeling when the bull rocked and bucked under him and he lay across the withers with one arm locked around the base of the horn and his hand holding the other horn tight, his fingers locked as his body tossed and wrenched and his left arm felt as though it would tear from the socket while he lay on the hot, dusty, bristly, tossing slope of muscle, the ear clenched tight in his teeth, and drove his knife again and again and again into the swelling, tossing bulge of the neck that was now spouting hot on his fist as he let his weight hang on the high slope of the withers and banged and banged into the neck.

The first time he had bit the ear like that and held onto it, his neck and jaws stiffened against the tossing, they had all made fun of him afterwards. But though they joked him about it they had great respect for him. And every year after that he had to repeat it. They called him the bulldog of Villaconejos and joked about him eating cattle raw. But every one in the village looked forward to seeing him do it and every year he knew that first the bull would come out, then there would be the charges and the tossing, and then when they yelled for the rush for the killing he would place himself to rush through the other attackers and leap for his hold. Then, when it was over, and the bull settled and sunk dead finally under the weight of the killers, he would stand up and walk away ashamed of the ear part, but also as proud as a man could be. And he would go through the carts to wash his hands at the stone fountain and men would clap him on the back and hand him wineskins and say, "Hurray for you, Bulldog. Long life to your mother."

Or they would say, "That's what it is to have a pair of *cojones!* Year after year!"

Andrés would be ashamed, empty-feeling, proud and happy, and he would shake them all off and wash his hands and his right arm and wash his knife well and then take one of the wineskins and rinse the ear-taste out of his mouth for that year; spitting the wine on the stone flags of the plaza before he lifted the wineskin high and let the wine spurt into the back of his mouth.

Surely. He was the Bulldog of Villaconejos and not for anything would he have missed doing it each year in his village. But he knew there was no better feeling than that one the sound of the rain gave when he knew he would not have to do it.

But I must go back, he told himself. There is no question but that I must go back for the affair of the posts and the bridge. My brother Eladio is there, who is of my own bone and flesh. Anselmo, Primitivo, Fernando, Agustín, Rafael, though clearly he is not serious, the two women, Pablo and the *Inglés*, though the *Inglés* does not count since he is a foreigner and under orders. They are all in for it. It is impossible that I should escape this proving through the accident of a message. I must deliver this message now quickly and well and then make all haste to return in time for the assault on the posts. It would be ignoble of me not to participate in this action because of the accident of this message. That could not be clearer. And besides, he told himself, as one who suddenly remembers that there will be pleasure too in an engagement only the onerous aspects of which he has been considering, and besides I will enjoy the killing of some fascists. It has been too long since we have destroyed any. Tomorrow can be a day of much valid action. Tomorrow can be a day of concrete acts. Tomorrow can be a day which is worth something. That tomorrow should come and that I should be there.

Just then, as kneedeep in the gorse he climbed the steep slope that led to the Republican lines, a partridge flew up from under his feet, exploding in a whirr of wingbeats in the dark and he felt a sudden breath-stopping fright. It is the suddenness, he thought. How can they move their wings that fast? She must be nesting now. I probably trod close to the eggs. If there were not this war I would tie a handkerchief to the bush and come back in the daytime and search out the nest and I could take the eggs and put them under a setting hen and when they hatched we would have little partridges in the poultry yard and I would watch them grow and, when they were grown, I'd use them for callers. I wouldn't blind them because they would be tame. Or do you suppose they would fly off? Probably. Then I would have to blind them.

But I don't like to do that after I have raised them. I could clip the wings or tether them by one leg when I used them for calling. If there was no war I would go with Eladio to get crayfish from that stream back there by the fascist post. One time we got four dozen from that stream in a day. If we go to the Sierra de Gredos after this of the bridge there are fine streams there for trout and for crayfish also. I hope we go to Gredos, he thought. We could make a good life in Gredos in the summer time and in the fall but it would be terribly cold in winter. But by winter maybe we will have won the war.

If our father had not been a Republican both Eladio and I would be soldiers now with the fascists and if one were a soldier with them then there would be no problem. One would obey orders and one would live or die and in the end it would be however it would be. It was easier to live under a regime than to fight it.

But this irregular fighting was a thing of much responsibility. There was much worry if you were one to worry. Eladio thinks more than I do. Also he worries. I believe truly in the cause and I do not worry. But it is a life of much responsibility.

I think that we are born into a time of great difficulty, he thought. I think any other time was probably easier. One suffers little because all of us have been formed to resist suffering. They who suffer are unsuited to this climate. But it is a time of difficult decisions. The fascists attacked and made our decision for us. We fight to live. But I would like to have it so that I could tie a handkerchief to that bush back there and come in the daylight and take the eggs and put them under a hen and be able to see the chicks of the partridge in my own courtyard. I would like such small and regular things.

But you have no house and no courtyard in your no-house, he thought. You have no family but a brother who goes to battle tomorrow and you own nothing but the wind and the sun and an empty belly. The wind is small, he thought, and there is no sun. You have four grenades in your pocket but they are only good to throw away. You have a carbine on your back but it is only good to give away bullets. You have a message to give away. And you're full of crap that you can give to the earth, he grinned in the dark. You can anoint it also with urine. Everything you have is to give. Thou art a phenomenon of philosophy and an unfortunate man, he told himself and grinned again.

But for all his noble thinking a little while before there was in him that reprieved feeling that had always come with the sound of rain in the village on the morning of the fiesta. Ahead of him now at the top of the ridge was the government position where he knew he would be challenged.

CHAPTER THIRTY-FIVE

ROBERT JORDAN lay in the robe beside the girl Maria who was still sleeping. He lay on his side turned away from the girl and he felt her long body against his back and the touch of it now was just an irony. You, you, he raged at himself. Yes, you. You told yourself the first time you saw him that when he would be friendly would be when the treachery would come. You damned fool. You utter blasted damned fool. Chuck all that. That's not what you have to do now.

What are the chances that he hid them or threw them away? Not so good. Besides you'd never find them in the dark. He would have kept them. He took some dynamite, too. Oh, the dirty, vile, treacherous sod. The dirty rotten crut. Why couldn't he have just mucked off and not have taken the exploder and the detonators? Why was I such an utter goddamned fool as to leave them with that bloody woman? The smart, treacherous ugly bastard. The dirty *cabrón*.

Cut it out and take it easy, he told himself. You had to take chances and that was the best there was. You're just mucked, he told himself. You're mucked for good and higher than a kite. Keep your damned head and get the anger out and stop this cheap lamenting like a damned wailing wall. It's gone. God damn you, it's gone. Oh damn the dirty swine to hell. You can muck your way out of it. You've got to, you know you've got to blow it if you have to stand there and—cut out that stuff, too. Why don't you ask your grandfather?

Oh, muck my grandfather and muck this whole treacherous muck-faced mucking country and every mucking Spaniard in it on either side and to hell forever. Muck them to hell together, Largo, Prieto, Asensio, Miaja, Rojo, all of them. Muck every one of them to death to hell. Much the whole treachery-ridden country. Muck their egotism and their selfishness and their selfishness and their egotism and their conceit and their treachery. Muck them to hell and always. Muck them before we die for them. Muck them after we die for them. Muck them to death and hell. God muck Pablo. Pablo is all of them. God pity the Spanish people. Any leader they have will muck them. One good man, Pablo Iglesias, in two thousand years and everybody else mucking them. How do we know how he would have stood up in this war? I remember when I thought Largo was O.K. Durruti was good and his own people shot him there at the Puente de los Franceses. Shot him because he wanted them to attack. Shot him in the glorious discipline of indiscipline. The cowardly swine. Oh muck them all to hell and be damned. And that Pablo that just mucked off with my exploder and my box of detonators. Oh muck him to deepest hell. But no. He's mucked us instead. They always muck you instead, from Cortez and Menendez de Avila down to Miaja. Look at what Miaja did to Kleber. The bald egotistical swine. The stupid egg-headed bastard. Muck all the insane, egotistical, treacherous swine that have always governed Spain and ruled her armies. Muck everybody but the people and then be damned careful what they turn into when they have power.

His rage began to thin as he exaggerated more and more and spread his scorn and contempt so widely and unjustly that he could no longer believe in it himself. If that were true what are you here for? It's not true and you know it. Look at all the good ones. Look at all the fine ones. He could not bear to be unjust. He hated injustice as he hated cruelty and he lay in his rage that blinded his mind until gradually the anger died down and the red, black, blinding, killing anger was all gone and his mind now as quiet, empty-calm and sharp, cold-seeing as a man is after he has had sexual intercourse with a woman that he does not love.

"And you, you poor rabbit," he leaned over and said to Maria, who smiled in her sleep and moved close against him. "I would have struck thee there awhile back if thou had spoken. What an animal a man is in a rage."

He lay close to the girl now with his arms around her and his chin on her shoulder and lying there he figured out exactly what he would have to do and how he would have to do it.

And it isn't so bad, he thought. It really isn't so bad at all. I don't know whether any one has ever done it before. But there will always be people who will do it from now on, given a similar jam. If we do it and if they hear about it. If they hear about it, yes. If they do not just wonder how it was we did it. We are too short of people but there is no sense to worry about that. I will do the bridge with what we have. God, I'm glad I got over being angry. It was like not being able to breathe in a storm. That being angry is another damned luxury you can't afford.

"It's all figured out, *guapa,*" he said softly against Maria's shoulder. "You haven't been bothered by any of it. You have not known about it. We'll be killed but we'll blow the bridge. You have not had to worry about it. That isn't much of a wedding present. But is not a good night's sleep supposed to be priceless? You had a good night's sleep. See if you can wear that like a ring on your finger. Sleep, *guapa.* Sleep well, my beloved. I do not wake thee. That is all I can do for thee now."

He lay there holding her very lightly, feeling her breathe and feeling her heart beat, and keeping track of the time on his wrist watch.

CHAPTER THIRTY-SIX

ANDRÉS had challenged at the government position. That is, he had lain down where the ground fell sharply away below the triple belt of wire and shouted up at the rock and earth parapet. There was no continual defensive line and he could easily have passed this position in the dark and made his way farther into the government territory before running into some one who would challenge him. But it seemed safer and simpler to get it over here.

"*Salud!*" he had shouted. "*Salud, milicianos!*"

He heard a bolt snick as it was pulled back. Then, from farther down the parapet, a rifle fired. There was a crashing crack and a downward stab of yellow in the dark. Andrés had flattened at the click, the top of his head hard against the ground.

"Don't shoot, Comrades," Andrés shouted. "Don't shoot! I want to come in."

"How many are you?" some one called from behind the parapet.

"One. Me. Alone."

"Who are you?"

"Andrés Lopez of Villaconejos. From the band of Pablo. With a message."

"Have you your rifle and equipment?"

"Yes, man."

"We can take in none without rifle and equipment," the voice said. "Nor in larger groups than three."

"I am alone," Andrés shouted. "It is important. Let me come in."

He could hear them talking behind the parapet but not what they were saying. Then the voice shouted again, "How many are you?"

"One. Me. Alone. For the love of God."

They were talking behind the parapet again. Then the voice came, "Listen, fascist."

"I am not a fascist," Andrés shouted. "I am a *guerrillero* from the band of Pablo. I come with a message for the General Staff."

"He's crazy," he heard some one say. "Toss a bomb at him."

"Listen," Andrés said. "I am alone. I am completely by myself. I obscenity in the midst of the holy mysteries that I am alone. Let me come in."

"He speaks like a Christian," he heard some one say and laugh.

Then some one else said, "The best thing is to toss a bomb down on him."

"No," Andrés shouted. "That would be a great mistake. This is important. Let me come in."

It was for this reason that he had never enjoyed trips back and forth between the lines. Sometimes it was better than others. But it was never good.

"You are alone?" the voice called down again.

"Me cago en la leche," Andrés shouted. "How many times must I tell thee? I AM ALONE."

"Then if you should be alone stand up and hold thy rifle over thy head."

Andrés stood up and put the carbine above his head, holding it in both hands.

"Now come through the wire. We have thee covered with the *máquina,"* the voice called.

Andrés was in the first zigzag belt of wire. "I need my hands to get through the wire," he shouted.

"Keep them up," the voice commanded.

"I am held fast by the wire," Andrés called.

"It would have been simpler to have thrown a bomb at him," a voice said.

"Let him sling his rifle," another voice said. "He cannot come through there with his hands above his head. Use a little reason."

"All these fascists are the same," the other voice said. "They demand one condition after another."

"Listen," Andrés shouted. "I am no fascist but a *guerrillero* from the band of Pablo. We've killed more fascists than the typhus."

"I have never heard of the band of Pablo," the man who was evidently in command of the post said. "Neither of Peter nor of Paul nor of any of the other saints nor apostles. Nor of their bands. Sling thy rifle over thy shoulder and use thy hands to come through the wire."

"Before we loose the *máquina* on thee," another shouted.

"Qué poco amables sois!" Andrés said. "You're not very amiable." He was working his way through the wire.

"Amables," some one shouted at him. "We are in a war, man."

"It begins to appear so," Andrés said.

"What's he say?"

Andrés heard a bolt click again.

"Nothing," he shouted. "I say nothing. Do not shoot until I get through this fornicating wire."

"Don't speak badly of our wire," some one shouted. "Or we'll toss a bomb on you."

"Quiero decir, qué buena alambrada," Andrés shouted. "What beautiful wire. God in a latrine. What lovely wire. Soon I will be with thee, brothers."

"Throw a bomb at him," he heard the one voice say. "I tell you that's the soundest way to deal with the whole thing."

"Brothers," Andrés said. He was wet through with sweat and he knew the bomb advocate was perfectly capable of tossing a grenade at any moment. "I have no importance."

"I believe it," the bomb man said.

"You are right," Andrés said. He was working carefully through the third belt of wire and he was very close to the parapet. "I have no importance of any kind. But the affair is serious. *Muy, muy serio.*"

"There is no more serious thing than liberty," the bomb man shouted. "Thou thinkest there is anything more serious than liberty?" he asked challengingly.

"No, man," Andrés said, relieved. He knew now he was up against the crazies; the ones with the black-and-red scarves. *"Viva la Libertad!"*

"Viva la F. A. I. Viva la C. N. T.," they shouted back at him from the parapet. *"Viva el anarco-sindicalismo* and liberty."

"Viva nosotros," Andrés shouted. "Long life to us."

"He is a coreligionary of ours," the bomb man said. "And I might have killed him with this."

He looked at the grenade in his hand and was deeply moved as Andrés climbed over the parapet. Putting his arms around him, the grenade still in one hand, so that it rested against Andrés's shoulder blade as he embraced him, the bomb man kissed him on both cheeks.

"I am content that nothing happened to thee, brother," he said. "I am very content."

"Where is thy officer?" Andrés asked.

"I command here," a man said. "Let me see thy papers."

He took them into a dugout and looked at them with the light of a candle. There was the little square of folded silk with the colors of the Republic and the seal of the S. I. M. in the center. There was the *Salvoconducto* or safe-conduct pass giving his name, age, height, birthplace and mission that Robert Jordan had written out on a sheet from his notebook and sealed with the S. I. M. rubber stamp and there were the four folded sheets of the dispatch to Golz which were tied around with a cord and sealed with wax and the impression of the metal S. I. M. seal that was set in the top end of the wooden handle of the rubber stamp.

"This I have seen," the man in command of the post said and handed back the piece of silk. "This you all have, I know. But its possession proves nothing without this." He lifted the *Salvoconducto* and read it through again. "Where were you born?"

"Villaconejos," Andrés said.

"And what do they raise there?"

"Melons," Andrés said. "As all the world knows."

"Who do you know there?"

"Why? Are you from there?"

"Nay. But I have been there. I am from Aranjuez."

"Ask me about any one."

"Describe José Rincon."

"Who keeps the bodega?"

"Naturally."

"With a shaved head and a big belly and a cast in one eye."

"Then this is valid," the man said and handed him back the paper. "But what do you do on their side?"

"Our father had installed himself at Villacastín before the movement," Andrés said. "Down there beyond the mountains on the plain. It was there we were surprised by the movement. Since the movement I have fought with the band of Pablo. But I am in a great hurry, man, to take that dispatch."

"How goes it in the country of the fascists?" the man commanding asked. He was in no hurry.

"Today we had much *tomate*," Andrés said proudly. "Today there was plenty of dust on the road all day. Today they wiped out the band of Sordo."

"And who is Sordo?" the other asked deprecatingly.

"The leader of one of the best bands in the mountains."

"All of you should come in to the Republic and join the army," the officer said. "There is too much of this silly guerilla nonsense going on. All of you should come in and submit to our Libertarian discipline. Then when we wished to send out guerillas we would send them out as they are needed."

Andrés was a man endowed with almost supreme patience. He had taken the coming in through the wire calmly. None of this examination had flustered him. He found it perfectly normal that this man should have no understanding of them nor of what they were doing and that he should talk idiocy was to be expected. That it should all go slowly should be expected too; but now he wished to go.

"Listen, *Compadre,*" he said. "It is very possible that you are right. But I have orders to deliver that dispatch to the General commanding the thirty-fifth Division, which makes an attack at daylight in these hills and it is already late at night and I must go."

"What attack? What do you know of an attack?"

"Nay. I know nothing. But I must go now to Navacerrada and go on from there. Wilt thou send me to thy commander who will give me transport to go on from there? Send one with me now to respond to him that there be no delay."

"I distrust all of this greatly," he said. "It might have been better to have shot thee as thou approached the wire."

"You have seen my papers, Comrade, and I have explained my mission," Andrés told him patiently.

"Papers can be forged," the officer said. "Any fascist could invent such a mission. I will go with thee myself to the Commander."

"Good," Andrés said. "That you should come. But that we should go quickly."

"Thou, Sanchez. Thou commandest in my place," the officer said. "Thou knowest thy duties as well as I do. I take this so-called Comrade to the Commander."

They started down the shallow trench behind the crest of the hill and in the dark Andrés smelt the foulness the defenders of the hill crest had made all through the bracken on that slope. He did not like these people who were like dangerous children; dirty, foul, undisciplined, kind, loving, silly and ignorant but always dangerous because they were armed. He, Andrés, was without politics except that he was for the Republic. He had heard these people talk many times and he thought what they said was often beautiful and fine to hear but he did not like them. It is not liberty not to bury the mess one makes, he thought. No animal has more liberty than the cat; but it buries the mess it makes. The cat is the best anarchist. Until they learn that from the cat I cannot respect them.

Ahead of him the officer stopped suddenly.

"You have your *carabine* still," he said.

"Yes," Andrés said. "Why not?"

"Give it to me," the officer said. "You could shoot me in the back with it."

"Why?" Andrés asked him. "Why would I shoot thee in the back?"

"One never knows," the officer said. "I trust no one. Give me the carbine."

Andrés unslung it and handed it to him.

"If it pleases thee to carry it," he said.

"It is better," the officer said. "We are safer that way."

They went on down the hill in the dark.

CHAPTER THIRTY-SEVEN

NOW ROBERT JORDAN lay with the girl and he watched time passing on his wrist. It went slowly, almost imperceptibly, for it was a small watch and he could not see the second hand. But as he watched the minute hand he found he could almost check its motion with his concentration. The girl's head was under his chin and when he moved his head to look at the watch he felt the cropped head against his cheek, and it was as soft but as alive and silkily rolling as when a marten's fur rises under the caress of your hand when you spread the trap jaws open and lift the marten clear and, holding it, stroke the fur smooth. His throat swelled when his cheek moved against Maria's hair and there was a hollow aching from his throat all through him as he held his arms around her; his head dropped, his eyes close to the watch where the lance-pointed, luminous splinter moved slowly up the left face of the dial. He could see its movement clearly and steadily now and he held Maria close now to slow it. He did not want to wake her but he could not leave her alone now in this last time and he put his lips behind her ear and moved them up along her neck, feeling the smooth skin and the soft touch of her hair on them. He could see the hand moving on the watch and he held her tighter and ran the tip of his tongue along her cheek and onto the lobe of her ear and along the lovely convolutions to the sweet, firm rim at the top, and his tongue was trembling. He felt the trembling run through all of the hollow aching and he saw the hand of the watch now mounting in sharp angle toward the top where the hour was. Now while she still slept he turned her head and put his lips to hers. They lay there, just touching lightly against the sleep-firm mouth and he swung them softly across it, feeling them brush lightly. He turned himself toward her and he felt her shiver along the long, light lovely body and then she sighed, sleeping, and then she, still sleeping, held him too and then, unsleeping, her lips were against his firm and hard and pressing and he said, "But the pain."

And she said, "Nay, there is no pain."

"Rabbit."

"Nay, speak not."

"My rabbit."

"Speak not. Speak not."

Then they were together so that as the hand on the watch moved, unseen now, they knew that nothing could ever happen to the one that did not happen to the other, that no other thing could happen more than this; that this was all and always; this was what had been and now and whatever was to come. This, that they were not to have, they were having. They were having now and before and always and now and now and now. Oh, now, now, now, the only now, and above all now, and there is no other now but thou now and now is thy prophet. Now and forever now. Come now, now, for there is no now but now. Yes, now. Now, please now, only now, not anything else only this now, and where are you and where am I and where is the other one, and not why, not ever why, only this now; and on and always please then always now, always now, for now always one now; one only one, there is no other one but one now, one, going now, rising now, sailing now, leaving now, wheeling now, soaring now, away now, all the way now, all of all the way now; one and one is one, is one, is one, is one, is still one, is still one, is one descendingly, is one softly, is one longingly, is one kindly, is one happily, is one in goodness, is one to cherish, is one now on earth with elbows against the cut and slept-on branches of the pine tree with the smell of the pine boughs and the night; to earth conclusively now, and with the morning of the day to come. Then he said, for the other was only in his head and he had said nothing, "Oh, Maria, I love thee and I thank thee for this."

Maria said, "Do not speak. It is better if we do not speak."

"I must tell thee for it is a great thing."

"Nay."

"Rabbit——"

But she held him tight and turned her head away and he asked softly, "Is it pain, rabbit?"

"Nay," she said. "It is that I am thankful too to have been another time in *la gloria*."

Then afterwards they lay quiet, side by side, all length of ankle, thigh, hip and shoulder touching, Robert Jordan now with the watch where he could see it again and Maria said, "We have had much good fortune."

"Yes," he said, "we are people of much luck."

"There is not time to sleep?"

"No," he said, "it starts soon now."

"Then if we must rise let us go to get something to eat."

"All right."

"Thou. Thou art not worried about anything?"

"No."

"Truly?"

"No. Not now."

"But thou hast worried before?"

"For a while."

"Is it aught I can help?"

"Nay," he said. "You have helped enough."

"That? That was for me."

"That was for us both," he said. "No one is there alone. Come, rabbit, let us dress."

But his mind, that was his best companion, was thinking La Gloria. She said La Gloria. It has nothing to do with glory nor La Gloire that the French write and speak about. It is the thing that is in the Cante Hondo and in the Saetas. It is in Greco and in San Juan de la Cruz, of course, and in the others. I am no mystic, but to deny it is as ignorant as though you denied the telephone or that the earth revolves around the sun or that there are other planets than this.

How little we know of what there is to know. I wish that I were going to live a long time instead of going to die today because I have learned much about life in these four days; more, I think, than in all the other time. I'd like to be an old man and to really know. I wonder if you keep on learning or if there is only a certain amount each man can understand. I thought I knew about so many things that I know nothing of. I wish there was more time.

"You taught me a lot, *guapa,*" he said in English.

"What did you say?"

"I have learned much from thee."

"*Qué va,*" she said, "it is thou who art educated."

Educated, he thought. I have the very smallest beginnings of an education. The very small beginnings. If I die on this day it is a waste because I know a few things now. I wonder if you only learn them now because you are oversensitized because of the shortness of the time? There is no such thing as a shortness of time, though. You should have sense enough to know that too. I have been all my life in these hills since I have been here. Anselmo is my oldest friend. I know him better than I know Charles, than I know Chub, than I know Guy, than I know Mike, and I know them well. Agustín, with his vile mouth, is my brother, and I never had a brother. Maria is my true love and my wife. I never had a true love. I never had a wife. She is also my sister, and I never had a sister, and my daughter, and I never will have a daughter. I hate to leave a thing that is so good. He finished tying his rope-soled shoes.

"I find life very interesting," he said to Maria. She was sitting beside him on the robe, her hands clasped around her ankles. Some one moved the blanket aside from the entrance to the cave and they both saw the light. It was night still and here was no promise of morning except that as he looked up through the pines he saw how low the stars had swung. The morning would be coming fast now in this month.

"Roberto," Maria said.

"Yes, *guapa.*"

"In this of today we will be together, will we not?"

"After the start, yes."

"Not at the start?"

"No. Thou wilt be with the horses."

"I cannot be with thee?"

"No. I have work that only I can do and I would worry about thee."

"But you will come fast when it is done?"

"Very fast," he said and grinned in the dark. "Come, *guapa,* let us go and eat."

"And thy robe?"

"Roll it up, if it pleases thee."

"It pleases me," she said.

"I will help thee."

"Nay. Let me do it alone."

She knelt to spread and roll the robe, then changed her mind and stood up and shook it so it flapped. Then she knelt down again to straighten it and roll it. Robert Jordan picked up the two packs, holding them carefully so that nothing would spill from the slits in them, and walked over through the pines to the cave-mouth where the smoky blanket hung. It was ten minutes to three by his watch when he pushed the blanket aside with his elbow and went into the cave.

CHAPTER THIRTY-EIGHT

THEY were in the cave and the men were standing before the fire Maria was fanning. Pilar had coffee ready in a pot. She had not gone back to bed at all since she had roused Robert Jordan and now she was sitting on a stool in the smoky cave sewing the rip in one of Jordan's packs. The other pack was already sewed. The firelight lit up her face.

"Take more of the stew," she said to Fernando. "What does it matter if thy belly should be full? There is no doctor to operate if you take a goring."

"Don't speak that way, woman," Agustín said. "Thou hast the tongue of the great whore."

He was leaning on the automatic rifle, its legs folded close against the fretted barrel, his pockets were full of grenades, a sack of pans hung from one shoulder, and a full bandolier of ammunition hung over the other shoulder. He was smoking a cigarette and he held a bowl of coffee in one hand and blew smoke onto its surface as he raised it to his lips.

"Thou art a walking hardware store," Pilar said to him. "Thou canst not walk a hundred yards with all that."

"*Qué va,* woman," Agustín said. "It is all downhill."

"There is a climb to the post," Fernando said. "Before the downward slope commences."

"I will climb it like a goat," Agustín said.

"And thy brother?" he asked Eladio. "Thy famous brother has mucked off?"

Eladio was standing against the wall.

"Shut up," he said.

He was nervous and he knew they all knew it. He was always nervous and irritable before action. He moved from the wall to the table and began filling his pockets with grenades from one of the raw-hide-covered panniers that leaned, open, against the table leg.

Robert Jordan squatted by the pannier beside him. He reached into the pannier and picked out four grenades. Three were the oval Mill bomb type, serrated, heavy iron with a spring level held down in position by a cotter pin with pulling rig attached.

"Where did these come from?" he asked Eladio.

"Those? Those are from the Republic. The old man brought them."

How are they?"

"*Valen más que pesan,*" Eladio said. "They are worth a fortune apiece."

"I brought those," Anselmo said. "Sixty in one pack. Ninety pounds, *Inglés.*"

"Have you used those?" Robert Jordan asked Pilar.

"*Qué va* have we used them?" the woman said. "It was with those Pablo slew the post at Otero."

When she mentioned Pablo, Agustín started cursing. Robert Jordan saw the look on Pilar's face in the firelight.

"Leave it," she said to Agustín sharply. "It does no good to talk."

"Have they always exploded?" Robert Jordan held the gray-painted grenade in his hand, trying the bend of the cotter pin with his thumbnail.

"Always," Eladio said. "There was not a dud in any of that lot we used."

"And how quickly?"

"In the distance one can throw it. Quickly. Quickly enough."

"And these?"

He held up a soup-tin-shaped bomb, with a tape wrapping around a wire loop.

"They are a garbage," Eladio told him. "They blow. Yes. But it is all flash and no fragments."

"But do they always blow?"

"*Qué va,* always," Pilar said. "There is no always either with our munitions or theirs."

"But you said the other always blew."

"Not me," Pilar told him. "You asked another, not me. I have seen no *always* in any of that stuff."

"They all blew," Eladio insisted. "Speak the truth, woman."

"How do you know they all blew?" Pilar asked him. "It was Pablo who threw them. You killed no one at Otero."

"That son of the great whore," Agustín began.

"Leave it alone," Pilar said sharply. Then she went on. "They are all much the same, *Inglés*. But the corrugated ones are more simple."

I'd better use one of each on each set, Robert Jordan thought. But the serrated type will lash easier and more securely.

"Are you going to be throwing bombs, *Inglés?*" Agustín asked.

"Why not?" Robert Jordan said.

But crouched there, sorting out the grenades, what he was thinking was: it is impossible. How I could have deceived myself about it I do not know. We were as sunk when they attacked Sordo as Sordo was sunk when the snow stopped. It is that you can't accept it. You have to go on and make a plan that you know is impossible to carry out. You made it and now you know it is no good. It's no good, now, in the morning. You can take either of the posts absolutely O.K. with what you've got here. But you can't take them both. You can't be sure of it, I mean. Don't deceive yourself. Not when the daylight comes.

Trying to take them both will never work. Pablo knew that all the time. I suppose he always intended to muck off but he knew we were cooked when Sordo was attacked. You can't base an operation on the presumption that miracles are going to happen. You will kill them all off and not even get your bridge blown if you have nothing better than what you have now. You will kill off Pilar, Anselmo, Agustín, Primitivo, this jumpy Eladio, the worthless gypsy and old Fernando, and you won't get your bridge blown. Do you suppose there will be a miracle and Golz will get the message from Andrés and stop it? If there isn't, you are going to kill them all off with those orders. Maria too. You'll kill her too with those orders. Can't you even get her out of it? God damn Pablo to hell, he thought.

No. Don't get angry. Getting angry is as bad as getting scared. But instead of sleeping with your girl you should have ridden all night through these hills with the woman to try to dig up enough people to make it work. Yes, he thought. And if anything happened to me so I was not here to blow it. Yes. That. That's why you weren't out. And you couldn't send anybody out because you couldn't run a chance of losing them and being short one more. You had to keep what you had and make a plan to do it with them.

But your plan stinks. It stinks, I tell you. It was a night plan and it's morning now. Night plans aren't any good in the morning. The way you think at night is no good in the morning. So now you know it is no good.

What if John Mosby did get away with things as impossible as this? Sure he did. Much more difficult. And remember, do not undervalue the element of surprise. Remember that. Remember it isn't goofy if you can make it stick. But that is not the way you are supposed to make it. You should make it not only possible but sure. But look at how it all has gone. Well, it was wrong in the first place and such things accentuate disaster as a snowball rolls up wet snow.

He looked up from where he was squatted by the table and saw Maria and she smiled at him. He grinned back with the front of his face and selected four more grenades and put them in his pockets. I could unscrew the detonators and just use them, he thought. But I don't think the fragmentation will have any bad effect. It will come instantaneously with the explosion of the charge and it won't disperse it. At least, I don't think it will. I'm sure it won't. Have a little confidence, he told himself. And you, last night, thinking about how you and your grandfather were so terrific and your father was a coward. Show yourself a little confidence now.

He grinned at Maria again but the grin was still no deeper than the skin that felt tight over his cheekbones and his mouth.

She thinks you're wonderful, he thought. I think you stink. And the *gloria* and all that nonsense that you had. You had wonderful ideas, didn't you? You had this world all taped, didn't you? The hell with all of that.

Take it easy, he told himself. Don't get into a rage. That's just a way out too. There are always ways out. You've got to bite on the nail now. There isn't any need to deny everything there's been just because you are going to lose it. Don't be like some damned snake with a broken back biting at itself; and your back isn't broken either, you hound. Wait until you're hurt before you start to cry. Wait until the fight before you get angry. There's lots of time for it in a fight. It will be some use to you in a fight.

Pilar came over to him with the bag.

"It is strong now," she said. "Those grenades are very good, *Inglés*. You can have confidence in them."

"How do you feel, woman?"

She looked at him and shook her head and smiled. He wondered how far into her face the smile went. It looked deep enough.

"Good," she said. *"Dentro de la gravedad."*

Then she said, squatting by him, "How does it seem to thee now that it is really starting?"

"That we are few," Robert Jordan said to her quickly.

"To me, too," she said. "Very few."

Then she said still to him alone, "The Maria can hold the horses by herself. I am not needed for that. We will hobble them. They are cavalry horses and the firing will not panic them. I will go to the lower post and do that which was the duty of Pablo. In this way we are one more."

"Good," he said. "I thought you might wish to."

"Nay, *Inglés,*" Pilar said looking at him closely. "Do not be worried. All will be well. Remember they expect no such thing to come to them."

"Yes," Robert Jordan said.

"One other thing, *Inglés,*" Pilar said as softly as her harsh whisper could be soft. "In that thing of the hand——"

"What thing of the hand?" he said angrily.

"Nay, listen. Do not be angry, little boy. In regard to that thing of the hand. That is all gypsy nonsense that I make to give myself an importance. There is no such thing."

"Leave it alone," he said coldly.

"Nay," she said harshly and lovingly. "It is just a lying nonsense that I make. I would not have thee worry in the day of battle."

"I am not worried," Robert Jordan said.

"Yes, *Inglés,*" she said. "Thou art very worried, for good cause. But all will be well, *Inglés.* It is for this that we are born."

"I don't need a political commissar," Robert Jordan told her.

She smiled at him again, smiling fairly and truly with the harsh lips and the wide mouth, and said, "I care for thee very much, *Inglés.*"

"I don't want that now," he said. *"Ni tu, ni Dios."*

"Yes," Pilar said in that husky whisper. "I know. I only wished to tell thee. And do not worry. We will do all very well."

"Why not?" Robert Jordan said and the very thinnest edge of the skin in front of his face smiled. "Of course we will. All will be well."

"When do we go?" Pilar asked.

Robert Jordan looked at his watch.

"Any time," he said.

He handed one of the packs to Anselmo.

"How are you doing, old one?" he asked.

The old man was finishing whittling the last of a pile of wedges he had copied from a model Robert Jordan had given him. These were extra wedges in case they should be needed.

"Well," the old man said and nodded. "So far, very well." He held his hand out. "Look," he said and smiled. His hands were perfectly steady.

"Bueno, y qué?" Robert Jordan said to him. "I can always keep the whole hand steady. Point with one finger."

Anselmo pointed. The finger was trembling. He looked at Robert Jordan and shook his head.

"Mine too," Robert Jordan showed him. "Always. That is normal."

"Not for me," Fernando said. He put his right forefinger out to show them. Then the left forefinger.

"Canst thou spit?" Agustín asked him and winked at Robert Jordan.

Fernando hawked and spat proudly onto the floor of the cave, then rubbed it in the dirt with his foot.

"You filthy mule," Pilar said to him. "Spit in the fire if thou must vaunt thy courage."

"I would not have spat on the floor, Pilar, if we were not leaving this place," Fernando said primly.

"Be careful where you spit today," Pilar told him. "It may be some place you will not be leaving."

"That one speaks like a black cat," Agustín said. He had the nervous necessity to joke that is another form of what they all felt.

"I joke," said Pilar.

"Me too," said Agustín. "But *me cago en la leche,* but I will be content when it starts."

"Where is the gypsy?" Robert Jordan asked Eladio.

"With the horses," Eladio said. "You can see him from the cave mouth."

"How is he?"

Eladio grinned. "With much fear," he said. It reassured him to speak of the fear of another.

"Listen, *Inglés*—" Pilar began. Robert Jordan looked toward her and as he did he saw her mouth open and the unbelieving look come on her face and he swung toward the cave mouth reaching for his pistol. There, holding the blanket aside with one hand, the short automatic rifle muzzle with its flash-cone jutting above his shoulder, was Pablo standing short, wide, bristly-faced, his small red-rimmed eyes looking toward no one in particular.

"Thou—" Pilar said to him unbelieving. "Thou."

"Me," said Pablo evenly. He came into the cave.

"*Hola, Inglés,*" he said. "I have five from the bands of Elias and Alejandro above with their horses."

"And the exploder and the detonators?" Robert Jordan said. "And the other material?"

"I threw them down the gorge into the river," Pablo said still looking at no one. "But I have thought of a way to detonate using a grenade."

"So have I," Robert Jordan said.

"Have you a drink of anything?" Pablo asked wearily.

Robert Jordan handed him the flask and he swallowed fast, then wiped his mouth on the back of his hand.

"What passes with you?" Pilar asked.

"*Nada,*" Pablo said, wiping his mouth again. "Nothing. I have come back."

"But what?"

"Nothing. I had a moment of weakness. I went away but I am come back."

He turned to Robert Jordan. "*En el fondo no soy cobarde,*" he said. "At bottom I am not a coward."

But you are very many other things, Robert Jordan thought. Damned if you're not. But I'm glad to see you, you son of a bitch.

"Five was all I could get from Elias and Alejandro," Pablo said. "I have ridden since I left here. Nine of you could never have done it. Never. I knew that last night when the *Inglés* explained it. Never. There are seven men and a corporal at the lower post. Suppose there is an alarm or that they fight?"

He looked at Robert Jordan now. "When I left I thought you

would know that it was impossible and would give it up. Then after I had thrown away thy material I saw it in another manner."

"I am glad to see thee," Robert Jordan said. He walked over to him. "We are all right with the grenades. That will work. The other does not matter now."

"Nay," Pablo said. "I do nothing for thee. Thou art a thing of bad omen. All of this comes from thee. Sordo also. But after I had thrown away thy material I found myself too lonely."

"Thy mother——" Pilar said.

"So I rode for the others to make it possible for it to be successful. I have brought the best that I could get. I have left them at the top so I could speak to you, first. They think I am the leader."

"Thou art," Pilar said. "If thee wishes." Pablo looked at her and said nothing. Then he said simply and quietly, "I have thought much since the thing of Sordo. I believe if we must finish we must finish together. But thou, *Inglés*. I hate thee for bringing this to us."

"But Pablo——" Fernando, his pockets full of grenades, a bandolier of cartridges over his shoulder, he still wiping in his pan of stew with a piece of bread, began. "Do you not believe the operation can be successful? Night before last you said you were convinced it would be."

"Give him some more stew," Pilar said viciously to Maria. Then to Pablo, her eyes softening, "So you have come back, eh?"

"Yes, woman," Pablo said.

"Well, thou art welcome," Pilar said to him. "I did not think thou couldst be the ruin thou appeared to be."

"Having done such a thing there is a loneliness that cannot be borne," Pablo said to her quietly.

"That cannot be borne," she mocked him. "That cannot be borne by thee for fifteen minutes."

"Do not mock me, woman. I have come back."

"And thou art welcome," she said. "Didst not hear me the first time? Drink thy coffee and let us go. So much theatre tires me."

"Is that coffee?" Pablo asked.

"Certainly," Fernando said.

"Give me some, Maria," Pablo said. "How art thou?" He did not look at her.

"Well," Maria told him and brought him a bowl of coffee. "Do you want stew?" Pablo shook his head.

"No me gusta estar solo," Pablo went on explaining to Pilar as though the others were not there. "I do not like to be alone. *Sabes?* Yesterday all day alone working for the good of all I was not lonely. But last night. *Hombre! Qué mal lo pasé!"*

"Thy predecessor the famous Judas Iscariot hanged himself," Pilar said.

"Don't talk to me that way, woman," Pablo said. "Have you not seen? I am back. Don't talk of Judas nor nothing of that. I am back."

"How are these people thee brought?" Pilar asked him. "Hast brought anything worth bringing?"

"Son buenos," Pablo said. He took a chance and looked at Pilar squarely, then looked away.

"Buenos y bobos. Good ones and stupids. Ready to die and all. *A tu gusto.* According to thy taste. The way you like them."

Pablo looked Pilar in the eyes again and this time he did not look away. He kept on looking at her squarely with his small, red-rimmed pig eyes.

"Thou," she said and her husky voice was fond again. "Thou. I suppose if a man has something once, always something of it remains."

"Listo," Pablo said, looking at her squarely and flatly now. "I am ready for what the day brings."

"I believe thou art back," Pilar said to him. "I believe it. But, *hombre,* thou wert a long way gone."

"Lend me another swallow from thy bottle," Pablo said to Robert Jordan. "And then let us be going."

CHAPTER THIRTY-NINE

IN THE dark they came up the hill through the timber to the narrow pass at the top. They were all loaded heavily and they climbed slowly. The horses had loads too, packed over the saddles.

"We can cut them loose if it is necessary," Pilar had said. "But with that, if we can keep it, we can make another camp."

"And the rest of the ammunition?" Robert Jordan had asked as they lashed the packs.

"In those saddle bags."

Robert Jordan felt the weight of his heavy pack, the dragging on his neck from the pull of his jacket with its pockets full of grenades, the weight of his pistol against his thigh, and the bulging of his trouser pockets where the clips for the submachine gun were. In his mouth was the taste of the coffee, in his right hand he carried the submachine gun and with his left hand he reached and pulled up the collar of his jacket to ease the pull of the pack straps.

"Inglés" Pablo said to him, walking close beside him in the dark.

"What, man?"

"These I have brought think this is to be successful because I have brought them," Pablo said. "Do not say anything to disillusion them."

"Good," Robert Jordan said. "But let us make it successful."

"They have five horses, *sabes?"* Pablo said cautiously.

"Good," said Robert Jordan. "We will keep all the horses together."

"Good," said Pablo, and nothing more.

I didn't think you had experienced any complete conversion on the road to Tarsus, old Pablo, Robert Jordan thought. No. Your coming back was miracle enough. I don't think there will ever be any problem about canonizing you.

"With those five I will deal with the lower post as well as Sordo would have," Pablo said. "I will cut the wire and fall back upon the bridge as we convened."

We went over this all ten minutes ago, Robert Jordan thought. I wonder why this now—

"There is a possibility of making it to Gredos," Pablo said. "Truly, I have thought much of it."

I believe you've had another flash in the last few minutes, Robert Jordan said to himself. You have had another revelation. But you're not going to convince me that I am invited. No, Pablo. Do not ask me to believe too much.

Ever since Pablo had come into the cave and said he had five men Robert Jordan felt increasingly better. Seeing Pablo again had broken the pattern of tragedy into which the whole operation had seemed grooved ever since the snow, and since Pablo had been back he felt not that his luck had turned, since he did not believe in luck, but that the whole thing had turned for the better and that now it was possible. Instead of the surety of failure he felt confidence rising in him as a tire begins to fill with air from a slow pump. There was little difference at first, although there was a definite beginning, as when the pump starts and the rubber of the tube crawls a little, but it came now as steadily as a tide rising or the sap rising in a tree until he began to feel the first edge of that negation of apprehension that often turned into actual happiness before action.

This was the greatest gift that he had, the talent that fitted him for war; that ability not to ignore but to despise whatever bad ending there could be. This quality was destroyed by too much responsibility for others or the necessity of undertaking something ill planned or badly conceived. For in such things the bad ending, failure, could not be ignored. It was not simply a possibility of harm to one's self, which *could* be ignored. He knew he himself was nothing, and he knew death was nothing. He knew that truly, as truly as he knew anything. In the last few days he had learned that he himself, with another person, could be everything. But inside himself he knew that this was the exception. That we have had, he thought. In that I have been most fortunate. That was given to me, perhaps, because I never asked for it. That cannot be taken away nor lost. But that is over and done with now on this morning and what there is to do now is our work.

And you, he said to himself, I am glad to see you getting a little something back that was badly missing for a time. But you were pretty bad back there. I was ashamed enough of you, there for a while. Only I was you. There wasn't any me to judge you. We were all in bad shape. You and me and both of us. Come on now. Quit thinking like a schizophrenic. One at a time, now. You're all right again now. But listen, you must not think of the girl all day ever. You can do nothing now to protect her except to keep her out of it, and that you are doing. There are evidently going to be plenty of horses if you can believe the signs. The best thing you can do for her is to do the job well and fast and get out, and thinking of her will only handicap you in this. So do not think of her ever.

Having thought this out he waited until Maria came up walking with Pilar and Rafael and the horses.

"Hi, *guapa,*" he said to her in the dark, "how are you?"

"I am well, Roberto," she said.

"Don't worry about anything," he said to her and shifting the gun to his left hand he put a hand on her shoulder.

"I do not," she said.

"It is all very well organized," he told her. "Rafael will be with thee with the horses."

"I would rather be with thee."

"Nay. The horses is where thou art most useful."

"Good," she said. "There I will be."

Just then one of the horses whinnied and from the open place below the opening through the rocks a horse answered, the neigh rising into a shrill sharply broken quaver.

Robert Jordan saw the bulk of the new horses ahead in the dark. He pressed forward and came up to them with Pablo. The men were standing by their mounts.

"*Salud,*" Robert Jordan said.

"*Salud,*" they answered in the dark. He could not see their faces.

"This is the *Inglés* who comes with us," Pablo said. "The dynamiter."

No one said anything to that. Perhaps they nodded in the dark.

"Let us get going, Pablo," one man said. "Soon we will have the daylight on us."

"Did you bring any more grenades?" another asked.

"Plenty," said Pablo. "Supply yourselves when we leave the animals."

"Then let us go," another said. "We've been waiting here half the night."

"*Hola,* Pilar," another said as the woman came up.

"*Que me maten,* if it is not Pepe," Pilar said huskily. "How are you, shepherd?"

"Good," said the man. "*Dentro de la gravedad.*"

"What are you riding?" Pilar asked him.

"The gray of Pablo," the man said. "It is much horse."

"Come on," another man said. "Let us go. There is no good in gossiping here."

"How art thou, Elicio?" Pilar said to him as he mounted.

"How would I be?" he said rudely. "Come on, woman, we have work to do."

Pablo mounted the big bay horse.

"Keep thy mouths shut and follow me," he said. "I will lead you to the place where we will leave the horses."

CHAPTER FORTY

DURING the time that Robert Jordan had slept through, the time he had spent planning the destruction of the bridge and the time that he had been with Maria, Andrés had made slow progress. Until he had reached the Republican lines he had travelled across country and through the fascist lines as fast as a countryman in good physical condition who knew the country well could travel in the dark. But once inside the Republican lines it went very slowly.

In theory he should only have had to show the safe-conduct given him by Robert Jordan stamped with the seal of the S. I. M. and the dispatch which bore the same seal and be passed along toward his destination with the greatest speed. But first he had encountered the company commander in the front line who had regarded the whole mission with owlishly grave suspicion.

He had followed this company commander to battalion headquarters where the battalion commander, who had been a barber before the movement, was filled with enthusiasm on hearing the account of his mission. This commander, who was named Gomez, cursed the company commander for his stupidity, patted Andrés on the back, gave him a drink of bad brandy and told him that he himself, the ex-barber, had always wanted to be a *guerrillero*. He had then roused his adjutant, turned over the battalion to him, and sent his orderly to wake up and bring his motorcyclist. Instead of sending Andrés back to brigade headquarters with the motorcyclist, Gomez had decided to take him there himself in order to expedite things and, with Andrés holding tight onto the seat ahead of him, they roared, bumping down the shell-pocked mountain road between the double row of big trees, the headlight of the motorcycle showing their whitewashed bases and the places on the trunks where the whitewash and the bark had been chipped and torn by shell fragments and bullets during the fighting along this road in the first summer of the movement. They turned into the little smashed-roofed mountain-resort town where brigade headquarters was and Gomez had braked the motorcycle like a dirt-track racer and leaned it against the wall of the house where a sleepy sentry came to attention as Gomez pushed by him into the big room where the walls were covered with maps and a very sleepy officer with a green eyeshade sat at a desk with a reading lamp, two telephones and a copy of *Mundo Obrero*.

This officer looked up at Gomez and said, "What doest thou here? Have you never heard of the telephone?"

"I must see the Lieutenant-Colonel," Gomez said.

"He is asleep," the officer said. "I could see the lights of that bicycle of thine for a mile coming down the road. Dost wish to bring on a shelling?"

"Call the Lieutenant-Colonel," Gomez said. "This is a matter of the utmost gravity."

"He is asleep, I tell thee," the officer said. "What sort of a bandit is that with thee?" he nodded toward Andrés.

"He is a *guerrillero* from the other side of the lines with a dispatch of the utmost importance for the General Golz who commands the attack that is to be made at dawn beyond Navacerrada," Gomez said excitedly and earnestly. "Rouse the *Teniente-Coronel* for the love of God."

The officer looked at him with his droopy eyes shaded by the green celluloid.

"All of you are crazy," he said. "I know of no General Golz nor of no attack. Take this sportsman and get back to your battalion."

"Rouse the *Teniente-Coronel,* I say," Gomez said and Andrés saw his mouth tightening.

"Go obscenity yourself," the officer said to him lazily and turned away.

Gomez took his heavy 9 mm. Star pistol out of its holster and shoved it against the officer's shoulder.

"Rouse him, you fascist bastard," he said. "Rouse him or I'll kill you."

"Calm yourself," the officer said. "All you barbers are emotional."

Andrés saw Gomez's face draw with hate in the light of the reading lamp. But all he said was, "Rouse him."

"Orderly," the officer called in a contemptuous voice.

A soldier came to the door and saluted and went out.

"His fiancée is with him," the officer said and went back to reading the paper. "It is certain he will be delighted to see you."

"It is those like thee who obstruct all effort to win this war," Gomez said to the staff officer.

The officer paid no attention to him. Then, as he read on, he remarked, as though to himself, "What a curious periodical this is!"

"Why don't you real *El Debate* then? That is your paper," Gomez said to him naming the leading Catholic-Conservative organ published in Madrid before the movement.

"Don't forget I am thy superior officer and that a report by me on thee carries weight," the officer said without looking up. "I never read *El Debate*. Do not make false accusations."

"No. You read A. B. C.," Gomez said. "The army is still rotten with such as thee. With professionals such as thee. But it will not always be. We are caught between the ignorant and the cynical. But we will educate the one and eliminate the other."

"'Purge' is the word you want," the officer said, still not looking up. "Here it reports the purging of more of thy famous Russians. They are purging more than the epsom salts in this epoch."

"By any name," Gomez said passionately. "By any name so that such as thee are liquidated."

"Liquidated," the officer said insolently as though speaking to himself. "Another new word that has little of Castilian in it."

"Shot, then," Gomez said. "That is Castilian. Canst understand it?"

"Yes, man, but do not talk so loudly. There are others beside the *Teniente-Coronel* asleep in this Brigade Staff and thy emotion bores me. It was for that reason that I always shaved myself. I never liked the conversation."

Gomez looked at Andrés and shook his head. His eyes were shining with the moistness that rage and hatred can bring. But he shook his head and said nothing as he stored it all away for some time in the future. He had stored much in the year and a half in which he had risen to the command of a battalion in the Sierra and now, as the Lieutenant-Colonel came into the room in his pajamas he drew himself stiff and saluted.

The Lieutenant-Colonel Miranda, who was a short, gray-faced man, who had been in the army all his life, who had lost the love of his wife in Madrid while he was losing his digestion in Morocco, and become a Republican when he found he could not divorce his wife (there was never any question of recovering his digestion), had entered the civil war as a Lieutenant-Colonel. He had only one ambition, to finish the war with the same rank. He had defended the Sierra well and he wanted to be left alone there to defend it whenever it was attacked. He felt much healthier in the war, probably due to the forced curtailment of the number of meat courses, he had an enormous stock of sodium-bicarbonate, he had his whiskey in the evening, his twenty-three-year-old mistress was having a baby, as were nearly all the other girls who had started out as *milicianas* in the July of the year before, and now he came into the room, nodded in answer to Gomez's salute and put out his hand.

"What brings thee, Gomez?" he asked and then, to the officer at the desk who was his chief of operation, "Give me a cigarette, please, Pepe."

Gomez showed him Andrés's papers and the dispatch. The Lieutenant-Colonel looked at the *Salvoconducto* quickly, looked at Andrés, nodded and smiled, and then looked at the dispatch hungrily. He felt of the seal, tested it with his forefinger, then handed both the safe-conduct and dispatch back to Andrés.

"Is the life very hard there in the hills?" he asked.

"No, my Lieutenant-Colonel," Andrés said.

"Did they tell thee where would be the closest point to find General Golz's headquarters?"

"Navacerrada, my Lieutenant-Colonel," Andrés said. "The *Inglés* said it would be somewhere close to Navacerrada behind the lines to the right of there."

"What *Inglés*?" the Lieutenant-Colonel asked quietly.

"The *Inglés* who is with us as a dynamiter."

The Lieutenant-Colonel nodded. It was just another sudden unexplained rarity of this war. "The *Inglés* who is with us as a dynamiter."

"You had better take him, Gomez, on the motor," the Lieutenant-Colonel said. "Write them a very strong *Salvoconducto* to the *Estado Mayor* of General Golz for me to sign," he said to the officer in the green celluloid eyeshade. "Write it on the machine, Pepe. Here are the details," he motioned for Andrés to hand over his safe-conduct, "and put on two seals." He turned to Gomez. "You will need something strong tonight. It is rightly so. People should be careful when an offensive is projected. I will give you something as strong as I can make it." Then to Andrés, very kindly, he said, "Dost wish anything? To eat or to drink?"

"No, my Lieutenant-Colonel," Andrés said. "I am not hungry. They gave me cognac at the last place of command and more would make me seasick."

"Did you see any movement or activity opposite my front as you came through?" the Lieutenant-Colonel asked Andrés politely.

"It was as usual, my Lieutenant-Colonel. Quiet. Quiet."

"Did I not meet thee in Cercedilla about three months back?" the Lieutenant-Colonel asked.

"Yes, my Lieutenant-Colonel."

"I thought so," the Lieutenant-Colonel patted him on the shoulder. "You were with the old man Anselmo. How is he?"

"He is well, my Lieutenant-Colonel," Andrés told him.

"Good. It makes me happy," the Lieutenant-Colonel said. The officer showed him what he had typed and he read it over and signed it. "You must go now quickly," he said to Gomez and Andrés. "Be careful with the motor," he said to Gomez. "Use your lights. Nothing will happen from a single motor and you must be careful. My compliments to Comrade General Golz. We met after Peguerinos." He shook hands with them both. "Button the papers inside thy shirt," he said. "There is much wind on a motor."

After they went out he went to a cabinet, took out a glass and a bottle, and poured himself some whiskey and poured plain water into it from an earthenware crock that stood on the floor against the wall. Then holding the glass and sipping the whiskey very slowly he stood in front of the big map on the wall and studied the offensive possibilities in the country above Navacerrada.

"I am glad it is Golz and not me," he said finally to the officer who sat at the table. The officer did not answer and looking away from the map and at the officer the Lieutenant-Colonel saw he was asleep with his head on his arms. The Lieutenant-Colonel went over to the desk and pushed the two phones close together so that one touched the officer's head on either side. Then he walked to the cupboard, poured himself another whiskey, put water in it, and went back to the map again.

Andrés, holding tight onto the seat where Gomez was forking the motor, bent his head against the wind as the motorcycle moved, noisily exploding, into the light-split darkness of the country road that opened ahead sharp with the high black of the poplars beside it, dimmed and yellow-soft now as the road dipped into the fog along a steam bed, sharpening hard again as the road rose and, ahead of them at the crossroads, the headlight showed the gray bulk of the empty trucks coming down from the mountains.

CHAPTER FORTY-ONE

PABLO stopped and dismounted in the dark. Robert Jordan heard the creaking and the heavy breathing as they all dismounted and the clinking of a bridle as a horse tossed his head. He smelled the horses and the unwashed and sour slept-in-clothing smell of the new men and the wood-smoky sleep-stale smell of the others who had been in the cave. Pablo was standing close to him and he smelled the brassy, dead-wine smell that came from him like the taste of a copper coin in your mouth. He lit a cigarette, cupping his hand to hide the light, pulled deep on it, and heard Pablo say very softly, "Get the grenade sack, Pilar, while we hobble these."

"Agustín," Robert Jordan said in a whisper, "you and Anselmo come now with me to the bridge. Have you the sack of pans for the *máquina?*"

"Yes," Agustín said. "Why not?"

Robert Jordan went over to where Pilar was unpacking one of the horses with the help of Primitivo.

"Listen, woman," he said softly.

"What now?" she whispered huskily, swinging a cinch hook clear from under the horse's belly.

"Thou understandest that there is to be no attack on the post until thou hearest the falling of the bombs?"

"How many times dost thou have to tell me?" Pilar said. "You are getting like an old woman, *Inglés.*"

"Only to check," Robert Jordan said. "And after the destruction of the post you fall back onto the bridge and cover the road from above and my left flank."

"The first time thou outlined it I understood it as well as I will ever understand it," Pilar whispered to him. "Get thee about thy business."

"That no one should make a move nor fire a shot nor throw a

bomb until the noise of the bombardment comes," Robert Jordan said softly.

"Do not molest me more," Pilar whispered angrily. "I have understood this since we were at Sordo's."

Robert Jordan went to where Pablo was tying the horses. "I have only hobbled those which are liable to panic," Pablo said. "These are tied so a pull of the rope will release them, see?"

"Good."

"I will tell the girl and the gypsy how to handle them," Pablo said. His new men were standing in a group by themselves leaning on their carbines.

"Dost understand all?" Robert Jordan asked.

"Why not?" Pablo said. "Destroy the post. Cut the wire. Fall back on the bridge. Cover the bridge until thou blowest."

"And nothing to start until the commencement of the bombardment."

"Thus it is."

"Well then, much luck."

Pablo grunted. Then he said, "Thou wilt cover us well with the *máquina* and with thy small *máquina* when we come back, eh, *Inglés?*"

"*De la primera,*" Robert Jordan said. "Off the top of the basket."

"Then," Pablo said. "Nothing more. But in that moment thou must be very careful, *Inglés.* It will not be simple to do that unless thou art very careful."

"I will handle the *máquina* myself," Robert Jordan said to him.

"Hast thou much experience? For I am of no mind to be shot by Agustín with his belly full of good intentions."

"I have much experience. Truly. And if Agustín uses either *máquina* I will see that he keeps it way above thee. Above, above and above."

"Then nothing more," Pablo said. Then he said softly and confidentially, "There is still a lack of horses."

The son of a bitch, Robert Jordan thought. Or does he think I did not understand him the first time.

"I go on foot," he said. "The horses are thy affair."

"Nay, there will be a horse for thee, *Inglés,*" Pablo said softly. "There will be horses for all of us."

"That is thy problem," Robert Jordan said. "Thou dost not have to count me. Hast enough rounds for thy new *máquina?*"

"Yes," Pablo said. "All that the cavalryman carried. I have fired only four to try it. I tried it yesterday in the high hills."

"We go now," Robert Jordan said. "We must be there early and well hidden."

"We all go now," Pablo said. *"Suerte, Inglés."*

I wonder what the bastard is planning now, Robert Jordan said. But I am pretty sure I know. Well, that is his, not mine. Thank God I do not know these new men.

He put his hand out and said, *"Suerte, Pablo,"* and their two hands gripped in the dark.

Robert Jordan, when he put his hand out, expected that it would be like grasping something reptilian or touching a leper. He did not know what Pablo's hand would feel like. But in the dark Pablo's hand gripped his hard and pressed it frankly and he returned the grip. Pablo had a good hand in the dark and feeling it gave Robert Jordan the strangest feeling he had felt that morning. We must be allies now, he thought. There was always much handshaking with allies. Not to mention decorations and kissing on both cheeks, he thought. I'm glad we do not have to do that. I suppose all allies are like this. They always hate each other *au fond.* But this Pablo is a strange man.

"Suerte, Pablo," he said and gripped the strange, firm, purposeful hand hard. "I will cover thee well. Do not worry."

"I am sorry for having taken thy material," Pablo said. "It was an equivocation."

"But thou has brought what we needed."

"I do not hold this of the bridge against thee, *Inglés,"* Pablo said. "I see a successful termination for it."

"What are you two doing? Becoming *maricones?"* Pilar said suddenly beside them in the dark. "That is all thou hast lacked," she said to Pablo. "Get along, *Inglés,* and cut thy good-bys short before this one steals the rest of thy explosive."

"Thou dost not understand me, woman," Pablo said. "The *Inglés* and I understand one another."

"Nobody understands thee. Neither God nor thy mother," Pilar said. "Nor I either. Get along, *Inglés.* Make thy good-bys with thy cropped head and go. *Me cago en tu padre,* but I begin to think thou art afraid to see the bull come out."

"Thy mother," Robert Jordan said.

"Thou never hadst one," Pilar whispered cheerfully. "Now go, because I have a great desire to start this and get it over with. Go with thy people," she said to Pablo. "Who knows how long their stern resolution is good for? Thou hast a couple that I would not trade thee for. Take them and go."

Robert Jordan slung his pack on his back and walked over to the horses to find Maria.

"Good-by, *guapa,*" he said. "I will see thee soon."

He had an unreal feeling about all of this now as though he had said it all before or as though it were a train that were going, especially as though it were a train and he was standing on the platform of a railway station.

"Good-by, Roberto," she said. "Take much care."

"Of course," he said. He bent his head to kiss her and his pack rolled forward against the back of his head so that his forehead bumped hers hard. As this happened he knew this had happened before too.

"Don't cry," he said, awkward not only from the load.

"I do not," she said. "But come back quickly."

"Do not worry when you hear the firing. There is bound to be much firing."

"Nay. Only come back quickly."

"Good-by, *guapa,*" he said awkwardly.

"*Salud,* Roberto."

Robert Jordan had not felt this young since he had taken the train at Red Lodge to go down to Billings to get the train there to go away to school for the first time. He had been afraid to go and he did not want any one to know it and, at the station, just before the conductor picked up the box he would step up on to reach the steps of the day coach, his father had kissed him good-by and said, "May the Lord watch between thee and me while we are absent the one from the other." His father had been a very religious man and he had said it simply and sincerely. But his moustache had been moist and his eyes were damp with emotion and Robert Jordan had been so embarrassed by all of it, the damp religious sound of the prayer, and by his father kissing him good-by, that he had felt suddenly so much older than his father and sorry for him that he could hardly bear it.

After the train started he had stood on the rear platform and watched the station and the water tower grow smaller and smaller and the rails crossed by the ties narrowed toward a point where the station and the water tower stood now minute and tiny in the steady clicking that was taking him away.

The brakeman said, "Dad seemed to take your going sort of hard, Bob."

"Yes," he had said watching the sagebrush that ran from the edge of the road bed between the passing telegraph poles across to the streaming-by dusty stretching of the road. He was looking for sage hens.

"You don't mind going away to school?"

"No," he had said and it was true.

It would not have been true before but it was true that minute and it was only now, at this parting, that he ever felt as young again as he had felt before that train left. He felt very young now and very awkward and he was saying good-by as awkwardly as one can be when saying good-by to a young girl when you are a boy in school, saying good-by at the front porch, not knowing whether to kiss the girl or not. Then he knew it was not the good-by he was being awkward about. It was the meeting he was going to. The good-by was only a part of the awkwardness he felt about the meeting.

You're getting them again, he told himself. But I suppose there is no one that does not feel that he is too young to do it. He would not put a name to it. Come on, he said to himself. Come on. It is too early for your second childhood.

"Good-by, *guapa,*" he said. "Good-by, rabbit."

"Good-by, my Roberto," she said and he went over to where Anselmo and Agustín were standing and said, *"Vámonos."*

Anselmo swung his heavy pack up. Agustín, fully loaded since the cave, was leaning against a tree, the automatic rifle jutting over the top of his load.

"Good," he said, *"Vámonos."*

The three of them started down the hill.

"*Buena suerte,* Don Roberto," Fernando said as the three of them passed him as they moved in single file between the trees. Fernando was crouched on his haunches a little way from where they passed but he spoke with great dignity.

"*Buena suerte* thyself, Fernando," Robert Jordan said.

"In everything thou doest," Agustín said.

"Thank you, Don Roberto," Fernando said, undisturbed by Agustín.

"That one is a phenomenon, *Inglés,*" Agustín whispered.

"I believe thee," Robert Jordan said. "Can I help thee? Thou art loaded like a horse."

"I am all right," Agustín said. "Man, but I am content we are started."

"Speak softly," Anselmo said. "From now on speak little and softly."

Walking carefully, downhill, Anselmo in the lead, Agustín next, Robert Jordan placing his feet carefully so that he would not slip, feeling the dead pine needles under his rope-soled shoes, bumping a tree root with one foot and putting a hand forward and feeling the cold metal jut of the automatic rifle barrel and the folded legs of the tripod, then working sideways down the hill, his shoes sliding and grooving the forest floor, putting his left hand out again and touching the rough bark of a tree trunk, then as he braced himself his hand feeling a smooth place, the base of the palm of his hand coming away sticky from the resinous sap where a blaze had been cut, they dropped down the steep wooded hillside to the point above the bridge where Robert Jordan and Anselmo had watched the first day.

Now Anselmo was halted by a pine tree in the dark and he took Robert Jordan's wrist and whispered, so low Jordan could hardly hear him, "Look. There is the fire in his brazier."

It was a point of light below where Robert Jordan knew the bridge joined the road.

"Here is where we watched," Anselmo said. He took Robert Jordan's hand and bent it down to touch a small fresh blaze low on a tree trunk. "This I marked while thou watched. To the right is where thou wished to put the *máquina.*"

"We will place it there."

"Good."

They put the packs down behind the base of the pine trunks and the two of them followed Anselmo over to the level place where there was a clump of seedling pines.

"It is here," Anselmo said. "Just here."

"From here, with daylight," Robert Jordan crouched behind the small trees whispered to Agustín, "thou wilt see a small stretch of road and the entrance to the bridge. Thou wilt see the length of the bridge and a small stretch of road at the other end before it rounds the curve of the rocks."

Agustín said nothing.

"Here thou wilt lie while we prepare the exploding and fire on anything that comes from above or below."

"Where is that light?" Agustín asked.

"In the sentry box at this end," Robert Jordan whispered.

"Who deals with the sentries?"

"The old man and I, as I told thee. But if we do not deal with them, thou must fire into the sentry boxes and at them if thou seest them."

"Yes. You told me that."

"After the explosion when the people of Pablo come around that corner, thou must fire over their heads if others come after them. Thou must fire high above them when they appear in any event that others must not come. Understandest thou?"

"Why not? It is as thou saidst last night."

"Hast any questions?"

"Nay. I have two sacks. I can load them from above where it will not be seen and bring them here."

"But do no digging here. Thou must be as well hid as we were at the top."

"Nay. I will bring the dirt in them in the dark. You will see. They will not show as I will fix them."

"Thou are very close. *Sabes?* In the daylight this clump shows clearly from below."

"Do not worry, *Inglés*. Where goest thou?"

"I go close below with the small *máquina* of mine. The old man will cross the gorge now to be ready for the box of the other end. It faces in that direction."

"Then nothing more," said Agustín. *"Salud, Inglés.* Hast thou tobacco?"

"Thou canst not smoke. It is too close."

"Nay. Just to hold in the mouth. To smoke later."

Robert Jordan gave him his cigarette case and Agustín took three cigarettes and put them inside the front flap of his herdsman's flat cap. He spread the legs of his tripod with the gun muzzle in the low pines and commenced unpacking his load by touch and laying the things where he wanted them.

"Nada mas," he said. "Well, nothing more."

Anselmo and Robert Jordan left him there and went back to where the packs were.

"Where had we best leave them?" Robert Jordan whispered.

"I think here. But canst thou be sure of the sentry with thy small *máquina* from here?"

"Is this exactly where we were on that day?"

"The same tree," Anselmo said so low Jordan could barely hear him and he knew he was speaking without moving his lips as he had spoken that first day. "I marked it with my knife."

Robert Jordan had the feeling again of it all having happened before, but this time it came from his own repetition of a query and Anselmo's answer. It had been the same with Agustín, who had asked a question about the sentries although he knew the answer.

"It is close enough. Even too close," he whispered. "But the light is behind us. We are all right here."

"Then I will go now to cross the gorge and be in position at the other end," Anselmo said. Then he said, "Pardon me, *Inglés.* So that there is no mistake. In case I am stupid."

"What?" breathed very softly.

"Only to repeat it so that I will do it exactly."

"When I fire, thou wilt fire. When thy man is eliminated, cross the bridge to me. I will have the packs down there and thou wilt do as I tell thee in the placing of the charges. Everything I will tell thee. If aught happens to me do it thyself as I showed thee. Take thy time and do it well, wedging all securely with the wooden wedges and lashing the grenades firmly."

"It is all clear to me," Anselmo said. "I remember it all. Now

I go. Keep thee well covered, *Inglés,* when daylight comes."

"When thou firest," Robert Jordan said, "take a rest and make very sure. Do not think of it as a man but as a target, *de acuerdo?* Do not shoot at the whole man but at a point. Shoot for the exact center of the belly—if he faces thee. At the middle of the back, if he is looking away. Listen, old one. When I fire if the man is sitting down he will stand up before he runs or crouches. Shoot then. If he is still sitting down shoot. Do not wait. But make sure. Get to within fifty yards. Thou art a hunter. Thou hast no problem."

"I will do as thou orderest," Anselmo said.

"Yes. I order it thus," Robert Jordan said.

I'm glad I remembered to make it an order, he thought. That helps him out. That takes some of the curse off. I hope it does, anyway. Some of it. I had forgotten about what he told me that first day about the killing.

"It is thus I have ordered," he said. "Now go."

"Me voy," said Anselmo. "Until soon, *Inglés."*

"Until soon, old one," Robert Jordan said.

He remembered his father in the railway station and the wetness of that farewell and he did not say *Salud* nor good-by nor good luck nor anything like that.

"Hast wiped the oil from the bore of thy gun, old one?" he whispered. "So it will not throw wild?"

"In the cave," Anselmo said. "I cleaned them all with the pull-through."

"Then until soon," Robert Jordan said and the old man went off, noiseless on his rope-soled shoes, swinging wide through the trees.

Robert Jordan lay on the pine-needle floor of the forest and listened to the first stirring in the branches of the pines of the wind that would come with daylight. He took the clip out of the submachine gun and worked the lock back and forth. Then he turned the gun, with the lock open and in the dark he put the muzzle to his lips and blew through the barrel, the metal tasting greasy and oily as his tongue touched the edge of the bore. He laid the gun across his forearm, the action up so that no pine needles or rubbish could get in it, and shucked all the cartridges out of the clip with his thumb and onto a handkerchief he had spread in front of him. Then, feeling each cartridge in the dark and turning it in his fingers, he pressed and slid them one at a time back into the clip. Now the clip was heavy again in his hand and he slid it back into the submachine gun and felt it click home. He lay on his belly behind the pine trunk, the gun across his left forearm and watched the point of light below him. Sometimes he could not see it and then he knew that the man in the sentry box had moved in front of the brazier. Robert Jordan lay there and waited for daylight.

CHAPTER FORTY-TWO

DURING the time that Pablo had ridden back from the hills to the cave and the time the band had dropped down to where they had left the horses Andrés had made rapid progress toward Golz's headquarters. Where they came onto the main highroad to Nava-cerrada on which the trucks were rolling back from the mountain there was a control. But when Gomez showed the sentry at the control his safe-conduct from the Lieutenant-Colonel Miranda the sentry put the light from a flashlight on it, showed it to the other sentry with him, then handed it back and saluted.

"*Siga,*" he said. "Continue. But without lights."

The motorcycle roared again and Andrés was holding tight onto the forward seat and they were moving along the highway, Gomez riding carefully in the traffic. None of the trucks had lights and they were moving down the road in a long convoy. There were loaded trucks moving up the road too, and all of them raised a dust that Andrés could not see in that dark but could only feel as a cloud that blew in his face and that he could bite between his teeth.

They were close behind the tailboard of a truck now, the motorcycle chugging, then Gomez speeded up and passed it and another, and another, and another with the other trucks roaring and rolling down past them on the left. There was a motorcar behind them now and it blasted into the truck noise and the dust with its klaxon again and again; then flashed on lights that showed the dust like a solid yellow cloud and surged past them in a whining rise of gears and a demanding, threatening, bludgeoning of klaxoning.

Then ahead all the trucks were stopped and riding on, working his way ahead past ambulances, staff cars, an armored car, another, and a third, all halted, like heavy, metal, gun-jutting turtles in the hot yet settled dust, they found another control where there had been a smash-up. A truck, halting, had not been seen by the truck which followed it and the following truck had run into it smashing the rear of the first truck in and scattering cases of small-arms ammunition over the road. One case had burst open on landing and as Gomez and Andrés stopped and wheeled the motorcycle forward through the stalled vehicles to show their safe-conduct at the control Andrés walked over the brass hulls of the thousand of cartridges scattered across the road in the dust. The second truck had its radiator completely smashed in. The truck behind it was touching its tail gate. A hundred more were piling up behind and an overbooted officer was running back along the road shouting to the drivers to back so that the smashed truck could be gotten off the road.

There were too many trucks for them to be able to back unless the officer reached the end of the ever mounting line and stopped it from increasing and Andrés saw him running, stumbling, with his flashlight, shouting and cursing and, in the dark, the trucks kept coming up.

The man at the control would not give the safe-conduct back. There were two of them, with rifles slung on their backs and flashlights in their hands and they were shouting too. The one carrying the safe-conduct in his hand crossed the road to a truck going in the downhill direction to tell it to proceed to the next control and tell them there to hold all trucks until his jam was straightened out. The truck driver listened and went on. Then, still holding the safe-conduct, the control patrol came over, shouting, to the truck driver whose load was spilled.

"Leave it and get ahead for the love of God so we can clear this!" he shouted at the driver.

"My transmission is smashed," the driver, who was bent over by the rear of his truck, said.

"Obscene your transmission. Go ahead, I say."

"They do not go ahead when the differential is smashed," the driver told him and bent down again.

"Get thyself pulled then, get ahead so that we can get this other obscenity off the road."

The driver looked at him sullenly as the control man shone the electric torch on the smashed rear of the truck.

"Get ahead. Get ahead," the man shouted, still holding the safe-conduct pass in his hand.

"And my paper," Gomez spoke to him. "My safe-conduct. We are in a hurry."

"Take thy safe-conduct to hell," the man said and handing it to him ran across the road to halt a down-coming truck.

"Turn thyself at the crossroads and put thyself in position to pull this wreck forward," he said to the driver.

"My orders are——"

"Obscenity thy orders. Do as I say."

The driver let his truck into gear and rolled straight ahead down the road and was gone in the dust.

As Gomez started the motorcycle ahead onto the now clear right-hand side of the road past the wrecked truck, Andrés, holding tight again, saw the control guard halting another truck and the driver leaning from the cab and listening to him.

Now they went fast, swooping along the road that mounted steadily toward the mountain. All forward traffic had been stalled at the control and there were only the descending trucks passing, passing and passing on their left as the motorcycle climbed fast and steadily now until it began to overtake the mounting traffic which had gone on ahead before the disaster at the control.

Still without lights they passed four more armored cars, then a long line of trucks loaded with troops. The troops were silent in the dark and at first Andrés only felt their presence rising above him, bulking above the truck bodies through the dust as they passed. Then another staff came behind them blasting with its klaxon and flicking its lights off and on, and each time the lights shone Andrés saw the troops, steel-helmeted, their rifles vertical, their machine guns pointed up against the dark sky, etched sharp against the night that they dropped into when the light flicked off. Once as he passed close to a troop truck and the lights flashed he saw their faces fixed and sad in the sudden light. In their steel helmets, riding in the trucks in the dark toward something that they only knew was an attack, their faces were drawn with each man's own problem in the dark and the light revealed them as they would not have looked in day, from shame to show it to each other, until the bombardment and the attack would commence, and no man would think about his face.

Andrés now passing them truck after truck, Gomez still keeping successfully ahead of the following staff car, did not think any of this about their faces. He only thought, "What an army. What equipment. What a mechanization. *Vaya gente!* Look at such people. Here we have the army of the Republic. Look at them. Camion after camion. All uniformed alike. All with casques of steel on their heads. Look at the *máquinas* rising from the trucks against the coming of planes. Look at the army that has been builded!"

And as the motorcycle passed the high gray trucks full of troops, gray trucks with high square cabs and square ugly radiators, steadily mounting the road in the dust and the flicking lights of the pursuing staff car, the red star of the army showing in the light when it passed over the tail gates, showing when the light came onto the sides of the dusty truck bodies, as they passed, climbing steadily now, the air colder and the road starting to turn in bends and switchbacks now, the trucks laboring and grinding, some steaming in the light flashes, the motorcycle laboring now too, and Andrés clinging tight to the front seat as they climbed, Andrés thought this ride on a motorcycle was *mucho, mucho.* He had never been on a motorcycle before and now they were climbing a mountain in the midst of all the movement that was going to an attack and, as they climbed, he knew now there was no problem of ever being back in time for the assault on the posts. In this movement and confusion he would be lucky to get back by the next night. He had never seen an offensive or any of the preparations for one before and as they rode up the road he marvelled at the size and power of this army that the Republic had built.

Now they rode on a long slanting, rising stretch of road that ran across the face of the mountain and the grade was so steep as they neared the top that Gomez told him to get down and together they pushed the motorcycle up the last steep grade of the pass. At the left, just past the top, there was a loop of road where cars could turn and there were lights winking in front of a big stone building that bulked long and dark against the night sky.

"Let us go to ask there where the headquarters is," Gomez said to Andrés and they wheeled the motorcycle over to where two sentries stood in front of the closed door of the great stone building. Gomez leaned the motorcycle against the wall as a motorcyclist in a leather suit, showing against the light from inside the building as the door opened, came out of the door with a dispatch case hung over his shoulder, a wooden-holstered Mauser pistol swung against his hip. As the light went off, he found his motorcycle in the dark by the door, pushed it until it sputtered and caught, then roared off up the road.

At the door Gomez spoke to one of the sentries. "Captain Gomez of the Sixty-Fifth Brigade," he said. "Can you tell me where to find the headquarters of General Golz commanding the Thirty-Fifth Division?"

"It isn't here," the sentry said.

"What is here?"

"The Comandancia."

"What comandancia?"

"Well, the Comandancia."

"The comandancia of what?"

"Who art thou to ask so many questions?" the sentry said to Gomez in the dark. Here on the top of the pass the sky was very clear with the stars out and Andrés, out of the dust now, could see quite clearly in the dark. Below them, where the road turned to the right, he could see clearly the outline of the trucks and cars that passed against the sky line.

"I am Captain Rogelio Gomez of the first battalion of the Sixty-Fifth Brigade and I ask where is the headquarters of General Golz," Gomez said.

The sentry opened the door a little way. "Call the corporal of the guard," he shouted inside.

Just then a big staff car came up over the turn of the road and circled toward the big stone building where Andrés and Gomez were standing waiting for the corporal of the guard. It came toward them and stopped outside the door.

A large man, old and heavy, in an oversized khaki beret, such as *chasseurs à pied* wear in the French Army, wearing an overcoat, carrying a map case and wearing a pistol strapped around his greatcoat, got out of the back of the car with two other men in the uniform of the International Brigades.

He spoke in French, which Andrés did not understand and of which Gomez, who had been a barber, knew only a few words, to his chauffeur telling him to get the car away from the door and into shelter.

As he came into the door with the other two officers, Gomez saw his face clearly in the light and recognized him. He had seen him at political meetings and he had often read articles by him in *Mundo Obrero* translated from the French. He recognized his bushy eyebrows, his watery gray eyes, his chin and the double chin under it, and he knew him for one of France's great modern revolutionary figures who had led the mutiny of the French Navy in the Black Sea. Gomez knew this man's high political place in the International Brigades and he knew this man would know where Golz's headquarters were and be able to direct him there. He did not know what this man had become with time, disappointment, bitterness both domestic and political, and thwarted ambition and that to question him was one of the most dangerous things that any man could do. Knowing nothing of this he stepped forward into the path of this man, saluted with his clenched fist and said, "Comrade Marty, we are the bearers of a dispatch for General Golz. Can you direct us to his headquarters? It is urgent."

The tall, heavy old man looked at Gomez with his outthrust head and considered him carefully with his watery eyes. Even here at the front in the light of a bare electric bulb, he having just come in from driving in an open car on a brisk night, his gray face had a look of decay. His face looked as though it were modelled from the waste material you find under the claws of a very old lion.

"You have what, Comrade?" he asked Gomez, speaking Spanish with a strong Catalan accent. His eyes glanced sideways at Andrés, slid over him, and went back to Gomez.

"A dispatch for General Golz to be delivered at his headquarters, Comrade Marty."

"Where is it from, Comrade?"

"From behind the fascist lines," Gomez said.

André Marty extended his hand for the dispatch and the other papers. He glanced at them and put them in his pocket.

"Arrest them both," he said to the corporal of the guard. "Have them searched and bring them to me when I send for them."

With the dispatch in his pocket he strode on into the interior of the big stone house.

Outside in the guard room Gomez and Andrés were being searched by the guard.

"What passes with that man?" Gomez said to one of the guards.

"Está loco," the guard said. "He is crazy."

"No. He is a political figure of great importance," Gomez said. "He is the chief commissar of the International Brigades."

"Apesar de eso, está loco," the corporal of the guard said. "All the same he's crazy. What do you behind the fascist lines?"

"This comrade is a guerilla from there," Gomez told him while the man searched him. "He brings a dispatch to General Golz. Guard well my papers. Be careful with that money and that bullet on the string. It is from my first wound at Guadarama."

"Don't worry," the corporal said. "Everything will be in this drawer. Why didn't you ask me where Golz was?"

"We tried to. I asked the sentry and he called you."

"But then came the crazy and you asked him. No one should ask him anything. He is crazy. Thy Golz is up the road three kilometers from here and to the right in the rocks of the forest."

"Can you not let us go to him now?"

"Nay. It would be my head. I must take thee to the crazy. Besides, he has thy dispatch."

"Can you not tell some one?"

"Yes," the corporal said. "I will tell the first responsible one I see. All know that he is crazy."

"I had always taken him for a great figure," Gomez said. "For one of the glories of France."

"He may be a glory and all," the corporal said and put his hand on Andrés's shoulder. "But he is crazy as a bedbug. He has a mania for shooting people."

"Truly shooting them?"

"Como lo oyes," the corporal said. "That old one kills more than the bubonic plague. *Mata más que la peste bubonica.* But he doesn't kill fascists like we do. *Qué va.* Not in joke. *Mata bichos raros.* He kills rare things. Trotzkyites. Divagationers. Any type of rare beasts."

Andrés did not understand any of this.

"When we were at Escorial we shot I don't know how many for him," the corporal said. "We always furnish the firing party. The men of the Brigades would not shoot their own men. Especially the French. To avoid difficulties it is always us who do it. We shot French. We have shot Belgians. We have shot others of divers nationality. Of all types. *Tiene mania de fusilar gente.* Always for political things. He's crazy. *Purifica más que el Salvarsán.* He purifies more than Salvarsan."

"But you will tell some one of this dispatch?"

"Yes, man. Surely. I know every one of these two Brigades. Every one comes through here. I know even up to and through the Russians, although only a few speak Spanish. We will keep this crazy from shooting Spaniards."

"But the dispatch."

"The dispatch, too. Do not worry, Comrade. We know how to deal with this crazy. He is only dangerous with his own people. We understand him now."

"Bring in the two prisoners," came the voice of André Marty.

"*Quereis echar un trago?*" the corporal asked. "Do you want a drink?"

"Why not?"

The corporal took a bottle of Anis from a cupboard and both Gomez and Andrés drank. So did the corporal. He wiped his mouth on his hand.

"*Vámonos,*" he said.

They went out of the guard room with the swallowed burn of the Anis warming their mouths, their bellies and their hearts and walked down the hall and entered the room where Marty sat behind a long table, his map spread in front of him, his red-and-blue pencil, with which he played at being a general officer, in his hand. To Andrés it was only one more thing. There had been many tonight. There were always many. If your papers were in order and your heart was good you were in no danger. Eventually they turned you loose and you were on your way. But the *Inglés* had said to hurry. He knew now he could never get back for the bridge but they had a dispatch to deliver and this old man there at the table had put it in his pocket.

"Stand there," Marty said without looking up.

"Listen, Comrade Marty," Gomez broke out, the Anis fortifying his anger. "Once tonight we have been impeded by the ignorance of the anarchists. Then by the sloth of a bureaucratic fascist. Now by the oversuspicion of a Communist."

"Close your mouth," Marty said without looking up. "This is not a meeting."

"Comrade Marty, this is a matter of utmost urgency," Gomez said. "Of the greatest importance."

The corporal and the soldier with them were taking a lively interest in this as though they were at a play they had seen many times but whose excellent moments they could always savor.

"Everything is of urgency," Marty said. "All things are of importance." Now he looked up at them, holding the pencil. "How did you know Golz was here? Do you understand how serious it is to come asking for an individual general before an attack? How could you know such a general would be here?"

"Tell him, *tu,*" Gomez said to Andrés.

"Comrade General," Andrés started—André Marty did not correct him in the mistake in rank—"I was given that packet on the other side of the lines——"

"On the other side of the lines?" Marty said. "Yes, I heard him say you came from the fascist lines."

"It was given to me, Comrade General, by an *Inglés* named Roberto who had come to us as a dynamiter for this of the bridge. Understandeth?"

"Continue thy story," Marty said to Andrés; using the term story as you would say lie, falsehood, or fabrication.

"Well, Comrade General, the *Inglés* told me to bring it to the General Golz with all speed. He makes an attack in these hills now on this day and all we ask is to take it to him now promptly if it pleases the Comrade General."

Marty shook his head again. He was looking at Andrés but he was not seeing him.

Golz, he thought in a mixture of horror and exultation as a man might feel hearing that a business enemy had been killed in a particularly nasty motor accident or that some one you hated but whose probity you had never doubted had been guilty of defalcation. That Golz should be one of them, too. That Golz should be in such obvious communication with the fascists. Golz that he had known for nearly twenty years. Golz who had captured the gold train that winter with Lucacz in Siberia. Golz who had fought against Kolchak, and in Poland. In the Caucasus. In China, and here since the first October. But he *had* been close to Tukachevsky. To Voroshilov, yes, too. But to Tukachevsky. And to who else? Here to Karkov, of course. And to Lucacz. But all the Hungarians had been intriguers. He hated Gall. Golz hated Gall. Remember that. Make a note of that. Golz has always hated Gall. But he favors Putz. Remember that. And Duval is his chief of staff. See what stems from that. You've heard him say Copic's a fool. That is definitive. That exists. And now this dispatch from the fascist lines. Only by pruning out of these rotten branches can the tree remain healthy and grow. The rot must become apparent for it is to be destroyed. But Golz of all men. That Golz should be one of the traitors. He knew that you could trust no one. No one. Ever. Not your wife. Not your brother. Not your oldest comrade. No one. Ever.

"Take them away," he said to the guards. "Guard them carefully." The corporal looked at the soldier. This had been very quiet for one of Marty's performances.

"Comrade Marty," Gomez said. "Do not be insane. Listen to me, a loyal officer and comrade. That is a dispatch that must be delivered. This comrade has brought it through the fascist lines to give to Comrade General Golz."

"Take them away," Marty said, now kindly, to the guard. He was sorry for them as human beings if it should be necessary to liquidate them. But it was the tragedy of Golz that oppressed him. That it should be Golz, he thought. He would take the fascist communication at once to Varloff. No, better he would take it to Golz himself and watch him as he received it. That was what he would do. How could he be sure of Varloff if Golz was one of them? No. This was a thing to be very careful about.

Andrés turned to Gomez, "You mean he is not going to send the dispatch?" he asked, unbelieving.

"Don't you see?" Gomez said.

"Me cago en su puta madre!" Andrés said. *"Está loco."*

"Yes," Gomez said. "He is crazy. You are crazy! Hear! Crazy!"

he shouted at Marty who was back now bending over the map with his red-and-blue pencil. "Hear me, you crazy murderer?"

"Take them away," Marty said to the guard. "Their minds are unhinged by their great guilt."

There was a phrase the corporal recognized. He had heard that before.

"You crazy murderer!" Gomez shouted.

"Hijo de la gran puta," Andrés said to him. *"Loco."*

The stupidity of this man angered him. If he was a crazy let him be removed as a crazy. Let the dispatch be taken from his pocket. God damn this crazy to hell. His heavy Spanish anger was rising out of his usual calm and good temper. In a little while it would blind him.

Marty, looking at his map, shook his head sadly as the guards took Gomez and Andrés out. The guards had enjoyed hearing him cursed but on the whole they had been disappointed in the performance. They had seen much better ones. André Marty did not mind the men cursing him. So many men had cursed him at the end. He was always genuinely sorry for them as human beings. He always told himself that and it was one of the last true ideas that was left to him that had ever been his own.

He sat there, his moustache and his eyes focused on the map, on the map that he never truly understood, on the brown tracing of the contours that were traced fine and concentric as a spider's web. He could see the heights and the valleys from the contours but he never really understood why it should be this height and why this valley was the one. But at the General Staff where, because of the system of Political Commissars, he could intervene as the political head of the Brigades, he would put his finger on such and such a numbered, brown-thin-lined encircled spot among the greens of woods cut by the lines of roads that parallel the never casual winding of a river and say, "There. That is the point of weakness."

Gall and Copic, who were men of politics and of ambition, would agree and later, men who never saw the map, but heard the number of the hill before they left their starting place and had the earth of diggings on it pointed out, would climb its side to find their death along its slope or, being halted by machine guns placed in olive groves would never get up it at all. Or on other fronts they might scale it easily and be no better off than they had been before. But when Marty put his finger on the map in Golz's staff the scar-headed, white-faced General's jaw muscles would tighten and he would think, "I should shoot you, André Marty, before I let you put that gray rotten finger on a contour map of mine. Damn you to hell for all the men you've killed by interfering in matters you know nothing of. Damn the day they named tractor factories and villages and co-operatives for you so that you are a symbol that I cannot touch. Go and suspect and exhort and intervene and denounce and butcher some other place and leave my staff alone."

But instead of saying that Golz would only lean back away from the leaning bulk, the pushing finger, the watery gray eyes, the gray-white moustache and the bad breath and say, "Yes, Comrade Marty. I see your point. It is not well taken, however, and I do not agree. You can try to go over my head if you like. Yes. You can make it a Party matter as you say. But I do not agree."

So now André Marty sat working over his map at the bare table with the raw light on the unshaded electric light bulb over his head, the overwide beret pulled forward to shade his eyes, refer-ring to the mimeographed copy of the orders for the attack and slowly and laboriously working them out on the map as a young officer might work a problem at a staff college. He was engaged in war. In his mind he was commanding troops; he had the right to interfere and this he believed to constitute command. So he sat there with Robert Jordan's dispatch to Golz in his pocket and Gomez and Andrés waited in the guard room and Robert Jordan lay in the woods above the bridge.

It is doubtful if the outcome of Andrés's mission would have been any different if he and Gomez had been allowed to proceed without André Marty's hindrance. There was no one at the front with sufficient authority to cancel the attack. The machinery had been in motion much too long for it to be stopped suddenly now. There is a great inertia about all military operations of any size. But once this inertia has been overcome and movement is under way they are almost as hard to arrest as to initiate.

But on this night the old man, his beret pulled forward, was still sitting at the table with his map when the door opened and Karkov the Russian journalist came in with two other Russians in civilian clothes, leather coats and caps. The corporal of the guard closed the door reluctantly behind them. Karkov had been the first responsible man he had been able to communicate with.

"Tovarich Marty," said Karkov in his politely disdainful lisping voice and smiled, showing his bad teeth.

Marty stood up. He did not like Karkov, but Karkov, coming from *Pravda* and in direct communication with Stalin, was at this moment one of the three most important men in Spain.

"Tovarich Karkov," he said.

"You are preparing the attack?" Karkov said insolently, nodding toward the map.

"I am studying it," Marty answered.

"Are you attacking? Or is it Golz?" Karkov asked smoothly.

"I am only a commissar, as you know," Marty told him.

"No," Karkov said. "You are modest. You are really a general. You have your map and your field glasses. But were you not an admiral once, Comrade Marty?"

"I was a gunner's mate," said Marty. It was a lie. He had really been a chief yeoman at the time of the mutiny. But he thought now, always, that he had been a gunner's mate.

"Ah. I thought you were a first-class yeoman," Karkov said. "I always get my facts wrong. It is the mark of the journalist."

The other Russians had taken no part in the conversation. They were both looking over Marty's shoulder at the map and occasionally making a remark to each other in their own language. Marty and Karkov spoke French after the first greeting.

"It is better not to get facts wrong in *Pravda*," Marty said. He said it brusquely to build himself up again. Karkov always punctured him. The French word is *dégonfler* and Marty was worried and made wary by him. It was hard, when Karkov spoke, to remember with what importance he, André Marty, came from the Central Committee of the French Communist Party. It was hard to remember, too, that he was untouchable. Karkov seemed always to touch him so lightly and whenever he wished. Now Karkov said, "I usually correct them before I send them to *Pravda*, I am quite accurate in *Pravda*. Tell me, Comrade Marty, have you heard anything of any message coming through for Golz from one of our *partizan* group operating toward Segovia? There is an American comrade there named Jordan that we should have heard from. There have been reports of fighting there behind the fascist lines. He would have sent a message through to Golz."

"An American?" Marty asked. Andrés had said an *Inglés*. So that is what it was. So he had been mistaken. Why had those fools spoken to him anyway?"

"Yes," Karkov looked at him contemptuously, "a young American of slight political development but a great way with the Spaniards and a fine *partizan* record. Just give me the dispatch, Comrade Marty. It has been delayed enough."

"What dispatch?" Marty asked. It was a very stupid thing to say and he knew it. But he was not able to admit he was wrong that quickly and he said it anyway to delay the moment of humiliation, not accepting any humiliation. "And the safe-conduct pass," Karkov said through his bad teeth.

André Marty put his hand in his pocket and laid the dispatch on the table. He looked Karkov squarely in the eye. All right. He was wrong and there was nothing he could do about it now but he was not accepting any humiliation. "And the safe-conduct pass," Karkov said softly.

Marty laid it beside the dispatch.

"Comrade Corporal," Karkov called in Spanish.

The corporal opened the door and came in. He looked quickly at André Marty, who stared back at him like an old boar which has been brought to bay by hounds. There was no fear on Marty's face and no humiliation. He was only angry, and he was only temporarily at bay. He knew these dogs could never hold him.

"Take these to the two comrades in the guard room and direct them to General Golz's headquarters," Karkov said. "There has been too much delay."

The corporal went out and Marty looked after him, then looked at Karkov.

"Tovarich Marty," Karkov said, "I am going to find out just how untouchable you are."

Marty looked straight at him and said nothing.

"Don't start to have any plans about the corporal, either," Karkov went on. "It was not the corporal. I saw the two men in the guard room and they spoke to me" (this was a lie). "I hope all men always will speak to me" (this was the truth although it was the corporal who had spoken). But Karkov had this belief in the good which could come from his own accessibility and the humanizing possibility of benevolent intervention. It was the one thing he was never cynical about.

"You know when I am in the U.S.S.R. people write to me in *Pravda* when there is an injustice in a town in Azerbaijan. Did you know that? They say 'Karkov will help us.'"

André Marty looked at him with no expression on his face except anger and dislike. There was nothing in his mind now but that Karkov had done something against him. All right, Karkov, power and all, could watch out.

"This is something else," Karkov went on, "but it is the same principle. I am going to find out just how untouchable you are, Comrade Marty. I would like to know if it could not be possible to change the name of that tractor factory."

André Marty looked away from him and back to the map.

"What did young Jordan say?" Karkov asked him.

"I did not read it," André Marty said. "*Et maintenant fiche moi la paix,* Comrade Karkov."

"Good," said Karkov. "I leave you to your military labors."

He stepped out of the room and walked to the guard room. Andrés and Gomez were already gone and he stood there a moment looking up the road and at the mountain tops beyond that showed now in the first gray of daylight. We must get on up there, he thought. It will be soon, now.

Andrés and Gomez were on the motorcycle on the road again and it was getting light. Now Andrés, holding again to the back of the seat ahead of him as the motorcycle climbed turn after switchback turn in a faint gray mist that lay over the top of the pass, felt the motorcycle speed under him, then skid and stop and they were standing by the motorcycle on a long, down-slope of road and in the woods, on their left, were tanks covered with pine branches. There were troops here all through the woods. Andrés saw men carrying the long poles of stretchers over their shoulders. Three staff cars were off the road to the right, in under the trees, with branches laid against their sides and other pine branches over their tops.

Gomez wheeled the motorcycle up to one of them. He leaned it against a pine tree and spoke to the chauffeur who was sitting by the car, his back against a tree.

"I'll take you to him," the chauffeur said. "Put thy *moto* out of sight and cover it with these." He pointed to a pile of cut branches.

With the sun just starting to come through the high branches of the pine trees, Gomez and Andrés followed the chauffeur, whose name was Vicente, through the pines across the road and up the slope to the entrance of a dugout from the roof of which signal wires ran on up over the wooded slope. They stood outside while the chauffeur went in and Andrés admired the construction of the dugout which showed only as a hole in the hillside, with no dirt scattered about, but which he could see, from the entrance, was both deep and profound with men moving around in it freely with no need to duck their heads under the heavy timbered roof.

Vicente, the chauffeur, came out.

"He is up above where they are deploying for the attack," he said. "I gave it to his Chief of Staff. He signed for it. Here."

He handed Gomez the receipted envelope. Gomez gave it to Andrés, who looked at it and put it inside his shirt.

"What is the name of him who signed?" he asked.

"Duval," Vicente said.

"Good," said Andrés. "He was one of the three to whom I might give it."

"Should we wait for an answer?" Gomez asked Andrés.

"It might be best. Though where I will find the *Inglés* and the others after that of the bridge neither God knows."

"Come wait with me," Vicente said, "until the General returns. And I will get thee coffee. Thou must be hungry."

"And these tanks," Gomez said to him.

They were passing the branch-covered, mud-colored tanks, each with two deep-ridged tracks over the pine needles showing where they had swung and backed from the road. Their 45-mm. guns jutted horizontally under the branches and the drivers and gunners in their leather coats and ridged helmets sat with their backs against the trees or lay sleeping on the ground.

"These are the reserve," Vicente said. "Also these troops are in reserve. Those who commence the attack are above."

"They are many," Andrés said.

"Yes," Vicente said. "It is a full division."

Inside the dugout Duval, holding the opened dispatch from Robert Jordan in his left hand, glancing at his wrist watch on the same hand, reading the dispatch for the fourth time, each time feeling the sweat come out from under his armpit and run down his flank, said into the telephone, "Get me position Segovia, then. He's left? Get me position Avila."

He kept on with the phone. It wasn't any good. He had talked to both brigades. Golz had been up to inspect the dispositions for the attack and was on his way to an observation post. He called the observation post and he was not there.

"Get me planes one," Duval said, suddenly taking all responsibility. He would take responsibility for holding it up. It was better to hold it up. You could not send them to a surprise attack against an enemy that was waiting for it. You couldn't do it. It was just murder. You couldn't. You mustn't. No matter what. They could shoot him if they wanted. He would call the airfield directly and get the bombardment cancelled. But suppose it's just a holding attack? Suppose we were supposed to draw off all that material and those forces? Suppose that is what it is for? They never tell you it is a holding attack when you make it.

"Cancel the call to planes one," he told the signaller. "Get me the 69th Brigade observation post."

He was still calling there when he heard the first sound of the planes.

It was just then he got through to the observation post.

"Yes," Golz said quietly.

He was sitting leaning back against the sandbag, his feet against a rock, a cigarette hung from his lower lip and he was looking up and over his shoulder while he was talking. He was seeing the expanding wedges of threes, silver and thundering in the sky that were coming over the far shoulder of the mountain where the first sun was striking. He watched them come shining and beautiful in the sun. He saw the twin circles of light where the sun shone on the propellers as they came.

"Yes," he said into the telephone, speaking in French because it was Duval on the wire. "*Nous sommes foutus. Oui. Comme toujours. Oui. C'est dommage. Oui.* It's a shame it came too late."

His eyes, watching the planes coming, were very proud. He saw the red wing markings now and he watched their steady, stately roaring advance. This was how it could be. These were our planes. They had come, crated on ships, from the Black Sea through the Straits of Marmora, through the Dardanelles, through the Mediterranean and to here, unloaded lovingly at Alicante, assembled ably, tested and found perfect and now flown in lovely hammering precision, the V's tight and pure as they came now high and silver in the morning sun to blast those ridges across there and blow them roaring high so that we can go through.

Golz knew that once they had passed overhead and on, the bombs would fall, looking like porpoises in the air as they tumbled. And then the ridge tops would spout and roar in jumping clouds and disappear in one great blowing cloud. Then the tanks would grind clanking up those two slopes and after them would go his two brigades. And if it had been a surprise they could go on and down and over and through, pausing, cleaning up, dealing with, much to do, much to be done intelligently with the tanks helping, with the tanks wheeling and returning, giving covering fire and others bringing the attackers up then slipping on and over and through and pushing down beyond. This was how it would be if there was no treason and if all did what they should.

There were the two ridges, and there were the tanks ahead and there were his two good brigades ready to leave the woods and here came the planes now. Everything he had to do had been done as it should be.

But as he watched the planes, almost up to him now, he felt sick at his stomach for he knew from having heard Jordan's dispatch over the phone that there would be no one on those two ridges. They'd be withdrawn a little way below in narrow trenches to escape the fragments, or hiding in the timber and when the bombers passed they'd get back up there with their machine guns and their automatic weapons and the anti-tank guns Jordan had said went up the road, and it would be one famous balls up more. But the planes, now coming deafeningly, were how it could have been and Golz watching them, looking up, said into the telephone, "No. *Rien à faire. Rien. Faut pas penser. Faut accepter.*"

Golz watched the planes with his hard proud eyes that knew

how things could be and how they would be instead and said, proud of how they could be, believing in how they could be, even if they never were, *"Bon. Nous ferons notre petit possible,"* and hung up.

But Duval did not hear him. Sitting at the table holding the receiver, all he heard was the roar of the planes and he thought, now, maybe this time, listen to them come, maybe the bombers will blow them all off, maybe we will get a break-through, maybe he will get the reserves he asked for, maybe this is it, maybe this is the time. Go on. Come on. Go on. The roar was such that he could not hear what he was thinking.

CHAPTER FORTY-THREE

ROBERT JORDAN lay behind the trunk of a pine tree on the slope of the hill above the road and the bridge and watched it become daylight. He loved this hour of the day always and now he watched it; feeling it gray within him, as though he were a part of the slow lightening that comes before the rising of the sun; when solid things darken and space lightens and the lights that have shone in the night go yellow and then fade as the day comes. The pine trunks below him were hard and clear now, their trunks solid and brown and the road was shiny with a wisp of mist over it. The dew had wet him and the forest floor was soft and he felt the give of the brown, dropped pine needles under his elbows. Below he saw, through the light mist that rose from the stream bed, the steel of the bridge, straight and rigid across the gap, with the wooden sentry boxes at each end. But as he looked the structure of the bridge was still spidery and fine in the mist that hung over the stream.

He saw the sentry now in his box as he stood, his back with the hanging blanket coat topped by the steel casque on his head showing as he leaned forward over the hole-punched petrol tin of the brazier, warming his hands. Robert Jordan heard the stream, far down in the rocks, and he saw a faint, thin smoke that rose from the sentry box.

He looked at his watch and thought, I wonder if Andrés got through to Golz? If we are going to blow it I would like to breathe very slowly and slow up the time again and feel it. Do you think he made it? Andrés? And if he did would they call it off? If they had time to call it off? *Qué va.* Do not worry. They will or they won't. There are no more decisions and in a little while you will know. Suppose the attack is successful. Golz said it could be. That there was a possibility. With our tanks coming down that road, the people coming through from the right and down and past La Granja and the whole left of the mountains turned. Why don't you ever think of how it is to win? You've been on the defensive for so long that you can't think of that. Sure. But that was before all that stuff went up this road. That was before all the planes came. Don't be so naïve. But remember this that as long as we can hold them here we keep the fascists tied up. They can't attack any other country until they finish with us and they can never finish with us. If the French help at all, if only they leave the frontier open and if we get planes from America they can never finish with us. Never, if we get anything at all. These people will fight forever if they're well armed.

No you must not expect victory here, not for several years maybe. This is just a holding attack. You must not get illusions about it now. Suppose we got a break-through today? This is our first big attack. Keep your sense of proportion. But what if we should have it? Don't get excited, he told himself. Remember what went up the road. You've done what you could about that. We should have portable short-wave sets, though. We will, in time. But we haven't yet. You just watch now and do what you should.

Today is only one day in all the days that will ever be. But what will happen in all the other days that ever come can depend on what you do today. It's been that way all this year. It's been that way so many times. All of this war is that way. You are getting very pompous in the early morning, he told himself. Look there what's coming now.

He saw the two men in blanket capes and steel helmets come around the corner of the road walking toward the bridge, their rifles slung over their shoulders. One stopped at the far end of the bridge and was out of sight in the sentry box. The other came on across the bridge, walking slowly and heavily. He stopped on the bridge and spat into the gorge, then came on slowly to the near end of the bridge where the other sentry spoke to him and then started off back over the bridge. The sentry who was relieved walked faster than the other had done (because he's going to coffee, Robert Jordan thought) but he too spat down into the gorge.

I wonder if that is superstition? Robert Jordan thought. I'll have to take me a spit in that gorge too. If I can spit by then. No. It can't be very powerful medicine. It can't work. I'll have to prove it doesn't work before I am out there.

The new sentry had gone inside the box and sat down. His rifle with the bayonet fixed was leaning against the wall. Robert Jordan took his glasses from his shirt pocket and turned the eyepieces until the end of the bridge showed sharp and gray-painted-metal clear. Then he moved them onto the sentry box.

The sentry sat leaning against the wall. His helmet hung on a peg and his face showed clearly. Robert Jordan saw he was the same man who had been there on guard two days before in the afternoon watch. He was wearing the same knitted stocking-cap. And he had not shaved. His cheeks were sunken and his cheek-bones prominent. He had bushy eyebrows that grew together in the center. He looked sleepy and as Robert Jordan watched him he yawned. Then he took out a tobacco pouch and a packet of papers and rolled himself a cigarette. He tried to make a lighter work and finally put it in his pocket and went over to the brazier, leaned over, reached inside, brought up a piece of charcoal, juggled it in one hand while he blew on it, then lit the cigarette and tossed the lump of charcoal back into the brazier.

Robert Jordan, looking through the Zeiss 8-power glasses, watched his face as he leaned against the wall of the sentry box drawing on the cigarette. Then he took the glasses down, folded them together and put them in his pocket.

I won't look at him again, he told himself.

He lay there and watched the road and tried not to think at all. A squirrel chittered from a pine tree below him and Robert Jordan watched the squirrel come down the tree trunk, stopping on his way down to turn his head and look toward where the man was watching. He saw the squirrel's eyes, small and bright, and watched his tail jerk in excitement. Then the squirrel crossed to another tree, moving on the ground in long, small-pawed, tail-exaggerated bounds. On the tree trunk he looked back at Robert Jordan, then pulled himself around the trunk and out of sight. Then Robert Jordan heard the squirrel chitter from a high branch of the pine tree and he watched him there, spread flat along the branch, his tail jerking.

Robert Jordan looked down through the pines to the sentry box again. He would like to have had the squirrel with him in his pocket. He would like to have had anything that he could touch. He rubbed his elbows against the pine needles but it was not the same. No-body knows how lonely you can be when you do this. Me, though,

I know. I hope that Rabbit will get out of this all right. Stop that now. Yes, sure. But I can hope that and I do. That I blow it well and that she gets out all right. Good. Sure. Just that. That is all I want now.

He lay there now and looked away from the road and the sentry box and across to the far mountain. Just do not think at all, he told himself. He lay there quietly and watched the morning come. It was a fine early summer morning and it came very fast now in the end of May. Once a motorcyclist in a leather coat and all-leather helmet with an automatic rifle in a holster by his left leg came across the bridge and went on up the road. Once an ambulance crossed the bridge, passed below him, and went up the road. But that was all. He smelled the pines and he heard the stream and the bridge showed clear now and beautiful in the morning light. He lay there behind the pine tree, with the submachine gun across his left forearm, and he never looked at the sentry box again until, long after it seemed that it was never coming, that nothing could happen on such a lovely late May morning, he heard the sudden, clustered, thudding of the bombs.

As he heard the bombs, the first thumping noise of them, before the echo of them came back in thunder from the mountain, Robert Jordan drew in a long breath and lifted the submachine gun from where it lay. His arm felt stiff from its weight and his fingers were heavy with reluctance.

The man in the sentry box stood up when he heard the bombs. Robert Jordan saw him reach for his rifle and step forward out of the box listening. He stood in the road with the sun shining on him. The knitted cap was on the side of his head and the sun was on his unshaved face as he looked up into the sky toward where the planes were bombing.

There was no mist on the road now and Robert Jordan saw the man, clearly and sharply, standing there on the road looking up at the sky. The sun shone bright on him through the trees.

Robert Jordan felt his own breath tight now as though a strand of wire bound his chest and, steadying his elbows, feeling the corrugations of the forward grip against his fingers, he put the oblong of the foresight, settled now in the notch of the rear, onto the center of the man's chest and squeezed the trigger gently.

He felt the quick, liquid, spastic lurching of the gun against his shoulder and on the road the man, looking surprised and hurt, slid forward on his knees and his forehead doubled to the road. His rifle fell by him and lay there with one of the man's fingers twisted through the trigger guard, his wrist bent forward. The rifle lay, bayonet forward on the road. Robert Jordan looked away from the man lying with his head doubled under on the road to the bridge, and the sentry box at the other end. He could not see the other sentry and he looked down the slope to the right where he knew Agustín was hidden. Then he heard Anselmo shoot, the shot smashing an echo back from the gorge. Then he heard him shoot again.

With that second shot came the cracking boom of grenades from around the corner below the bridge. Then there was the noise of grenades from well up the road to the left. Then he heard rifle-firing up the road and from below came the noise of Pablo's cavalry automatic rifle spat-spat-spat-spatting into the noise of grenades. He saw Anselmo scrambling down the steep cut to the far end of the bridge and he slung the submachine gun over his shoulder and picked up the two heavy packs from behind the pine trunks and with one in each hand, the packs pulling his arms so that he felt the tendons would pull out of his shoulders, he ran lurching down the steep slope to the road.

As he ran he heard Agustín shouting, *"Buena, caza, Inglés. Buena caza!"* and he thought, "Nice hunting, like hell, nice hunting," and just then he heard Anselmo shoot at the far end of the bridge, the noise of the shot clanging in the steel girders. He passed the sentry where he lay and ran onto the bridge, the packs swinging.

The old man came running toward him, holding his carbine in one hand. *"Sin novedad,"* he shouted. "There's nothing wrong. *Tuve que rematarlo.* I had to finish him."

Robert Jordan, kneeling, opening the packs in the center of the bridge taking out his material, saw that tears were running down Anselmo's cheeks through the gray beard stubble.

"Yo maté uno tambien," he said to Anselmo. "I killed one too," and jerked his head toward where the sentry lay hunched over in the road at the end of the bridge.

"Yes, man, yes," Anselmo said. "We have to kill them and we kill them."

Robert Jordan was climbing down into the framework of the bridge. The girders were cold and wet with dew under his hands and he climbed carefully, feeling the sun on his back, bracing himself in a bridge truss, hearing the noise of the tumbling water below him, hearing firing, too much firing, up the road at the upper post. He was sweating heavily now and it was cool under the bridge. He had a coil of wire around one arm and a pair of pliers hung by a thong from his wrist.

"Hand me that down a package at a time, *viejo,*" he called up to Anselmo. The old man leaned far over the edge handing down the oblong blocks of explosive and Robert Jordan reached up for them, shoved them in where he wanted them, packed them close, braced them, "Wedges, *viejo!* Give me wedges!" smelling the fresh shingle smell of the new whittled wedges as he tapped them in tight to hold the charge between the girders.

Now as he worked, placing, bracing, wedging, lashing tight with wire, thinking only of demolition, working fast and skillfully as a surgeon works, he heard a rattle of firing from below on the road. Then there was the noise of a grenade. Then another, booming through the rushing noise the water made. Then it was quiet from that direction.

"Damn," he thought. "I wonder what hit them then?"

There was still firing up the road at the upper post. Too damned much firing, and he was lashing two grenades side by side on top of the braced blocks of explosive, winding wire over their corrugations so they would hold tight and firm and lashing it tight; twisting it with the pliers. He felt of the whole thing and then, to make it more solid, tapped in a wedge above the grenades that blocked the whole charge firmly in against the steel.

"The other side now, *viejo,*" he shouted up to Anselmo and climbed across through the trestling, like a bloody Tarzan in a rolled steel forest, he thought, and then coming out from under the dark, the stream tumbling below him, he looked up and saw Anselmo's face as he reached the packages of explosive down to him. Goddamn good face, he thought. Not crying now. That's all to the good. And one side done. This side now and we're done.

This will drop it like what all. Come on. Don't get excited. Do it. Clean and fast as the last one. Don't fumble with it. Take your time. Don't try to do it faster than you can. You can't lose now. Nobody can keep you from blowing one side now. You're doing it just the way you should. This is a cool place. Christ, it feels cool as a wine cellar and there's no crap. Usually working under a stone bridge it's full of crap. This is a dream bridge. A bloody dream bridge. It's the old man on top who's in a bad spot. Don't try to do it faster than you can. I wish that shooting would be over up above. "Give me some wedges, *viejo.*" I don't like that shooting still. Pilar has got in trouble there. Some of the post must have been out. Out back; or behind the mill. They're still shooting. That means there's somebody still at the mill. And all that damned sawdust. Those big piles of sawdust. Sawdust, when it's old and packed, is good stuff to fight behind. There must be several of them still. It's quiet below with Pablo. I wonder what that second flare-up was. It must have been a car or a motorcyclist. I hope to God they don't have any armored cars come up or any tanks. Go on. Put it in just as fast as you can and wedge it tight and lash it fast. You're shaking, like a Goddamn woman. What the hell is the matter with you? You're trying to do it too fast. I'll bet that Goddamn woman up above isn't shaking. That Pilar. Maybe she is too. She sounds as though she were in plenty trouble. She'll shake if she gets in enough. Like everybody bloody else.

He leaned out and up into the sunlight and as he reached his hand up to take what Anselmo handed him, his head now above the noise of the falling water, the firing increased sharply up the road and then the noise of grenades again. Then more grenades.

"They rushed the sawmill then."

It's lucky I've got this stuff in blocks, he thought. Instead of sticks. What the hell. It's just neater. Although a lousy canvas sack full of jelly would be quicker. Two sacks. No. One of that would do. And if we just had detonators and the old exploder. That son of a bitch threw my exploder in the river. That old box and the places that it's been. In this river he threw it. That bastard Pablo. He gave them hell there below just now. "Give me some more of that, *viejo.*"

The old man's doing very well. He's in quite a place up there.

He hated to shoot that sentry. So did I but I didn't think about it. Nor do I think about it now. You have to do that. But then Anselmo got a cripple. I know about cripples. I think that killing a man with an automatic weapon makes it easier. I mean on the one doing it. It is different. After the first touch it is it that does it. Not you. Save that to go into some other time. You and your head. You have a nice thinking head old Jordan. Roll Jordan, Roll! They used to yell that at football when you lugged the ball. Do you know the damned Jordan is really not much bigger than that creek down there below. At the source, you mean. So is anything else at the source. This is a place here under this bridge. A home away from home. Come on Jordan, pull yourself together. This is serious Jordan. Don't you understand? Serious. It's less so all the time. Look at that other side. *Para qué?* I'm all right now however she goes. As Maine goes so goes the nation. As Jordan goes so go the bloody Israelites. The bridge, I mean. As Jordan goes, so goes the bloody bridge, other way around, really.

"Give me some more of that, Anselmo old boy," he said. The old man nodded. "Almost through," Robert Jordan said. The old man nodded again.

Finishing wiring the grenades down, he no longer heard the firing from up the road. Suddenly he was working only with the noise of the stream. He looked down and saw it boiling up white below him through the boulders and then dropping down to a clear pebbled pool where one of the wedges he had dropped swung around in the current. As he looked a trout rose for some insect and made a circle on the surface close to where the chip was turning. As he twisted the wire tight with the pliers that held these two grenades in place, he saw, through the metal of the bridge, the sunlight on the green slope of the mountain. It was brown three days ago, he thought.

Out from the cool dark under the bridge he leaned into the bright sun and shouted to Anselmo's bending face, "Give me the big coil of wire."

The old man handed it down.

For God's sake don't loosen them any yet. This will pull them. I wish you could string them through. But with the length of wire you are using it's O.K., Robert Jordan thought as he felt the cotter pins that held the rings that would release the levers on the hand grenades. He checked that the grenades, lashed on their sides, had room for the levers to spring when the pins were pulled (the wire that lashed them ran through under the levers), then he attached a length of wire to one ring, wired it onto the main wire that ran to the ring of the outside grenade, paid off some slack from the coil and passed it around a steel brace and then handed the coil up to Anselmo. "Hold it carefully," he said.

He climbed up onto the bridge, took the coil from the old man and walked back as fast as he could pay out wire toward where the sentry was slumped in the road, leaning over the side of the bridge and paying out wire from the coil as he walked.

"Bring the sacks," he shouted to Anselmo as he walked backwards. As he passed he stooped down and picked up the submachine gun and slung it over his shoulder again.

It was then, looking up from paying out wire, that he saw, well up the road, those who were coming back from the upper post.

There were four of them, he saw, and then he had to watch his wire so it would be clear and not foul against any of the outer work of the bridge. Eladio was not with them.

Robert Jordan carried the wire clear past the end of the bridge, took a loop around the last stanchion and then ran along the road until he stopped beside a stone marker. He cut the wire and handed it to Anselmo.

"Hold this, *viejo*," he said. "Now walk back with me to the bridge. Take up on it as you walk. No. I will."

At the bridge he pulled the wire back out through the hitch so it now ran clear and unfouled to the grenade rings and handed it, stretching alongside the bridge but running quite clear, to Anselmo.

"Take this back to that high stone," he said. "Hold it easily but firmly. Do not put any force on it. When thou pullest hard, hard, the bridge will blow. *Comprendes?*"

"Yes."

"Treat it softly but do not let it sag so it will foul. Keep it lightly firm but not pulling until thou pullest. *Comprendes?*"

"Yes."

"When thou pullest really pull. Do not jerk."

Robert Jordan while he spoke was looking up the road at the remainder of Pilar's band. They were close now and he saw Primitivo and Rafael were supporting Fernando. He looked to be shot through the groin for he was holding himself there with both hands while the man and the boy held him on either side. His right leg was dragging, the side of the shoe scraping on the road as they walked him. Pilar was climbing the bank into the timber carrying three rifles. Robert Jordan could not see her face but her head was up and she was climbing as fast as she could.

"How does it go?" Primitivo called.

"Good. We're almost finished," Robert Jordan shouted back.

There was no need to ask how it went with them. As he looked away the three were on the edge of the road and Fernando was shaking his head as they tried to get him up the bank.

"Give me a rifle here," Robert Jordan heard him say in a choky voice.

"No, *hombre*. We will get thee to the horses."

"What would I do with a horse?" Fernando said. "I am very well here."

Robert Jordan did not hear the rest for he was speaking to Anselmo.

"Blow it if tanks come," he said. "But only if they come onto it. Blow it if armored cars come. If they come onto it. Anything else Pablo will stop."

"I will not blow it with thee beneath it."

"Take no account of me. Blow it if thou needest to. I fix the other wire and come back. Then we will blow it together."

He started running for the center of the bridge.

Anselmo saw Robert Jordan run up the bridge, coil of wire over his arm, pliers hanging from one wrist and the submachine gun slung over his back. He saw him climb down under the rail of the bridge and out of sight. Anselmo held the wire in his hand, his right hand, and he crouched behind the stone marker and looked down the road and across the bridge. Halfway between him and the bridge was the sentry, who had settled now closer to the road, sinking closer onto the smooth road surface as the sun weighed on his back. His rifle, lying on the road, the bayonet fixed, pointed straight toward Anselmo. The old man looked past him along the surface of the bridge crossed by the shadows of the bridge rail to where the road swung to the left along the gorge and then turned out of sight behind the rocky wall. He looked at the far sentry box with the sun shining on it and then, conscious of the wire in his hand, he turned his head to where Fernando was speaking to Primitivo and the gypsy.

"Leave me here," Fernando said. "It hurts much and there is much hemorrhage inside. I feel it in the inside when I move."

"Let us get thee up the slope," Primitivo said. "Put thy arms around our shoulders and we will take thy legs."

"It is inutile," Fernando said. "Put me here behind a stone. I am as useful here as above."

"But when we go," Primitivo said.

"Leave me here," Fernando said. "There is no question of my travelling with this. Thus it gives one horse more. I am very well here. Certainly they will come soon."

"We can take thee up the hill," the gypsy said. "Easily."

He was, naturally, in a deadly hurry to be gone, as was Primitivo. But they had brought him this far.

"Nay," Fernando said. "I am very well here. What passes with Eladio?"

The gypsy put his finger on his head to show where the wound had been.

"Here," he said. "After thee. When we made the rush."

"Leave me," Fernando said. Anselmo could see he was suffering much. He held both hands against his groin now and put his head back against the bank, his legs straight out before him. His face was gray and sweating.

"Leave me now please, for a favor," he said. His eyes were shut with pain, the edges of the lips twitching. "I find myself very well here."

"Here is a rifle and cartridges," Primitivo said.

"Is it mine?" Fernando asked, his eyes shut.

"Nay, the Pilar has thine," Primitivo said. "This is mine."

"I would prefer my own," Fernando said. "I am more accustomed to it."

"I will bring it to thee," the gypsy lied to him. "Keep this until it comes."

"I am in a very good position here," Fernando said. "Both for up the road and for the bridge." He opened his eyes, turned his head and looked across the bridge, then shut them as the pain came.

The gypsy tapped his head and motioned with his thumb to Primitivo for them to be off.

"Then we will be down for thee," Primitivo said and started up the slope after the gypsy, who was climbing fast.

Fernando lay back against the bank. In front of him was one of the whitewashed stones that marked the edge of the road. His head was in the shadow but the sun shone on his plugged and bandaged wound and on his hands that were cupped over it. His legs and his feet also were in the sun. The rifle lay beside him and there were three clips of cartridges shining in the sun beside the rifle. A fly crawled on his hands but the small tickling did not come through the pain.

"Fernando!" Anselmo called to him from where he crouched, holding the wire. He had made a loop in the end of the wire and twisted it close so he could hold it in his fist.

"Fernando!" he called again.

Fernando opened his eyes and looked at him.

"How does it go?" Fernando asked.

"Very good," Anselmo said. "Now in a minute we will be blowing it."

"I am pleased. Anything you need me for advise me," Fernando said and shut his eyes again and the pain lurched in him.

Anselmo looked away from him and out onto the bridge.

He was watching for the first sight of the coil of wire being handed up onto the bridge and for the *Inglés*'s sunburnt head and face to follow it as he would pull himself up the side. At the same time he was watching beyond the bridge for anything to come around the far corner of the road. He did not feel afraid now at all and he had not been afraid all the day. It goes so fast and it is so normal, he thought. I hated the shooting of the guard and it made me an emotion but that is passed now. How could the *Inglés* say that the shooting of a man is like the shooting of an animal? In all hunting I have had an elation and no feeling of wrong. But to shoot a man gives a feeling as though one had struck one's own brother when you are grown men. And to shoot him various times to kill him. Nay, do not think of that. That gave thee too much emotion and thee ran blubbering down the bridge like a woman.

That is over, he told himself, and thou canst try to atone for it as for the others. But now thou has what thou asked for last night coming home across the hills. Thou art in battle and thou hast no problem. If I die on this morning now it is all right.

Then he looked at Fernando lying there against the bank with his hands cupped over the groove of his hip, his lips blue, his eyes tight shut, breathing heavily and slowly, and he thought, If I die may it be quickly. Nay I said I would ask nothing more if I were granted what I needed for today. So I will not ask. Understand? I ask nothing. Nothing in any way. Give me what I asked for and I leave all the rest according to discretion.

He listened to the noise that came, far away, of the battle at the pass and he said to himself, Truly this is a great day. I should realize and know what a day this is.

But there was no lift or any excitement in his heart. That was all gone and there was nothing but a calmness. And now, as he crouched behind the marker stone with the looped wire in his hand and another loop of it around his wrist and the gravel beside the road under his knees he was not lonely nor did he feel in any way alone. He was one with the wire in his hand and one with the bridge, and one with the charges the *Inglés* had placed. He was one with the *Inglés* still working under the bridge and he was one with all of the battle and with the Republic.

But there was no excitement. It was all calm now and the sun beat down on his neck and on his shoulders as he crouched and as he looked up he saw the high, cloudless sky and the slope of the mountain rising beyond the river and he was not happy but he was neither lonely nor afraid.

Up the hill slope Pilar lay behind a tree watching the road that came down from the pass. She had three loaded rifles by her and she handed one to Primitivo as he dropped down beside her.

"Get down there," she said. "Behind that tree. Thou, gypsy, over there," she pointed to another tree below. "Is he dead?"

"Nay. Not yet," Primitivo said.

"It was bad luck," Pilar said. "If we had had two more it need not have happened. He should have crawled around the sawdust pile. Is he all right there where he is?"

Primitivo shook his head.

"When the *Inglés* blows the bridge will fragments come this far?" the gypsy asked from behind his tree.

"I don't know," Pilar said. "But Agustín with the *máquina* is closer than thee. The *Inglés* would not have placed him there if it were too close."

"But I remember with the blowing of the train the lamp of the engine blew by over my head and pieces of steel flew by like swallows."

"Thou hast poetic memories," Pilar said. "Like swallows. *Joder!* They were like wash boilers. Listen, gypsy, thou hast comported thyself well today. Now do not let thy fear catch up with thee."

"Well, I only asked if it would blow this far so I might keep well behind the tree trunk," the gypsy said.

"Keep it thus," Pilar told him. "How many have we killed?"

"*Pues* five for us. Two here. Canst thou not see the other at the far end? Look there toward the bridge. See the box? Look! Dost see?" He pointed. "Then there were eight below for Pablo. I watched that post for the *Inglés*."

Pilar grunted. Then she said violently and raging, "What passes with that *Inglés*? What is he obscenitying off under that bridge. *Vaya mandanga!* Is he building a bridge or blowing one?"

She raised her head and looked down at Anselmo crouched behind the stone marker.

"Hey, *viejo!*" she shouted. "What passes with thy obscenity of an *Inglés*?"

"Patience, woman," Anselmo called up, holding the wire lightly but firmly. "He is terminating his work."

"But what in the name of the great whore does he take so much time about?"

"*Es muy conciénzudo!*" Anselmo shouted. "It is a scientific labor."

"I obscenity in the milk of science," Pilar raged to the gypsy. "Let the filth-faced obscenity blow it and be done. Maria!" she shouted in her deep voice up the hill. "Thy *Inglés*—" and she shouted a flood of obscenity about Jordan's imaginary actions under the bridge.

"Calm yourself, woman," Anselmo called from the road. "He is doing an enormous work. He is finishing it now."

"The hell with it," Pilar raged. "It is speed that counts."

Just then they all heard firing start down the road where Pablo was holding the post he had taken. Pilar stopped cursing and listened. "Ay," she said. "Ayee. Ayee. That's it."

Robert Jordan heard it as he swung the coil of wire up onto the bridge with one hand and then pulled himself up after it. As his knees rested on the edge of the iron of the bridge and his hands were on the surface he heard the machine gun firing around the bend below. It was a different sound from Pablo's automatic rifle. He got to his feet, leaned over, passed his coil of wire clear and commenced to pay out wire as he walked backwards and sideways along the bridge.

He heard the firing and as he walked he felt it in the pit of his stomach as though it echoed on his own diaphragm. It was closer now as he walked and he looked back at the bend of the road. But it was still clear of any car, or tank or men. It was still clear when he was halfway to the end of the bridge. It was still clear when he was three quarters of the way, his wire running clear and unfouled, and it was still clear as he climbed around behind the sentry box, holding his wire out to keep it from catching on the iron work. Then he was on the road and it was still clear below on the road and then he was moving fast backwards up the little washed-out gully by the lower side of the road as an outfielder goes backwards for a long fly ball, keeping the wire taut, and now he was almost opposite Anselmo's stone and it was still clear below the bridge.

Then he heard the truck coming down the road and he saw it over his shoulder just coming onto the long slope and he swung his wrist once around the wire and yelled to Anselmo, "Blow her!" and he dug his heels in and leaned back hard onto the tension of the wire with a turn of it around his wrist and the noise of the truck was coming behind and ahead there was the road with the dead sentry and the long bridge and the stretch of road below, still clear and then there was a cracking roar and the middle of the bridge rose up in the air like a wave breaking and he felt the blast from the explosion roll back against him as he dove on his face in the pebbly gully with his hands holding tight over his head. His face was down against the pebbles as the bridge settled where it had risen and the familiar yellow smell of it rolled over him in acrid smoke and then it commenced to rain pieces of steel.

After the steel stopped falling he was still alive and he raised his head and looked across the bridge. The center section of it was gone. There were jagged pieces of steel on the bridge with their bright, new torn edges and ends and these were all over the road. The truck had stopped up the road about a hundred yards. The driver and the two men who had been with him were running toward a culvert.

Fernando was still lying against the bank and he was still breathing. His arms straight by his sides, his hands relaxed.

Anselmo lay face down behind the white marking stone. His left arm was doubled under his head and his right arm was stretched straight out. The loop of wire was still around his right fist. Robert Jordan got to his feet, crossed the road, knelt by him and made sure that he was dead. He did not turn him over to see what the piece of steel had done. He was dead and that was all.

He looked very small, dead, Robert Jordan thought. He looked small and gray-headed and Robert Jordan thought, I wonder how he ever carried such big loads if that is the size he really was. Then he saw the shape of the calves and the thighs in the tight, gray herdsman's breeches and the worn soles of the rope-soled shoes and he picked up Anselmo's carbine and the two sacks, practically empty now and went over and picked up the rifle that lay beside Fernando. He kicked a jagged piece of steel off the surface of the road. Then he swung the two rifles over his shoulder, holding them by the muzzles, and started up the slope into the timber. He did not look back nor did he even look across the bridge at the road. They were still firing around the bend below but he cared nothing about that now.

He was coughing from the TNT fumes and he felt numb all through himself.

He put one of the rifles down by Pilar where she lay behind the tree. She looked and saw that made three rifles that she had again.

"You are too high up here," he said. "There's a truck up the road where you can't see it. They thought it was planes. You better get further down. I'm going down with Agustín to cover Pablo."

"The old one?" she asked him, looking at his face.

"Dead."

He coughed again, wrackingly, and spat on the ground.

"Thy bridge is blown, *Inglés,*" Pilar looked at him. "Don't forget that."

"I don't forget anything," he said. "You have a big voice," he said to Pilar. "I have heard thee bellow. Shout up to the Maria and tell her that I am all right."

"We lost two at the sawmill," Pilar said, trying to make him understand.

"So I saw," Robert Jordan said. "Did you do something stupid?"

"Go and obscenity thyself, *Inglés*," Pilar said. "Fernando and Eladio were men, too."

"Why don't you go up with the horses?" Robert Jordan said. "I can cover here better than thee."

"Thou art to cover Pablo."

"The hell with Pablo. Let him cover himself with *mierda*."

"Nay, *Inglés*. He came back. He has fought much below there. Thou hast not listened? He is fighting now. Against something bad. Do you not hear?"

"I'll cover him. But obscenity all of you. Thou and Pablo both."

"*Inglés*," Pilar said. "Calm thyself. I have been with thee in this as no one could be. Pablo did thee a wrong but he returned."

"If I had had the exploder the old man would not have been killed. I could have blown it from here."

"If, if, if—" Pilar said.

The anger and the emptiness and the hate that had come with the let-down after the bridge, when he had looked up from where he had lain and crouching, seen Anselmo dead, were still all through him. In him, too, was despair from the sorrow that soldiers turn to hatred in order that they may continue to be soldiers. Now it was over he was lonely, detached and unelated and he hated every one he saw.

"If there had been no snow—" Pilar said. And then, not suddenly, as a physical release could have been (if the woman would have put her arm around him, say) but slowly and from his head he began to accept it and let the hate go out. Sure, the snow. That had done it. The snow. Done it to others. Once you saw it again as it was to others, once you got rid of your own self, the always ridding of self that you had to do in war. Where there could be no self. Where yourself is only to be lost. Then, from his losing of it, he heard Pilar say, "Sordo——"

"What?" he said.

"Sordo——"

"Yes," Robert Jordan said. He grinned at her, a cracked, stiff, too-tightened-facial-tendoned grin. "Forget it. I was wrong. I am sorry, woman. Let us do this well and all together. And the bridge *is* blown, as thou sayest."

"Yes. Thou must think of things in their place."

"Then I go now to Agustín. Put thy gypsy much farther down so that he can see well up the road. Give those guns to Primitivo and take this *máquina*. Let me show thee."

"Keep the *máquina*," Pilar said. "We will not be here any time. Pablo should come now and we will be going."

"Rafael," Robert Jordan said, "come down here with me. Here. Good. See those coming out of the culvert. There, above the truck? Coming toward the truck? Hit me one of those. Sit. Take it easy."

The gypsy aimed carefully and fired and as he jerked the bolt back and ejected the shell Robert Jordan said, "Over. You threw against the rock above. See the rock dust? Lower, by two feet. Now, careful. They're running. Good. *Sigue tirando.*"

"I got one," the gypsy said. The man was down in the road halfway between the culvert and the truck. The other two did not stop to drag him. They ran for the culvert and ducked in.

"Don't shoot at him," Robert Jordan said. "Shoot for the top part of a front tire on the truck. So if you miss you'll hit the engine. Good." He watched with the glasses. "A little lower. Good. You shoot like hell. *Mucho! Mucho!* Shoot me the top of the radiator. Anywhere on the radiator. Thou art a champion. Look. Don't let anything come past that point there. See?"

"Watch me break the windshield in the truck," the gypsy said happily.

"Nay. The truck is already sick," Robert Jordan said. "Hold thy fire until anything comes down the road. Start firing when it is opposite the culvert. Try to hit the driver. That you all should fire, then," he spoke to Pilar who had come farther down the slope with Primitivo. "You are wonderfully placed here. See how that steepness guards thy flank?"

"That you should get about thy business with Agustín," Pilar said. "Desist from thy lecture. I have seen terrain in my time."

"Put Primitivo farther up there," Robert Jordan said. "There. See, man? This side of where the bank steepens."

"Leave me," said Pilar. "Get along, *Inglés*. Thou and thy perfection. Here there is no problem."

Just then they heard the planes.

Maria had been with the horses for a long time, but they were no comfort to her. Nor was she any to them. From where she was in the forest she could not see the road nor could she see the bridge and when the firing started she put her arm around the neck of the big white-faced bay stallion that she had gentled and brought gifts to many times when the horses had been in the corral in the trees below the camp. But her nervousness made the big stallion nervous, too, and he jerked his head, his nostrils widening at the firing and the noise of the bombs. Maria could not keep still and she walked around patting and gentling the horses and making them all more nervous and agitated.

She tried to think of the firing not as just a terrible thing that was happening, but to realize that it was Pablo below with the new men, and Pilar with the others above, and that she must not worry nor get into a panic but must have confidence in Roberto. But she could not do this and all the firing above and below the bridge and the distant sound of the battle that rolled down from the pass like the noise of a far-off storm with a dried, rolling rattle in it and the irregular beat of the bombs was simply a horrible thing that almost kept her from breathing.

Then later she heard Pilar's big voice from away below on the hillside shouting up some obscenity to her that she could not understand and she thought, Oh, God no, no. Don't talk like that with him in peril. Don't offend any one and make useless risks. Don't give any provocation.

Then she commenced to pray for Roberto quickly and automatically as she had done at school, saying the prayers as fast as she could and counting them on the fingers of her left hand, praying by tens of each of the two prayers she was repeating. Then the bridge blew and one horse snapped his halter when he rose and jerked his head at the cracking roar and he went off through the trees. Maria caught him finally and brought him back, shivering, trembling, his chest dark with sweat, the saddle down, and coming back through the trees she heard shooting below and she thought I cannot stand this longer. I cannot live not knowing any longer. I cannot breathe and my mouth is so dry. And I am afraid and I am no good and I frighten the horses and only caught this horse by hazard because he knocked the saddle down against a tree and caught himself kicking into the stirrups and now as I get the saddle up, Oh, God, I do not know. I cannot bear it. Oh please have him be all right for all my heart and all of me is at the bridge. The Republic is one thing and we must win is another thing. But, Oh, Sweet Blessed Virgin, bring him back to me from the bridge and I will do anything thou sayest ever. Because I am not here. There isn't any me. I am only with him. Take care of him for me and that will be me and then I will do the things for thee and he will not mind. Nor will it be against the Republic. Oh, please forgive me for I am very confused. I am too confused now. But if thou takest care of him I will do whatever is right. I will do what he says and what you say. With the two of me I will do it. But this now not knowing I cannot endure.

Then, the horse tied again, she with the saddle up now, the blanket smoothed, hauling tight on the cinch she heard the big, deep voice from the timber below, "Maria! Maria! Thy *Inglés* is all right. Hear me? All right. *Sin Novedad!*"

Maria held the saddle with both hands and pressed her cropped head hard against it and cried. She heard the deep voice shouting again and she turned from the saddle and shouted, choking, "Yes! Thank you!" Then, choking again, "Thank you! Thank you very much!"

When they heard the planes they all looked up and the planes were coming from Segovia very high in the sky, silvery in the high sky, their drumming rising over all the other sounds.

"Those!" Pilar said. "There has only lacked those!"

Robert Jordan put his arm on her shoulders as he watched them. "Nay, woman," he said. "Those do not come for us. Those have no time for us. Calm thyself."

"I hate them."

"Me too. But now I must go to Agustín."

He circled the hillside through the pines and all the time there was the throbbing, drumming of the planes and across the shattered bridge on the road below, around the bend of the road there was the intermittent hammering fire of a heavy machine gun.

Robert Jordan dropped down to where Agustín lay in the clump of scrub pines behind the automatic rifle and more planes were coming all the time.

"What passes below?" Agustín said. "What is Pablo doing? Doesn't he know the bridge is gone?"

"Maybe he can't leave."

"Then let us leave. The hell with him."

"He will come now if he is able," Robert Jordan said. "We should see him now."

"I have not heard him," Agustín said. "Not for five minutes. No. There! Listen! There he is. That's him."

There was a burst of the spot-spot-spotting fire of the cavalry submachine gun, then another, then another.

"That's the bastard," Robert Jordan said.

He watched still more planes coming over in the high cloudless blue sky and he watched Agustín's face as he looked up at them. Then he looked down at the shattered bridge and across to the stretch of road which still was clear. He coughed and spat and listened to the heavy machine gun hammer again below the bend. It sounded to be in the same place that it was before.

"And what's that?" Agustín asked. "What the unnameable is that?"

"It has been going since before I blew the bridge," Robert Jordan said. He looked down at the bridge now and he could see the stream through the torn gap where the center had fallen, hanging like a bent steel apron. He heard the first of the planes that had gone over now bombing up above at the pass and more were still coming. The noise of their motors filled all the high sky and looking up he saw their pursuit, minute and tiny, circling and wheeling high above them.

"I don't think they ever crossed the lines the other morning," Primitivo said. "They must have swung off to the west and then come back. They could not be making an attack if they had seen these."

"Most of these are new," Robert Jordan said.

He had the feeling of something that had started normally and had then brought great, outsized, giant repercussions. It was as though you had thrown a stone and the stone made a ripple and the ripple returned roaring and toppling as a tidal wave. Or as though you shouted and the echo came back in rolls and peals of thunder, and the thunder was deadly. Or as though you struck one man and he fell and as far as you could see other men rose up all armed and armored. He was glad he was not with Golz up at the pass.

Lying there, by Agustín, watching the planes going over, listening for firing behind him, watching the road below where he knew he would see something but not what it would be, he still felt numb with the surprise that he had not been killed at the bridge. He had accepted being killed so completely that all of this now seemed unreal. Shake out of that, he said to himself. Get rid of that. There is much, much, much to be done today. But it would not leave him and he felt, consciously, all of this becoming like a dream.

"You swallowed too much of that smoke," he told himself. But he knew it was not that. He could feel, solidly, how unreal it all was through the absolute reality and he looked down at the bridge and then back to the sentry lying on the road, to where Anselmo lay, to Fernando against the bank and back up the smooth, brown road to the stalled truck and still it was unreal.

"You better sell out your part of you quickly," he told himself. "You're like one of those cocks in the pit where nobody has seen the wound given and it doesn't show and he is already going cold with it."

"Nuts," he said to himself. "You are a little groggy is all, and you have a let-down after responsibility, is all. Take it easy."

Then Agustín grabbed his arm and pointed and he looked across the gorge and saw Pablo.

They saw Pablo come running around the corner of the bend in the road. At the sheer rock where the road went out of sight they saw him stop and lean against the rock and fire back up the road. Robert Jordan saw Pablo, short, heavy and stocky, his cap gone, leaning against the rock wall and firing the short cavalry automatic rifle and he could see the bright flicker of the cascading brass hulls as the sun caught them. They saw Pablo crouch and fire another burst. Then, without looking back, he came running, short, bow-legged, fast, his head bent down straight toward the bridge.

Robert Jordan had pushed Agustín over and he had the stock of the big automatic rifle against his shoulder and was sighting on the bend of the road. His own submachine gun lay by his left hand. It was not accurate enough for that range.

As Pablo came toward them Robert Jordan sighted on the bend but nothing came. Pablo had reached the bridge, looked over his shoulder once, glanced at the bridge, and then turned to his left and gone down into the gorge and out of sight. Robert Jordan was still watching the bend and nothing had come in sight. Agustín got up on one knee. He could see Pablo climbing down into the gorge like a goat. There had been no noise of firing below since they had first seen Pablo.

"You see anything up above? On the rocks above?" Robert Jordan asked.

"Nothing."

Robert Jordan watched the bend of the road. He knew the wall just below that was too steep for any one to climb but below it eased and some one might have circled up above.

If things had been unreal before, they were suddenly real enough now. It was as though a reflex lens camera had been suddenly brought into focus. It was then he saw the low-bodied, angled snout and squat green, gray and brown-splashed turret with the projecting machine gun come around the bend into the bright sun. He fired on it and he could hear the spang against the steel. The little whippet tank scuttled back behind the rock wall. Watching the corner, Robert Jordan saw the nose just reappear, then the edge of the turret showed and the turret swung so that the gun was pointing down the road.

"It seems like a mouse coming out of his hole," Agustín said. "Look, *Inglés.*"

"He has little confidence," Robert Jordan said.

"This is the big insect Pablo has been fighting," Agustín said. "Hit him again, *Inglés.*"

"Nay. I cannot hurt him. I don't want him to see where we are."

The tank commenced to fire down the road. The bullets hit the road surface and sung off and now they were pinging and clanging in the iron of the bridge. It was the same machine gun they had heard below.

"*Cabrón!*" Agustín said. "Is that the famous tanks, *Inglés?*"

"That's a baby one."

Cabrón. If I had a baby bottle full of gasoline I would climb up there and set fire to him. What will he do, *Inglés?*"

"After a while he will have another look."

"And these are what men fear," Agustín said. "Look, *Inglés!* He's rekilling the sentries."

"Since he has no other target," Robert Jordan said. "Do not reproach him."

But he was thinking, Sure, make fun of him. But suppose it was you, way back here in your own country and they held you up with firing on the main road. Then a bridge was blown. Wouldn't you think it was mined ahead or that there was a trap? Sure you would. He's done all right. He's waiting for something else to come up. He's engaging the enemy. It's only us. But he can't tell that. Look at the little bastard.

The little tank had nosed a little farther around the corner.

Just then Agustín saw Pablo coming over the edge of the gorge, pulling himself over on hands and knees, his bristly face running with sweat.

"Here comes the son of a bitch," he said.

"Who?"

"Pablo."

Robert Jordan looked, saw Pablo, and then he commenced firing at the part of the camouflaged turret of the tank where he knew the slit above the machine gun would be. The little tank whirred backwards, scuttling out of sight and Robert Jordan picked up the automatic rifle, clamped the tripod against the barrel and swung the gun with its still hot muzzle over his shoulder. The muzzle was so hot it burned his shoulder and he shoved it far behind him turning the stock flat in his hand.

"Bring the sack of pans and my little *máquina,*" he shouted, "and come running."

Robert Jordan ran up the hill through the pines. Agustín was close behind him and behind him Pablo was coming.

"Pilar!" Jordan shouted across the hill. "Come on, woman!"

The three of them were going as fast as they could up the steep slope. They could not run any more because the grade was too severe and Pablo, who had no load but the light cavalry submachine gun, had closed up with the other two.

"And thy people?" Agustín said to Pablo out of his dry mouth.

"All dead," Pablo said. He was almost unable to breathe. Agustín turned his head and looked at him.

"We have plenty of horses now, *Inglés,*" Pablo panted.

"Good," Robert Jordan said. The murderous bastard, he thought. "What did you encounter?"

"Everything," Pablo said. He was breathing in lunges. "What passed with Pilar?"

"She lost Fernando and the brother——"

"Eladio," Agustín said.

"And thou?" Pablo asked.

"I lost Anselmo."

"There are lots of horses," Pablo said. "Even for the baggage."

Agustín bit his lip, looked at Robert Jordan and shook his head. Below them, out of sight through the trees, they heard the tank firing on the road and bridge again.

Robert Jordan jerked his head. "What passed with that?" he said to Pablo. He did not like to look at Pablo, nor to smell him, but he wanted to hear him.

"I could not leave with that there," Pablo said. "We were barricaded at the lower bend of the post. Finally it went back to look for something and I came."

"What were you shooting at, at the bend?" Agustín asked bluntly.

Pablo looked at him, started to grin, thought better of it, and said nothing.

"Did you shoot them all?" Agustín asked. Robert Jordan was thinking, keep your mouth shut. It is none of your business now. They have done all that you could expect and more. This is an inter-tribal matter. Don't make moral judgments. What do you expect from a murderer? You're working with a murderer. Keep your mouth shut. You knew enough about him before. This is nothing new. But you dirty bastard, he thought. You dirty, rotten bastard.

His chest was aching with climbing as though it would split after the running and ahead now through the trees he saw the horses.

"Go ahead," Agustín was saying. "Why do you not say you shot them?"

"Shut up," Pablo said. "I have fought much today and well. Ask the *Inglés.*"

"And now get us through today," Robert Jordan said. "For it is thee who has the plan for this."

"I have a good plan," Pablo said. "With a little luck we will be all right."

He was beginning to breathe better.

"You're not going to kill any of us, are you?" Agustín said. "For I will kill thee now."

"Shut up," Pablo said. "I have to look after thy interest and that of the band. This is war. One cannot do what one would wish."

"Cabrón," said Agustín. "You take all the prizes."

"Tell me what thou encountered below," Robert Jordan said to Pablo.

"Everything," Pablo repeated. He was still breathing as though it were tearing his chest but he could talk steadily now and his face and head were running with sweat and his shoulders and chest were soaked with it. He looked at Robert Jordan cautiously to see if he were really friendly and then he grinned. "Everything," he said again. "First we took the post. Then came a motorcyclist. Then another. Then an ambulance. Then a camion. Then the tank. Just before thou didst the bridge."

"Then——"

"The tank could not hurt us but we could not leave for it commanded the road. Then it went away and I came."

"And thy people?" Agustín put in, still looking for trouble.

"Shut up," Pablo looked at him squarely, and his face was the face of a man who had fought well before any other thing had happened. "They were not of our band."

Now they could see the horses tied to the trees, the sun coming down on them through the pine branches and them tossing their heads and kicking against the botflies and Robert Jordan saw Maria and the next thing he was holding her tight, tight, with the automatic rifle leaning against his side, the flash-cone pressing against his ribs and Maria saying, "Thou, Roberto. Oh, thou."

"Yes, rabbit. My good, good rabbit. Now we go."

"Art thou here truly?"

"Yes. Yes. Truly. Oh, thou!"

He had never thought that you could know that there was a woman if there was battle; nor that any part of you could know it, or respond to it; nor that if there was a woman that she should have breasts small, round and tight against you through a shirt; nor that they, the breasts, could know about the two of them in battle. But it was true and he thought, good. That's good. I would not have believed that and he held her to him once hard, hard, but he did not look at her, and then he slapped her where he never had slapped her and said, "Mount. Mount. Get on that saddle, *guapa.*"

Then they were untying the halters and Robert Jordan had given the automatic rifle back to Agustín and slung his own submachine gun over his back, and he was putting bombs out of his pockets into the saddlebags, and he stuffed one empty pack inside the other and tied that one behind his saddle. Then Pilar came up, so breathless from the climb she could not talk, but only motioned.

Then Pablo stuffed three hobbles he had in his hand into a saddlebag, stood up and said, "*Qué tal,* woman?" and she only nodded, and then they were all mounting.

Robert Jordan was on the big gray he had first seen in the snow of the morning of the day before and he felt that it was much horse between his legs and under his hands. He was wearing rope-soled shoes and the stirrups were a little too short; his submachine gun was slung over his shoulder, his pockets were full of clips and he was sitting reloading the one used clip, the reins under one arm, tight, watching Pilar mount into a strange sort of seat on top of the duffle lashed onto the saddle of the buckskin.

"Cut that stuff loose for God's sake," Primitivo said. "Thou wilt fall and the horse cannot carry it."

"Shut up," said Pilar. "We go to make a life with this."

"Canst ride like that, woman?" Pablo asked her from the *guardia-civil* saddle on the great bay horse.

"Like any milk peddler," Pilar told him. "How do you go, old one?"

"Straight down. Across the road. Up the far slope and into the timber where it narrows."

"Across the road?" Agustín wheeled beside him, kicking his soft-heeled, canvas shoes against the stiff, unresponding belly of one of the horses Pablo had recruited in the night.

"Yes, man. It is the only way," Pablo said. He handed him one of the lead ropes. Primitivo and the gypsy had the others.

"Thou canst come at the end if thou will, *Inglés,*" Pablo said. "We cross high enough to be out of range of that *máquina*. But we will go separately and riding much and then be together where it narrows above."

"Good," said Robert Jordan.

They rode down through the timber toward the edge of the road. Robert Jordan rode just behind Maria. He could not ride beside her for the timber. He caressed the gray once with his thigh muscles, and then held him steady as they dropped down fast and sliding through the pines, telling the gray with his thighs as they dropped down what the spurs would have told him if they had been on level ground.

"Thou," he said to Maria, "go second as they cross the road. First is not so bad though it seems bad. Second is good. It is later that they are always watching for."

"But thou———"

"I will go suddenly. There will be no problem. It is the places in line that are bad."

He was watching the round, bristly head of Pablo, sunk in his shoulders as he rode, his automatic rifle slung over his shoulder. He was watching Pilar, her head bare, her shoulders broad, her knees higher than her thighs as her heels hooked into the bundles. She looked back at him once and shook her head.

"Pass the Pilar before you cross the road," Robert Jordan said to Maria.

Then he was looking through the thinning trees and he saw the oiled dark of the road below and beyond it the green slope of the hillside. We are above the culvert, he saw, and just below the height where the road drops down straight toward the bridge in that long sweep. We are around eight hundred yards above the bridge. That is not out of range for the Fiat in that little tank if they have come up to the bridge.

"Maria," he said. "Pass the Pilar before we reach the road and ride wide up that slope."

She looked back at him but did not say anything. He did not look at her except to see that she had understood.

"Comprendes?" he asked her.

She nodded.

"Move up," he said.

She shook her head.

"Move up!"

"Nay," she told him, turning around and shaking her head. "I go in the order that I am to go."

Just them Pablo dug both his spurs into the big bay and he plunged down the last pine-needled slope and cross the road in a pounding, sparking of shod hooves. The others came behind him and Robert Jordan saw them crossing the road and slamming on up the green slope and heard the machine gun hammer at the bridge. Then he heard a noise come sweeeish-crack-boom! The boom was a sharp crack that widened in the cracking and on the hillside he saw a small fountain of earth rise with a plume of gray smoke. Sweeish-crack-boom! It came again, the swishing like the noise of a rocket and there was another up-pulsing of dirt and smoke farther up the hillside.

Ahead of him the gypsy was stopped beside the road in the shelter of the last trees. He looked ahead at the slope and then he looked back toward Robert Jordan.

"Go ahead, Rafael," Robert Jordan said. "Gallop, man!"

The gypsy was holding the lead rope with the pack-horse pulling his head taut behind him.

"Drop the pack-horse and gallop!" Robert Jordan said.

He saw the gypsy's hand extended behind him, rising higher and higher, seeming to take forever as his heels kicked into the horse he was riding and the rope came taut, then dropped, and he was across the road and Robert Jordan was knee-ing against a frightened pack-horse that bumped back into him as the gypsy crossed the hard, dark road and he heard his horse's hooves clumping as he galloped up the slope.

Wheeeeeeish-ca-rack! The flat trajectory of the shell came and he saw the gypsy jink like a running boar as the earth spouted the little black and gray geyser ahead of him. He watched him galloping, slow and reaching now, up the long green slope and the gun threw behind him and ahead of him and he was under the fold of the hill with the others.

I can't take the damned pack-horse, Robert Jordan thought. Though I wish I could keep the son of a bitch on my off side. I'd like to have him between me and that 47 mm. they're throwing with. By God, I'll try to get him up there anyway.

He rode up to the pack-horse, caught hold of the hackamore, and then, holding the rope, the horse trotting behind him, rode fifty yards up through the trees. At the edge of the trees he looked down the road past the truck to the bridge. He could see men out on the bridge and behind it looked like a traffic jam on the road. Robert

Jordan looked around, saw what he wanted finally and reached up and broke a dead limb from a pine tree. He dropped the hackamore, edged the pack-horse up to the slope that slanted down to the road and then hit him hard across the rump with the tree branch. "Go on, you son of a bitch," he said, and threw the dead branch after him as the pack-horse crossed the road and started across the slope. The branch hit him and the horse broke from a run into a gallop.

Robert Jordan rode thirty yards farther up the road; beyond that the bank was too steep. The gun was firing now with the rocket whish and the cracking, dirt-spouting boom. "Come on, you big gray fascist bastard," Robert Jordan said to the horse and put him down the slope in a sliding plunge. Then he was out in the open, over the road that was so hard under the hooves he felt the pound of it come up all the way to his shoulders, his neck and his teeth, onto the smooth of the slope, the hooves finding it, cutting it, pounding it, reaching, throwing, going, and he looked down across the slope to where the bridge showed now at a new angle he had never seen. It crossed in profile now without foreshortening and in the center was the broken place and behind it on the road was the little tank and behind the little tank was a big tank with a gun that flashed now yellow-bright as a mirror and the screech as the air ripped apart seemed almost over the gray neck that stretched ahead of him, and he turned his head as the dirt fountained up the hillside. The pack-horse was ahead of him swinging too far to the right and slowing down and Robert Jordan, galloping, his head turned a little toward the bridge, saw the line of trucks halted behind the turn that showed now clearly as he was gaining height, and he saw the bright yellow flash that signalled the instant whish and boom, and the shell fell short, but he heard the metal sailing from where the dirt rose.

He saw them all ahead in the edge of the timber watching him and he said, "Arre caballo! Go on, horse!" and felt his big horse's chest surging with the steepening of the slope and saw the gray neck stretching and the gray ears ahead and he reached and patted the wet gray neck, and he looked back at the bridge and saw the bright flash from the heavy, squat, mud-colored tank there on the road and then he did not hear any whish but only a banging acrid smelling clang like a boiler being ripped apart and he was under the gray horse and the gray horse was kicking and he was trying to pull out from under the weight.

He could move all right. He could move toward the right. But his left leg stayed perfectly flat under the horse as he moved to the right. It was as though there was a new joint in it; not the hip joint but another one that went sideways like a hinge. Then he knew what it was all right and just then the gray horse knee-ed himself up and Robert Jordan's right leg, that had kicked the stirrup loose just as it should, slipped clear over the saddle and came down beside him and he felt with his two hands of his thigh bone where the left leg lay flat against the ground and his hands both felt the sharp bone and where it pressed against the skin.

The gray horse was standing almost over him and he could see his ribs heaving. The grass was green where he sat and there were meadow flowers in it and he looked down the slope across to the road and the bridge and the gorge and the road and saw the tank and waited for the next flash. It came almost at once with again no whish and in the burst of it, with the smell of the high explosive, the dirt clods scattering and the steel whirring off, he saw the big gray horse sit quietly down beside him as though it were a horse in a circus. And then, looking at the horse sitting there, he heard the sound the horse was making.

Then Primitivo and Agustín had him under the armpits and were dragging him up the last slope and the new joint in his leg let it swing any way the ground swung it. Once a shell whished close over them and they dropped him and fell flat, but the dirt scattered over them and and the metal sung off and they picked him up again. And then they had him up to the shelter of the long draw in the timber where the horses were, and Maria, Pilar and Pablo were standing over him.

Maria was kneeling by him and saying, "Roberto, what hast thou?"

He said, sweating heavily, "The left leg is broken, *guapa*."

"We will bind it up," Pilar said. "Thou canst ride that." She pointed to one of the horses that was packed. "Cut off the load."

Robert Jordan saw Pablo shake his head and he nodded at him.

"Get along," he said. Then he said, "Listen, Pablo. Come here."

The sweat-streaked, bristly face bent down by him and Robert Jordan smelt the full smell of Pablo.

"Let us speak," he said to Pilar and Maria. "I have to speak to Pablo."

"Does it hurt much?" Pablo asked. He was bending close over Robert Jordan.

"No. I think the nerve is crushed. Listen. Get along. I am mucked, see? I will talk to the girl for a moment. When I say to take her, take her. She will want to stay. I will only speak to her for a moment."

"Clearly, there is not much time," Pablo said.

"Clearly."

"I think you would do better in the Republic," Robert Jordan said.

"Nay. I am for Gredos."

"Use thy head."

"Talk to her now," Pablo said. "There is little time. I am sorry thou hast this, *Inglés.*"

"Since I have it—" Robert Jordan said. "Let us not speak of it. But use thy head. Thou hast much head. Use it."

"Why would I not?" said Pablo. "Talk now fast, *Inglés.* There is no time."

Pablo went over to the nearest tree and watched down the slope, across the slope and up the road across the gorge. Pablo was looking at the gray horse on the slope with true regret on his face and Pilar and Maria were with Robert Jordan where he sat against the tree trunk.

"Slit the trouser, will thee?" he said to Pilar. Maria crouched by him and did not speak. The sun was on her hair and her face was twisted as a child's contorts before it cries. But she was not crying.

Pilar took her knife and slit his trouser leg down below the left-hand pocket. Robert Jordan spread the cloth with his hands and looked at the stretch of his thigh. Ten inches below the hip joint there was a pointed, purple swelling like a sharp-peaked little tent and as he touched it with his fingers he could feel the snapped-off thigh bone tight against the skin. His leg was lying at an odd angle. He looked looked up at Pilar. Her face had the same expression as Maria's.

"*Anda,*" he said to her. "Go."

She went away with her head down without saying anything

nor looking back and Robert Jordan could see her shoulders shaking.

"*Guapa,*" he said to Maria and took hold of her two hands. "Listen. We will not be going to Madrid——"

Then she started to cry.

"No, *guapa,* don't," he said. "Listen. We will not go to Madrid now but I go always with thee wherever thou goest. Understand?"

She said nothing and pushed her head against his cheek with her arms around him.

"Listen to this well, rabbit," he said. He knew there was a great hurry and he was sweating very much, but this had to be said and understood. "Thou wilt go now, rabbit. But I go with thee. As long as there is one of us there is both of us. Do you understand?"

"Nay, I stay with thee."

"Nay, rabbit. What I do now I do alone. I could not do it well with thee. If thou goest then I go, too. Do you not see how it is? Whichever one there is, is both."

"I will stay with thee."

"Nay, rabbit. Listen. That people cannot do together. Each one must do it alone. But if thou goest then I go with thee. It is in that way that I go too. Thou wilt go now, I know. For thou art good and kind. Thou wilt go now for us both."

"But it is easier if I stay with thee," she said. "It is better for me."

"Yes. Therefore go for a favor. Do it for me since it is what thou canst do."

"But you don't understand, Roberto. What about *me?* It is worse for me to go."

"Surely," he said. "It is harder for thee. But I am thee also now."

She said nothing.

He looked at her and he was sweating heavily and he spoke now, trying harder to do something than he had ever tried in all his life.

"Now you will go for us both," he said. "You must not be self-ish, rabbit. You must do your duty now."

She shook her head.

"You are me now," he said. "Surely thou must feel it, rabbit.

"Rabbit, listen," he said. "Truly thus I go too. I swear it to thee."

She said nothing.

"Now you see it," he said. "Now I see it is clear. Now thou wilt go. Good. Now you are going. Now you have said you will go."

She had said nothing.

"Now I thank thee for it. Now you are going well and fast and far and we both go in thee. Now put thy hand here. Now put thy head down. Nay, put it down. That is right. Now I put my hand there. Good. Thou art so good. Now do not think more. Now art thou doing what thou should. Now thou art obeying. Not me but us both. The me in thee. Now you go for us both. Truly. We both go in thee now. This I have promised thee. Thou art very good to go and very kind."

He jerked his head at Pablo, who was half-looking at him from the tree and Pablo started over. He motioned with his thumb to Pilar.

"We will go to Madrid another time, rabbit," he said. "Truly. Now stand up and go and we both go. Stand up. See?"

"No," she said and held him tight around the neck.

He spoke now still calmly and reasonably but with great authority.

"Stand up," he said. "Thou art me too now. Thou art all there will be of me. Stand up."

She stood up slowly, crying, and with her head down. Then she dropped quickly beside him and then stood up again, slowly and tiredly, as he said, "Stand up, *guapa.*"

Pilar was holding her by the arm and she was standing there.

"*Vamonos,*" Pilar said. "Dost lack anything, *Inglés?*" She looked at him and shook her head.

"No," he said and went on talking to Maria.

"There is no good-by, *guapa,* because we are not apart. That it should be good in the Gredos. Go now. Go good. Nay," he spoke now still calmly and reasonably as Pilar walked the girl along. "Do not turn around. Put thy foot in. Yes. Thy foot in. Help her up," he said to Pilar. "Get her in the saddle. Swing up now."

He turned his head, sweating, and looked down the slope, then back toward where the girl was in the saddle with Pilar by her and Pablo just behind. "Now go," he said. "Go."

She started to look around. "Don't look around," Robert Jordan said. "Go." And Pablo hit the horse across the crupper with a hobbling strap and it looked as though Maria tried to slip from the saddle but Pilar and Pablo were riding close up against her and Pilar was holding her and the three horses were going up the draw.

"Roberto," Maria turned and shouted. "Let me stay! Let me stay!"

"I am with thee," Robert Jordan shouted. "I am with thee now. We are both there. Go!" Then they were out of sight around the corner of the draw and he was soaking wet with sweat and looking at nothing.

Agustín was standing by him.

"Do you want me to shoot thee, *Inglés?*" he asked, leaning down close. "*Quieres?* It is nothing."

"*No hace falta,*" Robert Jordan said. "Get along. I am very well here."

"*Me cago en la leche que me han dado!*" Agustín said. He was crying so he could not see Robert Jordan clearly. "*Salud, Inglés.*"

"*Salud,* old one," Robert Jordan said. He was looking down the slope now. "Look well after the cropped head, wilt thou?"

"There is no problem," Agustín said. "Thou has what thou needest?"

"There are very few shells for this *máquina,* so I will keep it," Robert Jordan said. "Thou canst now get more. For that other and the one of Pablo, yes."

"I cleaned out the barrel," Agustín said. "Where thou plugged it in the dirt with the fall."

"What became of the pack-horse?"

"The gypsy caught it."

Agustín was on the horse now but he did not want to go. He leaned far over toward the tree where Robert Jordan lay.

"Go on, *viejo,*" Robert Jordan said to him. "In war there are many things like this."

"*Qué puta es la guerra,*" Agustín said. "War is a bitchery."

"Yes, man, yes. But get on with thee."

"*Salud, Inglés,*" Agustín said, clenching his right fist.

"*Salud,*" Robert Jordan said. "But get along, man."

Agustín wheeled his horse and brought his right fist down as though he cursed again with the motion of it and rode up the draw. All the others had been out of sight long before. He looked back where the draw turned in the timber and waved his fist. Robert

Jordan waved and then Agustín, too, was out of sight.... Robert Jordan looked down the green slope of the hillside to the road and the bridge. I'm as well this way as any, he thought. It wouldn't be worth risking getting over on my belly yet, not as close as that thing was to the surface, and I can see better this way.

He felt empty and drained and exhausted from all of it and from them going and his mouth tasted of bile. Now, finally and at last, there was no problem. However all of it had been and however all of it would ever be now, for him, no longer was there any problem.

They were all gone now and he was alone with his back against a tree. He looked down across the green slope, seeing the gray horse where Agustín had shot him, and on down the slope to the road with the timber-covered country behind it. Then he looked at the bridge and across the bridge and watched the activity on the bridge and the road. He could see the trucks now, all down the lower road. The gray of the trucks showed through the trees. Then he looked back up the road to where it came down over the hill. They will be coming soon now, he thought.

Pilar will take care of her as well as any one can. You know that. Pablo must have a sound plan or he would not have tried it. You do not have to worry about Pablo. It does no good to think about Maria. Try to believe what you told her. That is the best. And who says it is not true? Not you. You don't say it, any more than you would say the things did not happen that happened. Stay with what you believe now. Don't get cynical. The time is too short and you have just sent her away. Each one does what he can. You can do nothing for yourself but perhaps you can do something for another. Well, we had all our luck in four days. Not four days. It was afternoon when I first got there and it will not be noon today. That makes not quite three days and three nights. Keep it accurate, he said. Quite accurate.

I think you better get down now, he thought. You better get fixed around some way where you will be useful instead of leaning against this tree like a tramp. You have had much luck. There are many worse things than this. Every one has to do this, one day or another. You are not afraid of it once you know you have to do it, are you? No, he said, truly. It was lucky the nerve was crushed, though. I cannot even feel that there is anything below the break. He touched the lower part of his leg and it was as though it were not part of his body.

He looked down the hill slope again and he thought, I hate to leave it, is all. I hate to leave it very much and I hope I have done some good in it. I have tried to with what talent I had. *Have, you mean. All right, have.*

I have fought for what I believed in for a year now. If we win here we will win everywhere. The world is a fine place and worth the fighting for and I hate very much to leave it. And you had a lot of luck, he told himself, to have had such a good life. You've had just as good a life as grandfather's though not as long. You've had as good a life as any one because of these last days. You do not want to complain when you have been so lucky. I wish there was some way to pass on what I've learned, though. Christ, I was learning fast there at the end. I'd like to talk to Karkov. That is in Madrid. Just over the hills there, and down across the plain. Down out of the gray rocks and the pines, the heather and the gorse, across the yellow high plateau you see it rising white and beautiful. That part is just as true as Pilar's old women drinking the blood down at the slaughterhouse. There's no *one* thing that's true. It's all true. The way the planes are beautiful whether they are ours or theirs. The hell they are, he thought.

You take it easy, now, he said. Get turned over now while you still have time. Listen, one thing. Do you remember? Pilar and the hand? Do you believe that crap? No, he said. Not with everything that's happened? No, I don't believe it. She was nice about it early this morning before the show started. She was afraid maybe I believed it. I don't, though. But she does. They see something. Or they feel something. Like a bird dog. What about extra-sensory perception? What about obscenity? he said. She wouldn't say good-by, he thought, because she knew if she did Maria would never go. That Pilar. Get yourself turned over, Jordan. But he was reluctant to try it.

Then he remembered that he had the small flask in his hip pocket and he thought, I'll take a good spot of the giant killer and then I'll try it. But the flask was not there when he felt for it. Then he felt that much more alone because he knew there was not going to be even that. I guess I'd counted on that, he said.

Do you suppose Pablo took it? Don't be silly. You must have lost it at the bridge. "Come on now, Jordan," he said. "Over you go."

Then he took hold of his left leg with both hands and pulled on it hard, pulling toward the foot while he lay down beside the tree he had been resting his back against. Then lying flat and pulling hard on the leg, so the broken end of the bone would not come up and cut through the thigh, he turned slowly around on his rump until the back of his head was facing downhill. Then with his broken leg, held by both hands, uphill, he put the sole of his right foot against the instep of his left foot and pressed hard while he rolled, sweating, over onto his face and chest. He got onto his elbows, stretched the left leg well behind him with both hands and a far, sweating, push with the right foot and there he was. He felt with his fingers on the left thigh and it was all right. The bone end had not punctured the skin and the broken end was well into the muscle now.

The big nerve must have been truly smashed when that damned horse rolled on it, he thought. It truly doesn't hurt at all. Except now in certain changes of positions. That's when the bone pinches something else. You see? he said. You see what luck is? You didn't need the giant killer at all.

He reached over for the submachine gun, took the clip out that was in the magazine, felt in his pocket for clips, opened the action and looked through the barrel, put the clip back into the groove of the magazine until it clicked, and then looked down the hill slope. Maybe half an hour, he thought. Now take it easy.

Then he looked at the hillside and he looked at the pines and he tried not to think at all.

Then he looked at the stream and he remembered how it had been under the bridge in the cool of the shadow. I wish they would come, he thought. I do not want to get in any sort of mixed-up state before they come.

Who do you suppose has it easier? Ones with religion or just taking it straight? It comforts them very much but we know there is no thing to fear. It is only missing it that's bad. Dying is only bad when it takes a long time and hurts so much that it humiliates you. That is where you have all the luck, see? You don't have any of that.

It's wonderful they've got away. I don't mind this at all now they are away. It *is* sort of the way I said. It is really very much that way. Look how different it would be if they were all scattered out across that hill where that gray horse is. Or if we were all cooped up here waiting for it. No. They're gone. They're away. Now if the attack were only a success. What do you want? Everything. I want everything and I will take whatever I get. If this attack is no good another one will be. I never noticed when the planes came back. *God, that was lucky I could make her go.*

I'd like to tell grandfather about this one. I'll bet he never had to go over and find his people and do a show like this. How do you know? He may have done fifty. No, he said. Be accurate. Nobody did any fifty like this one. Nobody did five. Nobody did one maybe not just like this. Sure. They must have.

I wish they would come now, he said. I wish they would come right now because the leg is starting to hurt now. It must be the swelling.

We were going awfully good when that thing hit us, he thought. But it was only luck it didn't come while I was under the bridge. When a thing is wrong something's bound to happen. You were bitched when they gave Golz those orders. That was what you knew and it was probably that which Pilar felt. But later on we will have these things much better organized. We ought to have portable short wave transmitters. *Yes, there's a lot of things we ought to have.* I ought to carry a spare leg, too.

He grinned at that sweatily because the leg, where the big nerve had been bruised by the fall, was hurting badly now. Oh, let them come, he said. I don't want to do that business that my father did. I will do it all right but I'd much prefer not to have to. I'm against that. Don't think about that. Don't think at all. I wish the bastards would come, he said. I wish so very much they'd come.

His leg was hurting very badly now. The pain had started suddenly with the swelling after he had moved and he said, Maybe I'll just do it now. I guess I'm not awfully good at pain. Listen, if I do that now you wouldn't misunderstand, would you? *Who are you talking to?* Nobody, he said. Grandfather, I guess. No. Nobody. Oh bloody it, I wish that they would come.

Listen, I may have to do that because if I pass out or anything like that I am no good at all and if they bring me to they will ask me a lot of questions and do things and all and that is no good. It's much best not to have them do those things. So why wouldn't it be all right to just do it now and then the whole thing would be over with? Because oh, listen, yes, listen, *let them come now.*

You're not good at this, Jordan, he said. Not so good at this. And who is so good at this? I don't know and I don't really care right now. But you are not. That's right. You're not at all. Oh not at all, at all. I think it would be all right to do it now? Don't you?

No, it isn't. Because there is something you can do yet. As long as you know what it is you have to do it. As long as you remember what it is you have to wait for that. *Come on. Let them come. Let them come. Let them come!*

Think about them being away, he said. Think about them going through the timber. Thik about them crossing a creek. Think about them riding through the heather. Think about them going up the slope. Think about them O. K. tonight. Think about them travelling, all night. Think about them hiding up tomorrow. Think about them. God damn it, think about them. *That's just as far as I can think about them,* he said.

Think about Montana. *I can't.* Think about Madrid. *I can't.* Think about a cool drink of water. *All right.* That's what it will be like. Like a cool drink of water. *You're a liar.* It will just be nothing. That's all it will be. Just nothing. Then do it. *Do it.* Do it now. It's all right to do it now. Go on and do it now. *No, you have to wait.* What for? You know all right. *Then wait.*

I can't wait any longer now, he said. If I wait any longer I'll pass out. I know because I've felt it starting to go three times now and I've held it. I held it all right. But I don't know about any more. What I think is you've got an internal hemorrhage there from where that thigh bone's cut around inside. Especially on that turning business. That makes the swelling and that's what weakens you and makes you start to pass. It would be all right to do it now. Really, I'm telling you that it would be all right.

And if you wait and hold them up even a little while or just get the officer that may make all the difference. One thing well done can make——

All right, he said. And he lay very quietly and tried to hold on to himself that he felt slipping away from himself as you feel snow starting to slip sometimes on a mountain slope, and he said, now quietly, then let me last until they come.

Robert Jordan's luck held very good because he saw, just then, the cavalry ride out of the timber and cross the road. He watched them coming riding up the slope. He saw the trooper who stopped by the gray horse and shouted to the officer who rode over to him. He watched them both looking down at the gray horse. They recognized him of course. He and his rider had been missing since the early morning of the day before.

Robert Jordan saw them there on the slope, close to him now, and below he saw the road and the bridge and the long lines of vehicles below it. He was completely integrated now and he took a good long look at everything. Then he looked up at the sky. There were big white clouds in it. He touched the palm of his hand against the pine needles where he lay and he touched the bark of the pine trunk that he lay behind.

Then he rested easily as he could with his two elbows in the pine needles and the muzzle of the submachine gun resting against the trunk of the pine tree.

As the officer came trotting now on the trail of the horses of the band he would pass twenty yards below where Robert Jordan lay. At that distance there would be no problem. The officer was Lieutenant Berrendo. He had come up from La Granja when they had been ordered up after the first report of the attack on the lower post. They had ridden hard and had then had to swing back, because the bridge had been blown, to cross the gorge high above and come around through the timber. Their horses were wet and blown and they had to be urged into the trot.

Lieutenant Berrendo, watching the trail, came riding up, his thin face serious and grave. His submachine gun lay across his saddle in the crook of his left arm. Robert Jordan lay behind the tree, holding onto himself very carefully and delicately to keep his hands steady. He was waiting until the officer reached the sunlit place where the first trees of the pine forest joined the green slope of the meadow. He could feel his heart beating against the pine needle floor of the forest.

ABOUT THE AUTHOR

Ernest Hemingway was born in Oak Park, Illinois, in 1899, and began his writing career with *The Kansas City Star* in 1917. During the First World War he volunteered as an ambulance driver on the Italian front but was invalided home, having been seriously wounded while serving with the Red Cross. In 1921 Hemingway settled in Paris, where he became part of the expatriate circle of Gertrude Stein, F. Scott Fitzgerald, Ezra Pound, and Ford Madox Ford. His first book, *Three Stories and Ten Poems,* was published in Paris in 1923 and was followed by the short story collection *In Our Time,* which marked his American debut in 1925. With the appearance of *The Sun Also Rises* in 1926, Hemingway became not only the voice of the "lost generation" but the preeminent writer of his time. This was followed by *Men Without Women* in 1927, when Hemingway returned to the United States, and his novel of the Italian front, *A Farewell to Arms* (1929). In the 1930s, Hemingway settled in Key West, and later in Cuba, but he traveled widely—to Spain, Italy, and Africa—and wrote about his experiences in *Death in the Afternoon* (1932), his classic treatise on bullfighting, and *Green Hills of Africa* (1935), an account of big-game hunting in Africa. Later he reported on the Spanish Civil War, which became the background for his brilliant war novel, *For Whom the Bell Tolls* (1940), hunted U-boats in the Caribbean, and covered the European front during the Second World War. Hemingway's most popular work, *The Old Man and the Sea* (1952), was awarded the Pulitzer Prize in 1953, and in 1954 Hemingway won the Nobel Prize in Literature "for his powerful, style-forming mastery of the art of narration." One of the most important influences on the development of the short story and novel in American fiction, Hemingway has seized the imagination of the American public like no other twentieth-century author. He died, by suicide, in Ketchum, Idaho, in 1961. His other works include *The Torrents of Spring* (1926), *Winner Take Nothing* (1933), *To Have and Have Not* (1937), *The Fifth Column and the First Forty-nine Stories* (1938), *Across the River and Into the Trees* (1950), and posthumously, *A Moveable Feast* (1964), *Islands in the Stream* (1970), *The Dangerous Summer* (1985), and *The Garden of Eden* (1986).